Wendy Holden

Filthy Rich

headline
review

First published in 2008
by HEADLINE REVIEW
An imprint of HEADLINE PUBLISHING GROUP

First published in paperback in 2008
by HEADLINE REVIEW

1

ISBN 978 0 7553 2513 9 (B-format)
ISBN 978 0 7553 4422 2 (A-format)

Typeset in Janson by Avon DataSet Ltd,
Bidford-on-Avon, Warwickshire

Printed and bound in Great Britain by Clays Ltd, St Ives plc

Headline's policy is to use papers that are natural, renewable and recyclable
products and made from wood grown in sustainable forests. The logging
and manufacturing processes are expected to conform to the
environmental regulations of the country of origin.

HEADLINE PUBLISHING GROUP
An Hachette Livre UK Company
338 Euston Road
London NW1 3BH

www.headline.co.uk
www.hachettelivre.co.uk

To my family, as ever

Chapter 1

Mary Longshott looked at herself in the mirror. It hung, bevel-edged and age-spotted, in its carved gilt frame, on the wall between two of the stately windows. The light through the long Georgian panes was bright yet subdued. It fell lovingly on Mary, giving the pale oval of her face a creamy glow and deepening the green of her thickly lashed, wide-apart eyes.

Her thick hair, tumbling about her shoulders and the dark brown of black coffee, shone too. Mary shook it, surprised at its shimmer considering it had not been brushed since this morning. Bed hair. Four-poster-bed hair in her case. Taking the scrunchie from her slim wrist, she pushed thick handfuls through it, tucking any further stray wisps behind her discreet white ears. She twitched her small, tip-tilted nose and smiled at herself, grateful for the still-fine cheekbones, the generous pink mouth and the lack of lines despite being over the threshold of thirty. She was still pretty. Very pretty, Monty said, but then he would, Mary thought indulgently. The green eyes in the mirror laughed back at her.

She was aware, as she stood, tall, slender and straight-backed before the row of windows, of the room extending behind her. The central salon was the house's most important room, built to receive esteemed guests and reinforce the family's status. Her predecessors as lady of the manor would have had their greatest successes here. Mary often imagined them at balls and parties, their diamonds winking in the candlelight, their pearls glowing, their silks rustling, their perfume trailing as they worked the ornate room, seemingly relaxed but with bright eyes everywhere, introducing this person to that person, tweaking that situation, supplying a rejoinder to this remark, laughing at that one and conducting, in the subtlest manner possible, the complex and demanding symphony of a brilliant social occasion.

There was no trace of such events now. The room was silent. The last notes of the orchestra had died out long ago, the candles blown out and the last guests had been gone for years.

Rather to Mary's relief, it had to be said. She was gentle and timid and parties terrified her. She would have been happy in the kitchen, sending up the syllabubs, rarebits, champagne jellies and whatever else people at such parties expected. But being out in the spotlight, the social motor of a brilliant occasion; it made her feel queasy to think about it.

Mary gazed down the flight of wide, shallow steps which led from the mansion's grey stone portico to the drive which, despite its patchy gravel and sprouting weeds, wound with a nonchalant magnificence between the trees in the park towards the far-distant gates and Weston Moor beyond them.

She imagined, without actually hearing it, the fizzing sound, faint but unmistakable, of a lark. There were lots of larks on the moor, singing away as if lacking a care in the world. They never failed to make her feel better, or to remind her how beautiful it was up here. Even on a drizzly afternoon in early June, like this one.

But drizzle could be delicious; wetness on leaves, grass or flowers seemed to release all the pent-up scent within. A rose after rainfall had to be the sweetest smell in the world; the diamond raindrops on the petals cold to the nose, the sweet, powdery scent as if the whole of summer had been distilled into the tight twists of one pink flower.

She couldn't just stand here, Mary knew. There were things to do, as there always were. But dragging herself away from the view was difficult. It was so familiar, and yet never the same. In the winter the landscape before the house brooded beneath skies that could be anything from palest duck-egg to deepest rose. The frosted oaks and chestnuts would hang with diamonds, frozen puddles would flash in the sun and snow would stipple the curving landscape, lying in the lee of dry-stone walls and revealing the contours of ancient ploughwork.

Early spring – in particular May, Mary's favourite of all the months – was a dream of green and white; the hedgerows heavy with scented hawthorn blossom, the cherry boughs ebullient with flowers, the sides of the road foaming with the delicate greenish white of cow parsley.

Then came June and summer – brasher and less virginal than May; the fields a brilliant green galaxy blazing with yellow meteors of dandelions. Poppies flamed in the hedgerows, foxgloves sent up fleshy fireworks of magenta and, more rarely, white. On the horizon the purple ridges of hills, so still and distant in winter, seemed nearer now, alive with the movement of clouds passing quickly overhead through the warm blue.

Mary pulled her gaze from the park gates back to the

parterre below the portico. There was little to show that these had once been formal gardens, planted with box and roses, dotted with statues, glittering with the curved jets of fountains. Nothing apart from coarse grass grew at Weston Underwood now. She would have tried her hand at horticulture, but it had been explained to her soon after her arrival that all the Weston Underwood land was barren. Creeping lead poisoning from the spoil heaps the once-booming lead mining industry had left scattered about the moor was to blame, apparently.

Considering that lead was the source from which her husband's ancestors had gained their wealth in the first place, the practical Mary had seen no point in bemoaning her gardening lot, or, rather, little. Had there not been lead mining, there would have been no Weston Underwood. And therefore no Monty, either. So, given all there was, the absence of a few courgettes and floribundas seemed a small price to pay.

Mary turned on her heel to return to her duties, but was instantly distracted again. Her eyes seemed pulled up by their own accord to another of her favourite views: the salon's ceiling. She could not look at it for long; the awkward pose made her neck ache, but never a day went by without her admiring it. It was seventeenth century, depicting a vast and gaudy sunset upon whose billowing pink-and-gold-tinged clouds a number of mythic occurrences were playing themselves out. There were the Eumenides, the Furies, one of whom was brandishing the scissors with which she would cut the thread of a man's life. There were the wild-eyed white horses and the golden chariot of the sun god, Apollo.

According to Monty, who had lived at Weston Underwood all his life, the characters on the ceiling had the faces of people employed in the house while the painter was working. The serene countenance of the saffron-robed Venus at the centre was reputedly based on the chatelaine of the time, the beautiful Lady Amelia Longshott. She had, Mary knew, a reputation for being as capable as she was lovely. Mary's glance flicked back to the mirror again to catch herself looking guilty. The thought of Lady Amelia always made her feel inadequate. When Mary thought of the balls in the central salon, it was Lady Amelia she most frequently imagined at the glittering centre.

She comforted herself by reflecting that Lady Amelia, for all her brilliance, had done considerably less well than Mary so far as husbands were concerned. The two men, however, shared the same name. Lady Amelia's Montague, so family legend had it, preferred to spend his time and money adventuring round the world in search of treasure, wars, fame or other excitements, which very possibly had included other women. Lady Amelia, nothing daunted, had apparently occupied herself in his absences by running the house with brisk efficiency.

Mary looked down at the wooden floor, rising and falling like the waves thanks to the centuries of damp beneath it, rubbed her neck and then looked up at the ceiling again. The handsome, somewhat self-satisfied face of the Icarus on the ceiling, the deluded youth who took stupid risks in pursuit of personal glory, was said to be that of Lady Amelia's frequently absent husband. He had been a big spender with it; his wife's enormous dowry was promptly blown on building a new house – the one Mary now stood in – and in financing her husband's exploits. Had Lady Amelia ever regretted marrying her Montague? Mary wondered.

Mary had never regretted marrying hers. Monty was very

far from being a normal sort of husband, admittedly, and their life together was, in the view of many, positively eccentric. But that was its attraction. Until she had met Monty, Mary's life had been about as normal as her age, education and situation could possibly have made it. And until she had met him, Mary had had no idea that this was not what she wanted, or that there were alternatives.

A twenty-something secretary in a London auction house, she had been sitting, as usual, at her desk outside her boss's shiny mahogany door, when the Head of Eighteenth-Century Paintings had suddenly demanded her presence. Smoothing her rather Sloaney printed skirt, and tweaking the pressed white collar of her blouse, Mary checked her black polished pumps and entered the presence.

Five minutes later she was looking, aghast, at the short, pink, prematurely bald, prematurely aged Head of Eighteenth-Century Paintings. He moved his florid neck uncomfortably in his pale blue and white checked shirt, set off by an unbecoming yellow tie. For someone who was supposed to be an art expert, he was, Mary had always thought, a terrible dresser.

'I'm awfully sorry, Mary.'

Mary had fixed him with as steely a glare as she had dared. That some impoverished aristocrat called Montague de Vere Longshott, in some place called Weston Underwood, near some town called Mineford, somewhere in the Midlands, wanted to put some of his collection up for sale had, up until that moment, been of interest to her only in so far as it affected her boss. In other words, as far as she had to make arrangements for him to go and inspect the works, which she duly had done, as she had done for similar 'go-sees', as he called them, many times before.

But the Head of Eighteenth-Century Paintings' wife had had other ideas about this particular go-see. She had demanded, on the same day he was expected at Weston Underwood, her husband's presence at their daughter's prep school's annual fête, an event of apparent great prestige attended by celebrity parents. The Head's wife, who even gentle Mary had realised was inordinately socially ambitious, had apparently volunteered her husband's services as a human fruit machine. 'Mary, I'm sorry, but I've got no choice,' the Head of Eighteenth-Century Paintings had admitted sheepishly through his fingers. 'Be a love and go and see Longshott for me, would you?'

'Me?' Mary had exclaimed. 'But I don't know the first thing about paintings.' It occurred to her that perhaps, actually, she ought to; she had been working in the department for six years.

From behind the safety of his large mahogany desk, the Head had looked at her dolefully with his protuberant blue eyes. 'Well I don't know the first thing about being a human fruit machine,' he had riposted. 'It rather worries me, to be frank. Where exactly does the money come out? Not to mention go in?'

Mary had no idea. Nor did she care. The point so far as she was concerned was that that night, that upcoming evening, had been a red-letter day for some time. It was the night she was doing dinner for six at the house of Richard, a rich if disdainful stockbroker she had met at the wedding of a mutual friend and embarked on a tentative relationship with.

He was a definite upgrade on the standard of looks and success she had thus far been used to. Despite her beauty, she was too shy to assert herself with men, and most of her previous liaisons had been with the predatory types who preyed on gentle girls. Chief among these had been a fattish, pompous, forty-something captain from Knightsbridge Barracks and an unsuccessful property developer who pretended to potential investors that the smart flat Mary's wealthy consultant neurosurgeon father had bought as a home for his only daughter was in fact his own. Both captain and developer had used the same tactics: portrayed themselves as lost causes in order to appeal to the shy, sensitive and motherly side they sensed was there, and then, having won her affections, bullied and exploited her.

Love and relationships had not turned out quite as Mary imagined them. The handsome prince whom, fuelled by her storybooks, she had imagined marrying in her earliest childhood had miserably failed to materialise. But Mary had never failed to hope that he might. 'Oh, Mary. Get real,' her friends would tell her, impatient and indulgent in equal measures.

Mary had tried her best. She had got real to the extent of accepting she was not clever enough to be the doctor or vet that had been her other great dream in childhood and trained as a secretary instead. But she had never stopped helping any vulnerable creature she happened to come across, whether it was a beggar outside the tube station, a child with a scraped knee, a cat with a cut paw. And her dream of a prince remained alive, too.

Was Richard that prince? Mary hoped he was. Given her chequered romantic history and advancing age – she was now twenty-five – it was, she knew, her stern if well-meaning parents' dearest wish to see her happily settled with a rich and handsome husband in a chintzy Chelsea townhouse. She was conscious that the dinner at Richard's house – which was both in Chelsea and abounded with chintz and striped wallpaper, not to mention bins festooned with hunting scenes – was her big chance to impress both parties. As well as Richard's friends, who all seemed as smart, successful and intimidating as he was and somewhat reluctant to accept her into their circle.

But Mary had a trump card which she planned to play that evening. However good Richard and his friends may be at assessing whether General Electrics would go up or down, or how Rio Tinto Zinc was doing, they could not, Mary knew, cook like she could.

Food was her one real skill. After school she had wondered about going into catering, but her father, who Mary was terrified of, told her it was a crowded market with low profit margins and she would almost certainly fail. Even though secretarial work, which he had recommended and which she had subsequently obediently trained in, didn't strike Mary as being exactly uncrowded nor particularly profitable. But she had kept up her interest in cooking, and delighted in giving dinner parties for work acquaintances she got on particularly well with, or her few schoolfriends who remained in London and had not yet married and disappeared to the country, the suburbs or abroad.

For Richard's dinner she had devised a menu of chicken in grapes and cream sauce followed by summer pudding. The combination had that rather eighties feel that always went down well with Richard's sort of City person. While Mary had made the summer pudding the night before – it was in a plastic lidded bowl in her bag – the rest had yet to be bought and she had planned to nip to Sainsbury's on the King's Road on the way round.

But now, to judge from the way the Head of Eighteenth-Century Paintings was looking at her, she was expected to drop everything for work reasons. Richard, of course, often had to do so – they had been together a mere four weeks and he had blown her out three times already: 'the bloody office, I'm afraid'. But he clearly would not expect it of her.

Mary felt panic rise. It was now mid-afternoon. If she had to take the train to the Midlands, do whatever it was she was expected to do and get back to London, she wasn't likely to return before the cheese course. Which at this stage had not yet been bought. Mary felt like bursting into tears. It was an unexpected blow to what had seemed a certain evening of triumph. She raised miserable, watery eyes to the Head of Eighteenth-Century Paintings.

'But I don't know anything about paintings,' she repeated.

'Don't worry,' her boss assured her. 'You don't have to.'

Mary stared back, almost jolted out of her misery by amazement. What was he saying? That he himself was a fraud? That, despite his billing, he didn't know anything about paintings either?

Guessing her thoughts, the blue protuberant eyes grew alarmed. 'No, hang on a minute, Mary, you've got the wrong end of the stick. I'm saying *you* don't have to know about paintings because *I* do. All I want you to do is go up and take pictures of them. That'll do for starters. Then I'll follow myself as soon as the diary permits. But for now, just take the train ticket and get up there,' the Head of Eighteenth-Century Paintings instructed. 'I don't want us to miss out on a Poussin or whatever. You never know with these provincial stately homes. They can be full of surprises.'

Chapter 2

Following a phone call to Richard who had been, predictably, incandescently angry; moreover, had used language no fairytale prince would ever employ, a dejected Mary had taken the Tube to St Pancras and the next train north. Dressed in her work clothes and with a summer pudding in a plastic bowl in her handbag.

She had not been expecting, given her agitated state of mind, to be soothed by, of all things, the scenery from the train windows on the way up. She had always imagined the Midlands to mean Birmingham and the Black Country; mile upon mile of tower block, chimney and cooling tower. Instead it was a lush landscape lolling in the heat of late summer, rolling green pasture stretching away to the horizon, beautiful trees, a flash of river here and there. And the Head of Eighteenth-Century Paintings had not been joking about these provincial stately homes being full of surprises.

By the time the taxi had taken her up into the lime-green hill country, through a pretty village called Allsop and along a moorland road with peerless views, before turning through a pair of urn-topped gates and starting the glide up a long and winding drive, Mary had revised her preconceptions. She gasped at the beauty of the house's classical façade, standing proudly in its park in the slanting shadows of the summer evening. It was one of the loveliest places she had ever seen. The atmosphere of unhurried peace took her breath away. As the car had got nearer, she had spotted a figure on the steps.

And this was the second surprise. Through the car window as it approached she could see a tall, spare, broad-shouldered figure bound down the wide portico steps as excitedly as a Labrador.

He opened the taxi door and looked surprised. 'Oh. I was expecting a middle-aged man.'

'So was I,' Mary stammered in reply. She had imagined Montague de Vere Longshott as some crusty old buffer in tweeds. Never had she pictured him as the handsomest man ever born.

Up close, his face was long, very pale, delicate and unmistakably aristocratic; a straight downward line of nose and, either side of the narrow bridge, large, extraordinarily luminous eyes of a pale Wedgwood blue. Far from having the distant, superior expression Mary was expecting as typical of a stately-home-dweller, they seemed warm, obliging and interested as they surveyed her from beneath pale blond brows. His messy mop of hair, which looked rather as if he cut it himself, was as blond as a toddler's.

Monty grinned. He had a wide, sweet, good-natured smile that sent Mary's stomach into a sudden somersault. Sternly, she tried to collect herself. She was here to take a few photographs. Then she would return to London and try and pick up the pieces of her relationship.

'They sent me,' she apologised. 'We tried to ring you to let you know, but the phone seems to be out of order.'

'Cut off, more like,' Monty sighed ruefully, as he helped her out.

She laughed as if this was a joke.

'I'm serious,' he said. There was a pause. 'Come on,' he added jauntily, recovering his good mood instantly. 'It's a lovely day. I'll show you round.'

Mary followed him as he bounded up the stairs to the portico, observing him greedily. He wore a battered tweed jacket and, over his immensely long legs, navy moleskin trousers with tears in the knees. His brown brogues, while disgracefully scuffed, had a Jermyn Street hand-made look about them that Mary, schooled in these matters, immediately recognised.

Now his features were becoming more familiar, she could register the details: his hair contained more shades of blond than she had known existed, his eyes were even more extraordinarily large, bright, blue and friendly than they seemed at first; the lashes thick and with a golden sheen. Nor was his skin as deathly pale as it had first appeared: his cheeks had two rather fetching smudges of rose towards the top and the straight, slim nose had an engaging spatter of freckles. He was almost as beautiful as his home, Mary thought, even if he didn't look as if he ate much.

As he ushered her into the house, she was horribly aware of her unbrushed hair and the make-up she had put on sketchily that morning. She had planned to re-make-up later, go the full lip-and-eyeliner as she rarely did, to mark the important occasion of Richard's dinner party. But the dinner party was almost certainly not happening, and here was some perspective on Richard himself, in addition. Mary had thought him extremely handsome – almost as fetching as Richard himself thought he was – but compared to Monty

Longshott, he was like a torch trying to compete with the sun.

Monty must, Mary calculated, have every heiress in the Midlands, if not further afield, hell-bent on rushing him up the aisle. Who wouldn't want to live here?

'This way,' Monty instructed, leading her into the entrance hall. After the balmy evening outside it was, Mary thought, like leaving a sauna to go into a fridge. The entrance hall was gloomy in the extreme; the only illumination that of its marble surfaces reflecting the tall, curtainless windows. The restricted light made Monty's large and shining eyes positively blaze.

'You live on your own? There's no one else here?' she asked him, with some surprise, half expecting some blonde fiancée with ancestral pearls and Boden cardigan to appear from a doorway.

'Well, apart from Mrs Shuffle.'

Mary raised an eyebrow. 'Who's that?' So she was right. There was a woman. A divorcee, by the sound of it. She pictured an experienced-looking brunette with a deep tan, a cracking figure and a holiday home in the south of France.

'The cleaner,' Monty smiled. 'She's very sweet. Looked after us for years.'

Mary glanced at the dusty surfaces, the grubby windows. Mrs Shuffle didn't seem to have made much of an impact. 'Oh, she only does the bits where I actually live,' Monty snorted, guessing her thoughts.

Mary regarded him wonderingly. He lived alone, with no one to look after him. She stifled a sudden, overwhelming desire to care for him, to shroud him in blankets, to cook him an enormous meal.

'You don't even have any dogs?' she asked. Aristocrats always had dogs, surely?

Monty shrugged. 'My father was allergic to them. He died last year. I suppose I could have got one, but it just seemed like another thing to look after. The house is quite demanding enough.'

'And your mother?' Mary was aware of being unusually inquisitive considering she had never met Monty before. But he was friendly and unthreatening and seemed glad of the chance to talk.

'Died five years ago. They were quite old parents,' Monty added, rather wistfully. 'They loved this place, though.'

'And you didn't want to leave?' Mary breathed, caught up in the romance of it all. The young, fair man with luminous eyes, solitary in this great dark box of a place. It was like Rapunzel. The Sleeping Beauty. Although there was nothing somnolent about Monty. He seemed very much awake; restless in fact.

Monty looked appalled. 'Leave? I couldn't. I mean, I went away to school and university, obviously, but I'm back for good now. Longshotts have lived at Weston Underwood for five hundred years. It's my home. Where else would I live?'

'Oh, absolutely,' Mary agreed quickly. 'It's spectacular,' she enthused, looking around. Then she remembered the reason for her coming. 'Expensive, too, I imagine,' she added. It was evident from the niches on the walls that the room had once been peopled with statues.

'They went to auction some time ago,' Monty confessed. 'I can't remember what the money went on. The rest of the death duties, probably. Or else putting about four square feet of new tiles on one of the roofs somewhere. Tiling's unbelievably expensive. Or perhaps some new buckets for the drips.'

Mary nodded. She had noticed on entry the several green plastic buckets standing around on the marble. She imagined the cleaner had left them.

'Here's the salon,' Monty said next, going ahead into a huge sitting room that had obviously once been magnificent. Beneath the grey, dusty glass of four enormous chandeliers, hanging on faded silk ropes from a riotously painted ceiling, groups of striped-silk-covered chairs and sofas on delicate curved legs stood companionably about. But mice had evidently made inroads into many of them. Her gaze lingered on the dark blue oblongs on the otherwise pale blue walls where pictures once had hung. A few were left: big hunting scenes in heavy gold frames; presumably the ones she was to photograph.

The sitting room led through to a room with a tatty billiard table, over which a broken lightshade hung askew. It was dusty and sad, Mary thought, and yet still retained something of the spirit of the cheerful evenings when Edwardian gentlemen with pointy beards and tweed waistcoats had repaired for sport and port after fifteen-course dinners. Which most certainly must have taken place; the entire house, after all, stood testament to an era when there was money enough to keep it going in some style. Her surprise at the house's dilapidation was fading; something of its character, and the happy times that it had witnessed, was replacing it. Strange though it seemed, she was beginning to see what kept Monty Longshott here.

The billiard room led out into another hall from which a huge staircase rose into the chill dark of the upper floors. Mary clacked after Monty up the shallow marble treads.

Upstairs was a sequence of bedrooms with dusty four-posters and damp-stained walls. Monty's own bedroom – which she rather blushed to be shown; it seemed private somehow – was extraordinarily messy, probably the messiest room Mary had ever seen. Clothes, books, bulging plastic bags and huge, flapping maps were strewn everywhere, but behind all the clutter was a really wonderful mullioned bay window and, rising out of the mess like a fantastical island, a Gibraltar hung with shabby red curtains, was a once magnificent four-poster bed, its four corners topped with dusty ostrich plumes.

Mary turned to Monty. 'I thought you said you had a cleaner,' she grinned, feeling somehow able to tease him.

He shrugged his big, broad shoulders guiltily. 'She comes tomorrow. Rescues me from being buried alive.'

She nodded indulgently, as she imagined Mrs Shuffle did too. Besides his angelic looks, Monty had an irrepressible boyish quality that was endearing.

'What are all the maps?' They were huge, Mary could see. Big, yellow and old-looking.

He looked gratified by her interest. 'Oh, they're fascinating. Absolutely fascinating. My great-great-uncle Hengist's maps of the North and South Poles. He was an explorer, you see,' Monty added, anticipating Mary's next question. She could hear the pride in his voice. 'I've always been rather interested in his voyages,' Monty told her. It looked like it, Mary thought. You could hardly see the bed for them. 'And they make quite a good extra layer on particularly cold nights,' he added with a grin. She grinned back, not entirely sure he was joking. The sun was shining outside, but in here she could see her breath.

Adjoining the bedroom was a bathroom; the last word in

Victorian plumbing technology, Mary guessed, admiring the mosaic walls above the colossal claw-foot bathtub and the massive, shallow square sink on its pedestal. The lavatory, shaped like a shell, had an enamelled pattern of flowers within it. All this, admittedly, was barely visible beneath piles of crumpled clothes and ancient newspaper supplements strewn about the base of the loo.

Another room, rather poignantly, contained rotting toys and a woodwormed rocking horse. 'The nursery,' Monty beamed, and Mary felt suddenly, powerfully and utterly unreasonably a rush in her chest and a tightening in her throat. Presumably this was where Monty had spent his earliest years and where he hoped the future of the line would be brought up. But she no longer felt convinced that every girl in the county was queuing up to mother it. Who, after all, she wondered, her eyes travelling the wrecked ceilings and slipped panes of glass in the window, would want to take all this on?

But as she followed Monty round, hearing him enthuse about something in every nook and cranny, Mary felt something in her respond. Was it because he was so charming? Or because the house had seen better days? It had been something magnificent and beautiful, but was now down on its luck, needing special care and attention. Infants, animals and hopeless cases, Mary reminded herself, had always had special appeal for her.

Over his shoulder, as he paced ahead of her down the shadowy corridors, Monty was telling her that special care for this house was unforthcoming. The heritage bodies only had so much and they had to spread it thinly. Tax breaks were out of the question as there was no capital around to fund projects on which tax could be claimed back. The only hope for a place like this, Monty sighed, were committed owners who spent their every waking moment raising money to keep it going. But it was an uphill struggle.

The straight-line formality of the house's Georgian frontage had now given way to a series of bendy corridors with uneven floors and windows of all sizes and periods. The view out of them was not across the drive and the park any more, but over what Mary supposed had once been the gardens at the back of the house.

She could make out what seemed to be the remains of two walled areas; one, with shattered fountains and formal paths, had obviously once been intended to be walked in, while beneath the rampant grass and rubbish of the other, a number of large, sloping beds could vaguely be discerned. A vegetable garden? Mary made out a shattered heap of glass festooned with broken pieces of wood that could once, conceivably, have been a greenhouse. And, actually, had been, as Monty went on to explain about the lead poisoning.

Back downstairs, he led her to the handful of paintings on the shabby grey-blue silk walls of the salon. 'They're the last ones,' he lamented. 'I'm having to sell everything that doesn't move.'

'Doesn't move?' Mary queried, puzzled. What did he mean?

'Anything that does move,' chortled Monty, 'probably has woodworm in it.'

Mary laughed, delighted by his irrepressible humour and absolute lack of pompousness, as well as touched by his obvious pride in the shabby but still impressive remnants of family glory. Living alone in his enormous, echoing mansion, determined to somehow restore the family home to its original splendour, he seemed to her not an eccentric figure as much as a romantic one. He captured her imagination completely. She longed to be able to help him in his enormous, daunting and impossibly glamorous task.

By the time it came for Mary to leave, it was with a sense of extraordinary calm that she recognised her entire romantic, gentle and simple soul had been lost, immediately and for ever, to this dashing – but unintentionally dashing – creature. And now she had to go back to London.

'Oh. Must you go?' Monty had commiserated. 'I was hoping we could have dinner together, although' – he waved a long, slim, hopeless hand about him – 'I don't have much food in at the moment.'

Mary considered. An idea had occurred to her, a spontaneous and crazy one, admittedly. 'I've got a summer pudding. In here.' She patted her large, capable secretary's bag.

'Wow.' In the dim light of the salon, the pale blue eyes lit excitedly. 'Now you're talking. I'll go and get some plates. And some wine, if I can find it.'

Chapter 3

Monty was as good as his word, returning with two Meissen bowls tucked nonchalantly under one arm, two glasses under the other, two tarnished spoons poking out of his pocket and grasping a bottle of Pol Roger.

'It says 1965 on here,' Mary gasped, spotting the label.

Monty looked perturbed. 'Oh. That not old enough for you? The only other bottle down there's a 1947. But 1965's supposed to be a good year.'

'I'm sure it is,' Mary spluttered, as the golden wine boiled over into the crystal glasses Monty arranged on a rickety, gold-painted side table he now dragged over. They sat alongside each other on the least raddled of the striped-silk sofas and watched a brilliant sunset through the row of great windows. In the magnificent high room with its painted ceiling, darkness fell.

They began to eat in a silence that felt companionable rather than awkward. Here they were, Mary thought, two people who had never met before but who were now sharing a most unorthodox supper in eccentric circumstances. And yet it felt entirely natural, not odd at all. She thought of the braying Chelsea dinner party that she should have been at and felt profoundly thankful she was not.

'This is a jolly good pudding, by the way.' He waved his silver spoon.

'Tell me more about the explorers,' Mary said, wanting to please Monty and remembering how he had waxed lyrical in the bedroom on this topic.

He beamed, his teeth white in the fading light. 'Oh, I'm so glad you're interested. Most people think it's boring, but I think it's fascinating.'

Mary nodded, wondering who 'most people' were. Most women? She felt a stab of jealousy.

She had now had a good look at Monty and could believe he came from exploring stock. For all his delicate beauty, there was a wiry strength and outdoorsiness to his tall, thin figure. She found her glance dwelling on the muscular length of his thigh, swallowed and found herself blushing again.

Monty pushed his pale hair back. 'Yes,' he said with obvious pride. 'My great-great-uncle Hengist de Vere Longshott went to both the North and South Poles and was the first man,' he added with a disarming grin, 'to mix a champagne cocktail at both ends.' He paused. 'And the last, actually. I'm not sure anyone's done it since.'

'Gosh.' Mary took another sip of the vintage Pol Roger. 'I expect it was nice and cold.' It was, she had noticed, rather cold in the house. She hoped Monty could not see her shivering; it seemed rude somehow, a rebuke of sorts. But the room was full of shadows. Monty's pale hair shone intensely in the dying light. Now the extent of decay could not be seen, the gleam of the mirrors, the glint of gilt and the pale glow of marble gave the vast, still and silent chamber something of its old magnificence. Mary felt rather awed.

'Forty-five degrees below, most of the time,' Monty said briskly. 'Oh, the cocktails, you mean? Yes, I expect they were. Uncle Hengist had to carry the bottles in his suit on the way there to make sure they didn't freeze altogether.'

Mary eyed him admiringly over the crystal rim of her glass. 'This may sound like a stupid question,' she smiled, emboldened by the wine, 'but is there actually a pole at the North Pole?'

Monty guffawed and slapped his long, moleskinned thigh. 'No, if they put one there it would just float away on the ice. There's no land there, you see. Just ice. It's the size of the United States in the winter and half of it melts in the summer – more now of course, with global warming and all that.'

Mary nodded soberly. Global warming seemed a world away in the centre of this chilly house.

'You're obviously very interested,' she observed. 'Have you ever thought of exploring yourself?'

Monty's eager face took on a rueful look. 'Well, I must admit I've always fancied having a go. But the only exploring I do at the moment is try to find money to keep this place standing.' The grin flashed again. 'And, actually, that's probably harder.' The Wedgwood-blue eyes rolled upwards to the ceiling of the salon. 'Grants, tax rebates, that sort of thing. It's very confusing.' He rubbed his eyes and, for a second, looked defeated. Mary found herself longing with all her obliging soul that she could help him. She was good with paperwork, typing letters and so on, after all.

'Well I'm glad you're not exploring,' she smiled at him. 'I'm sure it's dangerous.'

His eyes glittered in the last of the light. 'Oh it's that all right. You're navigating a moving and unstable ice pack, which is at the mercy of ocean currents below and winds above. You're enduring extreme weather conditions with sudden storms and temperatures down to minus forty degrees Centigrade. There are frequent "white-outs" – zero visibility – and if you're not in danger of plunging through the ice and dying of hypothermia, there's always the risk a polar bear might get you. Modern explorers travel with guns of course, but the question is whether they can get them quick enough if a bear attacks.'

He paused. Mary was clutching his wrist. 'Stop,' she pleaded. 'It sounds awful.' As he placed his free hand over hers to reassure her, Mary felt a violent jolt in her breasts, stomach and lower pelvic region all at the same time. She swallowed and looked down, her face stinging with heat.

'No point you going back now,' Monty said to Mary when the pudding was finished.

She shook her head. It was too dark for him to see her blush now, or, thankfully, for him to see in her eyes what she longed for him to do next. The champagne seemed to have concentrated all its force into her erogenous zones. Her lips burned to be kissed, her nipples seemed to be fizzing and the electricity between her legs, she felt, could probably have powered the house. It needed something to power it, certainly; the few lamps Monty now switched on were weak, flickering and incapable of lighting more than a radius of a few feet around them.

She watched, sipping more champagne – the 1947 bottle was open now – as Monty built a huge fire in the carved marble fireplace that could have held a motorbike. He piled up cushions on the carpet before it and they sat for a while staring at the flames. Then, in unison, they turned to each other. 'I hope you don't think this is a bit forward,' Monty muttered as his long mouth closed on hers. She shook her head as she pulled him down.

She had never gone back to London. Waking, that first morning, amid the heaps and mess of Monty's four-poster, Mary felt entirely happy for the first time in her life and realised she had never really liked the city. At the auction house, her heart had always been less with the Chanel-suited sophisticates who crowded in for the big sales than it was with the red-faced country landowners in battered tweed covered in dog hairs who occasionally appeared to have a Landseer valued or to sell a bit more silver plate.

As they left the auction house to get the bus to Paddington, Euston or whatever terminus chugged them back to their sprawling homes, Mary's heart would go with them. She would imagine the dogs rushing to meet them as they arrived, the fire leaping over the apple logs in the ancestral fireplace, the darkening acres outside the mullioned windows, the defiant chirrup of the last chaffinch. And now here she was, in just such acres. And there were plenty of chaffinches outside that morning.

She and Monty had married three weeks later in a register office in Derby. Mary had worn a pink sundress from Next. The witnesses had been two passers-by. Mary's parents, imagining themselves mere months away from a City financier son-in-law, had been appalled to discover their only daughter planned to marry an impoverished aristocrat whose house was apparently falling down about his ears. 'You need your head examining,' barked her neurosurgeon father. Her friends were equally suspicious, as well as offended at not being invited. 'You married after three *weeks*?' gasped one, who had been engaged to her stolid solicitor husband for three years. 'You had no engagement?'

'No.' What were engagements for, after all? For waiting while beads were hand-sewn on to the wedding dress and the hand-selected lilies to wind round the marquee posts were grown?

None of her friends had said in so many words that she was mad, but they had clearly thought it. However, ten years later, she and Monty were still married and most of the friends, long engagements notwithstanding, divorced.

And she and Monty were happy, for all their eccentric situation. Except for one thing, Mary knew. They never spoke about it and she was uncertain as to the extent that he still thought about it, but for her part, the children they had never had were a lingering sadness. She would have loved some; as, she knew, would Monty. He had never said so directly, but she sensed that filling the old, rotten, deserted nursery upstairs with a few white-blond heads of his own would be a dream come true on a par with saving the house itself. But the months had gone by, each with its relentless red smear appearing at the expected time, and then the years. The doctor had been able to find nothing wrong with either of them. In her more fancifully miserable moments, however, Mary wondered if the lead that had poisoned the land around Weston Underwood had not somehow entered her system too. God only knew what was in some of those pipes that fed the water tank.

It was hard sometimes, Mary thought, to see what she had actually achieved at all during the years of her marriage to Monty. No children, and, for all her hopes she would be able to help him with her secretarial skills, for all the letters to various grant bodies, all the research into tax breaks and heritage-related finance initiatives that formed her full-time, if unpaid employment, nothing of any significance had really resulted.

Even her early determination to tidy the place up a bit more soon faded in the face of the enormity of the task. It went against the grain of her domestic and orderly soul to admit defeat, but what Mary eventually had to admit was that Hercules's challenge in the Augean stables seemed peanuts – or perhaps horsenuts – compared to the job of bringing order to what were apparently over a hundred chaotic rooms. It was easier, Mary found, to hide her head in the sand – or the dust – and after a while she ceased to explore beyond the handful of rooms she and Monty normally used.

'Underpants'll survive,' Monty would declare cheerily. It was a traditional family joke to shorten Weston Underwood to 'Vest and Underpants' and from there to simply 'Underpants'. 'After all, it's survived for five hundred years,' he would add breezily, his pale blue eyes gleaming hopefully.

He was trying to rally her, she knew. And she appreciated his efforts, loved him for his unquenchable flow of enthusiasm and energy. But even so there was no question that, at the moment, things were dire. The direst they had ever been.

Chapter 4

Morag Archbutt-Pesk stood in her kitchen, hands on the hips of her lilac cotton drawstring trousers. The setting sun flamed through her tumbled aubergine bob, giving her the appearance of some vengeful purple goddess. And vengeful was what Morag, not unusually, was feeling.

Her thick brown brows were drawn in anger and she stared balefully with her protuberant brown eyes out of the kitchen window in the direction of the neighbours' house just above. 'I don't know what they're complaining about,' she snapped to her partner Gid. 'I mean, don't they want to save the human race? Don't they care about their fellow man and their mother planet?'

Gid shook his head in supportive bewilderment. The flesh of his face wobbled with the movement. He had once been handsome but was now beginning to soften and plump at the edges, his once pronounced cheekbones to fill in. 'Yeah, it's ridiculous. It's not our fault that our new low-eco-impact loo hasn't arrived from Reykjavik yet and we need to use theirs for the time being.'

The nostrils of Morag's sharp nose flared. 'It certainly isn't.

The Waterhouses should be delighted to assist us as we move towards a more sustainable lifestyle.'

'Absolutely,' Gid nodded. He always agreed with Morag. Partly because it was the safest and most convenient route, but mainly because he genuinely concurred. Morag with her high principles, endless energy and fearless approach to controversy was, so far as he was concerned, a modern Boadicea beside whom all other women paled. 'It's not very helpful,' he mused of his neighbours, 'for them to point out that us using their facilities quadruples the amount of flushed water in their house and negates in advance all the good our new system will do.'

Morag pressed her fleshy, unpainted lips together in fury. How dare Sally Waterhouse criticise the fact that the Archbutt-Pesks used the lavatory more frequently than the Waterhouses did themselves? It was obvious to anyone that this was because the Waterhouses ate far too much processed food and the Archbutt-Pesks had the more efficient diet. 'Typical of that selfish, loadsamoney incomer mentality,' she snarled.

Gid did not reply. While Morag was entirely correct in saying that the Waterhouses were incomers, i.e. people who had not been born in the village of Allsop, so too were he and Morag. Moreover, the Waterhouses had been in residence for a good few months before the Archbutt-Pesks had moved in; Gid to set up his biosustainable-lifestyle website selling minimum-impact existence solutions and Morag to be a full-time Woman, as she liked to shorthand her twin roles as partner to himself and mother to their daughter Merlin.

The sun shone through the small cottage window over Gid's left shoulder and caught the tips of his pointy ears and fleshy chin with its halo of stubble. Morag screwed her long thin face up harder against the rays. 'Oh well,' she shrugged. 'If people are too dim to see the obvious, so be it. You can lead a horse to water . . .'

'Although increasingly not, as sustainable land-water sources are drained through profligacy and overuse,' Gid slipped in.

Morag glanced at the kitchen clock. 'We'd better get moving, anyway. We're due at the Town Hall to protest.'

'Are we?' asked Gid.

Morag glared at him. 'Don't say you've forgotten!'

Gid looked sheepish. He hadn't forgotten that they were protesting; they protested most evenings after all and it was rare they did anything else. The detail of what they were protesting about had escaped him, however.

'The county council want to raise the remote-villages bus-service from once a week to twice for the crumblies to get to the supermarket.' Morag's voice was full of impatience, both with Gid and the crumblies. And, of course, the county council who wished to raise fossil fuel emissions in this way.

'Oh yes,' said Gid hurriedly.

'Oh *yes*. It's all very well for pensioners to want to get out more but they need to be reminded that their shopping trips have consequences for the universe,' Morag pronounced.

Gid nodded earnestly.

'And it's more than fuel emissions,' Morag warned.

'Oh, absolutely.' Gid waited to be told what else it was.

'They shouldn't be shopping in supermarkets. They should be sourcing their needs locally, at small artisanal bakeries and greengrocers selling organically grown vege-tables. Not pouring the pensions given to them by taxpayers into the pockets of multinational food corporations.'

Gid nodded. The question of whether small artisanal

bakeries and organic greengrocers actually existed in out-of-the-way villages flitted vaguely across his mind. In their infrequent trips to the real back of beyond he had never seen anything apart from the occasional Spar. He dismissed this treasonous thought, however.

Morag, meanwhile, had turned her strafing gaze on the thin strip of their own garden. Instantly her forehead creased again with frowns.

'Merlin's put that blasted princess tent your mother gave her up in front of the creature tower again,' she snarled. That their five-year-old daughter was far more interested in a mass-produced erection of bright pink nylon than in the admittedly rickety chimney-like construction of bark, twigs, sticks and other random natural materials Gid had built to encourage beetles, earwigs and other biodiversity to live in the garden was another source of annoyance.

Perhaps, Morag thought, she should have followed her heart and educated her daughter at home. She had been a fool to allow Gid to persuade her, last year, to send Merlin to that instrument of state repression, the local primary school.

'I'm still breastfeeding her,' Morag had objected at the time. 'And what about her raw-food diet? They'll try and vaccinate her as well.'

She had been mollified only when Gid had pointed out they could always send Merlin to school with a packed lunch of chopped organic carrots and home-made houmous. And that Merlin's introduction to formal education meant Morag's introduction to any number of parent committees and groups that needed someone with energy, commitment and strong, sensible ideas. This argument had eventually carried the day.

She continued to stare at the garden. Once, she had

planned to grow vegetables here to the highest biosustainable standards. But the creature tower and the princess tent now took up all available space. Morag flicked an angry eye up to the house above, where the Waterhouses' garden spread out from the back of their cottage like a floral cloak. Bloody flowers, Morag thought furiously. What was the point of them? Criminal waste of good vegetable-growing soil was what they were. That was the problem with bloody incomers. They just didn't get the country life at all. Didn't understand it. Hadn't a clue.

Take that new couple further down the lane. The Ferraros, or whatever they were called. Worse even than the Waterhouses, with their window boxes filled with twee miniature roses and their dustbin painted pale pink. Pink! And the woman – Beth – had got a painter and decorator to paint it too. 'A professionally painted pink dustbin!' Morag had spat at Gid, who had rolled his eyes obediently. 'But what else do you expect from Americans?' she had added.

'Capitalist imperialists,' Gid ventured.

'What are they doing in our village?' Morag stormed. 'They should bloody well go home. Back to where they came from. No one wants them here.'

Yet the Ferraros' worst crime, in Morag's eyes, was one they had not actually committed. And *because* they hadn't committed it, more to the point. Ever since the obviously wealthy American couple had first appeared in the lane, Morag had been watching their cottage like a hawk – from every window of her own house and every available vantage point outside – in the hope of spotting blatant floutings of building regulations. That the Ferraros should add Velux windows in a conservation area, dig a swimming pool in the back, wrench out some Jacobean beams or impose non-heritage roof lights was her dearest wish. Then she could unleash with full, targeted and legally justified force the entire extent of the loathing she felt for them.

Morag gave frequent, passionate and sometimes deafening airings to her longing for world peace, the end of poverty and the saving of the planet. But almost more than she longed for these, she longed for the appearance of the tell-tale pale blue paper in its protective plastic covering, tied to the Ferraros' drainpipe and advising all interested parties that under the terms of the Town and Country Planning Act, the couple sought approval for their intention to demolish the current property, dated 1659, and erect a futuristic glass-fronted split-level villa in its place. Anyone objecting should contact the council planning office.

But no such paper had yet appeared. Indeed, all the Ferraros had done so far was paint their exterior woodwork pale pink which, considering all hers was purple, and a rather more assertive register of colour into the bargain, Morag could not reasonably object to.

Therefore the sight of the pink dustbin, representing as it did all the evils of the world, especially those not committed, filled Morag with bilious fury every time she saw it. But owing to its location inside the deep recess of the Ferraros' cottage door, her efforts to hit it as she drove past had so far been thwarted.

Chapter 5

'That was a nightmare awful drive up,' Beth Ferraro exclaimed in her best English accent, flouncing into the cottage and dropping a flowery weekend bag on one of the many patterned sofas. As she bent to switch on the lamps her shining blond hair, caught up in a pink silk rose hair bobble, glowed; its pulled-back, Friday-night bunch revealing her thin and rather delicate face. Slipping her perfectly pedicured toes out of the jewelled flip-flops she liked to wear in the car, she wiggled them appreciatively against the simple, white-painted wooden floor, equipped below with the very latest underheating technology.

'You weren't even driving,' grumped her husband Benny, following her in, two bottles of red wine clamped in his big brown paws. 'You'd have something to complain about if you were.'

Benny, who habitually indulged his wife's every whim, had been happy to comply when Beth said they must, they absolutely must, have a cottage in some fashionable county of England. According to her, no one in London stayed in the city at weekends. You could have fooled him, Benny thought.

Oxford Street on a Saturday was a seething mass of humanity.

But Beth insisted that no one worth knowing stuck around beyond Friday and that the happening thing to do in England was to have a rural second home. So he'd got her one; rather, a relocation agent had, according to Beth's instructions that they required somewhere near lots of large country houses so they could make friends with dukes. Derbyshire, it turned out, was positively alive with such houses, although they were yet to make a single ducal acquaintance.

The village was pretty, admittedly. Totally English, on top of a hill, lots of cute, jumbly little grey-stone cottages with tiny flowery gardens all huddled together around an old church with a pointy tower. The cottages were of all ages – some hundreds of years old, others a mere fifty – all sizes and shapes and built at all angles, no one exactly like another. Their own cottage, on the block opposite the church, had 1659 on the date stone above the door, more or less before America existed, a thought which always rather struck Benny as he passed through the deep-walled doorway into the warreny cottage.

While the view out of the front was merely of the lane itself, that out of the back looked over steep green hills dotted with barns and sturdy, muscly cattle whose colour ranged from ginger to a kind of bluish grey, all new to Benny, who had imagined cows were black and white, period.

The view had obviously been the same for centuries. Some of the guys looking after the cows looked as if they had been here for centuries too. It was kind of hard, Benny thought, to imagine this sleepy, silent bunch of houses being here, being cute hundreds of years before the thrusting sheen and glare of Manhattan.

Yes, Allsop ticked every charming English country village box in the book. But there was no doubt the driving was a downer.

'London to Derbyshire without stopping . . .' He pronounced 'shire' to rhyme with 'fire'. Beth, who had worked hard since arriving in England at eradicating her American drawl, had an idea that this wasn't correct. But the 'Derb' in Derbyshire definitely rhymed with 'herb'. Of that she was certain.

Beth didn't drive. Beth didn't do anything she didn't want to. And that was the way he liked it, Benny reminded himself firmly as he uncorked the wine and slopped some into glasses. His beautiful, slender, golden-haired, clean-scented, delicate wife was his trophy. He earned the money and she spent it. It had been that way through the five years of their marriage, ever since, in a scenario worthy of *High Society*, or, as he secretly admitted was nearer the mark, of the video of *Uptown Girl*, he, a stocky, dark, not-particularly-handsome-but-nonetheless-millionaire financier of Italian-American extraction had wooed and won her, the educated, stylish daughter of a wealthy East Coast family.

Beth's part of the bargain was to look lovely, be amusing and make their home and social life reflect all that was currently tasteful and fashionable – with a unique twist all her own, of course. She had done this in various houses they had had in New York and Los Angeles already, and now, lured by new opportunities, Benny had crossed the herring pond and was living in London, she was doing it there too. And once she had decided that a cottage in the country was what all upmarket Brits had, she had done it in the country as well.

'I do think my English decor looks nice,' Beth remarked, looking round with satisfaction.

'Well you didn't actually do it yourself,' Benny could not resist pointing out. An interior design consultant had, as usual, done the hard work.

'No, but I did the difficult bit,' Beth said, enunciating with care. She had, Benny knew, accepted wholesale the British premise that a smart voice meant a smart person. 'I did the concept. The art direction. But it's come out pretty well,' she said, conscientiously pronouncing her T's. 'Take this room.' She waved a slender, beringed hand around the sitting room. 'I was going for that British look. Patterned chairs, wood piled in fireplace kinda thing, with distressed white cupboards and wooden floors.'

'And you got it,' grinned Benny, looking at the patterned chairs, the wood piled in the fireplace, the distressed white cupboards and the wooden floor. The sitting room, he felt, was actually the best room. The second best was the bathroom, where a big, generous roll-top Victorian tub had been installed.

He was less keen on the study she had made for him on the landing, with a sisal floor and some flowered wallpaper. He hated it – it gave him a migraine – but Beth countered his objections by insisting it was English country style. 'Sophisticated homespun,' she added.

Benny felt sophisticated homespun was making his head spin. Those stacks of violently colourful flowery cake tins in the kitchen even though Beth didn't eat cake and did her utmost to discourage him from doing so. Benny had a sweet tooth and, being dark, stocky and short thanks to his Italian forebears, tended to run to fat. There were multicoloured polka-dot plates in the cupboard. And apparently purposeless pink tins covered with stars on the shelf.

Upstairs was similarly riotous. There was a floral

eiderdown on the brass-framed double bed while the white-painted wardrobe was full of rose-printed dresses. And more, Benny knew, was planned. Much more.

'I saw some fabulous rose-printed cushions in the Cath Kidston catalogue,' Beth mused now, staring critically at the sofa, which she had bought new before having it reupholstered at great expense in faded striped material so it looked old. 'They'd look so cool there. So English.'

'Er . . .' Benny began to object.

His wife interrupted, face bright with excitement. 'And, hey, guess what?'

'What?' Benny asked fearfully.

'You know we still haven't come up with a name for this place?'

Benny nodded, swallowing. But Beth had come up with plenty of suggestions. He blushed beneath his tan to remember some of them.

'I hit on the perfect one this morning, when I was having a quick peek in Tiffany's,' Beth exulted, her blue eyes shining.

Benny fingered the collar of his weekend Armani polo shirt. 'Don't tell me. Holly Golightly cottage?'

'Bijou Cottage!' declared Beth, triumphantly. 'Because it's like a little jewel, don't you think?'

Benny did think, but only in the sense that the place had cost as much as a whole box of them. 'We-ell,' he started doubtfully. But then a high-pitched wailing ripped through the silence of the cottage.

Beth's large green eyes stretched wide. 'It's the car alarm!'

'Shit. Someone's fooling with it again.' Benny strode to the door. Boy, did this piss him off. Their shiny black four-wheel drive sat all week without incident outside their four-floor stucco terrace in Notting Hill, slap bang in the middle of central London. But the minute it got to Allsop, to the middle of bloody nowhere, it started going off like the fucking Fourth of July.

He flung open the ancient cottage door which was in two pieces, stable style. The bolt joining them had not been shot and so now the upper part of the door swung back and hit Benny in the face. He yelped with pain and irritation. Then, limping outside, he yelped with horror.

'What's up?' Beth called from inside the cottage.

'The fucking handbrake's slipped,' Benny muttered. 'Somehow.'

Beth crowed. 'Hey! Not the world's best driver after all, are we then?'

Benny tried to ignore her. There were greater matters in hand. Instead of being where he expected, on the gently inclining narrow lane right outside the door of the cottage, their big, shiny black car was at the bottom of the lane, front buried in the stones of the churchyard wall and completely obstructing any traffic that might want to pass along the road at the bottom. And, as it happened, someone did want to.

'Omigod!' Beth breathed, now leaning over the half-door. An ambulance had stopped just before the side of the Discovery. 'It can't get past our car! It could be life or death!' she declared dramatically.

'Gee, I never woulda realised,' Benny snapped, diving out of the door and heading down the lane. His heart was thundering. Was obstructing an ambulance actionable? Could the relatives of the deceased sue?

Chapter 6

A figure, Benny saw, was striding angrily up the road towards him. He noted its lack of the usual fluorescent green NHS boiler suit he thought all British ambulancemen wore. Or did on the TV soaps, anyhow. But this person, who appeared to be a woman, was wearing what looked, in the colour-flattening streetlight, to be purple trousers and a red waistcoat that seemed to be glittering with something.

Reassessing at speed, Benny concluded this must be the person who was with whoever was injured in the ambulance. He did not recognise them, but then he didn't really know anyone in Allsop yet apart from the landlord of the pub.

'Excuse me,' Benny began, genuinely apologetic. This person was after all entitled to be irritated. 'I'll get out of the way,' he assured her. 'Then you can get to the hospital.'

'Hospital?' snarled the woman. 'What do you mean, hospital?'

Benny stared at her in the swirling, misty gloom. 'Well, you've got an ambulance.' Although there wasn't an ambulance driver, he saw now. The front of the vehicle was empty, meaning this madwoman wasn't in the back with the victim, she had actually been driving it. Was that allowed? And who, he asked falteringly, was in the back?

'A lot of brown rice and mung beans from the health food shop, if you must know,' barked the woman. 'I've just been to pick up our monthly delivery which, I imagine, involves a great many fewer food miles than yours does.'

Benny rubbed his eyes. 'You mean,' he said, pointing at the vehicle, 'that *that's* what you actually drive about in? That ambulance is, like, your *car*?' Now he came to look at it closely the ambulance looked pretty old. It was also pretty filthy. Neither of which exactly screamed National Health Service.

'None of your business, but what if it is?' snarled the woman, placing her hands aggressively on her hips. 'It's decommissioned. A recycled vehicle. Better for the environment than that planet-annihilating *tank* you've got there.' She nodded contemptuously at the 4x4.

'But people have probably, like, *died* in that ambulance,' Benny could not stop himself blurting out.

'So what. Death's a natural process.' The woman stabbed an accusing finger at the 4x4. 'You going to move this or what?' she shouted.

'Sure,' muttered Benny, hurrying towards his car.

'Excuse me, but what *is* all this yelling about?' came Beth's best British voice from the lane behind him. She sounded, as she thought all smart English people habitually did, mildly amused.

Benny realised with a stab of panic that his wife was unlikely to defuse the incendiary situation. He had a distinct feeling that Beth was exactly the kind of woman this mad purple harridan hated most.

However, it was too late to do anything about it. He

watched helplessly as Beth came sashaying down the street, hugging her pale pink pashmina round her narrow frame. Under the lamplight her pale hair glowed mistily and her toes in their sparkling flip-flops wiggled in the cold. She extended a hand to Morag as if they were at the most fashionable W11 cocktail party imaginable. The pick of the work of a fashionable Knightsbridge jeweller glittered on her fingers.

'I'm Elizabeth Ferraro, how do you do?' Her clipped voice was amplified by the cottage walls around. In which, Benny imagined, everyone now had their ears pressed hungrily to the windows. 'It's a pleasure to meet you,' Beth added graciously.

His wife's words, as Benny had anticipated, had the effect on the purple-trousered woman that a lit match has on a drum of fuel.

'Well it's not a pleasure to meet *you*,' she snarled. 'We don't *want* Yanks here. Capitalist *oppressors*. Empire-building *exploiters*. With that bloody stupid pink dustbin,' she added contemptuously.

Beth looked horrified. 'Is it *that* obvious I'm American?'

Benny was torn. He could not decide which to be most offended by: the slights on the motherland or the disrespect to his dustbin, as people called ashcans here. Admittedly, he had been less than keen on Beth having the ashcan painted pale eggshell pink, but at the time he had decided it was the lesser of two evils. And Beth had at least held back from covering it with roses.

The woman glared. 'You should be ashamed of yourselves,' she ranted.

'What for?' Beth asked innocently. 'For painting the ashcan pink?'

'For taking cottages from local people and driving up property prices,' thundered their accuser.

'But we didn't drive up anything, we paid what they asked,' Beth protested with a winsome smile.

The other woman did not immediately reply. Benny had the sense of her taking in breaths, inflating, for some huge explosion. It came. 'It's people like you,' she roared at Beth, 'who are bringing the countryside to its knees. Flinging your filthy money about, thinking you can buy everything and everyone.'

Benny suddenly snapped out of his state of intimidated lethargy. This really was too much. In the course of the past five minutes he had been called a racist scumbag, a planet-wrecker, the representative of a repressive and immoral regime, and now he stood accused of single-handedly ruining the British rural economy. 'Let me deal with this,' he muttered.

But before Benny could challenge her on any of her remarks, the woman climbed back into the front of the ambulance and started it up with a series of splutters resolving into a terrifying, throaty roar. It may be decom-missioned and recycled, Benny mused, but just how good for the planet was it?

Benny mounted the people carrier's driving seat. The vehicle groaned and whined and the front end clanked and scraped. It did not, however, move. Somehow it had managed to jam itself into the churchyard wall. After revving harder and harder, more to relieve his feelings than anything else, Benny stabbed at the electric window button so furiously he hurt his index finger. When the pane had lowered itself to a level permitting, he thrust his large, rumpled head out. 'Hey,' he called towards the ambulance, as casually and collectedly as he could manage. 'I'm going to have to go make a phone call. I guess someone's going to have to come and pull us out.'

Later, after the nice AA man had left and the purple-trousered harridan finally gone, they sat by the fire in the cottage and stared glumly into the flames it had, as usual, taken an unfeasible amount of time to light. Benny was halfway through a bottle of red wine and trying not to worry about having seen the red tail-lights of the ambulance – well, the one that worked, in any case – heading up their lane and round the bend at the top where, he knew but had not inspected, there were more cottages. If Purple Trouser Woman was one of their near neighbours, that was not good news. Not good news at all. The couple they had bought from had been vague about their precise reasons for selling up and leaving the village. Could he now, Benny thought, have stumbled on the reason why?

Beth was silent, partly from tiredness and partly from shock at the unpleasantness of the handbrake-slipping episode. The period between the AA man being called and him actually arriving had been filled by the woman in purple unburdening herself of further fervent views on the subject of second-home-owners, especially American ones, and their careless and feckless ways.

Benny had tried to make her see reason. 'Don't you think you're prejudicing us with a bit of a negative stereotype?' he had suggested in as relaxed a tone as he could summon.

'Yeah, we just love English country style, as you can tell from the house,' Beth had added brightly, gesturing at the cottage, where she stood inside the stable door and the others outside.

This had merely been a cue for the woman to stick her tousled aubergine head through the hole in the door, look blazingly round the cottage sitting room and spit that stereotypes was the word, the whole place was a pathetic fucking cliché and who did they think they were kidding. English style, her arse. This had cut Beth to the quick. 'It's just the thought of her arse and my decor,' she had sighed afterwards.

There came now a sharp rap on the cottage door which caused both Beth and Benny to jump in terror off the sofa. 'You go,' hissed Beth, eyes wide with apprehension.

Benny crossed the white-painted wooden boards with their under-floor heating. He laid a shaking hand on the stable-door handle and gingerly opened it, trying to suppress visions of massed ranks of villagers waving pickaxes and baying for the blood of incomers.

A brilliant smile met him in the darkness. 'Your curry!' announced the man from the takeaway down in the valley. Neither of them had felt up to cooking, although the takeout choice around here was pretty limited. Beth had wanted sushi, but Indian was all that appeared to be on offer.

Benny gingerly took the brown paper bag, which featured a large grease patch on the side, and fumbled for his wallet. 'Thanks,' he muttered, handing over some notes. 'Keep the change.'

'There's something else,' the delivery man announced.

'What?' Benny asked jumpily.

Something hard and cold was suddenly thrust into his hands. Benny could not see what in the dark. 'What the hell is this?' he squealed, his much-strained nerves finally fraying as he imagined a Molotov cocktail primed to go off in his face.

'Bottle of Liebfraumilch!' beamed the man from the

takeaway as he slammed the stable door shut. 'Free with all orders over twenty-five pounds!'

Benny stared at the bottle. What in hell's name was Liebfraumilch? 'Er, thanks,' he said.

The man disappeared into the night. Once back in his van he continued to express his gratitude for their generous order with a series of loud honks Benny imagined would not exactly increase their popularity locally.

'It's pretty bad,' he said to Beth as they spooned a pink creamy soup containing a few chicken bits over their rice.

She pulled a face. 'I know. It must be five hundred per cent fat.'

'Not the food!' Benny exclaimed irritably, although he secretly felt a green polka-dot plate had not improved matters in that respect. 'I mean . . .' He waved a fork.

'Careful of the walls,' Beth interrupted. 'This stuff will stain.'

'I mean the village,' Benny pressed on exasperatedly. 'The fact we're not very popular.'

Beth shrugged. 'That woman probably hates everybody. She's got major anger issues.'

Unconvinced, Benny gazed glumly at the dining table, custom-made at vast expense in rustic style by a carpenter from Hoxton. Perhaps it would have been more diplomatic to source one locally. 'Sure, she's crazy. But there might be others who feel sort of the same way. I mean, we really haven't been making much of an effort. We should – well – try and integrate ourselves more. Make some friends. Make people realise we're not just dumb Yanks.' It was, he was beginning to feel, his patriotic duty.

'I guess so,' Beth yawned.

'Wouldn't you like to meet people?' Benny coaxed.

'Depends what sort of people. I want to meet the local aristocrats,' Beth said, eyes sparking with enthusiasm. 'It would be cool to get into that country-house scene. Dinners at fifty-foot-long tables. Footmen everywhere. Meets on the lawn on Boxing Day . . .'

Benny stared. 'Meets on the lawn – but they don't hunt in England any more. Well, they're allowed to chase after bits of paper, I think, but that's about it.'

'Shame,' said Beth.

'Not if you're a fox, I guess.'

Benny got up and paced over to the front window. On its sill sat the junk mail delivered during the week. As he had placed the pile there on entering the cottage that evening, he had unconsciously registered something he now realised could be useful. 'This has come,' he said, waving the item concerned at Beth.

Still thinking about stately homes, she looked at it with apprehension. 'What is it?' The former owners had sub-scribed to some worrying publications, including a plastics catalogue whose star item squeezed old bits of soap together to make a new bar.

'The village newsletter,' Benny said, striding back to the dining table. He sat down and reached for the distressed-wood lamp with the striped pink cotton shade. The shade promptly slid off the bulb, which shone a bare, circular beam on to the white stapled A4 pamphlet.

Benny pushed his plate of food to one side and began running his tanned index finger carefully up and down the pages.

Beth moodily munched on some chicken and watched him.

'There must be something here that we could join,' Benny

muttered. He looked up eagerly. 'Hey. There's a film club. They're showing *Pride and Prejudice*.'

'We saw that a million years ago,' sulked Beth.

'Mothers' Union?' Benny teased. 'Fancy a bit of jam-making?'

Beth winced at the idea of sugary preserve on her expensively white teeth. And not only at that. 'I'm not a mother, nor do I want to be, not yet, anyway.' She looked searchingly at her husband for confirmation that this was, indeed, the position they had reached on this important question.

'No,' agreed Benny, hurriedly.

Beth, now thinking about bed, stood up and prepared to take the plates to the rose-transferred, special-limited-edition dishwasher.

Benny's finger continued down the pages. 'There's a bell-ringing society . . .'

'*Bell-ringing?*'

He looked up now. 'Why not? What could be more English than the sound of bells across the meadows?'

'I am not,' Beth cut in crisply, leaning over the Hoxton dining table and fixing him with determined eyes, 'spending my weekends pulling noisy things on ropes up and down. If I wanted to do that, I'd get a goddam dog.'

Chapter 7

Mary Longshott sat writing letters in the kitchen at Weston Underwood. Being both the warmest and the least rotten-looking room on account of all the stone surfaces and general lack of furniture, it served as her office, Monty's office, dining room and sitting room.

From time to time Mary looked up, distracted by the silence. It was hard to imagine this silent, stone-floored chamber heaving, as it once had, with a team of twenty: pastry cooks, still-room maids, dairymaids and spit boys, with butlers, parlourmaids and footmen dashing in and out for the dishes. The massive fireplace still contained the spit once turned by the spit boy, and across one entire wall stretched a long, shallow stone sink with a wooden plate-rack hanging on by a whisker to the cracked wall above it.

Mary gazed around. Stone-framed doorways from the main kitchen led into a variety of other domestic offices: stillroom, storeroom, pastry room, butchery – with the rather grisly brick channel down the middle of the floor which had once run with the blood of pigs slaughtered on the premises.

There was also a laundry, empty now and with walls

scabbed with damp, but still with the enormous clothes-airer bolted to the ceiling and, in the corner, the curious flat-iron heater, a tall conical object some five feet tall, of black iron with ridged and faceted sides, which had once contained a fire and could heat fifty-six flat irons at once. The Weston laundry these days was an elderly twin-tub which threatened any day to give up the ghost, and the faithful Mrs Shuffle, who threatened nothing of the sort and seemed more sprightly with every passing year.

Mary looked up. The room was high to cope with the fierce heat that the great hearth had once generated. The only heat now came from the small electric radiator permanently affixed to the ancient Bakelite socket. The house as a whole, even in the summer, as now, never warmed up much inside. Sometimes Mary wondered what the enormous Victorian heating pipes were actually connected to. The fridge, probably.

This particular morning, however, even the fridge wasn't working. The electricity supply was suffering one of its periodic hiccups. As she worked, Mary found her thoughts drifting irresistibly to another of the rooms off the kitchen: the lamp room, in which oil lamps and candles for every room in the house had once been stored, maintained and dispensed by a servant whose entire responsibility it was. What luxury. An entire person in charge of the lighting system rather than some anonymous utility eternally impossible to get through to.

The kitchen table at which she sat was a small pine island in the midst of a huge stone sea. Mary tapped her pen against her lip, mulling over exactly how best to ask English Heritage about grants for heritage gutters. Once she had written off confidently asking for help with entire roofs and wings. She knew better now, but knowing better made her feel worse.

She knew the prospects even for gutter assistance were not good. A representative of the conservation body had assessed the house only the week before, and it had been heart-breaking to convey his verdict to Monty, who had been out buying Polyfilla at the time. The house's need for Polyfilla was so frequent and so huge, Mary often thought, that a pipeline connecting Underpants to wherever Polyfilla was made would save a lot of effort.

There had been no way to break the news gently. 'Monty,' Mary had said. 'This house is a wreck. Damp is an under-statement. We have a family of resident toads. Underpants is so wet that it would need an eight-year restoration project just to plug the holes.'

'Says who?' Monty challenged.

'The expert from English Heritage who came today to assess our chances of opening to the public.'

Monty's lean, handsome face lit up. The glassy blue eyes glowed. 'Fantastic.'

Mary shook her head. 'That's not what he thought. In fact, I'd rather not tell you what he thought.' The heritage expert had expressed his amazement that they lived from day to day, and when Mary had agreed that money was tight he had said, 'No, I'm amazed you don't get killed by something falling on you.'

Monty's expression radiated indignation and disappoint-ment. 'What?'

'The roofs and windows all leak badly and the water has penetrated the mortar which holds Underpants together,' Mary reported. These had been the headlines of the expert's assessment. 'It will take about five million pounds to stop it deteriorating further, let alone repair it,' she concluded miserably.

'We have to think of something,' Monty agreed.

Mary nodded. 'But, darling, what?'

The future looked hopeless. She and Monty had no money of their own, no grants were forthcoming from anyone else, and the only other option, which was selling it, was obviously impossible. No developer would be allowed to buy, knock down and build anew on what was after all a Grade 1 listed building on green-belt land. Even if Monty was prepared to sell it, which he obviously never, ever would. Nor did Mary want him to. She had married him and Underpants for better or worse, and while, at the moment, worse rather had the upper hand, things would get better eventually.

There was one small compensation, if so it could be called. Given the fact the place was to all intents and purposes a death trap, it was, Mary mused, just as well they didn't have any children.

'Morning, Mrs Longshott.'

Mrs Shuffle had arrived. Mary, grateful for the distraction, leapt to her feet in welcome.

Over the years, she had grown extremely fond of the cleaner who had served the Longshott family for so long and, it had to be said, for so little money. Of late, as Monty said, Mrs Shuffle was probably spending more in petrol than she was earning, but still the cleaner kept coming.

Mrs Shuffle was plump, cheerful, briskly capable and believed in looking her best at all times. She wore large ginger-rimmed glasses, gold earrings, was never without a slick of pink lipstick, and her hair, which had turned from vaguely sandy to brightest brass over the years, was always thoroughly tonged upwards to give an effect reminiscent of a chrysanthemum. She had a passion for clothes, specifically making and knitting her own, and the results could be mixed. This morning's yellow polo-neck featuring a bright purple poppy pattern was unmistakably, Mary recognised, a Shuffle original, and one she had not seen before.

About to offer the customary cup of tea, Mary remembered why she could not. 'Oh Mrs Shuffle, I'm so sorry. The electric's off again and so you won't be able to use the Hoover.'

Mrs Shuffle shrugged as if this were nothing out of the ordinary. Which it wasn't; she had not been able to use the vacuum cleaner for weeks now as the machine had terminally broken down. She had been awaiting the right moment to mention this to Mary, as a replacement was obviously out of the question.

'You'll have to use the dustpan and brush,' Mary lamented.

'That's all right.' Mrs Shuffle heroically forbore to point out that she had been exclusively using a dustpan and brush for some time.

Her good-natured tolerance made Mary's eyes suddenly prick. Mrs Shuffle's loyalty was from another era altogether, which most things at Underpants were, of course. But was it really loyalty that kept her coming, or simply fascination? Mrs Shuffle had a lively curiosity in the world and all its doings, especially the doings of Allsop, which she communicated to Mary in great detail on a weekly basis.

'I'd better ring the electric company up and get it back on,' Mary added resignedly.

'Good luck,' remarked Mrs Shuffle.

Her alerting of the utility company started reasonably

well. She called 0800, which had put her through to a nice man in Bombay who had then given her a number ostensibly for emergencies in her own area. Having dialled this number, Mary learnt all operators were busy and was put on hold. This conjured up the usual paranoid fantasies.

Despite knowing, rationally, that call centre work was among the most boring and unrewarding possible, whenever she was on hold Mary always imagined all the operators racing about on office chairs swigging champagne out of bottles and laughing at the customers paralysed in the system behind them. To be finally answered and told the nice man in Bombay wasn't so nice after all because he had given her the wrong number did little to obliterate her conviction that all forces in call centres, and in particular call centres connected to malfunctioning utilities, were forces of darkness. Again put on hold, Mary strove to be patient through eight more minutes of waiting, was eventually answered and given yet another number leading to yet more operators who were currently busy. Invited to save time and punch all her details into the system using the keypad on her telephone, Mary complied. She was rewarded a lengthy five minutes later when she reached a real person, a surly young woman who asked for her name, phone number, house number and postcode.

'But I've just entered all that in the handset,' Mary explained in tones which, for her, were quite testy.

'I need your name, phone number, house number and postcode,' the operator repeated obdurately.

Mary repeated them as politely as she could, the great well of suppressed rage she felt expressing itself only in the emphatic manner in which she pronounced the words.

'No need to shout,' the operator snapped.

'I'm trying not to, believe me. But it has been rather frustrating,' Mary said through clenched teeth.

'I'm warning you, if you shout I'm putting the phone straight down,' cried the operator.

'Can we just get on with it?' Mary asked, desperate to bring the matter to a resolution and secure help. 'Otherwise I'm afraid I'll be going to bed without food, light or hot water.'

'*I don't have to put up with someone talking to me like that!*' shouted the surly girl. Click. Burr. The line on which Mary had spent thirty of the most frustrating minutes of her life – and in Underpants that was saying something – was dead. After staring in furious disbelief for a few seconds, Mary reached the crushing realisation that to get back to the same point she would have to spend another thirty minutes – at least – going through an identical campaign of digital persuasion. It was difficult, feeling such frustration, to form a coherent thought, but the one that Mary managed was that trying endlessly to get through to the right person at the right utility call centre must be what hell was like.

But then, most unexpectedly, heaven intervened.

'Ooh,' Mrs Shuffle said, flicking one of the Bakelite switches on and off. 'I think the 'lectric's back.'

As power seeped slowly back through the building, various appliances shrilled and shrieked. The ancient phone gave its grinding ring and a perky-sounding double-glazing salesman assured Mary he would be 'in your area tomorrow and would be delighted to discuss any double-glazing requirements you might have'. It made Mary giggle despite herself.

'If only,' she said wistfully to Mrs Shuffle, having put the phone down with a polite refusal. 'But there are a hundred and ten windows and, believe it or not, it's a listed building.

We'd have English Heritage down on us like a ton of bricks – if the house itself doesn't come down on us like a ton of bricks in the meantime, that is.'

'Never mind,' said Mrs Shuffle comfortably. 'Now the 'lectric's back, let's put the kettle on.'

Mary agreed happily. A cup of tea with Mrs Shuffle meant only one thing. Besides the tea, that was. And the chocolate chip cookies the cleaner invariably brought for herself and shared with Mary. It meant news. Gossip. Monty, who was devoted to Mrs Shuffle as well, nonetheless disapproved of her gossiping tendencies. But he was out at a meeting with the local tourist board and Mrs Shuffle could therefore have her head.

As Mary found mugs and teabags, Mrs Shuffle opened the biscuits and began the weekly monologue. A lot was happening in the village, it seemed. The landlord of the Dun Cow was having an affair with the postwoman. There were ructions in the lane which ran up from the church, where a couple of recently installed rich Americans were apparently offending everyone.

'They've got a pink dustbin!' Mrs Shuffle reported, easing her broad beam in its blue nylon overall on to a kitchen chair and accepting the chipped mug of tea Mary passed her. 'And a fancy name plate on the door. "Bijou Cottage", they're calling it.'

'So, do they think everyone hates them?' Mary asked, her sympathies stirred on behalf of this unknown pair.

'Oh, it's not everyone hates them,' Mrs Shuffle assured her. 'Personally, I think they seem very nice. Good looking as well. But they've got on the wrong side of Morag Archhole-Whatsit, that's for sure.'

Mary raised her eyebrows. Morag Archhole-Whatsit

occasionally featured in Mrs Shuffle's reports. She sounded a terrifying, interfering, vengeful figure. 'Why've they got on the wrong side of her?' Mary asked.

Mrs Shuffle gave a sensational account of the four-wheel drive and ambulance incident. 'Stuck in't church wall, it were!'

'This Morag drives an ambulance?' Mary said faintly. She did her shopping in Mineford and drove through Allsop to get there. It looked a pretty enough village, its cottages all of the same rustic grey stone with similar tiny, square, deepset windows moustached with geraniums in boxes and over-looking small gardens colourful with lupins, hollyhocks, delphiniums and roses. The lanes were romantically hotch-potch in appearance, rambling north, west and east from the cluster in the centre grouped round the church, the school and the vicarage.

But Monty had an aristocratic horror of what he called small-time community politics and so Mary, naturally timid, had resisted, over the years, the occasional importunings from Allsop committees to organise the flower festival or take a stall at the school fête. As a consequence she had only the dimmest idea of what the inhabitants were like.

'She does that. It's an old one, though. Recycled, she says. Reckons she's very passionately eco-whatsit,' Mrs Shuffle remarked disdainfully, 'but it seems to me that what she really likes to do is order other folk around. She's allus popping into the school and trying to boss poor Miss Brooke about.'

'She's the new schoolteacher, isn't she?' Mary tried to remember.

'That's right. And very good, so everyone says. But not good enough for Morag Archhole-Whatsit, oh no.' Mrs Shuffle took a deep draught of tea. '*Everything's* wrong as far as she's concerned. This problem kid from a broken home the school's got this term, for instance. Morag's really got it in for 'im. Says he's an unstable and undermining influence and is threatening to take her own kid away. Encouraging the other parents to do the same. But if anyone's an unstable and undermining influence it's Morag Whatsit,' said Mrs Shuffle hotly.

'There's a problem kid from a broken home?' Mary found her eyes, quite unexpectedly, swimming with tears.

Mrs Shuffle eyed her over her mug of Nice Price Basics tea. That woman, she thought, not for the first time, needs a baby.

Chapter 8

Catherine Brooke, the headmistress of Allsop school, sat reading the *Education Guardian* in her office. It was a small, hot room, brightly striplit and painted a zinging yellow. Pinned here and there to its walls were clumps of A4 sheets detailing everything from PTA agendas to local council directives about bin-bag quotas.

From time to time Catherine raised her pink-cheeked face with its thoughtful grey eyes, shook her neat auburn bob and stared through her office window. Between the school building and the adjoining parent parish church stretched the graveyard; a grey stone thicket of slabs, stones and memorials of various types on which the early evening sunshine was smiling. Gold lettering glinted here; polished marble flashed there. The dark yews glowed with green colour. But it was a sombre view nonetheless and Catherine was in a sombre mood. Not for the first time she was wondering whether she had done the right thing by coming here.

Nothing about Allsop had turned out to be what she had expected. Perhaps, way back in the New Year when she had come for the interview, she had been too hasty. She had fallen in love with Allsop at first sight; perhaps she should have been more circumspect. But to someone like her, who had toiled for so long in the grimy inner city, it had seemed country village perfection; glittering in a brilliant frost beneath a pale blue sky, romantic little rows of pretty, well-kept grey-stone cottages, none quite the same as another. In the centre was a beautiful medieval church with a castellated tower whose spire soared like a rocket into the cold cloudless blue. Way up on top, a gold weathercock had flashed in the winter sun. As Catherine had walked the lanes around the village, the trees had seemed a fairyland of shimmering snow and icicles and the cold breaths of air had been as exhilarating as champagne.

Allsop had a pub, a village hall and a small playground, all hinting at a close and friendly community. Its situation was uplifting in every sense, high up, balanced on top of and between two green breasts of hill commanding wonderful views of dry-stone walls dividing rounded, sloping fields whose ancient ploughing patterns were clearly delineated in the frost. Beyond the fields, low hills, shading from lime green to khaki to purple, stretched to the horizon.

Catherine had been particularly charmed by the school, which was built with an architectural imagination completely lacking in the newbuild north London primary with its Portakabins. It was Victorian Gothic, all gables and traceried windows and with an arched Norman-style portal with a large iron ring handle set in the solid wooden door. The style was taken from the lovely church next door, to which the school was affiliated and which boasted genuine Norman and Gothic features as well as some romantic sixteenth-century mullioned windows and fine Victorian stained glass. The school was tiny, too, a mere seventy pupils compared to the three hundred she had left. A soft landing for her first headship, or so it had seemed, and situated in one of the prettiest villages she had ever seen.

School House, the Victorian cottage opposite Allsop Primary that the church fathers had built to accommodate their new school's head, had been equally charming. It was grey, like the school, and shared similar features: adorable pointed-arch Gothic windows as well as a round Norman front door which had struck Catherine as wildly romantic; infinitely more so than her current residence: a top-floor flat in a dull part of north London above a pair of DJs who slammed their doors a lot.

The estate agent, a fattish, fiftyish woman in high heels, a tight suit, unsuitable red lipstick and with hair far too long for her age, had hardly needed to talk in a grinding monotone about 'wow factor'. Catherine had been wowed by everything: by the wood-burning stove set in the recessed fireplace, the cosy, deep-silled bedroom and the ceiling of the dining room striped with polished oak beams. She had been wowed in particular by the fact it was for sale; she had been intending to rent, to see how the job went, but then it had seemed the height of romantic coincidence that the pretty little house, long ago sold and detached from the school, had come back on to the market at the same time she had been appointed Allsop Primary's new leader.

It had struck her as a good omen, and the price, although rather beyond her budget, had therefore seemed worth taking on. But was it? Catherine fretted now amid the bright yellow of her office. Had she been mad to stake hundreds of thousands of pounds on it? And had she been even madder to take the job?

Back then, Allsop and its school had seemed the answer to all her problems. The north London primary of which she was deputy head was a challenge at the best of times. An ill-advised romance with a colleague had proved the final straw. At the time of the Allsop interview, her circumstances had been in as much disarray as Allsop school's, whose former headmaster was, it seemed, uninterested, uninspiring and incapable of meeting required standards just as, albeit in different ways, Catherine's inamorato had been.

In the end, the problem had solved itself. Both unrewarding relationships had finally broken down. The Allsop headmaster had been sacked by the school and the north London primary schoolteacher boyfriend had been sacked by Catherine. The advertisement for Allsop's vacant headship had appeared in the *Education Guardian* the week after and had seemed to Catherine like Providence.

But now she was here . . . Catherine sighed and looked around. The heady rush in which she had applied, been interviewed, accepted, moved, had receded like the tide and left a beach strewn with problems.

It was of course tempting to blame the governors for their careful understatement of the condition she had subsequently discovered the school was in financially, structurally and in terms of the falling roll. But in her heart of hearts Catherine could not. Faced with an eager, qualified candidate, they had naturally jumped at the chance. As had she, to be fair.

Catherine knew she should go home, not lurk around here reading newspapers. It was Friday afternoon and the end of the school week. All around her people were excitedly preparing for the weekend. Catherine's weekend, meanwhile, stretched endlessly, featurelessly, datelessly ahead of her.

Village life had proved to be rather less social and inclusive than she had anticipated. Neither of her two colleagues, Miss Hanscombe and Mrs Watkins, lived in Allsop, and in any case they had families to go to after work. While being too friendly with parents of her pupils was difficult, for obvious reasons. PTA fundraising barbecues and discos were all very well, but they hardly took her away from her job. Nor did they constitute building a social life, however much they were ultimately building the new school computer suite. There was always the pub, of course, but she could hardly go there as a woman on her own. Besides, the landlord was of the exhibitionist sort who hailed people loudly from behind the bar.

Now summer was here she had set about some half-hearted gardening, but the plot behind School House was too small and stony for the carrots and onions she had seen herself growing in the first flush of her enthusiasm for country life. Besides, whenever she was at home in the cottage she only worried about the school. Being actually in the school gave her the illusion she was in the driving seat and in control, even if none of the controls actually worked and the seat itself had seen better days.

She walked to the door of the staff room, which gave on to the main school hall, a large, wooden-floored space whose walls were hung with gym equipment and which was the venue for everything from the morning assembly to the school plays she intended to put on.

A flash of pride shot through her gloomy mood as she looked around. She had made a difference to the inside of the school, in any case. On her arrival, it had reflected her predecessor's unimaginative approach by being a series of uncompromisingly stark, white rooms. The exterior woodwork had now been painted red and each of the three classrooms was a different shade of bright pastel to provide a more stimulating, jolly environment for the children. Catherine firmly believed that happy surroundings made for a happy school, and most of the Allsop Primary children certainly seemed cheerful enough. Apart from one, of course.

A sound made Catherine start. There was someone behind the door, in the hall.

She tried to still her instinctive and immediate panic. She was far too jumpy these days. It was probably only Mr Goodenough from the parish council, a pleasant elderly gentleman with white hair and rosy cheeks who occasionally popped in to see if she needed any help. Catherine was grateful for his friendliness and gave him the occasional lightbulb to fix, but unfortunately he could do little about the roof, the falling roll and the finances, where the real assistance was needed.

She opened the door into the hall. There was a figure in the centre of the floor but it was not Mr Goodenough.

'Sam!' Catherine breathed. 'What on earth are you doing here?'

The eight-year-old boy gave her a hostile stare from under his brows. Sam Binns was tall and wan and very skinny. He had a thin, pointed and rather flat face, wide-apart eyes narrowed in a slit and a small, tight mouth that rarely smiled. His hair was closely cropped in a manner possibly meant to look aggressive but which accentuated his slightly protruding ears in a way that made him seem fragile and vulnerable.

Catherine knew that this was the truth; that Sam Binns was fragile and vulnerable. He was a troubled child from a troubled home who had been taken into care by the local authority and was currently being fostered by a middle-aged couple in the village. They were, Catherine knew, finding it very hard going. Sorry though she was for them, Catherine was even more desperately sorry for Sam, who had arrived at the school around a month ago. Her efforts to be kind to him had fallen on stony ground, however; Sam's intention seemed to be as rude and unpleasant as possible to anyone and everyone. He was surly, uncommunicative and occasionally aggressive. The children had immediately voted with their feet and Sam had been shunned by his peers. The teachers had battled manfully on but the yellow staff room walls bore daily witness to the difficulties of coping with such a disruptive and difficult child.

'He's just so aggressive,' Mrs Watkins, one of the two other teachers, had complained only that morning.

'I know,' Catherine agreed, thinking that a mother who had died and a father in prison probably made you that way. She had kept the goriest details of Sam's circumstances from her colleagues, hoping that full disclosure would not be necessary. For Sam's sake she didn't want the whole village knowing about his father, and Mrs Watkins, for all her motherly kindness and genuine good intentions, had a tendency towards indiscretion.

Miss Hanscombe, the other, younger, snappier teacher, now pointed out that Sam Binns's presence in the school was hardly going to reverse the decline in numbers; if anything, it was going to increase it. 'What parent wants their precious darlings going to school with *him*?' she demanded.

Catherine's heart sank. As a matter of fact, the local children were not precious darlings in the literal sense, but the doughty, well-adjusted and good-natured offspring of local farmers and workers in the nearby towns. Even so, there was no reason to believe these mainly normal and sensible parents would be particularly sympathetic to the stormy boy currently causing turmoil in their children's learning time.

'Morag Archbutt-Pesk has already complained,' Miss Hanscombe added, pushing back a lock of springy burnished hair that had escaped from its colleagues in her ponytail.

Catherine suppressed the retort which sprang most immediately to her lips, that Morag could be relied on to complain about everything.

'Well we can't throw Sam out, can we?' she challenged. 'If we do, the same thing will only happen at the next school.'

'Let it,' said Miss Hanscombe, grimly.

'No.'

Miss Hanscombe looked at her searchingly. 'But it would be so easy to get him removed. No one's going to question it, not with the reputation he's got.' At this particular stage in his career, Sam Binns was the veteran of no fewer than seven schools.

But Catherine shook her head. 'I think it's our duty as educationalists to try and stop the vicious circle. He's in a calm place here.' She knew from experience how important quiet could be to children who had known only shouting and chaos. It was, she believed, a healer in itself.

'Calm? You think so?' sniffed Mrs Watkins. 'You should see my reading class when he's in it. Calm it isn't.'

'He'll learn. Improve,' Catherine said determinedly. Mrs Watkins and Miss Hanscombe were her own recruits; the first she had ever employed alone. After accepting the job, even before she had moved into Allsop, her first act had been to gently encourage early retirement for the inadequate and, blessedly, ancient and about-to-retire malcontent staff she had inherited from the old regime. Her new staff were present and correct for the start of the new term. She had successfully sold them her own dream of improving the school. She had not, however, sold them the dream of Sam Binns.

She looked at him now. He scowled back at her, his eyes narrowing further against a shaft of late-afternoon light slanting through the hall windows.

'What do you want, Sam?' Catherine asked gently.

The boy, as expected, did not reply. The hostile expression on his face reminded her that sympathy for Sam Binns was infinitely easier in theory than in practice.

'Won't Mr and Mrs Newton be wondering where you are?' the headmistress persisted.

The boy's face changed from hostility to contempt. Admittedly the change was slight. '*Them!*' he snorted.

Catherine had walked into the hall and was standing opposite him. She now sat down on a large chest that was used to store balls and beanbags for gym. 'Don't you like Mr and Mrs Newton?' she asked softly.

He shook his head violently.

'But they seem such nice people.' They *were* nice, Catherine knew. Mrs Newton was tall, sandy haired and had a face like an anxious hamster. She had been to the school to see Catherine about Sam. 'I'm so sorry, Miss Brooke,' she had exclaimed, looking at the headmistress with small, earnest, concerned eyes. 'Dave and I, we're at our wits' end, nearly. We're having the devil of a job getting through to him. He hardly ever says anything.'

'No, but he shouts a lot,' Catherine could imagine Miss Hanscombe replying.

The Newtons, it emerged, were experienced foster parents. 'We've had tricky ones before,' Mrs Newton told her. 'They turned out fine in the end. Sam, well, he's different. But we're hoping we'll get there.'

Which, Catherine thought, was another reason why she refused to fall at the first hurdle with Sam. If kindly Mrs Newton was hoping to get there, why should she not hope for the same thing?

'I'm locking the school up,' she told Sam now. 'You should go home.'

As she herded him to the door, she wondered why he had chosen to hang around the school. His only interest in lessons seemed to be in disrupting them, nor did he particularly respond to any teacher, herself included. Or was she being overly pessimistic? Hope now rose in her that his presence was an admission that he felt safe here and was finally responding to the kindness and sympathy she had been so solicitous about showing him.

'I'm glad you feel you can come here, Sam.' She smiled at him. Up close his skin was white and unhealthy looking, proof of Mrs Newton's dejected reports that, for all her efforts to tempt his appetite, he would rather eat sweets in his bedroom than her cooking in the dining room. 'Look,' Catherine added gently. 'You can come here – when it's open, I mean. Before school, after school, whenever you want. I'd like you to. I know what it's like, you see. Being new in a place,' she added hurriedly, in case he felt she was laying claim to all the horrors he had endured.

Sam looked back at her expressionlessly. 'I'm only here because it's warmer than the bus stop,' he said eventually, his flat tones spiked with spiteful triumph.

Catherine felt rather winded. 'Oh,' she said, disappointed. 'Well,' she added cheerfully, recovering herself, 'I suppose that's something.'

A loud knock at the door from the staff room made her jump again.

But not so much as it did Sam. The boy threw up his head in alarm and scuttled across the hall to the outside door, exiting in a flash. Under his bravado he was more nervous even than she was, Catherine realised, imagining with a pang the small heart banging inside that skinny body.

'Come in,' Catherine said to the knock, as authoritatively as she could manage given that she was not expecting anyone. She hoped it wasn't a serial killer, but then pushed the thought away as being hysterical and unworthy of someone, like her, who prided herself on her calm good sense. Or had done once. And did serial killers knock, anyway?

Chapter 9

The head that now appeared round the door was not, Catherine saw, a serial killer. But it was definitely a serial nuisance. One of the more difficult mothers. The most difficult, in fact. The mother who had not helped with painting the school on the grounds the paints had been bought from a wholesalers which was part of a retail group with insufficient Fair Trade take-up. The mother with large, inquisitive brown eyes which seemed to roll pryingly everywhere. The one with thick eyebrows and a slight shadow of moustache above lipstickless lips. The one with purple trousers and messy aubergine hair.

'Hello, Ms Archbutt-Pesk,' said Catherine, finding, as always, the title more difficult to say than it was to write. This particular mother had once spent a considerable amount of time explaining she had no time for the patriarchal institution of marriage and that the double barrel was the result of her decision with her partner that both their surnames should carry equal weight and importance with their daughter. It was just a shame, Catherine thought, that the names didn't go better together. And that the daughter was called Merlin into the bargain.

Merlin Archbutt-Pesk. It wasn't the best start in life. But Merlin managed to rise above the challenges of her nomenclature. She was a determined, plump, rosy-cheeked child with a penetrating gaze and ferocious ability to concentrate. She was fearsomely able at the school computer and more than once Catherine had caught her browsing on eBay.

'I'm glad I caught you before you rushed off,' said Merlin's mother.

Catherine tried to look less offended than she felt at the insinuation that, as soon as the door swung behind the last child, she fled from the building with all speed. But she had learnt that being in a state of more or less constant offendedness was concomitant with Morag Archbutt-Pesk's appearances.

Only a few days ago she had endured a tirade about nutrition at the end of which Morag had demanded whether she had checked the source of the fish in the fish pie that had been served to the children at lunch. The situation had not been helped by Catherine misunderstanding 'source' and answering that it had been parsley. Although why Morag was concerned at all on this point was a mystery; Merlin was supplied on a daily basis by her mother with carrot sticks and butterless houmous sandwiches.

'It's about Black History Month,' Morag stated, her eyes gleaming in a way which worried Catherine.

'Oh, right. What about it?' Catherine was confident of her ground here. The celebration of black culture was scheduled to start in a couple of weeks' time and she had lined up a selection of lessons, projects and displays that should impress even Morag.

'I thought I could help.'

Catherine flinched in alarm. 'Oh, really, that's awfully sweet, Ms Archbutt-Pesk, but there's no need . . .'

Morag waved her hand impatiently. 'I had a suggestion. How about having a black person actually coming into the school and talking about his experiences?'

Catherine stared. The fact that Allsop was entirely Anglo-Saxon white had amazed and worried her when, six months ago, she had first arrived from the inner city where she had previously taught. She had already set up links with multi-ethnic primary schools in a bid to address this and had various creative plans to use these links during Black History Month.

'You mean get someone black to come in just for the *day*?' She swallowed at the crudeness of the suggestion.

Morag nodded enthusiastically. 'Absolutely. Someone on the spot, who actually lives in the village.'

'Who lives *here*?' Catherine repeated. There was a black person in Allsop? Then a flash of understanding struck her. She had heard that an American couple had recently bought a weekend cottage. She had vaguely imagined that the well-groomed blonde she had spotted in the company of a stocky, dark and prosperous-looking man to be them. But it couldn't be, not if, as Morag seemed to be saying, they were black.

'Oh, you mean the new Americans?' she asked.

At the mention of the hated Ferraros, Morag's face flushed an angry puce. They had still not put a foot wrong so far as planning regulations were concerned. 'What are you talking about?'

'The new Americans are black,' Catherine muttered. Such a simple monosyllable, and yet what a difficult word it was to say.

'*Black!*' Morag's billiard-ball eyes bulged with fury. 'Of

course they're not bloody black. They're as WASP as they come. And they've been telling you they're black? That's outrageous. That's totally unacceptable. That's—'

'Hey, hang on a minute.' Catherine placed herself squarely before the juggernaut of Morag's tirade. 'They haven't said anything to me. I haven't met them.'

Morag stared resentfully back at her. 'So why are you talking about them?'

'I'm not, I just thought . . . oh, never mind,' Catherine sighed. She slid a glance at her watch. She had things to do, papers to mark, lessons to plan. She couldn't stand here all day discussing who was and who wasn't black in Allsop. 'Look, about this Black History Month. The, erm, black person you mentioned . . .'

'Yes?'

'Er . . .' Catherine tried to put it delicately. 'I didn't realise . . . I mean, I've never seen . . . er, who are you talking about?'

'Gid.'

'*Gid?*' Catherine wondered if she was hearing things. It had been a long day and it seemed like weeks since she had woken up. But even so, had Morag just claimed that her partner-and-father-of-her-child, Gideon, who had looked as white as snow whenever Catherine had seen him – was actually black?

'Yes,' said Morag.

'Er . . .' said Catherine.

'He has Malaysian forebears,' Morag explained. 'Way, way back. They were traders in tea. Colonial exploiters, of course, which is obviously embarrassing for him. But for the sake of everyone's education he's willing to come in and talk about it.'

'Well, that's a very helpful thought, Ms Archbutt-Pesk. Can I get back to you?'

'Do. And have you checked that fish pie yet, by the way? Was the fish line-caught and from sustainable sources?' Morag barked.

Catherine doubted it. She wondered about explaining about local authority centralised control of supplies. 'Er . . .'

Morag interrupted again. 'I don't mind telling you I'm concerned about school food and children's health, Miss Brooke. Or can I call you Catherine? Miss Brooke's so formal,' she added disapprovingly.

Or respectful, thought Catherine, who had no desire whatsoever to call this objectionable woman Morag. She felt the anger rise within her. 'Look, all the food served in the school is cooked on site, fresh every day . . .' she paused. She could see now the opportunity to raise a subject even dearer to her heart than the excellence of Allsop Primary food. 'But actually, as you've brought the subject of health up, may I just say that I consider your strong opposition to routine childhood vaccinations far more of a risk to the children, not to mention Merlin. Of course, it's your choice, but I just wanted to make sure you were informed of the facts. It's about herd immunity, you see.'

'You bet it's my choice,' Morag spat, almost foaming at the mouth. 'And I know all the facts, thanks. Vaccinations are unnatural.'

Catherine groaned. Where did one start with someone this wilfully stupid? 'Vaccination,' she explained patiently, 'is the process of injecting a small amount of an infectious disease into the body so it can build up resistance. It's entirely natural. It's also a brilliant trick.' And, she forbore to add, one without which Morag would not be in a position to shun it or anything else, as she would be dead of typhoid or TB. She tried not to dwell on this tempting thought.

Morag exited the school in high dudgeon. How dare the headmistress challenge her on vaccination? Vaccinations were sinister and dangerous, a conspiracy between the Government and the drugs companies. And who cared about herd immunity? She didn't want Merlin to be one of the herd. Merlin was an individual with her own beauty and creativity.

These thoughts whirling furiously round her brain, Morag stamped up the Tarmac lane which led from the school by the church back to her house. It was a fine evening and the rich light was shining on the cottages of Church Lane, warming the rough grey stone and making the polished windows gleam brilliantly.

As she stomped past in the large black boots she routinely wore, Morag cast a glance of purest loathing at Bijou Cottage's pink dustbin. She only just restrained herself from putting out a hand and ripping off the heads of the jaunty salmon-pink geraniums in the pink-painted window boxes. She peered, as she always did, into the interior; it being early Friday night the Ferraros would still be blocking the motorway and widening the ozone layer with their people carrier. But, as always, the interior looked blameless; in the planning sense, that was. There was plenty to blame in the ludicrous flowery decor, in Morag's view. Just playing at being rustic. That was what the Ferraros were doing.

She continued to stomp up the lane, passing her own purple door on the grounds her feelings were so heated they needed further expiation before she returned to home and hearth. There was no audience to receive her at home, anyway; no one to take her part against the outrage that was the headmistress. Gid would be out at his anti-sexist men's group and Merlin had gone to play with a friend who Morag had serious doubts about; the family had a television, for a start. With satellite.

The lupins, peonies and early roses in the cottage gardens she passed were glowing in the sunshine. Sunlight danced on the swaying tops of the trees lining the lane, brilliantly green against the deep blue sky. Cow parsley foamed in the hedgerows and the thorn bushes were covered with tiny pure white blooms, hanging as heavy as snow. The birds twittered and sang with piercing sweetness. But Morag heard or saw nothing of this beauty. Her head was filled with venomous views on Catherine and her gaze, as usual, was fixed on the large, round toes of her boots as they crunched up the lane.

Chapter 10

As the door shut behind his clients, Philip Prothcroe glanced out of the window of his Mineford office. The building opposite, an unlovely café with the even more objectionable local newspaper above it, was beautified by a richly golden Friday afternoon sun.

Philip rubbed his pale, tired face and raked his long white fingers through his crop of thick, floppy black hair. He stretched his gangly arms in their navy pinstripe suit upwards until he could feel the stitches strain. It had been a hard week. He was thirty-five, but he felt about fifty.

He replaced his thin rimless spectacles over the large dark eyes his wife had always joked were too poetic for a solicitor. His lips were too pretty as well, she always said; pink, full and girlish, totally rock star. He had laughed at this too. But he had liked it.

A movement opposite caught his eye. A black-haired girl was coming out of the *Mineford Mercury* doorway. She was, he knew, one of the paper's two reporters; the one who had written a ridiculously overblown account of Emily's accident. Watching her whip out a packet of cigarettes and shove one in her mouth, Philip felt a powerful wave of dislike. He felt relieved when the girl, having lit up, strolled off down the street and out of the view framed by his window.

He tapped his long, pale fingers on the cream surface of the wills the last clients had come in to sign. 'It seems a bit doomy, I suppose.' The young woman had smiled as she handed back the Mont Blanc he kept exclusively for such ceremonial purposes. It was amazing how many people came to sign their wills without pens. 'I mean,' she had continued, gesturing at her husband, 'we're not very old. But now, with the children, we feel we have to be responsible. You never know, after all . . .' Her smile and her lift of the chin as she finished the sentence seemed to imply that actually she did know and that the future was bright, but she was taking sensible precautions.

Philip, whose own future had once seemed just as bright, had nodded. He knew now, however, that one really did never know.

Last night an aeroplane had flown very low over the house. Too low, surely. The noise had been so great it had woken him up and he had lain there as the deafening grinding and throbbing grew louder, certain it was about to smash into the house. Then it had faded and gone. He had stretched an arm to the other side of the bed, to the terrible emptiness he still forgot was there, then remembered. It was exactly a year since Emily had died.

Philip took a deep breath and drummed his thin fingers on his desk. He didn't want to think about it. Not now. And part of the reason he was here, in his office, as he was most of the time, was so he would not think about it. It was strictly a workplace. There was nothing in it that reminded him of his wife.

The main feature, besides the big window, of the large, light first-floor room in which he worked was a big mahogany desk, the leather on its top worn to an ancient thinness and generally devoid of clutter apart from essentials such as the telephone, a pen and notepad and folders containing papers pertaining to expected clients. All were neatly set out.

The desk had a revolving chair behind it, his chair, while two chairs for clients stood before it. Otherwise there was an oil-fired plug-in radiator to supplement the ailing and aged heating system and a fireplace with a handsome mantelshelf. This shelf had once held the picture of Emily in a leather frame that currently languished in one of the filing cabinet drawers. He had put it in carefully, face up, the way she had always slept. The way she had looked when last he had seen her. Pale-faced beneath a heap of twisted and mangled metal, at the side of a dark motorway. 'Take her pulse,' Philip had cried at the ambulancemen. One had come up, put a hand on his shoulder. 'I'm sorry. She has no pulse.'

He had coped. 'How are you feeling *in yourself*?' people would ask if he met them in the flesh. What was he to say? Did they really want to know? Of course not, and he didn't want to tell them. How he could still feel the shattering, bomb-like blast as the car behind hit them, hear the scream of the emergency services as they arrived. The wail of an ambulance siren always brought back to Philip his dead wife's face beneath the wreckage. Now, whenever he heard one, his fingers would fly to his ears.

The psychiatrist charged with assessing, for legal reasons,

the extent of Philip's post-traumatic stress had been no help. The opposite, in fact. Amongst other things he had told Philip that grieving partners often found comfort in wearing their departed mate's clothes. 'But Emily was size eight,' a bewildered Philip had pointed out. And, in the end, what had all this useless advice and painful probing resulted in? A twelve-month driving ban on the twenty-one-year-old boy who had hit them in his father's Audi. Twelve months. No prison term. No fine.

The accident had been almost four years to the day since he had met her, at a colleague's thirtieth birthday summer garden party. He had been struck by her white teeth – not 'done', she had smilingly assured him – and her skin, which had had the velvety vitality of the tumbling roses around them. He had been struck by the fact she was an artist – an illustrator of children's books – and yet seemed interested in him, a dry solicitor. Very interested, as it turned out. But after three years together and two years of marriage – he had wasted no time in asking her – she was gone; his entire future wiped out.

Too roused now to think about work, Philip stared round his office. On the door hung the wooden coathanger to which he strode at one minute to eight every morning and invested with his navy blue Barbour and blue-toned checked wool scarf. At eight o'clock, a whole hour before the office opened, he was at his desk.

He always dressed smartly for work, even formally. A solicitor's office, in his view, had a certain solemn theatricality that one had to reflect in one's garb. To this end, he always wore dark suits, although one, a navy pinstripe Emily had helped him choose, had a rather daring bright red lining. He rarely wore it these days.

Philip's office had always been a solicitor's. To the right of his desk, across a sea of thin burgundy carpet, were shelves covering the whole wall, the top six or so being entirely filled with ledgers displayed with their fat spines outwards. These had come with the office when he bought it; the earliest ones among them dated back to the early nineteenth century when the original firm had been founded. Time and light had faded their cloth covers and paper labels to a surprisingly diverse range of beautiful soft browns and yellows.

A ladder rested against the top shelf as if Philip were constantly in the habit of referring to past cases, although he had never examined any of these volumes. But he had never wanted to get rid of them either, enjoying the view of them from his desk; there was something painterly and romantic about those soft warm fawns and creams. The other evidence of the office's long history as a solicitor's was the fluted bell mounted on the wall by the door that had once summoned the junior clerks down from the attics above into the main office where Philip now sat.

The phone intercom buzzed abruptly.

'It's her,' hissed his secretary, Mrs Sheen, whose disembodied voice he could hear simultaneously on the phone and in the flesh at her desk outside his door. 'Maureen Hughes. That estate agent.'

Philip's heart sank. While he routinely dealt with estate agents, and some of them could be troublesome, there was no doubt that this one was more troublesome than most. There seemed to be endless complications with this particular house sale and if he had been the fanciful type he would have fancied Maureen, a blowsy single woman who dressed considerably younger than her fifty-plus years, was making some of them up. But why would anyone do that?

'Do you want me to put her through?' Mrs Sheen asked. Philip felt grateful for her protection. His secretary, a doughty Mineford native, did not suffer fools gladly and Philip could tell from her voice that she felt Maureen Hughes was no better than she should be. And possibly a good deal less.

'I'm afraid so, Mrs Sheen,' Philip said reluctantly.

'You're through,' Mrs Sheen told Maureen Hughes.

The estate agent, from her office a mere hundred yards down the road, batted eyelids bruised with purple shadow and stretched out before her plump legs in dark tights and high heels. Maureen always wore heels; it made one bit of her at least look slim and elongated, just as wearing her favourite deep red lipstick 'Rouge Mystere' and keeping her hair long and dark gave her a smouldering air, whatever the woman at Snips & Lips might say about short being the only style for fifty-somethings like her.

'Well, *hello* there.' Maureen spoke in the breathy little-girl voice she reserved exclusively for flirtation.

'Hello?' barked Philip. Who was this? A crossed line? It sounded as if some strange toddler had got hold of the phone.

'Er, Maureen Hughes here,' Maureen said hurriedly in more normal tones. 'You're handling one of my clients.'

Maureen wished that Philip Protheroe was handling her as well. He was tall, dark and, on the handsome front, well above average for Mineford. Even more unusual for Mineford were his reticent good manners and unfailing politeness; there was also something rather attractively melancholy about him which Maureen thought possibly might have had something to do with his wife having died in a car accident a year or so previously.

Well, an acceptable amount of time had passed now. Philip Protheroe should be thinking about forming another relationship. A man like him shouldn't be on his own for ever. *Especially* a man like him. Young, attractive, no doubt vigorous. At the thought of his vigour, Maureen swallowed.

Philip was in the picture now. That strange voice had been Maureen after all. He resolved to get the call over with as quickly as possible. 'Oh yes. Hello, Mrs Hughes.'

'It's Miss,' growled Maureen. '*Miss* Hughes.' If she said it like that, Maureen realised, it sounded like 'miss you', which was entirely appropriate in the context. There was a lot she missed about men in general and which she would like Philip in particular to make up for.

'Yes, we need to talk about my client's completion date,' Philip Protheroe remarked in his grave, polite voice. He was aware of undercurrents at the other end of the line but had no idea what they signified.

'Yes, I know,' Maureen said hastily. 'But – well.' She giggled coquettishly into the phone and flicked her hair over her shoulders, as if he could see her. 'I just wanted you to know that there's a good-looking property on the market available to the right buyer.'

'I'm sorry?' Philip Protheroe was thoroughly confused. He had thought he was talking to the estate agent about a perfectly routine piece of business, but now she seemed to be trying to sell him something. Still, perhaps it wasn't so surprising.

'Men have . . . needs,' Maureen panted.

He could hardly make out the words for the heavy breathing.

'So do women,' Maureen added in a growl.

Philip was so surprised he now did the only thing he could think of. He put the telephone down abruptly. To one of his quick brain the absence of any other way for them to extract themselves from the conversation with dignity was immediately obvious. He sat at his desk for a few minutes, his fingers playing nervously round his mouth. He had no doubt at all that he had just been propositioned by Maureen Hughes.

Chapter 11

As the photographer fiddled with the lights, Alexandra tossed her glimmering platinum mane of hair back over her polished brown shoulders. She ran a pink tongue over a blaze of white-veneered teeth and arranged a fold of her tiger-print chiffon dress over the long brown legs which ended in a pair of gold leather cowboy boots.

Bending over, she dipped quickly into one of her boots and fished out the state-of-the-art mobile she had stuffed there and set on vibrate. If Max, her agent, needed to reach her in the middle of the shoot, he could, as could her hairdresser, waxer, tan therapist, nutritionist and personal assistant. Her personal stylist Petra was, of course, here at the shoot. Alexandra flipped the silver lid and stared at the sea-green illuminated display panel. Nothing. Nothing new, anyway. Disgruntled, she shoved the mobile back.

She shifted her lean waist around the huge brown leather belt whose circular gold medallions and vast gold buckle pressed into her ribcage. Her bad mood lifted slightly as she contemplated the bonily elegant dome of her kneecap. She'd always had very good, neat knees; nothing like those huge, sprouting cauliflower-like ones that some of the footballers' wives had. Poor Vicki Bostoff, for example. She'd actually had knee surgery in the end, but it only made things worse because now she had scars as well. As for Tina Morris's goofy teeth and Jo Smith's bushy eyebrows; all the designer clothes in the world couldn't make Jo look like anything other than Noel Gallagher with growth hormones.

What it was to be naturally beautiful, Alexandra mused complacently as she stretched out a slim arm and admired its deep caramel brown. Her new spray-on tan looked as if she had spent a month in St Lucia, not just a morning in a salon in Sloane Street. The cost, admittedly, was pretty much the same, but she was worth it. Her stunning good looks were getting her noticed. A recent *Daily Mail* article had made glancing mention of 'Alexandra Pigott . . . one of the England WAGS scrambling most desperately for Victoria Beckham's abandoned style crown'.

Alexandra glanced over to her footballer boyfriend. John sat awkwardly on a white chaise longue having his handsome black face dusted with powder by the make-up artist. That he was hating every single minute positively radiated from him. He hadn't wanted to do this celebrity magazine shoot, but she'd made him. 'It's for my *career*,' she had stormed.

For some reason, John seemed to be on a one-man mission to sabotage her efforts. He hardly ever touched alcohol and insisted on being in bed at eleven every night so he could be present and correct on the pitch the next day for training. Which was a lot of use when her own career required her to be present and correct in full Roberto Cavalli at whatever nightclub, restaurant or designer stationer's happened to be on the launch pad that night.

No one could accuse John of inconsistency, however. He

had, Alexandra accepted, been completely dedicated to football even when a schoolboy, which was when they had first met; falling in love at the back and the bottom of a Wanstead maths class. But John had made up in determination and discipline what he lacked in academic ability; playing football every weekend, training almost every night. Alexandra, meanwhile, had had her various beautician courses to fill in the time, and later, when the money started to roll in, she had gone to beauticians herself.

But after John started playing in the Premiership and was picked for England, merely having her nails and bikini line done failed to hit the spot. Even Alexandra could only have them done so often. East London was now far behind them, or at least it was far behind her; John retained a fondness for his roots that was incomprehensible to his girlfriend, who couldn't move up West fast enough. Now with her luxury Knightsbridge apartment, expensive shopping habit and celebrity hairdressers on speed-dial, she had started to crave a different sort of attention, the sort that only men with long lenses could assuage. Publicity. John was a star, and she wanted to be one too.

Alexandra whipped a compact out from where she had stuffed it in her other boot and examined her plump lips in their trademark Iced Skinny Latte pearlised lipstick. She was aware that some people, who had no idea how these things worked, might – and in actual fact did – sneer about openings of envelopes. Alexandra had also been named in several of the tabloids as a 'fully paid-up member of London's most consistently reliable rentacrowd'. But she was delighted to be 'breaking through', as her agent Max put it.

Exposure. Familiarity. *Photographs.* She went to everything and stopped at nothing, not even to read her diary properly, which was why she had once appeared in full warpaint and wet-look playsuit at a trade fair for undertakers. Still, at least the playsuit had been black, and the undertakers, in any event, had seemed delighted.

As a result of her efforts she had appeared in a number of magazine party pages, not to mention *Dying Today*, the undertakers' trade magazine. The pictures were not always correctly captioned, but that, Max assured her, would come too.

And this morning was the real breakthrough. Today, albeit after a certain amount of cajoling, and only because someone else had apparently dropped out (but Max insisted she focus on the positives), a major milestone on the road to stardom had been attained. A leading celebrity weekly had agreed to come and do an 'at home with the famous' feature in the roomy, light-filled penthouse a mere champagne cork's toss from Harvey Nicks that Alexandra had made John, much against his will, buy six months ago.

Alexandra was triumphant. Although no one had said so in so many words, there was obviously an excellent chance of the shoot making the cover. How could it not, when it featured her and her fabulous home?

She had been up since dawn drinking, as well as trying on, with the help of her stylist Petra, almost every item in her wardrobe before narrowing down her outfits for the shoot to a capsule ten. Together they had hit on a theme – Versace for the bedroom shots, Dior for the lounge, Cavalli for the hallway, Gucci for the dining room, Stella McCartney for the kitchen, Temperley for the bathrooms.

Petra had suggested they mix some of the labels up a bit for a funkier feel, but to Alexandra the funkiest feeling of all was for people to know she could afford to dress in head-to-

toe Gucci, and so the plan remained for one label per room.

She had then devoted her attention to making the penthouse look, in accordance with the magazine's instructions, 'natural, like a typical day at home'. She had rammed pink candles into silver branched candelabra and placed them everywhere, scattered serried ranks of crystalware about the never-yet-used mahogany dining table and arranged her most impressive-looking invitations in between the Lladro on the marble mantelpiece in the sitting room. Every shining gold cushion on the sitting room's white sofas had been plumped up and the cleaner, drafted in early to carry out instructions, had been instructed to polish the glass eyes on the heads of the three large fake tigerskin rugs.

An open bottle of Moët reclined in an engraved silver ice bucket on a stand in every room, including both bathrooms, where the bucket, positioned within a semicircle of glasses (one smeared with telltale Iced Skinny Latte lipstick), was on the side of the Jacuzzi. 'You've got more flutes than the bleedin' LSO,' the photographer had said, removing them and simultaneously dismissing Alexandra's suggestion that she pose in the empty bath wearing her Temperley ballgown. Or in the full one wearing nothing. 'This ain't *FHM*, love,' he had told her.

Dismissing the memory, Alexandra, invited to pose at long last for an actual photograph, now arranged herself against the plate-glass windows of the penthouse sitting room. She spread her long, slim brown legs in their gold leather cowboy high heels, satisfyingly aware that the light streaming from behind her would make her tiger-print chiffon dress almost completely transparent. She adjusted the belt, whose prong was piercing her lungs – or perhaps her pancreas, biology had never been her forte – pouted and pushed out her breasts. 'A bit less *Playboy*, love,' the photographer warned.

'I'm just trying to make it look more interesting,' Alexandra snapped.

There came from behind the lens what sounded suspiciously like a snort. 'Oh, it'll be interesting all right, love.'

Well the place looked its best, Alexandra reflected with satisfaction. The day before, Sloane Street's most expensive florist had arrived, heaving huge urns and man-height bunches of lilies into the mirrored, chandeliered hall. Vast formal flower arrangements foamed atop every table, from the squat marble-effect ones with carved, curved gold legs bearing the big white lamps in the sitting room, to the virgin mahogany in the dining room. The thick, carved, gold-sprayed curtain rails had been wrapped in yards of white tulle and net, over which had been pinned trails of dark green ivy. Swags of gerbera and red roses swung from the mantelpieces and above the doorways. Even the loo handle had its own laurel wreath, a single pink rose lay in the bidet and the scent of lilies from the huge urns flanking the entrance door in the hallway was enough to make the eyes water. It was certainly making the photographer's assistant's eyes water; he had been complaining about his hayfever since arriving. 'That's showbiz, honey,' Alexandra had snapped at him. 'If you can't stand the heat, stay out of the kitchen.'

'I was planning to,' the assistant sniffed. 'You've got a sinkful of hydrangeas in there and they always set me off.'

Out on the wrap-around veranda, which extended around all four sides of the penthouse and commanded panoramic views of the capital, even the patio heaters had been wound round with ivy and hypericum. As had the bay trees, which were trimmed into neat balls once a week by a man with scissors. It was one of Alexandra's few jokes that they had their hair done almost as often as she did. A single pink rose lay across the white cushions of each recliner and the outdoor dining table boasted a large arrangement of its own.

Yes, Alexandra thought. She'd pulled all the stops out, as the photographer had said. And the effort and expense would be worth it; no one who saw the finished pictures could have any doubt that Alexandra Pigott was a style and glamour force to be reckoned with. The foothills of fame were now hers; the main ascent and the glittering pinnacle would be next.

'Do you have to keep your sunglasses on?' asked the photographer.

'Yeah,' Alexandra shot back in a tone that brooked no argument.

She was shortsighted and had poor toleration of contact lenses, but flatly refused to wear glasses under any circumstances. She got round the problem by wearing sunglasses, enormous and intensely black to disguise the thick prescription lenses, at all times, even inside.

Her blazingly white teeth working over her favourite brand of silver pearlised gum, she looked exasperatedly at her boyfriend as he refused to let the make-up artist put clear lipgloss on his mouth. And now he was rebuffing the hairstylist, politely but firmly refusing to allow the wet-look glitter styling gel recommended by her personal stylist anywhere near him. He really had ridiculous ideas about his hair.

'Look, I'm black, it would look funny,' he would exclaim with all the good humour he could summon whenever she tried, as she frequently did, to persuade him to dye it platinum blond and wear it in spikes.

'Yes, but think of the publicity you'd get with a haircut like that,' Alexandra would argue back.

'I'm thinking of the piss I'd get ripped out of me in the changing rooms.'

'Oh for Christ's sake. What does that matter?'

'Are you joking? I want to be known for my football. Not my hairstyle.'

That John hadn't grasped even the rudiments of the art of fame-getting was painfully obvious.

'I don't do jewellery,' he was now telling Petra as she attempted to put a string of pearls around his dark neck.

Alexandra clenched her slim brown fists in frustration, or as much as she could clench them without endangering her nailbar-fresh manicure. Just why was John so defensive? Admittedly, he was a defender, that was his position in the team, so perhaps it went with the territory. And why did he hate shopping so much? Despite his commanding height, perfect physique and natural air of cool, his obvious boredom when she marched him round the male emporia of Savile Row and Bond Street was more acute even than when he trailed miserably after her down Sloane Street. He wasn't interested in watches. He cared nothing for male beauty products and refused point blank to entertain the services of a personal tattooist. Fashion left him cold. The only clothes he really cared about wearing, he explained to Alexandra, were his team's home and away strips.

Still, she reminded herself, there was light at the end of the tunnel. Their wedding was set to be spectacular.

Chapter 12

Alexandra had earmarked a million at least for the celebrations. She was definitely going to be a princess.

But exactly how was the question.

Outdoing everything that had already been done at other celebrity weddings was a challenge that kept her awake at nights. What would she wear? Versace or Dior? Meringue or sheath? Jimmy Choo or Manolo Blahnik? Or vintage, from some tiny boutique in New York? Should a Swarovski crystal tiara secure a cathedral-length veil, or should pink rosebuds riot romantically round her hair extensions?

And for the evening, her second grand entrance of the day, she'd need a whole entirely new outfit. But would a backless sparkling mini-dress be better than sequinned black leggings and a fitted black corset? Alexandra could not decide.

Church or register office? Church was classier, definitely, with choirs and organs and everything, even if she actually intended to go up and down the aisle to CDs. Whitney Houston's 'I Will Always Love You' for up, she'd thought, and 'You Are So Beautiful' by Joe Cocker for down. There would be huge candles everywhere and a green and white theme of flowers generally. Simple and unostentatious was the idea. Giant lilies, masses of white hydrangeas, thousands of huge white roses. Although a dark pink and opal theme in huge trumpet vases was a possibility as well.

The food had to be spectacular. Alexandra now had a huge collection of menu ideas. For canapés, she'd narrowed it down to three: fillet of beef with fondant potato and béarnaise sauce, tomato tarts with glazed goat's cheese, and sweet potato hash browns with beef, chilli and avocado salsa. On the other hand, sashimi of tuna wrapped in mooli with a wasabi dip sounded good, or white truffle and parmigiana soufflé. And what about filet mignon and Maine lobster tail? As for wine, should it be pink Laurent Perrier throughout, or should they switch to Château Lynch-Bages at some stage?

The choices were haunting her dreams. John had woken up several times, or so he claimed, to hear her murmuring in her sleep.

'What did I say?' she asked, panic-stricken.

'Something about fresh crab with caviar and sour cream and cornfed chicken and feta salad with mint in a water-melon box with aged balsamic vinegar.'

And then there were the main courses. So difficult to get right. There had been that wedding where the gold shiny menu card had proclaimed in scrolled letters that guests were about to enjoy Velouté of Provençale Grilled Roasted Tomatoes with a Tian and Heart Crouton with a Selection of Home-made Organic Breads. With considerable difficulty Alexandra had eventually translated this as tomato soup and a roll, but it had sounded classy. Much classier than the Nage of Pot Noodle followed by Velouté of Mushy Pea with Cocotte of Fish and Chip at the wedding of a footballer intent on keeping true to his working-class food preferences despite the palatial setting.

One thing she was set on. There would be three chocolate fountains. She'd been to a wedding that had had two: milk and strawberry chocolate. So she would have to think of a third. What other sort of chocolate was there? Mint? White? Plain? A mixture of all three?

Cakewise, the current front-runner was a ten-tier white chocolate tower rioting with chocolate roses painted with edible pearl and with a matching pearlised stepladder to climb to cut the top layer. Still, at least the question of the photographer had been settled. Alexandra had spent long nights awake trying to decide between Mario Testino and Annie Leibovitz before realising that of course all the pictures would be done by *OK!* and *Hello!* in an exclusive multi-million-pound deal with each of them.

But the party would be the real test of her ingenuity, Alexandra knew. It was essential to be different, bigger, better; raise the bar for everyone else. For months now she had been eagerly seeking inspiration from events she went to, or spotted in the celebrity press. Inspiration was now whirling round her head like an out-of-control carousel.

She had read about one gathering where guests were greeted by huge inflatables: an ice-cream cone, a banana, a lipstick and cherries, while a pink Cadillac provided a background for six Elvis impersonators singing Rat Pack classics on a stage that had been crafted to look like a white piano.

She had personally attended several events where a burlesque dancer had performed in a glass slipper or giant bucking lipstick. But would upmarket strippers still be hot stuff when she and John got married? Or would they be more over than . . . Alexandra racked her brains for some historical period that could be said to have ended, but nothing historical sprang to mind. Things rarely sprang in the region of Alexandra's mind unless her hairclips worked loose.

There would be a custom-made marquee complete with floral displays and water features – not forgetting that most crucial water feature of all, the luxury Portaloos complete with oil paintings and mahogany seats. And she loved the idea of 'chill zones' within the marquee, where guests could relax on Louis XVI-style chairs beside French glass occasional tables with bowls of roses and candles.

There'd been that Elton John party with all the hotels in Las Vegas carved out of ice, scattered with diamonds and illuminated with pink spotlights, which sounded good. Although nothing, Alexandra vowed, nothing in the world would convince her on the mirrored dance-floor front. At one wedding she had been to, the women who had sat by the wall and refused to dance, far from being the usual frumpy plump ones, were the ones in racy mini-dresses with no visible means of underwear. Alexandra herself had been among them.

Which stately home for the party, though? Blenheim and Cliveden had both been done to death, footballers' weddings-wise. Alexandra planned to go one better and was wondering about Windsor Castle. Plenty of room for everyone's helicopters, as well as space for her planned release of white doves and multicoloured butterflies. Not to mention the mega firework display synchronised to her favourite Mariah Carey ballads whose finale would be hers and John's names spelt out in sparklers in the middle of flaming hearts.

While she did not intend to share the limelight with any bridesmaids, John had to have a best man, and this, Alexandra was determined, should be someone understated and polite. She feared cracks at her expense in the wedding speech and was certainly not prepared to risk what poor Alex Gerrard, wife of Steven, had had to bear at her own elaborate nuptials: the best man announcing to the whole wedding crowd that the groom deserved 'a pat on the back for a lot of the good things you've done, none more so than when you got Alex's jugs done'. 'It was dead embarrassing,' the bride said afterwards. 'My nan didn't know.'

Alexandra reflected uncomfortably that not even John knew the extent of her own plastic surgery, which he had of course paid for. Her jugs had been only the start of it, although he had certainly known and approved of those.

No, there were a lot of decisions to make, Alexandra thought. But it was all going to be perfect, or at least it was once one other unresolved detail was settled.

She just had to persuade John to propose, that was all.

So far he had been evasive whenever the subject of marriage was raised. This despite their eight years together. It wasn't fair. What was holding him back? Hadn't she done her time? Stuck with him through thick and thin? Didn't she deserve the big prize now? Alexandra felt that she could forgive his complete indifference to male grooming if he would only take an interest in the one aspect of it that really mattered. Bridegrooming.

Chapter 13

'Pasta and pesto!' exclaimed Monty with every appearance of delight as he came whistling into the kitchen. For all the world as if he had never seen it before, Mary thought fondly. She made it at least three times a week.

Monty, for all she loved him, was not the most rewarding of people to cook for. Before they were married, his idea of dinner had been a visit to the Breville Snack and Sandwich toaster, in which, Mary discovered, he was in the habit of combining the most disgusting things – baked beans and raw onions, for example – and for which he had the kind of reverence most people reserve for the invention of the steam engine or the discovery of electricity.

Mary's first act on moving into Underpants had been to throw out the – horribly cheese- and bean-stained – Breville when Monty wasn't looking. She had had visions of her elegant but somewhat etiolated husband filling out beautifully on her own food, home-cooking of the best and most delicate type. Realising that he had not the least interest in eating, however, had been a hard and sometimes unbelievable lesson. Nonetheless, she learnt it, and slowly the soufflés, flambées, thermidors and fricassees which had characterised their early married life had disappeared, to be replaced by the spaghetti Bolognese and beans on toast Monty infinitely preferred.

Mary hadn't given up without a fight, however. She had once tried to make gourmet beans on home-made bread toast, only to discover that her husband liked Heinz and Mother's Pride much better; eventually, not having been able to beat them, she had eventually joined them. Being unable to grow fresh vegetables in the gardens at Underpants had been the final straw. There were no raw materials, there was no incentive, so what had been the point?

The result was that Mary had not cooked a serious three-course meal, the sort she had produced on a near-daily basis before marriage, in ages and occasionally wondered if she would still be able to if the occasion ever arose.

'How was the tourist board?' Mary asked, forcing a hopeful expression into her wide green eyes. Monty had had a meeting with the Mineford tourist board that afternoon in the hope of enlisting their help to extract loans from various bodies. Neither of them had harboured any great hopes of the meeting; the Mineford tourist board, with its array of tea towels and small sheep ornaments in the window, seemed closed as often as not.

But Monty seemed to radiate with positivity. His mop of pale blond hair gleamed as he took off his battered tweed jacket and hung it on the back of his small chair. He stretched his long arms in their blue check shirt endlessly upwards before, with a scrape of wooden legs on stone floor, he pulled the chair out, folded his long legs in their worn red cords, spread out the napkin on his knee – Mary sought to maintain some standards, at least – and beamed triumphantly at his wife.

'Mary, I've decided what to do about Weston Underwood. How we can save it.'

The enormous blue eyes either side of his long thin nose shone in the dim light. He looked very excited.

'Save it?' Mary sat down opposite and looked at him wonderingly.

'I'm getting a job! Yes! There, that surprised you.' Happily, Monty twisted some pasta in his fork.

Mary stared at him, her wide eyes wider than ever, her small pink mouth an 'o' of amazement. 'What, at the tourist board?' Had her husband finally cracked? Even the head of the entire country's tourist board network probably didn't earn enough to have Weston Underwood as much as rewired, and that was the minimum that was needed.

'Of course not, silly!' He forked up some more pasta and fixed his glowing eyes on hers. 'I'm going to follow my heart and the traditions of my family.'

Mary's fork fell with a clatter on the stone-flagged floor. Warning bells sounded in the heart-and-traditions stage of the sentence. She clapped a hand to her mouth and stared at him.

'Traditions of your family?' she repeated.

'Yes. Be an explorer. Like Uncle Hengist.'

Mary now knew rather more than she originally had done about Monty's gung-ho great-great-uncle Hengist de Vere Longshott and did not altogether like the sound of him. The number of wives he had got through – other people's as well as his own – seemed to indicate that his explorations went beyond the strictly geographical. She had no intention of allowing Monty to be anything like Uncle Hengist.

'You are joking,' she exclaimed, struggling to believe what she was hearing. Had Monty really chosen the moment of greatest financial and structural crisis in his ancestral home's history to announce that he was disappearing to the ends of the earth for months on end?

'Why ever not?' Monty asked in unfeigned amazement.

Mary stared down at the green-flecked strands of pasta. Where, exactly, did she start? That if Monty wanted to explore, let him explore ways of keeping Weston Underwood standing? Let him explore the attics and find the source of the river currently streaming down one of the back staircases?

Monty looked boldly back at her, his eyes dancing, his long mouth twitching. 'Think about it, Mary. It's the obvious way out.'

'But it's dangerous,' Mary wailed.

As a piece of plaster, falling unexpectedly from the ceiling, shot past his blond fringe and embedded itself in his pasta, Monty looked at her. 'No more dangerous than sitting here. And possibly a good deal less.'

He gently laid down his fork, stood up and came round to her side of the table. He placed his large yet sensitive hands on her shoulders and bent his face into her hair. 'Darling. I've got a confession to make,' she felt him mutter hotly into her scalp. 'I wasn't at the tourist board this afternoon.'

Fear stabbed Mary like a knife. 'Where were you?' she gasped, jerking his chin off her head and straining round to catch his expression. She was shocked to her simple, trusting core. Monty never lied to her. Ever. He never had.

The large, wet blue eyes looking back at her wore an apologetic expression. 'I just didn't want to raise your hopes.'

'Hopes!' Obscurely, immediately, madly, she thought this must be something to do with a child. Had he been to some sort of clinic?

Suddenly a grin blazed like a comet across Monty's

delicately beautiful face. 'I've done it!' he exclaimed, grabbing Mary by the waist and whirling her awkwardly round the kitchen.

'Done what?' Mary gasped, trying not to stumble over the long red corduroyed legs that seemed determined to trip her up. Dancing had never been Monty's forte.

'Got the money. For my expedition. Solo to the North Pole.'

'Solo!'

Eventually, after he had capered, whooped and waltzed some more, Monty was ready to divulge the facts. A business conglomerate had apparently offered the money. It was them he had been meeting with that afternoon.

'They're giving me all of it,' Monty beamed, naming what sounded to Mary an enormous sum.

'But we could have spent that on the West Wing,' she faltered.

His pale blond head was a whir of white as he shook it. It stilled and the blue eyes, now concerned, came into focus once more. 'No one was going to give it to us just for that. But if things go well I'll be in great demand for after-dinner speaking, the motivation industry as I believe it's called, all sorts of stuff. And things *will* go well, Mary.' He seized both her wrists and gazed passionately into her eyes. 'My profile will be raised and with it that of Underpants. We might be able to set up a fund to save it, with all the public interest. There might be TV programmes. Believe me, darling. People will be queueing up to give me money when I get back.'

'But . . . but . . .' Mary stammered, searching wildly for questions. It was all so surprising she hardly knew what to ask. 'But how did you find these sponsors? Who are they?'

'Amazing stroke of luck.' Monty's huge eyes widened even further and his long mouth spread in an incredulous smile. 'I was looking on the ongoing expedition websites at the library . . . um . . . *ahem* . . .'

As he cleared his throat guiltily, Mary realised in a flash that all those afternoons Monty seemed to be taking an extraordinarily long time at the DIY wholesalers, he had in fact been going the long way round via the free internet access offered by the Mineford library. She stared at him with a mixture of hurt and a sort of exasperated admiration that, despite the demands his ancestry was making on him in so many unwelcome ways, his enthusiasm for its glory days remained undimmed, if not stronger than ever.

'Turns out,' Monty added, 'that this firm had an expedition all set up and ready to go. But their previous person pulled out. So naturally I got in touch, right away. Then and there. Used the payphone at the library, in fact.' He sighed happily. 'It's a match made in heaven.'

'Why?' Mary asked instantly. Annoyance pricked at her. She and Monty were a match made in heaven. He often said so. How could he apply the term so readily to anything else?

'Because I wanted an expedition and they wanted someone to go on one.' The blue eyes turned on her, puzzled.

'No.' Mary shook her thick brown hair from side to side. 'I mean, why did the previous person pull out?'

Monty shrugged his wide yet slender shoulders. 'Personal problems, apparently. I couldn't pry, obviously.'

Mary's wide green eyes narrowed in a look of uncharacteristic suspicion. So far as she was concerned, anything involving her beloved husband had to be pried into without mercy.

He, however, was beaming. 'So they were looking for

someone like me and I was looking for someone like them. It's a miracle we got together.'

Mary felt jealous again. The last six words were ones Monty used exclusively to her as well. 'Who are these people?' she muttered crossly.

'Er, well they're sort of in the prison sector.'

Mary now discovered that the conglomerate offering to sponsor her husband was connected to a somewhat notorious organisation much involved in the privatisation of prison security. Under its auspices several dangerous criminals had escaped.

'Are you sure you want to be associated with them?' Mary asked, her smooth, girlish face creased with worry. 'They don't seem to have done a very good job.'

Monty folded his arms, looking as near to exasperated as he was able. 'Well it's all very well for people to criticise, but as the chairman, super chap by the way, was just saying to me, what no one seems to understand is that it's really very difficult keeping people somewhere they don't want to be. And I have to say I agree. My school had a hell of a job keeping me in, I can tell you. I escaped all the time.' He chuckled.

'I'm not sure it's quite the same thing . . .'

'Oh, Mary, listen.'

She listened to Monty explain that by sponsoring him and thereby allying themselves with a brave and very British struggle with some of the most inhospitable climes in nature, the firm hoped to weather their own public relations storm and redeem their public image. The theory of the corporate PR department seemed to be that the public could not jeer at Monty's efforts and the firm's simultaneously, and in getting behind one they would get behind the other.

'But . . .' Mary's eyes darted about the kitchen as she searched for further objections. 'You can't possibly be fit enough.'

Monty raised his pointed chin indignantly. 'Up to it? You jolly well betcha. Been careful to keep myself in tip-top condition.' He proudly stuck out his chest. 'A bit of training's all I need.'

He took a deep inward breath of satisfaction. 'Yes,' he added with conviction. 'We Longshotts are always ready for anything.'

Mary felt the only thing she was personally ready for was the house finally falling down. The previous night had been very windy and roof tiles had blown about like ticker tape. The first thing she had seen out of the windows that morning was something resembling a bloated grey-white body on the grass. An unpleasant few moments had passed while Mary rushed outside only to discover the corpse was a large and bulbous finial, late of a parapet over the Gentlemen's Wing.

'And they're going to train you?'

Monty nodded. 'I'll have a support team, of course. And they're going to give me full training,' he beamed. 'I'll be doing courses in aerobic fitness, water management, shooting . . .'

'Shooting!'

'Yeah, in case of polar bears . . . Oh, don't worry, Mary. It'll be fine. I've got my route all planned out. To be honest, I have had for years.' He gave her a guilty smile and looked abashed.

Mary could believe it. The piles of maps strewn all over the bed when she had seen Monty's room for the first time still remained, in a pile in the bedroom's corner. They were frequently referred to. And, for years, he had pored avidly over any newspaper story concerning polar expeditions. Similarly, any TV programme on the subject had him rapt in a corner of the kitchen, perched on a small wooden chair watching the tiny portable balanced on the hacked and uneven surface of the former butcher's block. His interest had never gone away.

'But . . . but . . . where is this training going to take place?'

'London,' Monty replied firmly.

Mary felt a shock of misery. He would be leaving her. Going away to London. The city she had left to live with him. 'Where in London?' she asked sadly, trying not to feel somehow betrayed.

'An army base,' Monty said excitedly.

Mary looked unhappily back at him. It was obviously all sorted out. There was no room for doubt. 'But . . .' she searched for objections, all the same. 'Solo to the North Pole.' The thought of her beloved Monty alone in the icy wilderness brought the tears starting to her eyes. What chance did he have amongst polar bears, treacherous ice and extreme temperatures?

Gently, Monty shared his view that the freezing temperatures of Underpants, even in summer as it allegedly was now, were ideal for acclimatisation. 'And I'm pretty fit – you have to be to live here, ha ha.'

Mary's lips, rather than sharing his joky grin, trembled.

'You'll be all by yourself. In the most hostile environment known to man. Alone and without help. Anything could happen at any time.'

He gave her a wry grin. 'Alone and without help in a hostile environment . . . well, to be honest, darling, we've lived like that for years at Underpants, haven't we?'

Chapter 14

Alexandra and John sat in the penthouse's huge gold and white sitting room, watching the outsize LCD television that was neither gold nor white, despite Alexandra's strenuous efforts to find one that was.

But John saw nothing of the tense detective drama that was unfolding. The only drama he was aware of was the one that would follow the news he was about to break. He felt his heart-rate increase and his palms go clammy. Going down the tunnel before a cup final was nothing on this. 'I've got something to tell you,' he said, and told her.

Alexandra leapt up, clutching about her the designer Matthew Williamson robe she always wore for quiet nights in along with a pair of leopardskin mules. Her face reminded him of the way a detonated building hangs in the air before collapsing. It did not, however, collapse, due to a dried-to-stiffness bright green face pack which gave the bright green eyes currently glaring at him a terrifying heightened quality.

'You're joking,' she shrieked over a woman shrieking on the police drama. He reached for the remote and turned it off.

'No. I'm not.' He didn't do jokes and, actually, there would have been no point if he did, as Alexandra didn't do humour. He had once tried telling her the only one he knew, about the naughty inflatable boy at the inflatable school being told by the inflatable headmaster that he had let the school down but worst of all he had let himself down, but Alexandra had not even smiled.

She was not smiling now either. He could tell that from the way her feet in their leopardskin mules had plonked themselves in the patch of white carpet at which he was staring. He found himself examining with unprecedented curiosity the small topaz jewel on the mule's upper, trimmed with a fawn-coloured feather.

'Leave London?' Alexandra waved her hands wildly. Her nails were still drying.

John sighed. 'You know this transfer's been under discussion. I've talked to you about it. The idea's been on the table for a while.'

Alexandra glared at him, her recognition of any such conversation as blurred as her vision. Not even Alexandra could wear sunglasses over a facepack.

'I *can't* leave London,' she cried hysterically.

John bowed his head lower, staring miserably at his muscular legs, spread wide apart on the outsize white leather pouffe. His gaze lingered on the large outcrops of knee beneath the white linen trousers Alexandra liked him to wear but which he was not too sure about himself.

'Look, there's not much I can do about it, to be honest. They're selling me.'

Personally he was quite relaxed about moving from the London club where competition for the starting line-up got worse each week, to the Midlands club which had had its share of troubles but was now not only back in the Premiership but swiftly scaling it. And he could, he knew, be part of the scaling; speed it up, too, and with never a suggestion of him sitting on the reserves bench either. He was happy about the deal; Alexandra, on the other hand, had different views, rather as he had suspected she might.

'What about my career?' Alexandra wailed. He watched the mules raising and stamping with fury in the deep white pile carpet and cringed to think of the pressure on her calves.

'What career?' he asked candidly, his honest eyes clouded with doubt.

Wrong response, he realised immediately. Her eyes flashed with emerald ominousness, losing none of their angry power to the fact that she could hardly see him. 'My agent says lots of exciting things are being discussed.'

'What sort of exciting things?' he asked disbelievingly. Alexandra's agent had got her all excited not long ago about a possible job as a judge on a cable TV show about a modelling competition. Nothing had come of it apart from to confirm his low opinion of the agent. 'Not that modelling thing again?'

Alexandra tossed her white hair impatiently to one side of her head. 'That modelling thing, as you call it, would have been the perfect vehicle for me. Being in the beauty industry, like I used to be, and intending to go into TV presenting.

'But, since you ask, it's not that,' she continued, tossing her hair to the other side of her head as she did so. It looked beautiful, he thought admiringly, as well it might considering she was in the salon twice a week; she saw more of Robby Trendy, her hairdresser, than she did of him.

'So what is it then?'

'New things,' Alexandra snapped, adding force to her

remarks by putting her hands on her hips, diamond-laden fingers spread in the way her stylist had shown her.

'What sort of new things?'

She tossed her head again. 'There's a fly-on-the-wall show about shopaholics that I'm in the frame for . . .'

He felt a pang of alarm. All he really knew was football; the world of fame and television celebrity interested him far less than many of his fellow players. Nonetheless, even he was aware of how the fly on the wall could end up biting you on the bum, and wondered if parading her addiction to Sloane Street in general and Gucci and Chanel in particular would do Alexandra any favours.

'Are you sure that's a good idea?' he ventured carefully.

'My agent's very keen,' she shot back. Well of course, John reflected, the agent would be. He was the one who stood to pocket the commission.

'Look,' he said quickly. 'There's no reason why you can't, um, develop your, um, career when we move. We'll be near lots of big cities. Manchester. Birmingham. Sheffield . . .'

'*Sheffield!*' she shrieked.

'It's near lots of nice countryside,' he ploughed on, not entirely sure of his facts.

'*Countryside!*' Alexandra bellowed in horror.

She strode furiously and not without difficulty through the immensely thick pile carpet, flinging herself petulantly on the outsize white-silk-upholstered sofa.

'If we move to the country we can have a big house,' he urged her. 'A real house.'

'What's not real about this house?' Alexandra wailed, flinging an arm which rattled with bracelets in the direction of the fake tigerskin rugs and some polystyrene real-effect marble statues on plinths which stood in the corner.

John paused, trying to think of a reply. The truth – that the Knightsbridge penthouse had never been his thing, really – would infuriate Alexandra, he knew. She had been less than keen when he had pushed for a stockbroker-belt mansion like all the other lads, preferably near the other lads so they could have regular rounds of golf.

'It would be different if we were married,' Alexandra said silkily, having decided to drop the hints and take the direct route. 'All these years together and I haven't even got a ring to show for it,' she added, stretching out the hand where in fact a great many rings flashed and dazzled.

'You've got lots of rings,' he pointed out quickly.

He loved his girlfriend but was in no hurry to have one of those obscenely vast and lavish footballer's weddings with carved ice sculptures, silver chairs, chocolate fountains and enough pink champagne to swim in. He had been to plenty of them, and he hated them. There was one in particular he remembered, of a team-mate he was fond of. At the reception, John had looked over from where he was sitting to see the friend behind a top table laden with so many flowers and white silk it had looked like a bier. The bride, drowning in designer frills, had been flanked by her terrifying-looking mother in a custom-built creation, swilling champagne by the bucketful and looking ominously down at the other diners. John's kind heart had gone out to his friend.

'There's plenty of time for all that,' he said pleasantly.

Alexandra knew better than to nag him on this most sensitive of subjects. With an immense effort she accepted that to have any hope of securing the eventual union, she had little choice but to go with him to his new club.

'Just think about it,' John was urging her, his handsome face all persuasion. 'We could get some massive pile in some country village. You could be lady of the manor. Do it all up, any way you like.' He swallowed slightly as he said this. Alexandra spent money like water. It was truly terrifying what she had lavished on the penthouse already.

Alexandra tucked a stray platinum strand behind her tiny, tanned and diamond-studded ear. There were possibilities, definitely, she was thinking. Massive pile, John had said. Lady of the manor. Pictures began to form in her head. Suddenly, Alexandra was seeing stables. She was seeing gleaming, high-spirited thoroughbred steeds, irrespective of the fact she had never as much as sat on one. She was seeing parkland almost as manicured as her nails. She was seeing crests and crowns and four-poster beds.

And more than any of this she was seeing a venue for the wedding of the decade. For where else would the reception be held other than in her very own stately home? Perhaps she could get married in her own estate chapel drawn by her own horses and carriage. That would knock Jordan's wedding into a cocked hat, whatever that was. One of those hairbands with illuminated penises on that people wore on their hen nights, probably. Not that she would do anything so vulgar on *her* hen night. A girlie trip to Las Vegas was more what she was thinking.

Alexandra descended from these happy fantasies with a bump. Of course, none of this could happen until John had proposed. But moving to the country might at least bring this one step nearer. What other option was there?

Chapter 15

'I've got it!' Benny announced excitedly.

It was Friday night and they had just arrived at the cottage. Beth, in the kitchen, where she was admiring the effect of the new rose-printed cover on the ironing board, looked up. Benny was leafing through the post. 'Got what?'

'The answer. What we should do to make ourselves more popular in this village.'

'Move out of it, I should think,' his wife said lightly, gazing with satisfaction on the new rose-printed peg bag that matched the ironing-board cover and also the lining of the new wicker laundry basket. She had ordered it all from the internet and found it, as expected, on their arrival outside the cottage door in a big cardboard box marked with the Cath Kidston logo; marked, too, with evidence that some large and scruffy vehicle had apparently run into it. Mercifully the contents were unharmed.

Benny envied his wife her detachment. Beth was so utterly, blithely oblivious to anything and anyone who did not interest her. If people were rude, she ignored them. Following the encounter with the purple-trousered woman the week before she had immediately ceased to think about it. Certainly it had not occurred to her, as it had occurred immediately to him, that the tyre marks on her Cath Kidston box were not an accident and had almost certainly come from the decommissioned ambulance.

'No, no. Moving out would mean bigots like that woman get the better of us,' Benny insisted.

'What woman . . . oh, *that* woman.' Beth turned her eyes reluctantly from the peg bag. 'Must we talk about her? I want to enjoy being in our *adorable* Bijou Cottage.'

Benny flinched at mention of the dreaded name. Beth had insisted, however, and had ordered what she described as a 'tasteful, hand-painted nameplate' from a chi-chi interiors emporium on Westbourne Grove. This had not yet arrived and would, Benny imagined, be the last straw for Morag Archbutt-Pesk when it did. He could imagine her attacking it with a chisel, teeth bared with fury. And then attacking him and Beth with the chisel as well.

Benny now noticed for the first time what Beth had unpacked from the box. He blinked at the ironing board. He had never seen Beth use an iron in her life. In London, it was all done by their cleaner.

'I adore Bijou Cottage,' Beth declared, stroking her ironing-board cover happily.

'But Allsop doesn't adore us, that's the problem,' Benny said dolefully.

'Don't be so paranoid,' yawned Beth.

He looked at her hopefully. 'You think I am being? You don't think they hate us because we're American?'

She shrugged. 'No.'

He looked relieved.

'How could they?' Beth enunciated carefully. 'I'm more

English than the English. You're always saying so.' Really, Benny was taking all this far too seriously. Who cared what the oiks in this village thought?

Benny grinned despite himself and, pulling Beth to him, pressed his face into her hair and smelt all the expensive, delicious lotions she used. Beth was the cleanest-smelling person he had ever known. She radiated freshness like a pile of newly ironed linen sheets in the sunshine. Not by accident, however. The bathroom cabinet in London was full of her bottles, and the one here was going rapidly the same way. There was no room for his things any more and Beth was already starting to talk about having a second bathroom built so they would have one each, as they did in Kensington Park Road.

'So what's your great idea?' Beth muttered into his shoulder. 'To make ourselves loved?'

'There's a piece in the newsletter about a village allotment scheme for Allsop.'

Beth pulled her head from under his chin and stared up into his eyes in surprise. She frowned. 'A what?'

'An allotment. A vegetable plot,' explained Benny. 'It's, like, a field full of them. You get one and then you go there and plant, like, vegetables.'

Comprehension dawned on Beth. 'Oh, I've seen them. They're, like, a mess. Sticks everywhere, plastic and really grungy sheds.' She stuck out her pretty lower lip in objection.

'But *our* allotment wouldn't be,' Benny promised. 'We'd keep it beautifully. And if it's an all-new site, no one else's would be messy either. And just think, you could grow your own vegetables to cook with.'

Beth raised a perfectly waxed eyebrow. She did like

cooking, that was true. Eating possibly wasn't her forte, but she enjoyed the preparation.

'You'll meet people, too,' Benny pointed out, sensing he had struck a seam of interest.

'I don't want to meet people who grow vegetables,' Beth objected. 'I want to meet smart people with stately homes.'

'Yeah, but you know how much you like organically grown stuff.' Her husband retreated hurriedly. 'You *love* farmer markets in London. You're always saying you can't beat, where is it, Marylebone . . . ?'

Beth nodded. 'Yeah, for unpasteurised buffalo cream. And I found some world-class shiitake in Borough last week. They have amazing samphire at our local one in Notting Hill.'

'Well there you are then. So let's grow our own samphire.'

'I think you've got to grow samphire in the sea,' Beth demurred uncertainly. Still, she was finding the idea more palatable now. She saw herself in a large straw hat, designer jeans, hair soft-lifted by a flattering breeze, pulling a perfect organic carrot from the freshly tilled earth and gently brushing the dirt from it. She suppressed the sure knowledge that, so far, she had never even managed to grow cress from cress seeds. The back garden of the cottage was testament to the non-greenness of her fingers.

Benny's finger, meanwhile, traced the paragraphs of the newsletter. 'Anyone who's interested in having an allotment needs to come to the inaugural meeting of the Allsop Allotments Association, President Elect Mr St John Goodenough, Chairman of the Parish Council.' He looked up, beaming. 'So let's go to the meeting. Get in there and get an allotment. That'll give us something in common with everyone else. Get us involved.'

*

St John Goodenough, Chairman of Allsop Parish Council and President Elect of the Allsop Allotments Association, was having lunch with his wife Veronica when the telephone rang in the hall.

St John chewed his mouthful of liver and onion hurriedly, put down his knife and fork and wiped his mouth with a snowy napkin. Even when it was just the two of them having lunch, he and Veronica had standards. They had a cooked lunch, eaten in the dining room with a tablecloth on the polished oak table, using the lunchtime willow-pattern china, as opposed to the breakfast-time earthenware Veronica put out every night before going to bed so it would be ready for the morning.

He was not particularly surprised, on answering the shrilling instrument, to find an agitated-sounding female at the other end of it. No one civilised telephoned during lunch, so far as he was concerned. It must be an emergency of sorts.

'We need a direction,' the woman thundered.

'Direction?' St John repeated, puzzled. It was unusual for people to ring him up for this reason, but if it was a damsel in distress, he could make an exception. 'Where do you want directions for?' asked St John, gallantly.

'The allotments, of course,' snapped the woman.

'Ah.' The allotments. St John's pinker face went pink with pleasure. His rosy bald head positively glowed and his white moustaches bristled with pride. This person may have interrupted him during his favourite lunch – Veronica's tour de force liver and onions with mashed potato – but if they wanted to talk about his favourite subject, all was forgiven.

It had been he, St John Goodenough Esquire, Chairman

of Allsop Parish Council, who had been the initial force behind the plan to convert a strip of disused common land on the hill behind the village into an area where the inhabitants of Allsop, many of whom felt constrained by their small cottage gardens, could grow vegetables. It had taken some time – yes, and some determination too – to find the site and get the practicalities of the plan approved by the relevant authorities. But he had got there in the end. And soon they would have the glorious unveiling of everything he had worked for.

'Well, of course they're not allotments yet, not strictly speaking,' St John now informed his mysterious female caller. 'They haven't been, er, allotted yet, as it were. We're due to have a meeting about that. Next Friday in fact. A week from today.'

St John could hardly stop himself jigging when he thought about the meeting. It would be the moment when he revealed to a collected village the efforts he had made and basked in their collective gratitude.

'However, in answer to your original question, the directions to the allotments site are as follows,' St John continued chirpily. 'Go down to the village cross, then over the road, up the path into the fields and they're on your right through the gate.'

'I'm not talking about that sort of direction,' hissed the other end of the phone, exasperated. 'The direction we need for the allotments is *political* direction.'

'*Poli—?*' boggled the Chairman of the Parish Council and President Elect of the Allsop Allotments Association. 'Who is this speaking, please?' he asked now, his mild tones disguising mounting concern he was being targeted by a madwoman.

'Morag Archbutt-Pesk.'

St John gasped faintly. He knew who this was. That terrifying female in purple trousers. He *was* being targeted by a madwoman.

'What exactly do you mean by political direction?' he asked carefully, his eyes fixed on, yet not seeing, the gently ticking grandfather clock in the shady, oak-panelled hall.

'No one should be allowed to use slug pellets,' announced Morag in lordly fashion, 'and the field should be made ready in the traditional way with a horse and plough.'

St John struggled for a reply. 'We've made no decisions about any of those things,' he blustered eventually.

'*We?*' countered Morag immediately. 'Who's we? Who's in charge?'

'Well, that's not been decided yet either. Not formally. But *I* am President Elect,' St John announced, supporting himself on the hall's oak sideboard as he puffed his chest out with pride.

'Elected by *who?*' demanded Morag crisply. 'Not by *me*. *I* never elected you to be President Elect.'

St John was generally easygoing but he now felt himself coming to a kettle-like boil. Did this ungrateful, obstreperous woman not realise the efforts he had made for the good of the village? He tried not to think what Veronica's answer to this would be.

'I feel particularly strongly about the horse-ploughing,' Morag declared stridently.

Panic swept St John. He was planning to use the mini-tractor he used on his lawn on his own allotment. Then he shook himself. He was not going to be cowed by this woman. Or horsed, come to that.

It was, however, difficult to get a word in edgeways. Impossible, in fact. 'Modern farming methods can traumatise the land,' Morag thundered. 'We are stewards of the ground, not torturers of it. We should grow our vegetables in happy earth.'

St John sighed. Veronica, who had clearly had enough of eating on her own by now, had come out of the dining room. She looked at him with a mild but quizzical expression in answer to which, using long-established code, St John pointed his index finger to his temple and revolved it in a way that signified a person of unsound mind was on the other end. Veronica Goodenough nodded. St John occasionally received crank calls. It was part and parcel of parish council duties.

'There is, as I said, to be a public meeting about the allotments next week,' St John told Morag in his best official voice, his eyes following Veronica's Paisley skirt and white cardigan as they retreated into the dining room. 'Anyone wishing to acquire one or express their views about them will have the opportunity then.'

Morag wished to take the opportunity now, however. Admittedly the village allotments project had not been her idea, not exactly or entirely, although she *had* thought about growing vegetables in their own garden to the latest and highest biosustainable standards. But the garden was tiny; the creature tower and the princess tent took up all the available room.

St John may have stolen the concept from her. But the allotments would go no further without her guiding the way. She was determined to move in now with what she considered to be much-needed ideological backbone.

'I hear what you're saying,' St John said wearily, when, after what seemed like years, she stopped to draw breath. He imagined everyone else in Allsop could hear too; Morag

Archbutt-Pesk had a voice like a foghorn. 'But, as I mentioned, I can't do anything about it now. You'll need to come and put your views at the meeting on Friday.'

He put the telephone down feeling concerned. The allotment idea had been such a simple one: turn disused land that belonged to no one into something everyone could use and enjoy. Why did shouty women in purple trousers have to complicate matters?

Reseating himself at the table, he found his liver had gone cold into the bargain.

Chapter 16

Maureen Hughes, estate agent, had been about to shut up shop when the call came through. Business was slow, although this was not in itself the reason for closure. If it was, as Maureen often said herself to the owner of Snips & Lips, the beauty shop next door, the whole of Mineford would be permanently shut.

The town was struggling. One only had to look at the number of new businesses that set up and shut down within twelve months to realise that. The most recent failure had been a rather nice deli, with a rather nice young man behind the counter more to the point, but his cappuccinos had been *very* overpriced, everyone agreed on that, and eventually he had gone the way of the art gallery and the designer kitchenware that had preceded him.

She herself made a reasonable enough living, and it wasn't as if there were seriously rich pickings to be had anyway. She didn't do big, she didn't do glitz. But then neither did Mineford and its environs generally. Properties in the area tended to be small and unambitious: terraces, starter homes, that sort of thing. The fanciest end of the market were the factory conversions – executive homes in former spinning mills – or cottages of the rambling and romantic variety. And when one of the latter arrived on the market they were soon snapped up, as that place in Allsop had just been, by that young American couple. But that was about as good as it got.

Maureen switched off the lights – well, the ones whose bulbs had not blown some time ago – in the main showroom and, as the spotlights faded over the house details displayed in lopsided laminated rows along the walls and in the windows, went into the kitchenette to get the plastic bag containing her swimwear. As she did, the phone rang.

Maureen groaned. She hadn't yet put the answerphone on, and depending on the determination of the person on the other end, it could ring for ages. She picked it up.

'I need a house,' barked someone on the other end. As well as being impatient, it was female. And young, Maureen estimated. With a Cockney sort of accent. Unusual for Mineford all round.

'What sort of a house?' asked Maureen.

'A big one.'

'Oh. We don't have big ones.' Perhaps another agent would have tried to finesse this, to suggest alternatives, but Maureen had never been one for this approach. Her view was shared by most shopkeepers in Mineford, which was why, when the town was looking for a slogan to put on its entry sign, one wag had written to the paper suggesting 'Mineford: Delighted To Disappoint'. This had been overruled in favour of 'Mineford: A Healthy Place', although a look in any of the doctors' waiting rooms first thing on a Monday morning might hint otherwise.

'You don't have big ones?' demanded the voice, clearly disappointed and equally clearly not at all delighted about it.

'No.'

Well, not in that sense. Maureen smiled a secret smile as she caught her reflection in one of the plastic displays. Her male admirers had always in particular admired her chest area, or upper level. It had invariably been viewed as greatly enhancing the overall appeal of the property. Not that anyone had seen fit to buy it yet, although there had been a number of long-term leasees and she had recently had hopes that the young solicitor might be one of them. But since Philip Protheroe had indicated his lack of interest in anything other than a professional relationship, she was engaged in a programme of overall refurbishment, of which the aquarobics formed part. Hopefully, eventually, this initiative would result in a successful transaction.

'Not even biggish ones?'

''Fraid not. Now if you'll excuse me, I really must . . .'

Maureen's eye beneath its purple eyeshadow rolled towards the clock. She had five minutes to get to the pool if she wanted to be in time. Anything less and she risked measuring her length on the cracked Mineford pavement in her heels.

The woman at the other end of the phone was not giving up so easily, however. 'But I've got a lot of money to spend,' she snapped disbelievingly. 'Don't you want any of it? I'm talking millions. *Mil-l-i-ons*,' she repeated, as if communicating with a simpleton.

It was a landmark for Hughes and Hughes. No one had ever mentioned such huge sums down the telephone before. But if they think I'm going to be impressed by that, Maureen thought, they're very much mistaken. 'Well that's nice for you, I'm sure,' she said tartly, 'but I'm afraid it doesn't change the actual position vis-à-vis the housing market as it stands at the moment in terms of the general availability or non-availability of actual property—'

'What?' interrupted the other end.

'If you want big ones,' Maureen said firmly, 'you should try another agent. Perhaps over towards Derby or Manchester. That's where the folk with big houses live.'

'I've tried all the other agents,' complained the voice on the other end. 'You're the last one.'

Maureen was not especially offended by this. She was most people's last one, and thought of it as a compliment in a way. When all else failed, people turned to Hughes and Hughes.

'There's nothing for sale anywhere,' Alexandra complained. Agent after agent had broken the unwelcome news that the market was unprecedentedly slow at the moment and the people with big houses were hanging on to them. There certainly weren't any mansions with their own gym, stables, swimming pool and helicopter pad, one particularly snooty agent had told her, unless you counted Chatsworth, and as far as he knew that was not on the market.

''Fraid I can't help you then,' sniffed Maureen.

Alexandra ground her expensively veneered teeth. It was on the tip of her tongue to demand whether Maureen knew who she was, but it was undeniable even for one of her unlimited self-belief that her plans for world domination had taken something of a setback recently. The celebrity magazine had not put the At Home on the cover after all but towards the back, just before a feature in which 'Britain's Eurovision hopefuls' shared their favourite TV snacks with the nation.

Alexandra had immediately fired her PA, which was the reason she herself was having to make the calls to estate agents now. There had been other people around, but the cleaner and ironing woman were Filipinos, and while they were apparently doctors and lawyers in their home country, neither was up to tracking down a mansion in the Midlands. Her personal stylist, meanwhile, had become furiously busy as soon as the subject had been raised and her agent Max had flatly pointed out that his job was to make her famous, not arrange accommodation.

'There's *really* nothing?' she demanded of Maureen Hughes now. 'I repeat, I've got millions to spend.' Alexandra lived in a world where mentioning millions achieved the desired result with lightning speed. 'There must be some nice villages around,' she argued, annoyed at almost having to plead with this lumpen fool on the other end. But if she drew a blank with this woman, after wasting so much time with so many others, not only would her hopes of being lady of the manor bite the dust, but she would be in trouble with John as well. They needed somewhere to live. The transfer deal was signed, the new season looming, and even someone with Alexandra's limited interest in football could recognise that something of a countdown was underway.

And of course, if she was in trouble with John, her chances of getting him up the aisle would be yet more remote than they seemed at present. 'Millions,' she repeated rather desperately to Maureen.

Maureen groaned. The clock had gone past five; she was never going to make aquarobics now. There was nothing for it but to resign herself to this annoying but persistent person.

'Nice villages?' she sniffed, leaning over to grasp a handful of details and blowing the dust off them. 'Well, there's Allsop, I suppose.'

'Well, has it got anywhere big in it? You know, a rectum or something.'

'Rectum?' Maureen repeated faintly.

'You know. Where the vicar lives.'

'You mean a rectory.'

'Whatever. Point is, they're usually big, aren't they?'

'There's a vicarage, yes. But it's not for sale.'

'What about a manor house?'

'Not for sale either.' Maureen gave a lofty sniff. 'The family has lived there for hundreds of years.'

'About time they moved out then,' Alexandra retorted. Her patience had finally, after this unprecedentedly lengthy airing, run out. 'So there's nothing in Allsop, is that what you're saying?'

Something stirred within Maureen then. It was a feeling she had not experienced for a long time. The desire to sell something to someone was deeply buried but not, she now realised, extinguished altogether. She remembered that, lurking deep within her register of properties for sale, was a cottage in Allsop that for some reason had never appealed to anyone. The reason might have had something to do with its lack of garden, the hideous glass porch which seemed to encapsulate all that was wrong with the architecture of the 1970s, its complete lack of utilities and general state of rotting collapse. But for the right buyer, these would be challenges, not drawbacks.

'Well there is somewhere,' the dormant sales beast within Maureen said now. 'And, actually, Allsop's quite an interesting village. It's got a very pretty medieval church that's mentioned in something or other. And of course there's the betrothal stone.'

'What's that?'

It was a good question, Maureen thought. It had been so long since she had thought to mention the stone to any potential buyer that the facts surrounding it momentarily escaped her. No one in Allsop took the least notice of it and certainly no one in her lifetime had ever actually used it, to Maureen's knowledge. Whatever the betrothal stone had once been, whatever erstwhile significance it had enjoyed, it was now a joke, at best. She had not even bothered to tell the Americans about it; admittedly, the woman's keenness on the cottage was such that she had not needed extra encouragement.

Maureen ransacked her memory in vain for what she could remember about the Allsop betrothal stone. Fortunately, the sales beast came to her rescue.

'A quaint local tradition,' it simpered. 'Ladies can propose marriage to their gentlemen friends at this stone. And . . .' the beast dropped its voice, aware that it had the full and rapt attention of the person at the other end, 'it's unlucky for the gentleman to refuse.'

In Knightsbridge, Alexandra swallowed. Her narrow brown hand gripped the telephone. 'Really?' she gasped.

Alexandra's direct, if not visceral, approach to life and what she wanted belied her child-like suggestibility. She believed, for example, every word of her magazine horoscopes, even when different magazines said exactly opposite things. She believed every word she read in the celebrity press, particularly if it concerned Victoria Beckham. And now, instantly, she believed in the betrothal stone in this unknown village in some far-off corner of the country. Women could propose to their boyfriends at this stone. And it was unlucky for the men to say no.

'Absolutely,' the beast assured her.

'And you say you have a property for sale in this . . . Slopley?'

'Allsop. I do indeed. It's opposite the betrothal stone, as a matter of fact. And that's important. The stone only works for residents of Allsop. You have to live in the village for it to have any effect.'

Maureen was astounded. Personally, she had completely forgotten about this particular stipulation concerning the stone. But the beast seemed to know what it was doing. The woman was clearly interested. In fact, had Maureen been given to such flights of fancy, she might have thought the person on the other end was panting.

'Is this property big?' Alexandra demanded.

'Betrothal Cottage is . . . biggish.' If you happened to be a beetle, thought the beast. But getting the client to actually see a place was half the battle. Every agent knew that.

'It's actually called Betrothal Cottage?' Okay, Alexandra thought, so the cottage bit didn't sound great, but it could be misleading. There was a football stadium called Craven Cottage, for example, which was enormous and looked nothing like a cottage.

'It is, yes.'

'When can I see it?' Alexandra demanded.

Chapter 17

'Mrs Sheen will show you out,' Philip told his clients as his secretary appeared at the door. He watched as Mrs Sheen, neat in her dark blue suit, short red hair, technical-looking glasses and sober expression, collected the couple he had been advising and led them out of the door.

It was a shoplifter he had agreed to represent at the county court, plus her mother. 'She's a Victim of the Consumer Culture,' the mother had boomed on arrival. She was a redoubtable, excitable female with indignant round eyes beneath a clump of black hair, muddy skin and an enormous body encased in a large pink towelling track-suit. The girl, who wore jeans exposing her own billowing midriff, was a plump teenager with brown hair scraped back to reveal a pink shapeless face radiating resentment.

'A victim?' Philip had echoed in surprise. 'How exactly do you mean?' The shop whose make-up section had been decimated regarded itself, he knew, as significantly more injured.

The mother fixed Philip with an unblinking, hot-eyed

stare. 'Well she is a Victim. She's got no money at all and she Wants Things.'

It was, Philip thought, an ingenious defence and not without truth. In fact, he doubted he could improve on it.

Mrs Sheen's sharp, bird-like face appeared round the door. She was, he knew, about to announce her departure. Mrs Sheen always went at five on the dot, but she was always at her desk at nine on the dot and took lunch at one on the dot to two on the dot, so he could hardly complain.

'I'll be going now, Mr Protheroe.'

He had asked her to call him Philip several times but his secretary preferred formality. Calling her Shirley was therefore out of the question.

'See you tomorrow, Mrs Sheen. Have a good evening.'

'You too, Mr Protheroe.' The red head withdrew.

A good evening, Philip mused to himself as he tidied his desk. There was little chance of that. He hadn't had a good evening for a year now. He would never have a good evening again. The same applied to good days and good mornings and, in particular, to good weekends. Any time he wasn't at work could not, by definition, be good any more; it was the time he was by himself, in the abyss, dependent on his own resources, alone; forever alone.

He locked the office, descended the wide stairs and walked out into the street and the nearby station car park where he habitually left his BMW.

Crossing Mineford's medieval bridge, three arches over the rushing river, Philip drove up by the handsome villa now housing the Royal Bank of Scotland and took the hedge-bordered road into the hills.

Rather to his surprise, he reached the end of the single-track road leading towards Allsop without once having to stop and reverse to allow a tractor or large four-wheel drive to pass. The number of people who felt themselves able to drive without ever having mastered the art of reversing amazed Philip. In particular those old men who opened the driver's door for a better view as they weaved backwards over the highway.

He drove into Allsop and up the winding main street, towards the church with its foursquare clock tower topped with soaring spire. Allsop's setting, Philip had to admit, was lovely, nestling as it did in the cleavage between two large green hills, striped and squared with fields and fluffy with trees. Above it stretched the length of Weston Moor, an expanse of grey-green grass pitted with former lead-mine workings and alive with larks in the spring and summer.

This was not the village in which he had lived with Emily, however. That, Bradwell, was some ten miles away, equally distant from Mineford, and the cottage they had lived in together there was infinitely more tasteful: white-walled, calming, its furniture a palette of muted sages and pebbles. But Emily was too powerfully there, or, rather, the fact she was no longer there was there. For months afterwards, especially on the sheets which he could not bear to change, he thought he detected snatches of her fresh lemony scent – Eau d'Hadrien had been her favourite, discovered in the Place Victoire on an unforgettable trip to Paris and remained steadfastly loyal to during what remained of her life. He kept the gold-topped fluted glass bottle carefully in his sock drawer, hoping the dark would preserve what remained of the perfume she had loved.

In the end, the memories had proved too much. With a wrench to his heart, Philip had put the Bradwell cottage on the market and looked for another in any village near to

Mineford and his office. The one in Allsop had been the first to come up.

Yet even in the Allsop cottage, in a place she had never set foot in, Emily was in every corner. He could never enter without picturing her horror at the battered black plastic sofa, the swirly patterned carpet, the soggy jade shagpile in the bathroom and the blaring ceiling light fittings everywhere. She would, he knew, have hated them especially; Emily preferred muted lighting. Big lamps, arranged near bookcases and comfortable chairs and sofas, had been a feature of the Bradwell cottage.

There was no escape from memories in the area, Philip had realised. Perhaps there was no escape anywhere, and did he want to escape anyway? But just in case there was, and he did, he planned to sell the Mineford business too at some stage and move to another part of the country and set up there. Perhaps even abroad. But not yet. It was too early. He was too tired, but he was always tired these days. He woke up too early. But what, now, was there to stay in bed for?

Philip parked his car at the bottom of Church Lane, where his rented cottage was, and walked the fifty yards up it to his front door. His next-door neighbours were the new American couple above, who he had so far had little to do with. They seemed nice enough. The man was short and bullish and the woman a manicured and rather scrubbed-looking blonde very different from Emily's more breezy, natural style.

Below Philip, at the very bottom of the row, was Mrs Palfrey, an ancient lady who combined the appearance of frailty with the toughness of the proverbial old boot. Her face was creased like tissue paper and had a yellowish tinge and yet her hair was always neat, her teeth in and her lean, wiry form, without fail, smart in a dress or skirt over which, when at home, she always wore an apron. He had never once seen her in trousers.

She was possessed of a tireless energy; Philip could look out of his small kitchen window which overlooked her back yard and see in all weathers the neat, determined figure violently smashing a small axe into pieces of wood for the sitting-room fire. This roared away even in high summer, sending large flecks of black soot up the chimney and, if the wind was in the wrong direction, all over the washing of anyone who had pegged some out nearby. Devoted to her nutty slack, Mrs Palfrey did not believe in the type of fancy coal that burned cleanly and that Philip suspected was a legal requirement in the area.

Mrs Palfrey, Philip thought, had an indomitability, an indestructibility, even, that for all her destruction of the environment, one could not help but admire. Thus he did not mind the small extent to which this independent old lady depended on him, such as when he was called round to witness her scrabbling on the floor in front of her new television attempting to determine whither the Sky card went. Or the slightly more dramatic occasion on which she had banged on his door claiming that Mr Palfrey had died, when in fact, on hasty examination by Philip, he turned out to be profoundly asleep and breathing deep and silent, having ingested a more than usually enormous breakfast.

Mrs Palfrey's husband was a weary-looking man with untidy white hair, a large flabby body and eyes buried in deep, tired brown holes. His air of defeat, Philip suspected, was in part due to the continuing presence of his predecessor all around him.

The immediately previous Mr Palfrey had been called Albert, and beside the front door was a nameplate proclaiming 'Tarbel'; an anagram which, while possibly ingenious, had never struck Philip as particularly respectful of the feelings of Albert's successor. The present Mr Palfrey also had to endure the fixed stare of a large black and white photograph of Albert mounted on the wall of the room in which he slept. While Philip felt sorry for him, he was amused by Mr Palfrey's plight as heavily underscored second husband. He was, he thought, a sort of elderly northern male version of the second Mrs de Winter in *Rebecca*, which had been Emily's favourite book.

Mrs Palfrey's fire was at full blast now – in every sense – Philip saw, noticing the smuts flying from her battered stack as he walked slowly up the lane with his briefcase. Her curtains, as always at the first flush of evening, were drawn to stop anyone looking in and seeing the Palfreys, irradiated by the ever-roaring fire, staring at the television. They could be heard, however; the TV was invariably turned up to a deafening level, not that this disturbed Philip. The two-feet-thick walls of his cottage enabled him to go about his evening unaware of whatever light entertainment choice the Palfreys had settled on.

The lane, as it often was, was empty, but Philip was under no illusions that he was unobserved. He knew from experience that eyes were surveying him from behind every net curtain. *That's the solicitor*, he sensed them saying. *The one whose wife . . .*

'You're the solicitor, aren't you?' came a loud voice behind him.

Philip turned round to see, coming from the direction of the school at the bottom of the lane, that aggressive harridan who always seemed to have the same pair of purple drawstring trousers on. Evidently knowing he was a solicitor, she had tried to buttonhole him on several occasions about Mrs Palfrey's fuel choices. Her aim had seemed to be free legal advice, but Philip, who had no wish to be involved and was in any case fond of Mrs Palfrey, had advised her to write to the council with her concerns.

'I want to talk to you,' the aggressive woman in purple trousers announced rudely.

Philip could not return the sentiment. He did not want to talk to Morag Archbutt-Pesk. Not in the slightest.

'I've got a problem,' Morag announced, setting broad hands on her purple hips and glaring at him from fierce brown eyes.

Just the one? Philip mused ironically, and of course silently. He waited.

'Have you any idea what's going on up there?' Morag challenged now, stabbing her finger upwards to where Mrs Palfrey's smoke billowed blackly out into the blue heavens. 'She's changing the climate single-handedly.'

Philip sighed. No doubt Morag had a point, but there was something about the way she made it that instilled in him the urge to rush inside, turn all his taps on full blast and switch every light on before rushing out again to catch a long-haul flight somewhere. Instead, he raised an eyebrow and waited.

'It's an excrescence. A joke,' growled Morag.

Philip regarded her with dislike. Morag Archbutt-Pesk was an excrescence and a joke so far as he was concerned. The prime contender for the title of Allsop's busiest body, that was for sure. Mrs Palfrey's nutty slack was hardly responsible, admittedly, but if it annoyed Morag this much, it had something going for it at least.

Morag had moved a step or so closer. He felt speared in the gaze of her bulging brown eyes. She wore a faded pink vest top that exposed a great deal of fleshy, tattooed upper arm, and she had, he noticed, very thick and heavy eyebrows. A nose-stud nestled at the side of her nostril like a large gold pimple. As, apparently to underscore her agitation, she lifted both hands to rake busily through her clumpy purple-red hair, an unpleasant smell of garlic and sweat wafted from her. Philip felt a sudden twinge of sympathy for her daughter, who he had seen in the street and who looked quite normal and even pretty.

'I want you to take legal action against her,' Morag hissed into Philip's face. Some spittle settled on his glasses which disgusted him but which etiquette did not permit him to wipe off.

'Me? Against *Mrs Palfrey*? My *neighbour*?'

The eyebrows and the nose-stud came closer. 'Yes. Don't worry. You'll get paid. Legal Aid'll cover it.'

Philip cleared his throat, straightened up and tugged at his tie. 'Legal Aid isn't available for absolutely every case anyone decides to bring, you know,' he informed her, correcting what he found an especially irritating popular misconception. 'And I'm afraid it's not the sort of case I handle either,' he added, correcting another peculiar to Morag. 'I'm sorry, but I've just got home from work and so, if you'll just excuse me . . .'

Fumbling with his keys, he shot into his cottage, feeling that he had just crossed no-man's-land and was now safe in his trench. For the moment.

Chapter 18

She had lost Monty already, Mary realised sadly. He was not yet gone physically, admittedly; there remained a week or so before his training was due to start, but mentally he was already far away. 'I'll just have another look at the route,' he would say at breakfast, munching his toast over the map of the Arctic Ocean on the kitchen table. Mary worried that an inadvertent blob of jam might be mistaken for an island or other geological feature and Monty be sent off in the wrong direction completely.

Mary tried to rally herself by remembering the absences that Lady Amelia Longshott had had to endure, in this very house. But from what tradition handed down about her husband, surely Lady Amelia could not love him as Mary herself loved Monty. Doubtless the wife of the philandering Hengist de Vere Longshott had suffered here too, although not necessarily entirely because of the South Pole. Another pole, rather closer to Hengist, had probably caused her just as much if not more misery.

As Monty hunched over his maps, Mary wandered about the house, trying not to think about the separation to come.

Determinedly she shut out the picture of Monty by himself in an icy wilderness and tried to continue with the two main tasks that customarily took up all her time: writing letters asking for grants and dashing about the house placing buckets under drips and Polyfilla-ing any new cracks. She found herself returning repeatedly to the sitting room and looking up at Lady Amelia on the ceiling. The steady, encouraging gaze of her long-dead predecessor seemed to instil a certain strength in her. But not enough to get her through entirely.

'You all right?' Mrs Shuffle asked Mary. 'You worrying about this holiday of Mr Longshott's?'

'Expedition,' corrected Mary quickly.

Mrs Shuffle shrugged. Holidays, expeditions, they were all the same these days. People who had once gone to Cleethorpes for a fortnight now felt impelled to charge round the world white-water rafting and big-game hunting. It was madness if you asked her. What was so wrong with sitting on the sand for two weeks?

Mary sighed. She wasn't in the habit of opening her heart to her cleaner, but as her heart felt more than usually boilingly full at the moment it might be wise to relieve some of the pressure. 'I suppose I'll be a bit lonely,' she admitted. 'But it's nothing,' she added immediately in bright, nonchalant tones. 'Monty's going to be in constant touch. Communications are excellent these days. I can send him emails from the Mineford library, I've already looked into that. And of course I'll get a hobby or something, to occupy myself.'

'That's the stuff,' said Mrs Shuffle approvingly. 'Now, look here. I've brought you summat.' She rummaged in what Mary now noticed was a rather bulging plastic bag hooked over her arm. She also noticed that the plastic bag bore the logo of the local Sainsbury's, out of her own financial reach. Mrs Shuffle's car, a new-ish Yaris, was also better than their own ancient Volvo, lion-hearted though it was.

Mrs Shuffle rummaged and produced a large woolly jumper made of brilliantly coloured patchwork. 'Thought it might come in useful.'

'I'm sure it will,' Mary said brightly, imagining the cleaner intended to use it on the house in some capacity.

Mrs Shuffle glowed with gratification. 'I was going to take it down to the Red Cross in Mineford. But then I thought it'd be better here.'

Mary nodded, smiling but puzzled. Better for what, exactly?

'It'll keep you warm, that's for sure.'

'*Me!* Er, Mrs Shuffle . . .'

'You don't need to thank me. I don't wear jumpers so much now I've started with my hot flushes.'

'Oh, right.' Mary tried to look suitably appreciative of this glimpse into her cleaner's menstrual status.

'And I think the colours will suit you.'

Mary stared down at the blazing knitwear as the connection – and the humiliation – registered. Mrs Shuffle – her cleaner – was offering her, Mary Longshott, chatelaine of Weston Underwood, her own cast-off clothes. 'You're very kind,' Mary muttered, recognising that Mrs Shuffle was trying to be motherly but unsure whether the tears springing to her eyes came from gratitude or self-pity. Perhaps both.

'Let's have a nice cup of tea,' said Mrs Shuffle.

Mary cheered up. There was one and one advantage only of Monty's absence. Mrs Shuffle could now gossip at will.

Mary, eager for distraction was more keen than usual for

knowledge of events in Allsop, in particular news of the misfit child at the school. Mrs Shuffle, disappointingly, had nothing new to report on this front. There was, however, plenty of Morag news.

'She's got it in for poor old Sinjin Goodenough, you know, he's my neighbour. Nice chap. Chairman of the parish council. He's just got these allotments going and she's in there already, trying to dictate everything. There's about ten of 'em,' Mrs Shuffle added. 'Matter o' fact, I'm thinking of applying for one meself.'

The cleaner put down her tea and fixed Mary with hazel eyes bright in her reddish face. 'You know, it's just struck me, you should get an allotment as well. You were going to grow veg up 'ere once, weren't you?'

Mary nodded. She remembered telling the sorry tale of the poisoned land to Mrs Shuffle. 'Oh, I was. There's a whole ruined vegetable garden round the back. I had visions of growing everything from cabbages to cardoons.'

'Car-whats?' Mrs Shuffle's homely red face was creased with puzzlement.

'A sort of enormous celery. Very popular in Victorian gardens. You see, I had all sorts of ideas about growing historical vegetables in keeping with the house.' Mary shrugged. 'And then trying to cook them as well.' She blinked. It seemed extraordinary now she had had such energy and imagination.

Mrs Shuffle, capable hands on plump sides, was looking at her quizzically. 'Well, there you are then. Wouldn't you like an allotment?'

Mary shrugged. 'I suppose so. But you have to rent them and I, we, well . . .' She felt the colour rising. 'I just can't afford it.'

'They're free, though, these village ones,' the cleaner told her now.

'*Free?*'

'Yes. To anyone as wants one. They're being doled out at a meeting in the village 'all on Friday night. You should come,' Mrs Shuffle urged. 'Do you good to get out and meet people.'

Mary considered. Mrs Shuffle was quite right, of course. She did need to get out. She was starting to worry that, left entirely alone at Underpants, she would go mad. On the other hand, did she really want to attend the type of public meeting she had shunned for so long – alone? People, knowing the assumed splendour she came from, would stare at her old clothes, her air of rack and ruin. Although, actually, she need not go alone, Mary realised. Monty would still be around on Friday night. He could come with her, support her.

She grinned at her cleaner. 'You're right, Mrs Shuffle. I should get an allotment. Friday night did you say the meeting was?'

Chapter 19

'Sam! Will you please *stop* that?' Alerted by a sharp squeal, Catherine turned from the whiteboard to see the school naughty boy pulling hard on one of the immaculate blond pigtails of the school good girl, Olivia Cooke.

'He's hurting me, miss,' Olivia complained, her large blue eyes screwed up with pain.

Catherine rose to her feet hurriedly and swept across the classroom like an avenging Valkyrie. Which was, she supposed, appropriate given that this morning her Year Fours were doing Norse mythology.

Catherine was disappointed at Sam's inattentiveness. She had picked the Norse creation myth in the specific hope that its improbable luridity would interest the problem child of the class. What eight-year-old boy, after all, could fail to be amazed by the idea that the whole earth sprang from an enormous cow and a frost giant who grew trolls from his sweaty feet? (She had been hoping to make a few jokes about smelly trainers there.) And that the frost giant was killed and his body became the earth, his blood the sea, his bones the mountains and his brains the clouds . . .

oh well. The rest of the class had loved it.

'Leave Olivia alone,' Catherine commanded, looking Sam challengingly in the eyes. He stared insolently back at her for a few moments before dropping his gaze. The headteacher returned to the front of the classroom. She would have preferred to leave the children to read and absorb the information sheets she had prepared for a little while longer, but it was clear she would have to take control.

'Okay,' she said, smiling. 'Let's have a little test and see how much you've taken in.' She looked around the light-filled classroom at eight eager faces and one surly, uneager one.

'The Norsemen,' Catherine said encouragingly, 'believed that the earth was created by a frost giant and a big cow. What was the name of the giant?'

Three or four hands shot up. Predictably, Sam's was not among them. 'Ymir,' said Olivia Cooke breathlessly.

Catherine smiled at the little blonde girl, who looked like something out of a Norse legend herself. 'Very good, Olivia. Ymir is absolutely right. And what was the name of the big cow?'

Hands shot up again. To her amazement Catherine saw Sam's thin, rather red one among them. Her heart thumped with excitement at this evidence that her patience and encouragement had finally induced the shy and hostile boy to hazard his knowledge in public. She was starting to break through. 'Yes, Sam?' she asked delightedly. 'What was the name of the enormous cow?'

'Miss Brooke,' Sam said in tones of harsh triumph.

There was a ripple of shocked laughter followed by an embarrassed silence. Eight pairs of wide eyes and one narrow, sneering one focused on Catherine. She felt sick – not with fear; she had handled many a discipline issue, especially recently – but with disappointment. Why was Sam Binns so hostile? Could he not see that she was trying to help him?

Just at that moment, however, the classroom door opened and the vicar appeared wearing his usual half-smile. 'Ah, good morning, Miss Brooke. Good morning, children.'

'Good morning, Vicar,' the children mumbled.

'I hope you don't mind me just coming in,' the vicar said to Catherine in tones which clearly assumed she would not.

Catherine did mind, however. She took her teaching extremely seriously and did not appreciate being barged in on, especially at such a crucial juncture in the lesson. She wished the Reverend Tribble would not sweep into the school as if he owned the place, even if, it being a Church of England assisted primary and he vicar of the Church of England's nearest branch, she supposed he did to some extent.

The Reverend Tribble was middle-aged, thin and wiry, with dull black hair scraped over his scalp and sharp, rather close-set, somehow lightless dark eyes which moved constantly about. He was, as usual, dressed in black with a dog collar. Catherine had never known quite what to make of him although he was clearly determined to make a go of the post to which, like her, he had been appointed relatively recently.

She knew of various schemes that had been put into practice in order to increase the dwindling number of, as the Reverend rather baldly referred to it, bums on pews. Coffee and biscuits were served after family services. Youth groups were mooted and parishioners, or so Catherine had heard from Mr Goodenough, who also served as a churchwarden, continually urged to take part in residential study groups in

Skegness. One could, Catherine supposed, only applaud the Reverend's energy. Although the fact that he had spent much of the special school service on the first day of term sitting at the back of the church texting rather made one wonder. To whom had he been sending messages? The Almighty?

The vicar's watchful eyes had made several circuits of the classroom and had settled on the whiteboard. 'And what are we learning this morning, Miss Brooke?' he asked brightly, his eyes widening as he read the words 'sweaty feet' and 'trolls' in fat red marker pen in Catherine's big round hand.

'The Norse creation myth,' Catherine smiled. 'I thought, as part of our comparative religion studies, it might be interesting.'

The Reverend Tribble had folded his arms and put a thin finger to his colourless lips. Although he was nodding, a slight frown had gathered above his bony nose. 'Hmm, very creative, Miss Brooke,' he murmured. 'And very interesting that you don't think studies of comparative religion should embrace rather more relevant areas of alternative theology. Islam, for instance.'

Catherine flinched at the implicit criticism. She had quite enough of that – and the more explicit variety too – from Morag Archbutt-Pesk. Why couldn't people leave her alone to get on with her job? She didn't interfere with the vicar's, although she sensed her non-attendance at church was rather frowned on. It was not, however, an official part of her duties and Catherine, who got up at half past six five days a week, cherished her weekend lie-ins.

'Well of course we study Islam too,' she said hurriedly. 'We cover all major world belief systems. I just thought Norse myths would be interesting from a historical perspective, they're full of amazing stories to interest children this age . . .'

'So I see,' smiled the vicar thinly. 'I suppose that makes up for their declining relevance.'

'I'm not sure they're irrelevant,' Catherine defended. 'Take the names of the days of the week, for instance. All named after Norse gods, Wednesday, Wodin's Day, Thursday, Thor's Day . . .'

'Yes, thank you, Miss Brooke. I am aware of the etymology.' The vicar's quick, lightless eyes darted back to the whiteboard. They narrowed. 'What's this?' the Reverend Tribble said, peering at the writing. 'Worms?'

A small hand shot up from one of the tables. 'The god Odin turned worms into elves and goblins,' supplied Olivia Cooke, beaming at him with her gappy front teeth. Catherine smiled at her. Good old Olivia. She was so willing and bright, exactly the sort of child one needed at a school swaying on the edge of the dreaded Special Measures and struggling to get back into respectability. If only there were more like her; hopefully, if all went according to plan, there would be.

The vicar looked at Olivia. 'Did he indeed?' He smiled thinly. 'Well that is something I shall bear in mind when I start digging over my new allotment! Are you going to the meeting on Friday, Miss Brooke?'

Catherine looked bemused.

'It's in the village magazine,' the vicar supplied. 'The parish council are giving out allotments to interested parties. Do you never read the community newsletter, Miss Brooke?' he added, his head on one side, his flat black eyes critical.

Catherine stared back at him. It was on the tip of her tongue to bark that she never had time to read magazines and she was surprised that he did himself. She restrained herself, however.

*

The Reverend returned to the vicarage, slumped against the heavy wooden desk of his dark study and heaved a sigh. The inescapable feeling that, once again, he had been given the brush-off descended on him. He had high hopes of Catherine Brooke when first he had seen her. Young, pretty, energetic and obviously keen. But not on him, unfortunately. Yet he could not give up. He had to keep trying. Catherine Brooke was his only hope.

When, six months ago, the Bishop had summoned him and asked him if he was ready for a challenge, the Reverend had fallen over himself to assure His Grace in the affirmative. His expectations were high; the Bishop, or so the Reverend Tribble had always believed, saw him as one of the Church's young Turks – so to speak – a priest of promise on the fast track to the ecclesiastical big time.

Standing in the Bishop's stained-glass-and-oak-panelled office, he had anticipated promotion to canon at the very least. But the challenge was, instead, a posting to this backwater with its handful of old ladies, with the brief to increase the congregation.

And with what tools? An organist and choir so unencumbered by musical ability that the one couple he had married since arriving had actually paid them to stay away. Another wedding was planned in a few weeks' time where they had decided to do without hymns altogether. Nor did the Reverend Tribble blame them; whenever he heard the quavering, the wrong notes, the misjudged timing he would close his eyes, not in prayer, but in anguish, mourning the carved stalls of the Cathedral, the thundering organ, the gilt, the monuments and above all the prestige.

He had made it plain to the Bishop that rather more than Allsop had been expected, but the Bishop had merely smiled in his ethereal fashion and uttered that tired old cop-out about God moving in mysterious ways. The hope began to grow within the Reverend that, like a tyro politician hoping for a safe seat, he had been given a difficult one to fight first before receiving his just and splendid reward. But merely doing bird in Allsop would not be enough, the Bishop had hinted.

'Have you ever considered how much a companion might help you in your ministry?' the old man had murmured. 'Someone to lean on.' Well, the Bishop, who obviously needed to lean on most things, could speak for himself, the Reverend thought, affronted.

'You mean get married?' he had asked, horrified. Women and the Reverend had never really got on. He had managed a few relationships in his twenties, but these had fizzled out to a mere one or two in his thirties and none whatsoever since he had turned forty, which was two years ago. He had, on the whole, little respect for the breed; they were hysterical and unpredictable if young and fussy and querulous if old. Had it not been the act of a woman, after all, that had expelled mankind from Paradise?

'Matrimony,' said the bishop, his faded eyes glowing with benevolence, 'is a holy state, woman an earthly comfort.'

There was, the Reverend Tribble sensed, an altogether unnecessary emphasis on the word 'woman'. What was the Bishop trying to imply? That he was gay or something?

The Reverend Tribble glared at his ecclesiastical superior. Not for the first time he wondered whether he was wasted in the Church of England. The Catholics were, after all, crying out for priests with no interest in women, or anyone else either, for that matter. If he crossed the floor, as it were, went to the other side, he'd be in a strong position. But it would be a complicated business, and whichever way one looked at it, the Catholics weren't the powers in the land they once had been. He could go to Rome, of course, but his Italian was hopeless.

'Ministry is a lonely business.' The Bishop began the attack again with his gentle smile. Well it certainly was in Allsop, the Reverend thought resentfully. He'd been in an entirely empty church on at least two occasions. A wife, if nothing else, would provide company in the pews.

But where was he supposed to find one in Allsop? Who would want to come and live in, not to mention *clean*, this enormous echoing mausoleum of a vicarage? With its vast sitting room and dining room whose towering height immediately sucked up any heat, leaving him to sit or sleep in the chilly regions below.

There were six bedrooms, none of them comfortable, and an ancient bathroom with a haphazard water supply. The building's exterior was like the Rock of Ages itself: cliff-like sides of dark stone, abounding with the gables, trefoils and tracery characteristic of the Victorian Gothic, which was far from being his favourite architectural period. The fact he had to inhabit this enormous place, and not some rather more desirable piece of ecumenical real estate such as the sunny, rambling wisteria-clad Georgian rectories that routinely appeared in Jane Austen films was another source of discontent for the Reverend.

Noticing his hands had a bluish tinge, the vicar bent to light the fire in his study. This he accomplished with the usual difficulty and mess – thankfully his working clothes were all black anyway. No, he hadn't quite got Moses's touch with burning bushes. He vowed to add the observation to a future sermon. The one old lady who heard it might find it amusing.

Chapter 20

As usual, Robby Trendy Hair was busy, filled with the young, the moneyed and, most particularly, the blond. Robby Trendy's was in fact London's first blond salon, specialising entirely in blondness. Robby himself sported an arrestingly full platinum quiff, below which his eyes, the electric blue of a Riviera swimming pool, were startling in his spray-tanned face. The various stylists, or technicians, as the master called them, ran the full gamut of blondness, even the black ones. Noting one male Asian cutter's pound-coin-coloured mohican, Alexandra thought moodily again about John's absolute refusal to adopt such a hairstyle and thereby deny her acres of useful publicity. Robby, when she had told him about it, had regretted it too. 'Ooh, I'd love him in here, dear. Tell him to come any time. I'll welcome him with open legs . . . sorry, arms.'

The purple damask boudoir chairs of the Trendy VIP area seemed largely empty this morning. VIP, I don't think so, Alexandra snorted to herself, eyes following the generous rear of a former breakfast TV presenter as it crossed the marble swathes from mirror to basin. VPL though, definitely.

Perhaps it was time she moved on from Robby Trendy. There was a salon in Shoreditch she had heard about, which did caviar hair treatments and had an in-house cocktail mixologist.

Robby, in his tight black trousers and matching, straining shirt, was cooing over a client who held a shih-tzu on her lap. 'This is Elvis,' the woman announced, patting the dog with one skinny brown arm. As Robby fussed extravagantly over the animal, Alexandra stared. She knew for a fact that he hated dogs.

'Lovely pink,' Robby crooned. Alexandra felt a faint wave of relief. Her eyes through her sunglasses had not been deceiving her. The tiny dog's hair was indeed a light rose which exactly matched the woman's strappy, clinging and not necessarily flattering sundress.

The woman beamed. 'Everyone's dyeing their pets to match their clothes right now.'

Panic shot through Alexandra. Were they? Should she get a shih-tzu herself and dye it leopardskin?

But coloured dogs and her lack of one was not the only worrying business on Alexandra's mind. She had visited Allsop now and seen the house for sale. The visit had not been a success.

The place was so dark, she had thought, peering through the rain and her solidly black sunglasses at the cottages of Allsop as Maureen Hughes walked her through it on a drizzling wet afternoon earlier that week.

'Is that the place that's for sale?' Alexandra had asked, pointing at a large house of dark stone behind a big wall next to the church.

'No. That's the vicarage,' Maureen said, delighted to disappoint.

Alexandra snorted, frustrated. This place she was being taken to see had better be good, she fumed, shoving the hand that wasn't holding her candy-pink umbrella deep into her silver mackintosh pocket.

'Has this village got a gym?' she demanded of Maureen as they walked upwards from the church past a row of cramped cottages where a woman with dyed aubergine hair and purple drawstring trousers was hanging a windchime outside a violet-painted door. The woman, evidently overhearing Alexandra's question, looked at her with scornful and very protuberant brown eyes.

'Gym!' she repeated sneeringly. 'The whole of the countryside's a gym. It's one big outdoor exercise facility.'

Alexandra turned her rain-spattered sunglasses on the woman. 'Well it's not my idea of a gym,' she retorted. 'Where's the sauna, for a start? And the Jacuzzi? The beauty treatment rooms?'

'I don't know what you're talking about,' the woman in purple trousers said sourly, her bulging gaze taking in every detail of Alexandra's appearance.

Alexandra smirked. 'No,' she said, giving as good as she got on the stare front. 'I can see that you don't.'

The woman's eyes narrowed. She finished tying up the windchime and it swung agitatedly in the breeze. As Alexandra continued up the road, she could feel the bulge-eyed gaze boring into her back. 'Oh well,' she said loudly over her silver shoulder, 'I guess it's no disaster if there's no gym here. I was only wanting something to tide me over until I built my own.'

The purple door slammed.

Alexandra stared. 'Locals aren't very friendly, I must say,' she remarked loudly.

Maureen, clacking up the path ahead, turned. 'Oh, that's Morag Archbutt-Pesk, she's not local,' she said nonchalantly. 'I sold them that place a couple of years ago. They're from Surrey.'

The purple door flew open again and a furious aubergine head thrust itself out. 'How dare you!' it snarled. 'We're extremely involved in all local matters, play a central role in village life, and to imply we're outsiders of any sort is deeply insulting.'

As Maureen, her mottled face flushed with shock and her Rouge Mystere'd mouth opening and shutting like an amazed goldfish, groped for a reply, Alexandra, chewing nonchalantly on her pearlised gum, regarded Morag Archbutt-Pesk in surprise. 'Keep your hair on,' she remarked. 'Although,' she added consideringly, head on one side as she examined it through her sunglasses, 'on second thoughts that colour's not great. And the condition's pretty bad too. You could do worse than chop it all off and start again.'

The woman regarded them burningly before slamming the door even louder than before. The windchime swung wildly about.

'Is it really up here?' Alexandra peered doubtfully up the road in front, which seemed to be narrowing and disappearing under some overhanging trees. 'The place next to the wosname stone?'

'Betrothal Cottage?' Maureen pointed a stubby finger along the road in front of them. 'This way.'

The cottages became less close together and eventually straggled out altogether. There was, Alexandra now noticed, only one remaining building, a mouldy-looking shack covered in moss where it wasn't covered in damp grey pebbledash, cracked in places, and whose roof, which even from this distance was clearly full of holes, sagged ominously and was patched with rusty corrugated iron. It stood, or perhaps leant, on a scrap of rough land sprouting with weeds and pitted with partially upturned bricks, from its own walls by the look of it.

'Here it is,' Maureen announced with satisfaction. She was relieved and rather surprised to see that the nasty seventies porch had disappeared. Had the owner removed it for aesthetic reasons? Oh no, there it was, collapsed in a heap of shattered glass and rotting wood in front of the gaping black hole where the entrance door had once hung.

Alexandra, meanwhile, looked down at the small, grey, rectangular granite block soggy in the rain and surrounded by clumps of weeds. Somehow she had imagined something large, white, carved and marble. Sort of like the Albert Memorial. But . . . this – lump didn't look anything special. She felt disappointed. The top of it barely reached her knees. Fine if you were one dwarf wanting to marry another. On the other hand, weren't people much smaller in the olden days?

Would it, she wondered, tracing its rugged top with the tip of her finger, despite its unimpressive appearance, bring her what she most wanted? If the stone really did have magic powers, that would be very useful. Of course, everything would depend on John believing in its magic powers too, but he was no stranger to crediting fantasies – just look at the extravagant promises each new manager who bought him told him about being top of the Premiership, in Europe and the rest of it. John believed it all, which was why he was moving north now. So why shouldn't he believe in the betrothal stone? Footballers were notoriously superstitious creatures.

The likelihood of success seemed strong to Alexandra,

even if the method was less romantic than she would have liked. Her fantasy scenario had been John falling to one knee in a luxury hotel suite and producing a ring he had designed himself. But she was beginning to accept now that he fell to his knees only for sliding tackles. And a ring designed by John was unlikely to be the circlet of pink diamonds in white gold or white diamonds in pink gold she was currently favouring. Left to himself, he would come up with something in his football club colours, whatever they were.

She turned expectantly to Maureen Hughes. 'So where's this house you were telling me about?'

Maureen beamed. 'Betrothal Cottage is there.' She waved a hand at the ruined shack with the sagging and rusty roof.

Alexandra stared with disbelief at the battered building, taking in the cracks, the smashed windows and splintered frames, the peeling paint of the door, the weeds bursting out everywhere like mocking laughter. There was even grass growing out of the chimney. The only thing for a building like this was to put it out of its misery and knock it down.

Alexandra turned to look at Maureen. 'You mean that's the place for sale? You must be fucking joking.'

She groaned now as Robby minced over and flipped through the silver-foiled strands of hair on top of her head. 'You're not quite cooked yet, darling. Another ten to fifteen minutes to *complete* goddessdom, I'm afraid. Just you sit tight – not that you can do anything else in *those* trousers, darling. Armani, are they?' he put in quickly, before Alexandra could react. 'Mm. Thought so. Can see Giorgio coming a mile off. Although chance would be a fine thing, frankly. Ooh, just listen to me! Am I the worst or am I the worst?' He clapped his hands on her shoulders. 'So just you sit there and I'll get someone to bring you something to drink. Glass of champagne, sweetie?' he murmured lovingly into Alexandra's hair. 'Or a cup of coffee? I've got some lovely rich Italian at the moment, and no one should pass up the chance of getting a rich Italian inside them in my view. Ooh, just *listen* to me!' He slapped his tanned hand and cackled.

'Glass of champagne,' Alexandra said. It had taken four hours to put the hair extensions in and do the highlights and if anyone deserved a drink, it was her.

The champagne arrived. Alexandra took it and sipped it, watching the salon in the mirror. Actually, there was someone famous there, she realised now, albeit someone rather common. A well-known glamour model was having her silver highlighting foils removed by a plump, white-quiffed boy stuffed into the black string vest and tight black trousers that was the Robby Trendy uniform. The woman's famously enormous breasts strained through her tight white T-shirt while her thin, bare brown legs in her tiny denim mini were wide apart.

'She looks like she wants someone to take her right now,' Robby whispered, suddenly materialising at Alexandra's side. 'And you know,' he added, breathing hard, 'if I wasn't on the other bus I might oblige. *Great* tits.'

Alexandra looked critically at the celebrated breasts, wondering whether promoting her own from a C cup to a double D might help in her quest for fame. 'I sometimes wonder about having another boob job,' she confided to Robby.

Robby gestured towards the glamour model in a flutter of fingers. 'Wonder no more.'

'But do I really want to be famous just for having massive knockers?' Alexandra mused.

'Well, there are worse reasons,' Robby said crisply. 'Look at the Yorkshire Ripper, dear. No one remembers *him* for his figure.'

'Hmm.' Alexandra looked at herself in the mirror. 'But I don't want people to get the wrong idea about me.'

'Wrong idea, sweetie?' Robby, leaning over her chair from the back, cocked an eyebrow at himself in the mirror.

'Yes. People think that because I'm blonde, I must be thick.'

Behind her in the mirror, Robby looked outraged. 'That's disgusting. Blonde-ist.'

'Exactly.'

'The fact that you're thick,' he pronounced, 'has nothing to do with the fact you're blonde.'

Alexandra stared. '*What* did you say?'

He nudged her and cackled. 'Joke, dear. So, what were you saying? What do you want people to know you for?'

'My intelligence and creativity, of course.'

He gave her his twitchy smile and raised an eyebrow. 'Of course,' he said in a caring voice. 'Of *course*.'

'My agent's been getting some very exciting vibes,' Alexandra announced.

'*Has* he now. Lucky old devil!' Robby bunched his mouth suggestively. 'You must tell me where he goes. Joke, ha ha. Tell me, dearest. What's he been getting for you?'

'Oh, this and that,' Alexandra said quickly. She had no intention of telling Robby that none of the TV irons had yet emerged from the fire and the most definite offer to come the way of her agent was the request she be the face of British Sausage Week.

'Get stuffed,' had been Alexandra's angry response.

'Yes, how did you know, that's the campaign slogan,' Max had exclaimed in surprise. His client now tried to console herself by recalling the agent's promise that there were 'lots of exciting things in the pipeline. And, babe, I don't mean chipolatas.'

'Now,' Robby added, flipping through the silver foil index again, 'you're all done up here. Let's get these out and restore you to your full-blown – well, dry-blown, anyway – natural beauty.'

She watched him examine his handiwork, looking carefully at the point at which the differing hair shafts had melted together in the heat. 'Mm. I've done a great job if I say so myself. Although I've always said I'm a dab hand at welding,' he remarked in satisfaction. 'I've missed my vocation, really. Think of the time I'd have with all those lovely boys in the steelworks.'

Steelworks. Wasn't Sheffield something to do with that? Alexandra, her troubles momentarily dispelled by the contemplation of her coiffure, now felt her thoughts hurtling back down the long dark tunnel to the Midlands and the house she had not yet managed to buy.

'What's up, sweetie?' Robby asked. Time to ask a few questions, he realised, as Alexandra began to unburden herself. Being able to talk at great length about themselves was what his customers came for – apart from the peroxide.

'So the only place for sale is this shitty shack,' she finished dolefully.

'You're saying that's the only place for sale in the whole of the county?'

'Well, the only one in the village I want.'

'Can't you live in any other village? That one doesn't

sound very glam, darling. Any gastropubs? Any former rock star cheese-makers? Have you ever seen Kate Moss there?'

'Um, no,' Alexandra muttered. She hadn't mentioned the betrothal stone. Something had warned her that confiding this to Robby would be an even worse idea than British Sausage Week. Both might smack of desperation.

'But that's where I want to live,' she said. 'And as you know, Robby,' she added, turning the sunglasses determinedly on him, 'I always get what I want.'

Robby's eyes sparked. Time was nearly up. 'Absolutely. So, what's holding you back? Buy the shack, woman.'

She whirled round to look at him so fast that the recently applied extensions whirled like a cat-o'-nine-tails and slapped her in the face. 'Buy it!' exclaimed Alexandra. 'Ow. Ow. *Owww!*' she yelped, as the agitated hair continued to hit.

Robby had his hands on his narrow black-trousered hips and his chin cocked. 'Call yourself a footballer's wife!' he teased.

Alexandra ignored this. Instead she demanded, 'What do you mean, buy it?'

'Buy it and knock it down, of course. Then build your dream château. Isn't that what all the footballers do? They buy some swoonsome old Tudor pile, bulldoze it, mullions and chapel and all, and then fling up some tasteless excrescence with indoor and outdoor pools, underground garaging for twenty four-wheel drives, a home gym, a games room, a helipad, an indoor golf range and a multiplex-size home cinema . . .' He reined himself in, conscious he might be going too far. 'Erm, what I mean to say, of course, is that they build a stylish contemporary home with every modern convenience.'

Alexandra was not insulted. Quite apart from having the

hide of an elephant in that respect anyway, she had hardly
heard past the first couple of sentences. Now she felt as if a
very large, very bright bulb had just been switched on in her
head. She stared at Robby, the light from this new knowledge
streaming out of her eyes, through her sunglasses. 'God!
You're right, aren't you!'

Of course that was what footballers did. And it was what
she could do too. Why hadn't she thought of it before?
'Robby,' she gasped, 'you're a genius.'

Chapter 21

Maureen Hughes was about to close for lunch and head off to the fish and chip shop when the call came through.

'I'll have it,' barked the voice at the other end. 'I want it *now*.'

The very words Maureen longed to hear. Apart from one thing.

They did not come from Philip Protheroe, or any other male currently in Maureen's sights. The person on the other end of the phone was a woman; a woman with a Cockney accent. The woman in the tarty silver coat and ridiculous snakeskin boots, Maureen recognised, remembering indignantly how rude she had been when shown the cottage in Allsop. What did *she* want? Well, whatever it was, she was going to get a piece of Maureen's mind first.

Alexandra, however, was uninterested in Maureen's mind. 'That dump by the betrothal stone,' she cut in commandingly as Maureen launched her speech. 'I want to buy it. I'll give you the asking price.'

'*Buy* it?' Maureen repeated, pulled up short. She blinked, a rare sense of wonder cutting through her outrage. Maureen was not a religious woman but she had imagined the mountains would fall and the seas rise before the cottage in Allsop was sold. Let alone for the asking price.

'I'll come up this afternoon and sign the papers. You've got everything up there, right?'

Maureen thought for a second. There was no chain. The old man who owned the cottage had been in a home for years. His daughter, who lived in Mineford, would be over like a shot at the news of a sale. None of them had ever expected it to happen. 'I suppose the procedure could be speeded up,' Maureen said grudgingly, reluctant, as ever, to oblige. 'On the other hand,' she added with satisfaction, suddenly remembering, 'I'm closing early tonight. It's Friday and I've got my salsa class.'

'Sod your salsa class,' Alexandra snapped. 'Do you want to sell this dump or don't you?'

'I don't see what the rush is,' Maureen objected, her mind still on her salsa class. The instructor, who claimed to have once competed on *Come Dancing*, had a Latino whiff about him, particularly after an hour or so's energetic twisting his hips.

'I've got plans for this place,' Alexandra retorted. 'I'm going to knock it down and build my idea of a house.'

'Ah,' said Maureen quickly. She might have known there was a catch. 'Well, you won't be able to,' she said swiftly, unable to resist being the bearer of bad tidings even when there was a sale at stake.

'Why not?' Alexandra was indignant. People never told her she wasn't able to do anything.

'Nothing new's been built in Allsop for, ooh . . .' Maureen sucked air through her teeth. 'About two hundred years at least.'

'About time it was then,' Alexandra retorted.

'You need to get planning permission,' Maureen warned.

At the London end of the line, Alexandra yawned. 'So, fine. I'll get planning permission. Where do I buy it from?'

'It's not a designer dress, you know,' Maureen said spitefully. 'You can't get it just like that. You have to apply for it.'

'Yeah, well you can't always get designer stuff all that easily,' Alexandra said disdainfully. 'You ever heard of waiting lists?'

Maureen hadn't. 'It's not a matter of just waiting,' she said crisply. 'There's a whole procedure you have to go through. Put signs up at the property, submit it to planning meetings, deal with objections.'

'Oh, there won't be any objections,' Alexandra said airily.

Maureen sniffed disbelievingly. 'People can be very difficult, you know. Especially in old villages. There are bound to be objections.'

'There won't be,' Alexandra said confidently. 'No one could possibly have anything against the house I want to build.'

'Come on!' Morag roared up the stairs to where Gid cowered in their small bedroom which also doubled as his office.

The blood beat in her ears. The light of battle glinted in her protuberant eyes. Tonight was the night. The moment of truth. When she entered the village hall, it would be as head of a conquering army.

The familiar tumbling sound of Gid descending the cottage's tiny narrow staircase echoed through the sitting room. He appeared, breathless and flustered, in the doorway and looked enquiringly at his partner. 'What's up? Oh God. It's not the allotment meeting tonight, is it?'

He was dreading it. Morag was clearly squaring up for a fight and he knew from personal experience just how devastating fighting Morag could be. This allotments business had really gripped her. She was determined to get what she called her 'vision' accepted by the allotments' ruling committee, which she also intended to be part of. She had spent hours on the phone persuading various cronies to get involved. Mouth set in a grim line, she had worked through the hemp-covered address book given free by the local health food shop to particularly valued customers.

'Of course it's the allotment meeting,' snapped Morag, the testosterone pumping through her despite the calming dung tea she had drunk. 'It's *now*. We've got to go!'

Gid tried not to be offended. He was used to being put down by Morag and he knew from an earlier glance at the menstrual calendar Blu-Tacked to the door of their ethically small fridge that her Woman Time was approaching. She was never in the best of humours then. He'd give her a special flaxseed head massage later to combat the stress. 'Who's looking after Merlin while we're out at the meeting by the way?' he asked.

'Oh.' Morag sniffed dismissively. 'Sarah Gilman. I called her and asked if Merlin could go and play with the Gilman girls.'

Gid looked faintly surprised. 'And was that cool? I mean, we don't really know them. Merlin's never been to play with them before. Did Sarah Gilman mind?'

Morag was outraged. 'Mind? Of course she didn't mind. I pointed out that by keeping an eye on Merlin she's helping us save the planet. Who could argue with that?'

'Who indeed,' agreed Gid. Who could argue with Morag, full stop?

Chapter 22

It was Friday night. Philip locked up the office himself. Mrs Sheen, as always, had gone at five on the dot and the last clients had taken longer than anticipated.

Mineford was clearly in weekend-starts-here mood. Much of it was already dressed for a night out. Boys with gelled hair and girls with a great deal of flesh showing were clattering through the streets. Philip blinked at the billowing white midriffs and large cleavages so extravagantly on display. It was sunny, admittedly, but hardly tropical.

Philip headed for the car park, stepping off the narrow pavement to allow more scantily clad would-be revellers to barge past. Shutting himself inside the neat and familiar cab of his black BMW he pushed the button that activated Radio Four and drove off without listening to it. He drove out of the town and up into the hills, again without really seeing how the rich evening sun slanted over the fields, picking out the ancient plough and furrow pattern. The thorn boughs heavy with tiny white scented flowers and the foam of cow parsley fringing the hedges similarly escaped him. Emily had loved cow parsley. She had loved thorn too, the whole green and white of the early summer. But then, she had loved high summer, as well as the drifting mists of autumn and the sharp, bright frosts of winter. She had loved all seasons and all growing things.

She had especially loved the garden of their cottage. When he thought of Emily now the first image was not as he had last seen her, at the accident, but as he had loved to see her, her slight, supple frame bent over the flower beds, her red hair blowing about her freckled face, secateurs in hand, clipping at the exuberant lavender bush, bemoaning the lack of parsley – which had never seemed to grow for some reason – or exclaiming over the smell of the honeysuckle. There was an orange blossom bush which strayed over the fence from the neighbour's garden that was her particular delight. Its heavy white scented flowers tumbled, Emily said, like a peal of bells. At the time she had died, she had been thinking about growing vegetables.

Philip suddenly twisted his steering wheel violently. He was driving along the narrow grey lanes between the dry-stone walls and had almost hit a duck belonging to some farm. Collecting himself once again, he thought about the weekend. As usual, he had no plans; as usual, he was taking work home to avoid the necessity of making any.

Reaching Allsop he parked, as usual, along the churchyard wall and walked past Mrs Palfrey's cottage where, also as usual, the television was booming. Letting himself in to his own, he switched the lights on – it was always dark in the cottage, however light outside – and walked to the kitchen to make a cup of tea. His eye fell on a white oblong on the mat.

The village newsletter, Philip saw, picking it up. Not an organ he took any interest in as a rule, having long ago dismissed it as a mere list of things for sale combined with notices of Mothers' Union meetings and crummy bands about to perform at the two local pubs. He had, however, occasionally thought there might be money in the festering inter-neighbour disputes occasionally rearing their heads in Letters to the Editor, some of which were definitely actionable. But Philip had no need to look elsewhere for money. The fact his business was flourishing made the idea of moving yet more complicated.

Now, as he sipped his mug of tea, he sat down at the kitchen table and began to leaf through the newsletter. A notice on the back page caught his eye. WOULD YOU LIKE AN ALLOTMENT? it asked politely.

Philip read on and discovered that some common land was to be divided into allotments for the use of the villagers. The number available were limited and to be allocated on a first-come-first-served basis. A meeting inviting people to express their interest was to be held in the village hall. Looking at the date, and the time, Philip realised with a mild shock that it was starting in fifteen minutes exactly.

He considered. Did he want an allotment? Emily, he knew, would have been first in the queue for one. She had said several times that the vegetable beds she was planning for the garden were not as big as she would have liked them. But what about him? He, personally, had hardly ever wielded a spade in earnest; content to leave it to his green-fingered wife, he had done the odd spate of weeding and left it at that. But now something prompted him to consider the allotment idea. Besides in some way connecting him with one of his wife's greatest loves, it would also give him something to do and provide him with fresh air and exercise. It might even provide him with some vegetables, who knew.

This uncharacteristically positive sequence of thoughts

did not last. The familiar voice of caution now took up arms, pointing out the risks. Was it worth it? He might not be staying in the village for much longer, after all; his and Emily's cottage in Bradwell could sell at any time.

But his last conversation with the estate agents – not Maureen Hughes exactly, but not markedly better – had not been overly promising in this respect. A couple who had seemed very interested on site had reported back to the agent that seventeenth-century beams and character fireplaces were all very well but the property's lack of fitted kitchen and garaging was 'a deal-breaker'.

'Melamine surfaces and off-road sheltered parking for two cars weren't really priorities back then,' Philip had remarked to Lesley, the agent's representative.

'I know, but it's what people want,' she had replied.

But it wasn't, Philip thought as he put the phone down, what he and Emily had wanted. An allotment, on the other hand, Emily would have adored. Should he get one? If she were able to see him, from wherever she was, she would be richly amused by the sight of him gardening. Trying to grow things. Was it madness, he wondered, to think about making a ghost laugh?

Was it madness, full stop? He could, if he wanted, always cultivate the garden at the back of this house – although, frankly, it was half the size of Emily's one at the Bradwell cottage and full of rubbish to boot.

He looked at the notice about the allotments again. Then he reached for the coat he had only just taken off, opened the door he had just closed and, after a cursory glance up and down for Morag Archbutt-Pesk, set off down the lane he had just walked up. He was heading for the village hall.

Chapter 23

That evening, even though it was Friday, Catherine did not go directly home. She remained in her office, pretending to work, but in reality still dwelling on Sam Binns's latest rabbit punch to her professional ego. He had not repeated the huge cow remark, admittedly, but possibly only because he had not been present to do so. He had played truant several times this week, not in the least attempting to disguise the fact by strutting, whistling, past the school building. When told, Mrs Newton had been devastated to hear about it. 'Oh Miss Brooke! I really don't know what we're going to do with him. We're trying our best, honestly, but . . .'

'We're all trying our best,' Catherine had reassured her, whilst feeling just as miserable as Mrs Newton.

She had not told Miss Hanscombe and Mrs Watkins about the huge cow incident, nor about him pulling Olivia Cooke's hair. Supportive and generally excellent though her colleagues were on almost all occasions, they would, in both these cases, only roll their eyes and ask her what else she expected of Sam Binns. It was a question to which she had no answer.

Among the rubbish on her desk, Catherine now saw, was the village magazine. She flicked through it in desultory fashion, reached the page asking if anyone wanted an allotment and, uninterested, stared into space through the window. Unexpectedly, however, her mind returned to the question on the page. Might she want an allotment? It would give her exercise and something to think about that wasn't school. She didn't know the first thing about growing vegetables, though. So what was the point?

At a loud knock on the door Catherine jumped. It opened and in came the fleshy, sullen face of Lorraine the cleaner. As the school invariably looked dirtier after Lorraine had been, Catherine intended, at some stage, to dispense with the services of this unsatisfactory school servant but had so far not summoned up the energy. There were other challenges to deal with first.

'Parent to see you,' Lorraine said sulkily. Even as the muscles of Catherine's stomach clenched in concern, expecting Morag Archbutt-Pesk for the millionth time, the grey door of the office now opened wider to admit a blonde woman in jeans and a gilet. Catherine recognised her as one of Allsop Primary's small number of yummy mummies, sleek, well off and invariably looking down on the world through the smoked-glass windows of gleaming four-wheel drives.

'Hello,' said the blonde, rather forcefully. 'I'm Olivia's mother.'

'Yes, of course,' Catherine smiled. Julia Cooke, as always, was caked in make-up, rioting with highlights and impeccably turned out in yummy mummy uniform: new, clinging jeans, sheepskin-trimmed suede gilet and high-heeled leopardskin-print ankle boots. While the style struck

Catherine as excessive for Allsop, it was hard not to feel dowdy in comparison.

In the interests of time and simplicity she usually wore dark blue trousers and a white shirt as her school 'uniform', despite suspecting it made her look like a naval rating or a policewoman. She rarely wore make-up; her skin had always been good and, however mixed her feelings about rural life, there was no doubting country air had restored to her face a bloom and youthfulness it had lacked in the city. But a touch of mascara would help, Catherine thought, even if not necessarily as much as Julia, who looked as if a centipede was trapped in each of her eyelids.

Her auburn hair, she knew, looked neat and clean in its customary short bob, but also more businesslike and less glamorous than Julia's lavishly highlighted tresses.

'Do sit down,' Catherine invited.

'I'd rather not. This isn't a social call.' Julia Cooke twisted her full, brown-lipsticked lips. 'Sam Binns has been pulling Olivia's hair.'

Catherine nodded resignedly. She had, she supposed, expected something of the sort. She smiled comfortingly at Julia. 'There was a minor incident. It wasn't anything serious.'

The blonde frowned. 'I'm very surprised to hear you say that, Miss Brooke. Olivia was quite traumatised by the whole thing.'

It was Catherine's turn to be surprised. Olivia had not seemed traumatised. Rather, once it had stopped, she had seemed to shrug it off. That she was not a child for histrionics was, in Catherine's view, one of her many strengths. She did not say this, however. The sixth sense she had developed from many years encountering parents now warned her that this was not the whole story and that something else was coming.

Julia Cooke spoke again. 'That boy is a menace,' she said agitatedly. 'All the parents say so. We don't want him in the school, in the village, even. Aren't you going to get rid of him?'

Catherine disguised her shock of anger as best she could. She shook her head. 'There are no plans to, Mrs Cooke, no.'

Julia Cooke gave an angry snort through nostrils which might have been surgically enhanced. 'Oh, I suppose I may as well come straight out with it,' she exclaimed. 'I'm withdrawing Olivia from Allsop Primary.'

Catherine gasped. She felt as if someone had socked her in the guts. For Olivia's mother to be angry was, she supposed, not unreasonable. But this . . . this was unreasonable. Olivia Cooke was to be taken away from her. Olivia Cooke, the willing bright spark, star of Year Four and general all-round Good Thing. Just for a minor hair-pulling incident. It made no sense.

'We – her father and I – feel that St Aidan's will be much better for her,' Julia now stated.

So this was what it was all about. Catherine's heart sank. St Aidan's was a successful nearby private prep school whose clientele were the wealthy from many miles around.

'Are you sure about this?' Catherine looked Olivia's mother right in the eye. 'Does Olivia want to go? She seems very happy here, the hair-pulling incident notwithstanding.'

The blonde's eyes flashed. Catherine suddenly suspected that what Olivia wanted probably had very little to do with it. Had her mother just used Sam Binns as an excuse? The hair-pulling as an opportunity? 'St Aidan's is very high up the league tables,' Julia said defensively. 'Whereas Allsop Primary is almost in Special Measures.'

Whump! But Catherine disguised the fact the blow had

hit home. 'It does do well in the league tables. But, Mrs Cooke, there is more to education than league tables. And, as you know, Allsop Primary is under a new management team now and we are working very hard on improving our performance.'

There was a silence after this. 'You're right,' Julia Cooke said unexpectedly. 'There is more to education than league tables.'

Catherine nodded, surprised and gratified.

'There are social considerations as well. We want Olivia to go to school with people who have bigger ambitions than driving tractors like their fathers.' Julia's very violet eyes – which may have had coloured contact lenses – glittered. 'Practically all the pupils here are farmers' children. What sort of aspirations do they have?'

'All kinds,' Catherine said indignantly. 'Some want to be astronauts, some ballet dancers, some Formula One drivers . . .'

'Oh come on, Miss Brooke.' The blonde tittered gratingly. 'That's not very realistic, is it?'

'I'm not sure how realistic any of us are about our careers when we're nine,' Catherine hit back. Although, actually, Sarah in Year Five was unswerving in her determination to be a doctor, and she herself had wanted to be a teacher for as long as she could remember.

Julia Cooke was shaking her head and smiling. 'Why are you bothering, Miss Brooke?'

'Bothering?'

'With this school, I mean.'

It was a good question, Catherine knew, and one which she was increasingly asking herself. Particularly after situations like this one. She had only been at Allsop a few months. She could get an easier job elsewhere; return to her old school, even. The headmistress had not found a satisfactory permanent replacement and would welcome her back with open arms.

'From what Olivia tells me, you're a really good teacher. Why not go somewhere better? St Aidan's, for instance?'

The rush of anger Catherine now felt fused with a new determination and surge of protectiveness towards her primary. She wouldn't give up on it. She couldn't. She took a deep breath. 'I believe in state education, Mrs Cooke. It's essential to me, this idea that everyone, however poor, has access to an education that will help them live up to their potential and ambitions.'

'Or live down to their lack of potential and lack of ambition,' sniffed Olivia's mother derisively.

Catherine eyed her. She wondered what ambitions Julia Cooke had ever harboured apart from marrying someone comfortably off. Martin Cooke was an aggregates millionaire and looked as if he could break his own stone with his face.

'You should be aware,' Catherine now warned her, 'that taking a girl as able as Olivia away from Allsop Primary will have an effect on the community. The community in which *you* live.' So far as the Cookes, in their large restored house at the very edge of the village, could be said to do so.

'In what way?' demanded the blonde.

'It will damage the school. Our pupil roll is falling. We need girls like her.'

Julia Cooke tossed her head. 'Why should my daughter prop everyone else up? She's going to St Aidan's and that's the end of it. I just thought I should let you know personally.'

'Thank you, Mrs Cooke. That was really very considerate of you.'

It occurred to her that in tugging Olivia's little plaits, Sam had been committing bodily harm on quite the wrong blonde in the Cooke family.

After Olivia's mother had left, Catherine paced her tiny office, willing her heartbeat rate to slow down. She was going to make herself ill with stress at this rate. Learning not to take things personally was almost the first rule of primary school teaching. On the other hand, it was difficult not to take Julia Cooke's behaviour personally, still less Sam Binns's. But what could she do about it? How could she change things? Her hopes had been so high. But now it all seemed such a waste of time. And she was so tired, for all she had achieved nothing.

Catherine slumped in her worn office chair and, as the lump rose in her throat and the tears pricked her eyes, lowered her head miserably on to her desk. Thus it was, in an attitude of despair, that she found herself staring, eyeballs rolling over the paper a mere few millimetres away, once again at the notice asking villagers who might be interested in having an allotment to attend a meeting at the village hall. With a start, Catherine realised the meeting was – well, *now*. About to start. She sat up slowly. Starting to bloom in her head was the idea that a vegetable plot might give her some solace. Somewhere else in the village to go that was not the school. Somewhere else to deploy her energies. Somewhere to stop her going completely mad. Not a rest, but a change.

Chapter 24

Alexandra shifted her tight-white-trousered bottom on the leopardskin-effect driving seat as her pink, pearlised four-wheel drive with the blacked-out windows shot up the motorway. It was Friday night and busy, but she was determined to reach Mineford before Maureen Hughes disappeared to her salsa class. And after that, after everything was signed and sealed and Betrothal Cottage was hers, Alexandra had decided to go and view her property, do a bit of planning, decide exactly where the helipad and the horizon pool should go. And the bars. There would be an old-fashioned London-style boozer with cowskin snooker table and tequila counter for John, and a nightclub-style champagne bar for herself with gold walls and pink velvet heart-shaped cushions.

She had outlined her plans to John, who had been as relaxed as she expected about the idea of building a new house. No footballer liked a second-hand home, Alexandra knew, and all John's team-mates had bulldozed old places to make way for their varying architectural visions. She had not mentioned the betrothal stone, however.

'Yeah, go ahead, babe,' John had told her, packing to go and play an international friendly in some country Alexandra was not entirely sure she had heard of. 'Just make sure we can live in at least some of it when the new season starts, that's all,' he had added, rummaging in the bathroom cupboard for his toothbrush.

Alexandra had hoped for some input from her personal stylist for the momentous occasion of her trip to Mineford, but Petra was busy styling some boy band from Dagenham who were appearing on Jonathan Ross. Alexandra had managed to dress herself, and looked a damn sight better than usual, she considered. There was no doubt that the combination of tight white jeans, knee-length silver boots, and white and gold Hermès shirt topped off with her usual sunglasses and mass of white hair about her shoulders struck the ideal rural note. The snaffles and saddles on the shirt especially.

A lack of personal stylist was not the only disaster to hamper her progress, however. Alexandra's usual chauffeur, the one she used for events in London, had mysteriously become unavailable; there had, admittedly, been a slight incident in his limo earlier in the week involving too many cocktails on an empty stomach following the launch of a new skincare line. The skincare line had somehow leaked into the incident as well. But that, as Alexandra had told the car company, was just showbiz, although telling them this did not seem to have helped matters.

Finally Alexandra reached the motorway junction and veered off it at speed. More by luck than management she managed to whizz off the roundabout on to the correct road for Mineford.

Her mobile phone burst into life. Alexandra, reaching

over with one hand to the passenger seat, searched for it in her large, slouchy designer bag. Given its size, depth and the complexity of its construction this was not a simple matter. Alexandra was red-faced and panting by the time she dragged it out, and one of her nails was broken.

'Are you sitting down?' her agent asked.

Alexandra, holding the phone to one ear while she steered at speed with the other hand, confirmed that she was.

'Well, it's your big break, girl,' Max said. 'Your big TV moment.'

'What?' Alexandra swerved with violence towards the wall bordering the road. As she slammed both her feet on the clutch and the brake the car skidded, the engine cut out and the mobile shot through the air to the back seat.

Alexandra restarted the engine, moved the car to a convenient space before a farm gate and, after an undignified rummage in the back-seat footwell, raised the phone to her ear once again. What was Max about to announce? *Celebrity Big Brother*? *I'm A Celebrity, Get Me Out Of Here*? *Celebrity Love Island*? All had been pitched for. Alexandra waited, heart banging like a gate in a gale.

'You're going to prison, babe,' Max announced with evident satisfaction.

Alexandra squealed. 'But I haven't done anything!' she hissed into the phone.

'Not real prison.' Max emitted the laugh he had prepared for this highly predictable moment. 'It's a celeb reality show. In a specially designed TV prison. Sort of like the *Big Brother* house but with bars. The idea is that you do the prison day – you know, up at six for breakfast.'

'Six!' It wasn't an hour Alexandra really believed existed. 'And then what do I do?'

'Oh, well, you're sort of in this cell. You can watch telly for an hour a day . . .'

'An *hour*? That's *all*?'

'And read the rest of the time.'

'*Read!*' screamed Alexandra in absolute horror.

Max paused. His many years of showbiz experience now alerted him to the fact he was not handling this well. He needed to start again, from another angle.

'You won't be on your own, babe,' he assured her, all concern. 'You'll be with someone else. Another celebrity.'

At the words 'another celebrity', Alexandra's agitated heart immediately calmed down.

'Matter of fact,' Max continued, 'I've got some names of who else is on the producer's wish list right here.' There was a rustle as he fished out a piece of paper from the inside of one of the hand-made pastel suits he generally wore. The sugared almond colours, he believed, made the best contrast with his tan.

His client waited with bated breath to hear who the other stars of the show might be. Someone classy and glamorous, preferably. Angelina Jolie. Nicole Kidman. Kate Winslet.

'I've never heard of any of them,' she snapped when Max reached the end of the wish list.

'Oh well. *Crossroads* probably was a bit before your time. And *Robin's Nest*. But believe me, Peter Purves used to be huge.'

'Sure,' Alexandra growled disbelievingly.

'Come on, Alex,' Max urged. 'The cell sounds lovely and cosy. You have a mirror – polished metal rather than glass, in case you try to top yourself, ha ha. And there's a basin and loo in there as well. All mod cons.'

'Loo! You mean the viewers would see me . . . you know . . .'

'Well, there are ways round that,' Max said briskly. 'You could cover yourself with a towel or something. But it's a great opportunity for you, sweetheart. Sort of like *Big Brother*, except that the viewers vote for the person they like to get out, rather than stay in.'

Alexandra was not entirely sure she followed. Nonetheless, she now cut to the chase, to the one question that really mattered. 'What are the clothes like?'

'Well, prison gear really. It being a prison reality show and all that. You've got to look authentic.'

'What . . . you mean striped pyjamas and leg irons?' Alexandra exclaimed.

'It's moved on a bit now, babe. More jumpsuits these days.'

'Jumpsuits! How eighties is that?' shrieked Alexandra in horror.

'Well the eighties is kind of trendy, isn't it?' Max shot back. 'You won't be short of anything. They give you a standard-issue kit with a toothbrush, razor, comb, that sort of thing.'

Alexandra pictured the serried chrome ranks of hair straighteners, tongs and hairdryers filling one entire wall of her penthouse dressing room. Manage with just one comb? It was impossible.

Had she known it, she had Max's sympathy on this point more than on any of the others. He too had serried ranks of blow-drying equipment. But he was going to allow nothing to discourage her. 'You get a sachet of hair colouring if your roots start to show,' he assured her. 'And two pairs of regulation socks and knickers.'

'I've never heard of Regulation,' Alexandra grumbled. 'Is it a new label?'

Max, lounging in his squashy leather revolving chair in his light-filled Soho office whose walls were covered in signed photographs of former clients, snorted impatiently. He was handing it to her on a plate, could the stupid woman not see that? Admittedly there was a degree of personal humiliation involved, but there always was these days, you didn't get anything for nothing now.

Time was, you had to have a talent, actually be good at something to get on the telly, but these days the only attribute sought was the hide of a rhinoceros. And there was money in this, money he wanted, and he was going to persuade Alexandra to do it if it was the last thing he ever did. He took a deep breath and emitted a stream of blandishments. He promised her the earth, the moon and the stars and a good deal of the galaxy beyond as well.

'Yes, but . . .' Alexandra muttered. Half her brain felt dizzy with excitement – on telly at last! The other half was less certain. A shared cell with a loo that millions could watch you use. It wasn't partnering Bruce Forsyth exactly, was it?

'Well, no,' said Max. 'But would you want to share a cell with him anyway? I'm sure I wouldn't. And think of all those other people whose careers have skyrocketed since they did bird,' he purred. 'Paris Hilton. Martha Stewart. Jeffrey Archer. The Krays.' He had gone into full-on persuasive mode, Alexandra recognised. She could almost smell his aftershave down the telephone wire. Being the focus of so much attention was deeply flattering and really rather addictive.

'What's the show called?' she asked.

'*The Clink*,' Max said delightedly, as if there could be no finer name in the world. 'Think of it as the clink of money,' he added quickly, before Alexandra could extort the confession that the name referred to a notorious Southwark jail.

'*The Clink*,' Alexandra mused. Then her face convulsed in what she one day hoped would be described as her famous smile. 'Great,' she enthused. 'I'll do it.'

As she rattled over the country roads, music thumping, she sang loudly along with Madonna, one of the many entertainers still being auditioned for the wedding slot. She had not yet definitely decided on Elton and there was still everything to play for. The evening outside the car's black windows was soft and green and beautiful, but Alexandra, in her sunglasses, could hardly see it through two layers of tinted glass.

Her career, she reflected with satisfaction, was on track. Now all she had to do was get to Maureen Hughes before she shut up shop and went to salsa. Alexandra's foot in its high-heeled silver boot pressed hard on the accelerator. Things flashed at her as she went along, there were funny markings in the road, but no doubt this was some strange rustic custom.

Chapter 25

Tamara Ogden, twenty-eight, short, plump, dark haired, tight clothed and news reporter for the *Mineford Mercury*, drove her battered Peugeot 106 through the main street of Mineford.

It was Friday night and she had drawn the office short straw, which was to attend and provide an account of some meeting about allotments being held in Allsop village hall.

Which was, Tamara thought glumly, just great. In an area which as a whole generated few news sensations, Allsop generated fewer than most. There had been a wedding there about a year ago, and even though it had celebrated the union of no one more glamorous than a local butcher and his home help wife, Tamara had given the story everything she had and had been severely pulled up by Derek Savage afterwards for 'bloody Mills and Boon-itis'. The editor was always telling her off for writing short stories instead of newspaper reports.

Tamara's face sizzled with embarrassment at the memory. So what if she went slightly over the top in her dispatches? She was only trying to make things interesting. It didn't justify Derek reading the whole thing out in a silly voice to the entire office and then taking his red pen and slashing through most of her finely wrought description. But she'd get even. She'd show him. Somehow.

He'd be sneering on the other side of his sharp and whiskery face when she was editing a national newspaper or glossy magazine in London. How exactly she would get there Tamara had not yet worked out. But she would. She had to. She had no intention of spending the rest of her days in an office above a greasy-spoon café where the scent of rancid bacon permeated everything from the milk in the fridge to the clothes and hair of the staff. The hair of the staff who still had hair, that was.

But until she could escape, Tamara knew, she would be covering stories about sewage pipe replacement schemes and supermarket expansion plans. Oh, and meetings about allotments. Hardly showbiz, was it? A fat lot of glitz and glamour there was going to be in that.

Tamara jerked herself out of her reflections just in time to avoid running over an old man on the pedestrian crossing opposite Nice Price, a budget supermarket Tamara had never seen anything particularly nice about. There was a rumour that they scribbled out the sell-by dates, but she had never set foot in there to verify this. Mineford, Tamara thought, was depressing enough without going into Nice Price.

She drove off past Club Foot, a few shopfronts along from Nice Price. Mineford's leading – and only – nightspot was famous for its blue cocktails which, it was said, got their colour and flavour from screenwash. And having tasted them, Tamara could believe it. She passed the enormous, sprawling Edwardian pub, the Crown. Basically Tudorbethan, it sprouted Gothic protuberances – pointy towers, bulging balconies, extraneous clocks – like warts and was topped off with a roof of unpleasant bright orange tiles. The Crown was home to Mineford's not inconsiderable band of professional all-day lager drinkers. It was also home to Tamara, whose three-room flat was on its top floor.

Tamara drove over the bridge, took the turning by the bank and zoomed up the single-track road whose thickly bushed borders made it more difficult than ever to see oncoming traffic. She had more than one near miss with various four-wheel drives but succeeded in making everyone else reverse for her and was feeling triumphant as, finally, she drove into Allsop.

The village looked really quite pretty tonight, Tamara thought as she sped through it at a velocity far in excess of the thirty miles an hour counselled on signs at Allsop's entrance along with pleas to 'Drive Carefully Through Our Village'. It was a lovely evening; the sky was sunny and blue and the strong light brightened the colour of the cottages from the soggy charcoal they were when it rained to a really quite pretty and definitely dry pale grey. The flowers in the gardens seemed to have an almost nuclear glow, but then, Tamara saw, looking closer, the red-hot-poker season was in full fig.

Allsop was well known for its flowers, Tamara knew. Not for nothing had the village won the East Midlands Water Community in Bloom 2007 (Runner-Up) Award, all the breathless excitement of which Tamara had brought to her readers. And there was more to it than just gardens; out on Weston Moor, the narrow lanes were snowy with hawthorn blossom in May, and other wild varieties flourished on the spoil heaps of the former lead mines. Tamara knew all this through, reluctantly, having to write the seasonal 'Notes' columns in the *Mercury*, which had made her more familiar than she had ever wanted to be with the habits of cowslips and violets. But what really interested Tamara about Weston Moor was the only splash of local glamour, the big house up there, Weston Underwood.

It was not open to the public, however, and the lord and lady of the manor, Mr and Mrs Monty Longshott, kept themselves very much to themselves. Unfortunately, try as she might over the years to invent a pretext, the *Mercury* never had any reason to visit. Mary Longshott had, disappointingly, failed to be interested in Tamara's invitations to write a 'Lady Mary Entertains' column for the *Mercury*, although she had always refused very nicely. On bog-standard Basildon Bond though, Tamara had been disappointed to see, rather than the expected hand-laid paper embossed with a gold crest.

Allsop was definitely the most attractive spot on her beat, even so. Sometimes Tamara wondered about moving here, even if, given what Savage paid her, there was little chance of her being able to buy anywhere soon that wasn't the cramped, damp flat above the Crown. She had her sights set far beyond a village. Villages were boring. It would be a penthouse in Docklands once she was editor of a newspaper or a big fat successful glossy.

The lane heading north up the hill from the church contained possibly the only building Tamara was likely ever to be able to afford in Allsop: the rusting hovel opposite the betrothal stone. It had been for sale for years but, hardly surprisingly, no one had bought it. The amount of work that would be needed to make the place even vaguely habitable did not bear thinking about. As for the betrothal stone itself – an undistinguished lump shrouded in weeds – Tamara did not believe a word of the apparently ancient tradition that ladies in Allsop could propose to men here and it was unlucky for the men to turn them down. It was a load of guff, Tamara decided robustly. A curio, not that anyone in the village seemed to be curious about it any more, if they ever had been in the first place. What woman in her right mind would propose to a man from Allsop anyway?

Personally, Tamara often wondered why she bothered putting on make-up every morning, having a fake tan whenever she could afford it, getting her thin, dark hair to grow as long as it was capable of and possibly beyond – all for the benefit of the bullet-headed, fat-bellied youths of Allsop and Mineford, none of whom had ambitions beyond being farmers or builders like their fathers, and marrying puddingy women like their mothers.

Of course, the local youth weren't all thickset and stupid; some were quite clever and good looking, like Jamie Clark, for example, who had been an intern at the *Mercury* during his gap year before university. But therein lay the problem. All the good ones left and were never seen again. A pearl before swine was what she was, both professionally and personally, Tamara thought with a dramatic sigh as she drew up with a screech of brakes outside the village hall.

Allsop village hall, where the allotments meeting was to take place, was next to the village playground. It was a long corrugated-iron hut painted a strong green and with wooden windows picked out in white. Tamara, now looking for a parking space, was surprised to see the road outside was a sea of vehicles. Some very strange looking: a Dormobile painted purple with yellow stars, for instance.

Amazing, Tamara thought. Two people and a dog was all she had imagined would turn up for something as dull as a meeting about allotments. She was slightly late, as she habitually was for everything, but had not expected it to matter. Now she began to wonder if, incredibly, she might actually be missing something. As there was clearly no time to lose, she double-parked and rushed into the hall, clasping her notebook to her breast.

Inside was hot and full of people sitting on rows of grey plastic chairs. There was nowhere to stand but the back. Most of Allsop must be here, an amazed Tamara registered. The back rows, much as expected, contained several old men in knitted waistcoats, booted feet apart, gnarled hands on brown-trousered knees, white shirts with collars unbuttoned round red and wrinkled throats. Competitive carrot-growers and celery champions to a man, Tamara knew. She had covered enough Allsop Annual Horticultural Shows.

At the front, behind a wooden table, facing the expectant rows, sat an old chap with a pink face and impressive white moustaches. The chairman of the parish council. Beside him, in a pale blue Paisley-patterned blouse with a bow at the neck, was his mousy-looking wife.

But the front row was completely different. Rather festival, Tamara thought. Quite Glastonbury. They were presumably the ones who had come in the Dormobile.

At the end of the front row was a thin-faced, big-nosed man whose lank, long brown hair was crowned with a navy blue velvet stovepipe hat. This was the subject of a certain amount of audience interest. It had yellow stars sewn on it, along with bells which jangled whenever he jerked his head, which was often. Next to him was a woman with big teeth and a bright pink vest top. Tamara's gaze moved on to Pink Top's neighbour: a plump-faced man with very short hair, pointy ears, an earnest gaze and a waistcoat with mirrors all over it. He sat with a defeated air beside the woman next to him, who was standing up and looking beadily round at everyone. Morag Archbutt-Pesk, Tamara recognised. The row made more sense now. The mirrored man was her partner and the others presumably her friends.

Morag seemed, as always, to bristle with aggression, which was odd when you thought about it. Most alternative lifestylers generally affected an exaggerated level of calm to distinguish themselves from the stressed-out capitalists they were the alternative to. Tamara ran her eyes over Morag's badly hennaed shaggy bob and what even from this distance looked like a moustache. Her purple trousers were topped off with a pink and green tie-dye T-shirt. She could use a bra, Tamara thought. But then, she had probably burnt it decades ago. As Morag's burning brown orbs swung in her direction, Tamara dropped her eyes. She did not want to be buttonholed by Morag Archbutt-Pesk. There were at least ten Letters to the Editor weekly from Morag, objecting in vituperative terms to various harmless-sounding requests for planning permission. Not all of them made their way into the *Mercury*. Very few of them did, in fact.

Tamara concentrated her gaze now on Catherine Brooke. The headmistress sat behind Morag Archbutt-Pesk and seemed, Tamara thought, rather tired. The reporter felt a stab of guilty pleasure. The headmistress had, when Tamara had interviewed her for the *Mercury* to mark her arrival at the school, been so full of plans and enthusiasm she had made Tamara feel rather jealous and useless. But Catherine's formerly satin-smooth, poker-straight bob, which had projected such a sense of purpose, now looked less perfect, and her grey eyes, while still steady, looked more harassed.

Then again, perhaps she had good reason. Catherine Brooke, after all, had the Reverend Alan Tribble sitting next to her. Tamara recalled without pleasure the interview she had done with the vicar marking his appointment to the diocese, during which he had shown a disturbingly keen interest in her unmarried status. She was of course desperate, but not *that* desperate; the vicar was far too ancient for her, in the unlikely event she would have been interested in a vicar at all, let alone one with a puddingy face, hair in a greasy black scrapeover and eyes too close together.

Tamara wondered what he wanted an allotment for. Or why the headmistress did, come to that. Or anyone, frankly. Anything more boring than gardening Tamara could not imagine. Apart from working on the *Mineford Mercury*, of course.

She noticed a man with dark hair and a lean, pale, sensitive face beneath his glasses. The solicitor, Tamara recognised, from the office across the road from the *Mercury*; the one whose wife had died in the crash. She hadn't realised he lived in Allsop; he'd lived somewhere else at the time. Interesting; she wouldn't have had him down as the allotment type. He always seemed to be working; he was there in his office whenever she arrived at hers, and there without fail when she left.

Tamara tried to catch his eye, but he seemed to be studiously avoiding it, as he always did. She'd smiled and waved cheerfully enough to him the first few times after the death of his wife, but he had never responded. Even if he'd thought her report a bit dramatic, as Savage had, you'd have thought he would be over it by now. It was well over a year ago, after all.

Tamara looked at the solicitor consideringly. For Mineford, Philip Protheroe was hot stuff, despite being so buttoned up in his three-piece dark suit. She liked his floppy black hair though, and those glasses were rimless so you could hardly see them. His business always seemed busy; he must be well off too. Her gaze lingered on his unexpectedly full and girlish lips. What would it be like to kiss him?

Her attention was now caught by a tall woman coming in and looking shyly around. She was, Tamara saw, extremely pretty in that unpolished, natural, haphazard way that only true beauties could get away with. Tamara, who never stirred without the most careful make-up herself, looked jealously at the woman's full, rosy mouth, wide-apart eyes and lovely cheekbones, framed by enviably thick brown hair. And that she was as nice as she was pretty was obvious too; there was something appealingly gentle about the way she was politely smiling and apologising as she squeezed her tall frame past the row of grumpy old men, every one of whom now looked charmed.

She wore strange clothes though, Tamara thought, especially that turquoise jumper with huge yellow polka dots. The woman was taking it off now, no doubt because of the heat in the room, to reveal straight shoulders and firm little breasts under a white T-shirt. Tamara narrowed her eyes at the newcomer, unable to imagine who it might be.

A man had followed the pretty, dark-haired woman in and was squeezing after her along the rows. He was, Tamara saw, even taller, and even more gorgeous. Were these the New Yorkers she had heard about? Maureen Hughes had told Marcus the ad salesman that a wealthy American couple from London had bought a place in Allsop not long ago.

What was certain was that he was the best-looking man she had ever seen in Allsop. Tamara gazed hungrily at the exquisite lines of the long, thin face, the blond hair, eyes that even from this distance appeared large and glassily blue, the aristocratic length of his limbs as he sat down, his knees touching the back of the chair in front. Her own admiration, Tamara could see, was shared by the woman, who was turning confidingly to her handsome companion, clasping his hand, smiling a soft, private smile that even jaundiced Tamara could see was love.

She tried to take solace in the fact that the man was oddly dressed too: battered tweed jacket and navy moleskin trousers with tears in the knees. But the dilapidation of his clothes only seemed to make him look more handsome than ever. She was, a swooning Tamara recognised, hopelessly in the grip of Mills and Boon-itis. But she did not care.

Who were this couple? She was not the only person who had noticed the pair. Tamara strained her ear to catch the whispers now circulating and gathered, with growing excitement, that this was the couple from Weston Underwood. The Longshotts, who no one ever saw because they came so rarely into the village.

Tamara's interest in the couple skyrocketed. There was some ancient photograph of the Longshotts in the paper's archives, admittedly, but it had been taken ages ago in what looked like a snowstorm and hardly did them justice. Hardly hinted that Monty, in particular, lounging in his plastic chair, was an aristocratic sex god. Well, Tamara thought, licking her lips and trying in vain to catch his eye, he could have *droit de seigneur* over her any time. She'd be over like a shot after the meeting to ask him for an interview.

Chapter 26

Morag, at the front of the meeting, shifted her purple-cotton-clad bottom on the grey plastic seat of her village hall chair and stared challengingly round. She was aware that some of the more conservative villagers were looking askance at her row of friends. But creative, alternative people, people with the right ideas about the stewardship of the land, did not, Morag thought angrily, tend to wear green corduroy trousers, navy blue jumpers and graph-paper shirts.

To her alarm, more people were entering the allotment meeting all the time. Even those grasping bastards from the stately home, ruthless exploiters and shameless benefi-ciaries of a discredited and anachronistic feudal system, had come. Morag wanted to spit, and only with great difficulty stopped herself doing so. With a space that size, they were hardly in need of a vegetable patch. Was there no end to their greed?

The other burning question was how the hell had all these people found out about it? Having decided on a strategy to dominate the gathering – and subsequently the allotments – with people of the same outlook as herself, Morag had been hell-bent on preventing any other potentially interested parties knowing that the meeting was taking place at all. Gid had, accordingly, been sent out in the dead of night to remove all posters advertising it from the telegraph poles to which Mr Goodenough had fixed them.

The doors of the hall were closed now and Morag looked twitchily, assessingly, round. There were, she had discovered, some ten allotments available and there must be at least forty people present in the hall.

Competition would obviously be stiff. Yet Morag knew that the first rule of leadership was to disguise panic. She must appear calm and in control if she were to successfully rally her troops for battle.

She glanced down her row of supporters, baring her not-terribly-white teeth encouragingly at Dweeb, who described himself as a chainsaw artist, cutting trees into animal shapes for a living and residing in a ramshackle cottage called Bugger's Muddle along the road between Mineford and Allsop. She nodded next at Dweeb's girlfriend Vicky, a professional children's face-painter. They had been among the first Morag had inspired with her call to arms. 'Come up and get an allotment,' she had suggested. 'Fierce,' Dweeb had replied, which Morag had taken as an affirmative. She knew from bumping into them both in the health food shop that she, Dweeb and Vicky shared some of the same dreams – certainly a preference for the same high-bran-content breakfast cereal. Besides, Bugger's Muddle was right by the road and didn't have a garden. Morag had no idea if either Dweeb or Vicky knew the first thing about horticulture, but this was hardly the point. The point was to make sure the allotments went in the right direction, philosophically speaking.

Dweeb nodded back, the bells on his hat jingling as he did so. Vicky, beside him, grinned, exposing a wealth of tongue studdage. Morag's satisfied glance moved on to Tecwen and Gudrun.

Tecwen gestured upwards with both thumbs at Morag. He did something mysterious with computers which possibly involved the sale of soft drugs, and shared his Allsop cottage with Gudrun, a professional T-shirt printer with a pronounced nose and almost as pronounced a fondness for pink. They had been as enthusiastic as Dweeb and Vicky about the allotments and, Morag supposed, showed some evidence of horticultural leanings in the fact that the yellow window boxes leaning against their rose-pink window frames were 'planted' with a considerable number of large, brightly painted wooden flowers on sticks that were the work of Gudrun, as was the rainbow-striped front door. Inside, everything was very brightly coloured, which could have been the reason Tecwen sported sunglasses all the time. He wore them now: purple metallic wraparounds which gleamed rather devilishly in the village hall striplights' powerful beam. Beside him Gudrun grinned excitedly, her large nose shining in the light.

A couple of rows behind Gudrun was that solicitor whose wife had died, Morag recognised. She stared at Philip with open curiosity and not a little hostility. Funny how he still stayed in the village. Surely anyone normal would have been off to pastures new, not hanging around taking allotments other people wanted and occupying cottages with three bedrooms when people like herself, Gid and Merlin were squashed into ones with just two. What did he want an allotment for anyway?

Philip, aware of the stare of Morag Archbutt-Pesk, as well as that of the girl he disliked from the local newspaper, did not meet either. He sat up in his chair, hands folded in his lap, head slightly bent. He felt rather like he used to in school assembly almost a quarter of a century ago. The village hall, which he had never entered before, had a similar feel – striplights bouncing off a thickly varnished wooden floor and tables with thin metal legs and sharp edges.

He rather regretted coming now. He had never seen so many villagers in one place before; had never known so many people lived in Allsop in fact. The village had always seemed more or less deserted, although he could, he supposed, have guessed at the true number of inhabitants simply by totting up the number of dwellings, all of which were clearly occupied. But never had he imagined any of them to be occupied by some of the people here tonight, the woman with tongue studs further down and the velvet top hat at the end especially.

He concentrated on the row in front of him and found himself gazing at the back of a female head. She had reddish-brown hair cut in a neat, shiny bob. Philip stared at the hair, which was not as brown as it first seemed. It had gold threads, black threads and even red threads. He wondered who it belonged to. Below it, a neatly ironed white cotton shirt covered a pair of impressively straight shoulders.

As the head turned slightly to the side and looked down to its lap, Philip caught a glimpse of lips and eyelashes and realised he knew this woman. He had seen her around the village school; she was, he was sure, one of the teachers. She lived, he knew, in the cottage opposite the school, round the corner from Church Lane. Sometimes, when leaving his own cottage, he had seen her crossing the road to work at the impressively early time of half past seven. Perhaps she was the headmistress.

Morag Archbutt-Pesk had also spotted Catherine. Looking, Morag thought, as if the world was on her shoulders, and yet what did she have to worry about? Huge salary from the Department of Education just to teach a handful of kids in a village school. And not all that well, either, in Morag's opinion. Catherine's inclusion of Christianity in the world religion lessons was a mistake; openly pandering to a repressive patriarchy. And her agreeing to have that disruptive misfit Sam Binns in the school, well that was ridiculous and had to be stopped. Worst of all, she had not, despite Morag's stupendous, generous and imaginative offer, involved Gid in Black History Month.

Catherine, aware of Morag's stare but determined not to look at her, fumbled for a tissue in her handbag and pushed it to her nose. It always streamed at the wrong time, usually through stress. The sight of Morag Archbutt-Pesk always stressed Catherine, for all her efforts to maintain a steely personal self-control in her presence. Had she known, Catherine thought, that Morag was involved with the allotments she probably would not have come, but two seconds' consideration would have told her that of course Morag would be involved. She was involved with everything.

Chapter 27

Benny had been uncertain from the first about Beth's idea that they come up this weekend in the red Mercedes convertible rather than the four-wheel drive. 'But it will make us more popular,' Beth insisted.

'How do you work that out?'

'Well Morag Whateverhernameis was incandescent about the Discovery. She can hardly be more angry about the Merc.'

Benny was by no means certain about this, but as it was a hot evening it made sense in more straightforward ways to take the top down and cruise up the motorway. Now they were here, however, his former doubts about how a forty-thousand-pound luxury roadster might favourably influence hearts and minds had returned.

As he looked for a parking space outside the village hall, Benny was aware of a slouching, skinny boy who wore trainers, baggy jeans and a dark hooded top despite the hot evening. As a result, it was hard to make out his features properly.

Benny got an impression of skin stretched tightly over a fragile, bony face, long, pale, slitted eyes, ears that stuck out, and shorn light-brown hair. The boy had narrow shoulders, a crouching, concave, defensive posture, and was looking at them in a manner suggesting that his heart and mind, at least, were unconquered.

'That your car?' he growled at Beth and Benny.

'Sure it is,' trilled Beth, adjusting the Dior sunglasses she felt lent an air of Grace Kelly and peering at the boy in amusement.

The boy sniggered in a way evidently meant to imply that, in the universe he inhabited, owners were not necessarily occupiers. Benny was surprised. Awareness of carjacking at the tender age of – what was this boy? Seven? Eight? – seemed to be pushing it, even nowadays. What was this – the Bronx? The boy then compounded this impression by asking if he could drive it.

'Of course you can't drive it,' expostulated Beth. 'You're seven years old.'

'Eight,' shot back the boy. 'And I can easily drive a car like that,' he added with a contemptuous drawl from the side of his mouth.

'Come on, Beth!' Benny interrupted. 'We're late for this meeting as it is.' He forbore to add that this was less because of the traffic than because Beth had wasted half an hour before they set off trying to decide on exactly the right footwear for a village hall meeting about allotments. He had, at least, persuaded her away from the new rose-printed wellies she had been considering, in favour of some white plimsolls that no one could possibly object to.

Beth grinned. 'Hey. Relax. Chill. It's fashionable to be late in England.'

*

St John Goodenough had risen to his feet. His mood was one of triumphant astonishment. Even his fear of Morag Archbutt-Pesk faded away amid his genuine surprise and delight that so many people were enthusiastic about what had originally been his idea and would not exist without him. He felt quite giddy at the sight of the massed ranks before him. While admittedly not comparable to a packed Trafalgar Square, forty-plus bodies in the village hall was an unprecedented show of interest in a project. The Queen's Golden Jubilee Commemorative Village Mug Committee, for example, had managed only eight, and he could never get anyone to help organise the carnival.

It was the most wholehearted personal vote of confidence St John Goodenough had ever received and it had a powerful effect. His head spun with questions about whether or not he should be aiming for higher and greater rungs on the ladder of local politics; the county council, perhaps. Westminster even. His mind rioted with the possibilities while, beside him, Veronica smiled calmly.

St John drew a deep breath and prepared to orate. 'Ladies and gentlemen, good evening. We are gathered here, of course, because of a most welcome addition to Allsop's amenities . . .'

But then St John's expression of happy anticipation faded. Something was happening that was as unpleasant as it was unexpected. Morag Archbutt-Pesk was standing up.

'We may as well cut to the chase,' she announced loudly, turning from side to side to address the audience. Like any good commander she had decided to seize the initiative and triumph through surprise. 'There are only ten allotments and about four times that number of people here who presumably want them. So what I propose is—'

St John, by now, had recovered sufficiently to be outraged at this interruption to his savouring of his moment of glory. 'Now just a minute,' he said sternly to Morag. 'It is I who am chairing this meeting and I . . .'

Another interruption diverted the attention of both of them to the swing doors at the village hall entrance.

Tamara, slouching at the back, straightened immediately. The Americans, definitely, this time. You could just tell; they had that clean, rather proper air about them. The woman was a pretty blonde, slim and pale in a rose-print dress. On the end of her smooth, pale legs gleamed a pair of dazzlingly white new plimsolls. The man was thirtyish, short, tanned and shaped rather like a bull on its hind legs – thick neck, broad chest, short, powerful thighs and calves and a big head of dark hair. A well-dressed bull, however, with a fresh pink check shirt tucked into his jeans. He wore expensive-looking shiny black loafers with no socks; a metropolitan touch Tamara particularly appreciated.

Beside his wife, Benny tried to look less flustered than he felt. Their chaotic arrival was not, he suspected, a good start to their charm offensive on the village. Everyone was staring at them, and not all the stares were friendly ones. That woman standing up, for instance, looked furious. His heart plummeted when, registering the colour of the trousers, he realised who the woman was.

Morag *was* furious. She could hardly believe what she was seeing. The *cheek* of it. Not only had the grasping oppressors from the big house come, but now also making their way to a seat were the Ferraros. The capitalist imperialists with the pink dustbin had had the temerity to show their faces. Who the hell did they think they were? They weren't locals. They weren't even *British* . . . Morag's eyes bulged and her chest thumped alarmingly.

Beth smiled brightly at her. 'Don't stop what you were saying on our account,' she urged politely. Morag ground her teeth so hard she almost felt splinters of enamel in her mouth.

'I wasn't,' she snarled, turning back to St John Goodenough. The only positive outcome of the oppressors' interruption was that it had surprised him and she could therefore seize back the initiative.

'As there are now even *more* people requiring the very small number of allotments available,' Morag announced, with a spiteful glance at Benny and Beth, 'my proposal is that everyone who wants one should be required to make a short speech outlining exactly what their plans for their plot are and why they deserve to be awarded one. A manifesto, in other words.'

It was, she felt, an irresistible scheme and one which would almost certainly see her triumph. No one else, after all, approached the project with the altruistic depth of purpose that she did; no one else had such imaginative, earth-sensitive plans and could show such commitment to the eco-future. No one else had prepared a speech, either.

Apart from Dweeb, Vicky, Gudrun and Tecwen that was, not forgetting Gid. Together they were the moral majority and their arguments would carry the day – and the allotments.

St John Goodenough raised a plump red hand. 'I'm afraid that's quite out of the question,' he said, more firmly than he felt. 'There are for a start about forty people in this hall and it would take all night to hear everyone's speeches. This is not a sixth-form debating society, it's a meeting about growing vegetables.'

Morag turned on the president-elect with blazing eyes. 'Don't try and bully me with your privileged public-school education,' she snapped back at St John. 'Sixth-form debating society *indeed.*'

As St John reddened with fury, a mild, calm voice from the back row spoke up. 'There's nothing particularly public school about debating societies,' it remarked. 'I went to a comprehensive and we had one there.'

Everyone looked round in surprise apart from Morag, who glared murderously about for whoever had dared to argue with her. It was, she saw, the widowed solicitor who had spoken. Philip, having said his piece, was disconcerted to find his heart thumping powerfully. But what that woman had said had been both incorrect and bigoted and on both counts he had felt obliged to speak.

'Actually,' added someone else, 'I'm planning to introduce debates in school to get the Year Sixes used to the idea of reasoned argument.' Catherine reddened violently as she closed her sentence. She had felt compelled to support what the person behind had rightly said. She did not look round, but had spotted on arrival that he was the tall, dark-haired man who lived at one of the cottages on the row just up from the church, round the corner from herself, in fact. She had an idea he was a solicitor. He appeared to live on his own, just like she did, although he seemed to keep himself to himself. Until now, that was.

Beth, who with Benny had taken places at the end of the second row, was following proceedings in amazement. She had not expected such drama. 'I thought village meetings would be boring,' she hissed in a stage whisper to Benny, whose toes in their Gucci loafers clenched in shame.

Tamara licked her lips. A fight! A dispute! She began to scribble excitedly.

St John was swift to capitalise on Morag's confusion and seize back command. Yet he realised his moment of glory was past. The self-congratulatory speeches window was now firmly shut. She had succeeded in moving the evening to what was indeed the crux of it, the allotting of the allotments. 'So the idea of debates must be shelved,' he concluded. 'And as chairman of the meeting my proposal is that we adopt the only fair procedure in such circumstances, which is to draw lots.'

'Lots!' Morag was outraged. 'A method relying on mere chance when what I proposed was a system based on logic and merit.'

'Not necessarily,' Philip found himself pointing out. 'It is, after all, the culmination of a sequence of mere chances that you're standing in this hall.'

'Ha ha,' applauded the American blonde. 'Very well put,' she added delightedly as Benny nudged her furiously.

St John, in the meantime, was busying himself. Some pieces of lined A4 paper had been produced from somewhere and were being torn efficiently into strips by Veronica, who had a flair for handicrafts and was especially good at embroidery.

These were then handed round by her husband with the instructions that the recipients write their names on and fold them in half. There was a mass scrabbling in bags and pockets for pens.

'And now,' St John announced, making the most of what little opportunity there remained to direct things, 'we need something to put everyone's names in and draw them out of.' Looking round, his earnest, squinting gaze mellowed into delight as it fell upon the tall blue velvet creation on top of

Dweeb. 'Borrow your titfer, sir?' St John requested gaily, whisking the hat from Dweeb's head before the chainsaw artist, whose responses were slow at the best of times, could object. Dweeb's close associates looked with interest on the balding pate thus exposed.

St John then went around encouraging everyone to thrust their names quickly inside. Philip, who was extremely fastidious, withdrew his hand as speedily as possible, disliking the rather greasy feel of the velvet and the powerful patchouli scent the hat emitted.

St John now looked excitedly about the hall. 'I need a lovely assistant to help me,' he beamed, his good humour quite restored now he was back in the driving seat. His benevolent round eyes settled on Beth, watching proceedings with a fascinated expression.

'You, madam,' purred St John, swooping to her side. 'Perhaps you could oblige me by pulling out the names of the lucky ten to get an allotment?'

'Sure,' exclaimed Beth, jumping to her feet. 'I must say,' she added in her rather tortured English accent, 'that it rather reminds me of that dinner party game where everyone puts in the name of a famous person and—'

'Just get on with it, Beth,' muttered Benny.

'Excuse me.' Morag, from the front row, was holding up a hand. Her face was almost as purple as her trousers. Her eyes bulged with the strain of forcing an even vaguely convincing smile across her face.

'What's the matter?' asked St John irritably. He was approaching Beth and wanted to concentrate his efforts on this attractive, smiling young woman, who clearly knew the meaning of femininity, rather than a purple-trousered harridan with strange red patches in her hair.

'The matter is,' Morag announced in a tight voice, 'that it is surely unfair to allow someone who, ahem, *does not live in the village full-time and is in fact foreign* . . .' she paused here for effect, 'to assume such a position of power over a matter such as this which affects a great many *permanent, native* residents.'

St John frowned. He paused. While he didn't like what the woman had said, he had no idea how to reply to it. Fortunately that pale young man in the back row came to the rescue.

'I was not aware,' Philip said, conscience having provoked him once again to challenge what he saw as an unjust remark, 'that the allotments were to be awarded to full-time residents only. Or that there was a qualifying clause about nationality.' He looked questioningly at St John.

'Nor are they,' St John blustered in reply. 'The idea was that they are open to anyone who has an interest. The idea was originally that they were available on a first-come-first-served basis. Of course, rather more have come than can be served, hence the draw. Now, if you wouldn't mind, my dear . . .' He inclined a beaming head at Beth.

'Delighted,' breathed Beth, extending a slender hand on which the rings flashed in the striplights. 'Oh,' she added, disconcerted, feeling herself aggressively jolted.

Morag had shot to her side. She stared challengingly with baleful and bulging eyes into St John's watery blue ones. 'I still feel,' she hissed, 'that a full-time local should preside over this important ceremony. Me, for instance.'

'There now arose a loud cheer from the alternative lifestyle sector of the audience . . .' Tamara scribbled.

'Go, girl,' drawled Dweeb, rustling about in the huge black overcoat he wore. The movement sent more sickly waves of patchouli Philip's way.

*

Morag was not the only one who was going, however. Alexandra, having completed her business at the estate agent's, was now heading to examine her new purchase.

As the pearlised pink car shot by something oblong and white, she realised a second later that it had said 'Allsop'.

Alexandra careered up the main street, trying to remember where the church was. The betrothal stone and adjacent shack were, she was sure, just up from there.

She suddenly found herself screeching to an unscheduled and unwelcome halt. Cars were parked in the narrow road outside a scruffy-looking green hut. Double parked. It was, Alexandra saw angrily, a complete sea of cars. A Dormobile painted purple with yellow stars stood directly in her path, with a rusty old Peugeot 106 parked next to it. A car of normal width could probably have got between them, even so, but Alexandra's pearlised battle wagon had no chance. She was stuck.

'You can't get through there,' a skinny boy in a hoodie informed her from the front seat of a shiny red open-top sports car.

Alexandra stared at him. 'That's not your car.'

'Is.' He wobbled the gearstick and waggled the steering wheel. 'What's it to you anyway, Paris fucking Hilton?'

Alexandra tottered off towards the green hut in her silver boots, tossing her head disdainfully to disguise her intense pleasure. Paris fucking Hilton was, after all, exactly what she was going for. Particularly now she was doing *The Clink*.

Inside the hut, as St John and Beth looked on helplessly, Morag seized the blue velvet, star-covered hat. Triumphantly she thrust in an arm and drew it out. 'And the first allotment goes to . . .'

She did not, however, finish the sentence. There now came from behind a deafening crash as the village hall's wooden doors slammed back on their hinges into the corrugated metal walls. Alexandra had arrived.

Chapter 28

Everyone turned to look. What they saw was that a young woman, very tall, very thin and very blonde, heavily made up beneath her huge black sunglasses and wearing tight white trousers ending in knee-length silver boots, stood at the back of the village hall. Under her arm was a huge brown leather bag, much buckled, fringed and studded, and her teeth, blaringly white between lips of frosted beige, chewed aggressively on silver-coloured chewing gum.

Tamara gasped in ecstasy. The third glamorous vision – and the most blingtastic of all – to appear in Allsop this evening. What had happened to the place?

Morag looked furious. Who was this woman? Walking right into the middle of her, Morag's, territory. Making spiteful and irresponsible remarks about Dweeb's planet-saving transport solutions.

Alexandra, while rather satisfied with the absolute stunned silence she had created, took a purposeful step forward in her high-heeled silver boots. She couldn't stand here all night being admired. She had houses to plan.

'Look,' she shouted. 'I don't care what's going on here. But will whoever's parked that shitty purple Dormobile and that filthy old Peugeot outside just get the hell out of here and move them so I can get my car through?'

There was another stunned silence. Then Morag spoke, or, rather, screeched. The first shot had been fired over the bows. Now it was her turn. 'How dare you?' she ranted. 'This is a private community public business meeting you've barged into here.'

'Yeah, well it's blocking the road,' Alexandra hit back.

St John, who had clamped his hands to his head in a gesture part anguish, part self-protection, now raised both arms. 'Ladies,' he called despairingly, as the precious culmination of all he had worked for threatened to collapse about him. 'Ladies. This is not a public planning meeting. This is a meeting concerned with the question of distributing allotments. Now can we *please* get on with it?'

Alexandra took a deep breath and drew herself up. She folded her arms below her bosom. Behind her impenetrably black lenses, her eyes blazed like lasers. 'A meeting giving out allotments, did you say?' she rasped.

Her mind was whirring as it had seldom whirred before. She was not remotely interested in gardening and hated getting her hands dirty. But if more land was up for grabs, she wanted it. Allotments were quite big, weren't they? The right sort of size for a swimming pool, if not a helipad.

'To members of the *community*,' Morag snarled triumphantly.

Alexandra lifted her chin. There was battle in the glint of her sunglasses. She was a member of this community now, wasn't she?

*

'Well it could have been worse,' Gid said brightly to Morag as they headed home. As always, they were walking with a purpose; fast, arms pumping. For Morag the purpose was to work off some of the incandescent anger she felt. She disagreed with Gid. So far as she was concerned, the meeting could not have been much worse. It had been almost as bad as it was possible to be.

Striding up the main street of the village, she relived the heart-freezing moment when, after pulling the names of Catherine Brooke and Philip Protheroe out of Dweeb's hat – and that had been bad enough – she had next selected Beth and Benny Ferraro.

Morag's ears had surged with fury. She had awarded precious allotments not only to the injections-obsessed, school-dinner championing headmistress and that horrible argumentative solicitor – who, incidentally, thoroughly deserved to have lost his wife; she'd had a lucky escape, quite frankly – but to that pair of evil imperialists into the bargain. As her shaking fingers entered the hat and seized the fourth piece of paper, Morag had closed her eyes and pulled it thinking that this time, please, Goddess, it had to be her and Gid.

And yet it hadn't been. The paper on which Morag now turned her amazed and infuriated gaze bore the name Mary Longshott – the stately-home owner, no less. Could anything be worse?

Yes, as it turned out. Morag's hand, tattooed on the back with her, Gid's and Merlin's names written in Sanskrit, went once more into the hat and produced a hastily scribbled piece of paper bearing the name 'Alexandra Pigott'.

'I can't understand it,' Morag stormed now. 'What does that *tart* want an allotment for anyway?'

To annoy you? Gid thought, but knew better than to put his suspicions into words. Nonetheless it was his firm belief that if Morag had not been so aggressive, the blonde apparition in their midst would have gone as abruptly as she had arrived. Once Dweeb's Dormobile had been moved, that was.

'Why has she bought that place up at the top of the lane?' Morag demanded suspiciously. It was at the point when Alexandra informed the meeting of her recent actions in the real estate field that Morag realised she had seen her before. Alexandra was the woman in the silver coat who had told her to get her hair cut. Who had been asking about gyms. Did she intend to build a gym up there, at the top of the lane? Morag's thick, dry lips twisted balefully. She had another think coming, if so.

'It's that bloody solicitor's fault,' Morag snarled.

Up to a point, Gid privately allowed. When Morag had tried to prevent Alexandra's name going into the hat on the grounds that the draw was under way and new entries could not be allowed, Philip Protheroe had indeed risen to his feet and argued that, as she owned land in Allsop, Alexandra should be allowed to take part.

And so it had come to pass, that, within four minutes of entering the village hall and insulting Dweeb's Dormobile, Alexandra was in possession of one of the evening's coveted prizes. An allotment. An allotment, moreover, that neither Morag nor her supporters had yet secured. None of their names had come out of the hat.

As the draw she was herself drawing continued producing the names of neither herself nor her supporters, Morag's body temperature had rocketed. The name Ernest Peaseblossom was the next out, provoking a mild cheering among the old men at the back, of whose number Ernest evidently was. Morag, hand clenched over Dweeb's hat, stared at the row of seniors with loathing. Old gits. Parasites. Encumbrances. Irrelevant husks. They had no part in the future of the planet. They shouldn't be allowed to have allotments. Or anything else, including bus services. They shouldn't be allowed to live.

Morag had the sensation that her face was about to explode. And then, thank Goddess, it all came right. Hers and Gid's names were the seventh slip out of the hat, followed by Tecwen and Gudrun. The ninth slip was Dweeb and Vicky.

And then, just as she had slipped her hand in once again, the vicar had stood up. 'There's no need,' he had said calmly.

'No need for what?' snapped Morag, eyeing him with dislike. He may be wearing a long black dress and a collar but he needn't think it impressed her.

'No need to draw another name,' said the Reverend Tribble.

'I've only taken out nine,' Morag sneered. Couldn't the man count? She thought these churchmen were supposed to be educated.

The vicar's gaze was polite but unbending, as was his voice. 'Yes, but the tenth is mine.'

'*Yours?*'

The vicar bowed his head, a faint, polite smile playing around his small mouth as it had from the beginning of the exchange. 'I am here to exercise the ancient right of the Church in these parts to one tenth of the common land,' the Reverend Tribble explained. As Morag's face went white with horror and anger, his smile widened. 'I thought it would be a marvellous way to get to know more of the community.'

'But at least you got an allotment. We all did,' Gid pointed out, breaking into her boiling thoughts.

Morag reluctantly admitted to herself that, for once, Gid was right. Things *could* have been worse. It was admittedly infuriating that, despite all her efforts, St John Goodenough had been elected as President of the Allsop Allotments Association at the meeting. This had been mainly compensatory: having failed to secure a plot through the draw, the chairman of the parish council had effectively been left out of his own idea and would now have to go on a waiting list.

But the bumbling idiot needn't think he was in charge, Morag resolved with blistering force. Far from it. Morag had got her own power base, and let him not forget it. Oh yes, Goodenough was in for a battle if he came between her and her Vision.

Thanks to Dweeb and the rest getting theirs, she was in direct charge of a third of the allotments at least, and she could always bully the headmistress into doing what she wanted. That gave her four, a majority. After the first panic she had decided to discount the Ferraros. Feckless urbanites like them would probably turn up once and never bother again. She'd do her best to make sure that was the case. Then their allotment could be taken over – by her, obviously – within a matter of weeks. That made five. Fifty per cent. Morag punched the air. She had the controlling share. Of the remaining five, that bloody solicitor would be difficult, of course, and the vicar didn't look good either. But Mary Longshott looked like a pushover and Ernest Peaseblossom was so ancient she probably *could* push him over when no one was looking, Morag thought. But hopefully he'd keel over himself soon enough.

As for Alexandra Pigott, she had better look out on a

number of fronts. Although she was not yet sure how, Morag was determined to make it so Alexandra Pigott, whoever she was, would never want to show that make-up-plastered face of hers in the village ever again. Meaning that her allotment too would be up for grabs.

The balm of satisfaction started to calm Morag's troubled soul. Tomorrow she would call Dweeb and Tecwen and they'd go up to the allotments and survey their new kingdom. Project Earth Mother, as she fondly thought of it, could get under way in earnest.

She and Gid had now reached Church Lane. As she passed the Ferraros' Bijou Cottage, Morag could not resist relieving her feelings by driving a furious booted foot into the pink dustbin.

Chapter 29

Beth and Benny wasted no time. The morning after the allotment meeting found them in the gardening section of the nearest B&Q, which was, it emerged after a long drive and several missed towns, not that near after all. Benny pulled out a large and shining spade from a rack, blinking at the weight of it. Jesus H. Were all the tools that heavy?

He experienced a slight and uncharacteristic moment of doubt. What was he letting himself in for? Was months of backbreaking work in all weathers too high a price to pay for acceptance within the village? Of course it was, which was why he had already ordered a mini-tractor to which he planned to attach his mini-rotivator and plough up their patch that way.

Beth had walked straight past the spades. She had also walked past the hoes and forks, but was now examining a length of reclaimed concrete balustrade in a shade of rather blatant cream.

'Honey, it's an allotment,' Benny groaned. 'Not a patio.' He pronounced it to rhyme with Horatio.

Nonetheless, generally speaking, he was satisfied with the

allotment initiative. The timing had been perfect. Things had worked out so they had been given a plot at the exact time that Bijou Cottage had, in Beth's eyes at least, reached its ultimate pitch of perfection. Inside, scarcely a surface remained that hadn't got some vintage print rioting all over it. The finishing touch, the hand-painted nameplate, had arrived from Notting Hill and been screwed to the outside wall. So far, Morag Archbutt-Pesk had not attacked it, but she no doubt had other matters to attend to just now.

To Benny's delight, Beth seemed to have moved seamlessly on from the cottage to the allotments. She had, just as he had hoped, picked up the gauntlet, or rather the daisy-patterned gardening gloves, with relish. Not to mention the garden kneeler in rose-printed oilcloth which had arrived along with the gloves from an online horticultural emporium called The Flowerpot Men. It seemed to Benny that, while Beth hadn't been desperately keen at first, the whole idea of gardening had quickly grown on her. Perhaps all those printed roses had by force of association kick-started some genuine horticultural interest. Or perhaps it was just something else to shop for.

Well, anything that filled her time was just fine by him. It kept her off his back; she got annoyed if he worked too hard and late. But he needed to, given the money she got through, and she was approaching the allotment project like she approached everything else. Unstintingly. With no expense spared. But wasn't that, Benny thought indulgently, what he worked for anyway? So his beautiful, spirited and tasteful wife could spend her time and his money creating a beautiful, spirited and tasteful life for them both?

So long as she didn't go too much over the top. With a twinge of trepidation he watched her trace her long, bejewelled fingers over a statue of a Greek goddess. 'Wow, this is just so stately home. I can just see that under one of those.' She walked musingly towards a small concrete Classical-style temple.

'It's a vegetable plot. Not the park at Chatsworth,' Benny cautioned.

'Sure,' Beth replied, heading off in the direction of a three-tier fountain festooned with lion heads. Benny rolled his eyes and whipped out his BlackBerry. This was clearly going to take some time.

Beth had now spotted some large cream-painted panels of criss-cross lattice. 'Hey! These are neat. Why don't we put some of this round our patch? Wall ourselves off. Then we won't have to look at any of the others.'

'Rather defeats the object, don't you think?' drawled Benny, frowning at his portable email. 'The whole point of having an allotment is to make ourselves more popular with the locals.'

A smile played about Beth's small pink mouth. 'I'm not sure we are, though, honey. Did you see Purple Pants' face when she read out our names?'

'Sure.' Benny remembered the hot wave of murderous anger that had come his way as Morag had announced his and Beth's allotment. 'She's not the only person involved,' Benny said stoutly now. 'And the other guys will come round when they see us getting stuck in, getting the earth under our fingernails and the rest of it.'

Beth looked shocked. 'Eew. I'm not doing anything of the sort.' She surveyed her immaculate finger-ends.

'I'm speaking metaphorically,' Benny said hurriedly, although he wondered if he was, exactly. He doubted that even the hi-tech, chemically enhanced, labour-saving, ultramodern manner in which he intended to cultivate their allotment and the rather more Gosford Park way that Beth planned to could cut out worms, slime, dirt and the rest of it entirely. Although, given the things she seemed to be planning to crowd on to it, there wouldn't be much earth to dig – or for the tractor, when it arrived, to dig – before long.

'Well we've made some new friends already, anyway,' Beth reminded him proudly. 'Monty and Mary from Weston Underwood.'

'Mmm,' said Benny, heaving their groaning trolley along. This, of course, was the other reason Beth was suddenly so interested in the allotments. At the meeting, of all places, she had finally met someone smart, someone who fulfilled her expectations about the English countryside. The Long-stockings, or whatever their name was. The man looked like a woman and the woman was pretty but her clothes didn't seem to fit. But Beth had loved them. She was so excited, Benny noticed, she had even forgotten to put on her English accent. As she proceeded to bombard Mary with questions about her house, he could see it was a match made in heaven. The evening had ended with the Longshotts being asked to Bijou Cottage to dinner.

'It's wonderful to know people who actually live in a stately home, don't you think?' Beth sighed happily, bending down to peer at a sundial. 'Such a gorgeous one too.'

'Honey, it's gross,' Benny said, staring at the dial and feeling he had to speak up. There was kitsch and there was concrete with swags of flowers and robins all over it.

'Not the sundial!' Bella tittered. 'The stately home.'

Weston Underwood was impressive, Benny had to admit. At Beth's insistence, he had driven past it the day after the allotment meeting, or as near to past it as one could get on public roads. Beth, who had been enchanted at the sight of the magnificent classical grey stone façade, had been all for going up the drive and knocking on the enormous front door set in the centre of the portico, but Benny had refused. He was neither as impulsive nor as rampantly aspirational as his wife. But he agreed the Longstockings were good contacts. They had lived in the area for centuries and were bound to be well thought of. Useful allies in the quest for acceptance, or lack of hostility at any rate.

Beth wondered whether a water feature might be a bit excessive. And even if it was, it would have the advantage of making trips to the stand pipe unnecessary. God only knew how far away that was.

'So glamorous, Monty being about to go off exploring,' she breathed.

Benny thought this was just plain weird. Hell, didn't exploring belong back in the nineteenth century with top hats, crinolines, coffee filter papers and paying for things with cash? He had no idea people still did it and couldn't see why anyone would want to. It must cost a fortune and it sounded dangerous. Not to mention cold, which he hated.

'I wonder how many bedrooms it's got,' Beth mused as they headed past the slug pellets. 'Hundreds, by the looks of it. I wonder if ours will have a four-poster.'

'Ours?' queried Benny, applying his powerful biceps to pushing their overloaded trolley along. It went faster than he expected and he seized it, desperately trying to avoid smashing into his wife's exposed, well-exfoliated heels.

'When they invite us to stay there,' Beth sang back happily. 'When they invite us to theirs, after we've asked them to ours. I just know we're going to be such good friends. You can't say that everyone hates us now.'

Benny, weaving after her down the shiny lino aisle, supposed this was true. 'When are the Longstockings coming round?' he asked.

'Long*shotts*. Next week.'

'So soon?'

Beth's honey-gold hair swished in an affirmative. 'Sure. We've got to grab them before Monty goes to start his training.'

Benny suppressed a groan. He hated dinner parties. They were hard work to him, and as hard work was what he did every weekday, he'd expected more of weekends. Less, rather. He forced his mind off the unpleasant subject.

'Hey,' he grinned, as a more entertaining idea struck him. 'I wonder if we'll bump into that crazy blonde in the white trousers in this garden store. You know, buying some mulch or something.'

Beth frowned. There she had been, in the village hall, arm halfway inserted into a smelly blue velvet hat, when in had burst a woman wearing more make-up than the whole cosmetics department of Selfridges, with cascading platinum hair and trousers so tight an eel would have to lie on its back to get into them. 'She looked like a hooker,' Beth concluded. 'Hey,' she added, catching her husband's expression and adopting a teasing tone. 'You didn't *fancy* her, did you?'

Benny shook his huge head in horror. Alexandra Pigott – could that really have been her name? – certainly had something of the platinum Playboy bunny about her. She wasn't his type, though. Beth was his ideal woman, his trophy, his adored and pampered all-in-all. She was tasteful and educated, fastidious; pure, delicate and refined as a lily. Alexandra was the opposite: a hot pink peony, all show, curves and cleavage. He wasn't tempted, not at all.

'And why the hell does she want an allotment?' Beth asked in humorous wonder as she eyed some bird tables on Corinthian column bases. 'Anyone can see she doesn't know anything about gardening. Can you imagine her bent over her carrots in a pair of goddam hotpants?'

Benny swallowed. He could, as it happened. Quite easily. What was more, he felt a prick of admiration for Alexandra. There had been something pretty cool about the way she had materialised out of the blue, shouted about that tatty Dormobile and then, in a matter of minutes it seemed, disappeared in her silver boots having claimed one of the precious few allotments. It was hard not to be impressed by her sheer balls. Benny suspected he had not been the only one in the village hall very much appreciating the spectacle of Morag Archbutt-Pesk receiving a taste of her own very nasty medicine.

Chapter 30

'I've got an allotment,' Philip told Mrs Palfrey over the garden wall the next morning. His voice echoed with the surprise he still felt. He recalled Morag Archbutt-Pesk's face when she had read out his name. The only funnier moments had been when she realised she had also given an allotment to the second-home owners. Or the stately-home owner. Or the footballer's wife whose interests he had found himself, for the sake of justice, defending despite her obvious unsuitability for horticulture.

'An allotment, eh?' Mrs Palfrey muttered. She was, as usual whenever she was in her garden, engaged in violently hurling any snail she found on her flowerbeds over the back wall into the neighbouring field. She had, Philip considered, a bowling action that could interest the England selectors. 'Albert used to have one of them,' Mrs Palfrey added. Albert, Philip remembered, was the first Mr Palfrey. The Rebecca to the second Mr Palfrey's second Mrs de Winter.

As Mrs Palfrey straightened up and began outlining her former husband's great achievements in the field of onion-growing and carrot cultivation, the second Mr Palfrey emerged from the house armed with a coal bucket which he began moodily filling from the store in the little brick outhouse next to Mrs Palfrey's battered greenhouse.

As Mrs Palfrey spoke, she nodded her head, on which the hair was thin and grey and, at regular intervals, wound over a roller. Something about the rollers, the spaces between them and the general greyness reminded Philip suddenly and irresistibly of the pods on the Millennium Wheel. He and Emily had taken a trip on it the last time they had gone to London. Philip swallowed and determinedly followed what Mrs Palfrey was saying.

'You'll be growing potatoes then?' she was asking. 'In your allotment?'

'Er . . . yes . . . I suppose so.'

She fixed him with a beady glare. 'And carrots and onions. They do all right in soil like this. Lettuces don't do bad either.'

He wished he had a notebook to write it all down. 'That sounds great,' he said, hoping he sounded confident.

'Yer don't seem very sure,' Mrs Palfrey accused.

'I'm not really,' Philip confessed. 'I don't know much about growing things, to be honest. That was much more the sort of thing my w—' He clamped his mouth shut.

Mrs Palfrey continued to look at him shrewdly for a few moments. 'Well, you won't need to go buying hexpensive hequipment. I've got a shed full of it there.' She pointed at a ramshackle wooden construction that was part of her garden shanty town also containing the place where she kept and split her logs and the coal shed where Mr Palfrey still rattled. 'There's a wheelbarrow, spades, 'oes, the lot. I don't need 'em in my size of garden. You're welcome to 'em.'

'Thank you,' said Philip, surprised and grateful. He had

been anticipating a trip to a gardening supply shop without enthusiasm. He had only the vaguest idea what he might require and was resigned to making expensive mistakes. 'You must let me buy them off you.'

'Not on your nelly,' said Mrs Palfrey. 'You're welcome to 'em. Albert would be right glad to know they were being used again.' She paused and a misty look came into her eyes. 'It'd be a sort of link with 'im, I suppose. If you know what I mean.'

Philip nodded. He knew all right. All too well. There was a clatter as the second Mr Palfrey knocked over the coal bucket.

Some hours later, in the kitchen at Weston Underwood, Mary and Monty had just finished lunch. 'Great meeting last night,' Monty was enthusing, looking up from the map of the North Pole that covered the table and which could be better examined now he had pushed his plate aside.

He was, Mary could see, both delighted and relieved that she had found a hobby to sustain her throughout his absence.

While she felt a pang of betrayal still, and an ever-growing dread as the actual moment of parting neared, Mary managed to smile over the remains of her cheese on toast. The meal was perilously close to what had formerly come out of the Breville, but this was not uppermost in her thoughts. She was genuinely surprised and delighted about her allotment. It seemed a miracle she had managed to get one in the face of such stiff competition.

Of late, three things had seized her thoughts at bedtime. The prospect of the house without Monty. The house full stop, with all its problems. The problems Monty would encounter on his own in the Arctic. This unhappy trinity kept her awake at night, churning her brain and stomach with miserable scenarios, reducing her to silent tears as Monty snored beside her. Last night, however, for the first time since the expedition had been mooted, she had not gone to sleep weeping.

Last night, she had forcibly pushed away the fact that her beloved husband would be away for at least two months, even, which at times seemed unlikely, if he didn't die of hypothermia, starvation or at the claws of a polar bear first. She suppressed the image of the great red bed empty of anyone but her, the image of Monty struggling through the precarious landscape alone apart from the sled which contained all his provisions, the image of her running from cracked wall to leaking roof in an ever-faster race round Underpants, brandishing buckets and Polyfilla.

Instead, she had lain there and forced her thoughts to her new allotment. It had been difficult; more than once her mind had threatened to veer off the horticultural and plunge back into the familiar, ghastly abyss of howling blizzards and marauding, murderous mammals. But she had determinedly steered it back and had made some initial decisions. Carrots, to start with. And onions. And potatoes. If she planted them soon they might even be ready in the autumn. And courgettes too; they were supposed to be easy for beginners.

'And those people were nice,' Monty remarked brightly, rubbing a smear of mustard off the North Siberian Islands.

Mary remembered the meeting. She had not realised Allsop contained so many inhabitants. It had always been empty whenever she went through it. She had certainly never suspected anyone as decorative as Alexandra Pigott was planning to live there. That had been an extraordinary scene, the one between her and Morag Archbutt-Pesk, who Mary recognised effortlessly from Mrs Shuffle's many descriptions. She had always suspected Mrs Shuffle to have been exaggerating, but now realised that exaggerating Morag was impossible.

As for Alexandra, she looked, Mary thought, straight out of the Playboy Mansion, an article about which she had recently read at the dentist's. She had been suffused with envy, not necessarily of the girls' lifestyles, but certainly of the secure ceilings and crack-free windowpanes clearly to be seen in all the photographs of the place. Whatever the mansion's moral structure, its physical structure was unimpeachable and to that extent at least utterly admirable.

'They'll be friends for you,' Monty added, glancing up from his map, his blue eyes shining encouragingly.

Mary met his gaze in surprise. Morag and Alexandra Pigott? Friends? Then she realised he was talking about someone else altogether. 'Oh yes. Beth and, um, what was her husband called?'

'Benny.'

'They're very, um, American,' Mary smiled.

They looked at each other and grinned. Once St John had introduced Mary, who'd gone rather red in the face about it for some reason, as 'chatelaine of our local stately home', Beth had turned to her excitedly. 'Wow! That's so cool! A real stately home!'

'How do you do,' Mary had muttered, blushing further.

'No, how do you do!' Beth gushed, remembering her accent again. 'I was beginning to lose hope I'd ever find anyone civilised round here!'

'Beth!' Benny had growled, looking meaningfully from his

wife to St John, who stood between her and Mary wearing a crushed expression.

'Oh, I don't mean you!' Beth gasped, swooping on the President of the Allotments Association. 'You're an absolute poppet, St John!'

She had pronounced it, Mary remembered now, as in the Apostle.

'They've asked us to dinner,' Monty declared, shaking his blond head, which never failed to shine no matter how infrequently he washed it, in wonder.

It was, Mary agreed, an exciting prospect. They had not been out for dinner in living memory. It would be fun to have some new friends, especially now Monty was going away.

She carried the plates to the sink and ran the ancient and clanking brass tap. As the water swirled into the old steel sink she felt thankful she had followed Mrs Shuffle's advice. This time last week there had been nothing in prospect apart from the departure of her husband, and while that ghastly eventuality still loomed, the overall dark misery of the picture had been alleviated with dashes of colour, small but not without significance.

Mary was a natural optimist who sought to make the best of things, and it was hard not to feel slightly buoyed by the fact that she now had an allotment of her own and had met the glamorous, wealthy and lively Ferraros. And there was the prospect of dinner out, to boot. Mary felt the former foodie within her stir. It would be interesting to taste someone else's cooking for a change. And Beth was obviously a person of style. Yes, she was looking forward to it.

Chapter 31

Catherine walked through the village. It was a scented June evening, the air heavy with wafts of honeysuckle, jasmine and orange blossom from the low garden walls bordering the High Street. From a blue, untroubled sky the sun shone richly on the ancient stone walls of the cottages and glittered in the leaves of the trees in the churchyard. The headmistress's soul, however, was a good deal less placid than the scenes of summer before her.

A good dig on her allotment would hopefully get the frustrations of the last few days out of her system. The news of Olivia Cooke's defection to St Aidan's had been greeted by Mrs Watkins and Miss Hanscombe with even more dismay than Catherine had anticipated. The dismay had deepened when they had discovered the reason. 'You've just got to get rid of that boy,' Miss Hanscombe had cried. 'He's dragging the whole school down.'

Catherine had, in the end, promised to think about it. Anything less would have resulted in mutiny. Yet having to expel needy, troubled Sam Binns because one spoilt mother wanted to send her child to prep school stuck in her craw. She would never do it. It went against all her principles.

As she reached the market cross in the village centre she was surprised to see the object of her thoughts in person.

'I can see you, Sam Binns,' Catherine called out to the skinny figure in its hooded top lurking in the bushes outside the cottage opposite. 'Don't hide there, Sam. Mrs McManus is old and she'll be scared.' As Catherine spoke, however, the cottage door opened and a truly fearsome-looking dame with thick jet-black eyebrows and snow-white hair streaming backwards like a cloud appeared shaking a stout stick. Sam took one look, leapt over the wall and scurried back up the road towards where his foster mother Mrs Newton, who Catherine had just passed, was wandering forlornly about calling his name and the fact that dinner was ready.

As she walked, Catherine wondered if Mrs McManus was too old to be a classroom assistant. It was the first time she had seen Sam Binns scared of anything.

What if the Reverend Tribble were there? While Mary Longshott, who seemed nice enough, flanked her plot on one side, the vicar was Catherine's neighbour on the other and his visits to his plot seemed to coincide hideously frequently with her own. Even more frequently, for all her efforts to avoid him on a plot that was, like all the others, twenty feet across by thirty feet long, Catherine seemed to be regularly finding herself planting out her bean stakes in an area near where the vicar was digging. And, as he dug, talking relentlessly.

There was something, too, about the way he looked at her in her jeans. She knew he was a single man, and the knowledge, as she felt his eyes follow her bottom down her bean rows, was not comforting.

Her heart sank as she entered the allotment field to find

him there now, his black gown billowing in the gentle evening breeze. He saw her, waved, and hopped off the black upturned earth of his growing area on to the narrow strip of grassy path that divided his plot from hers.

'Good evening, Miss Brooke.'

'Hello, Vicar.' Catherine suddenly wished she hadn't put on quite such a clinging pink T-shirt.

'And how are the pagans getting on?' The Reverend Tribble's thin face positively beamed with the brilliance of his sally, even though he made the same one on a practically daily basis.

'Fine, thank you,' Catherine said shortly, wishing he would go away. It was late as it was; she had come up to try and get the last of the evening sun, the very same one the vicar was now standing squarely in front of. Her heart sank as the Reverend Tribble's tightly laced black shoes failed to move, as hoped, along the path from her plot to his, or, better still, away altogether.

Catherine strove for inward patience. Social interaction literally went with the territory on allotments, which had been one of its initial attractions. But she wished the vicar would interact with her slightly less. Every evening he seemed to be here and always ready with a gay sally about her teaching or a question about the vicarage, which he was currently refurbishing. He had bored her senseless with carpet samples for the past week, and last night she had endured a lengthy interrogation about what colour curtains she thought he should have.

She wished Beth and Benny would appear with their tractor now. But it was midweek and they would be in London. A shame.

Catherine could not help recalling with a smile the first

time the Ferraro tractor had appeared on the allotments. It had been a Saturday afternoon and everyone had been occupied with the initial business of hoeing and digging over, many exclaiming in dismay at the stoniness of the soil.

Then a sudden explosion of noise made them all look up. Over the hill above the field had appeared a shining new red mini-tractor with virgin tyres and a rear bristling with gleaming digging equipment. On the tractor seat rode an exhilarated-looking Benny with Beth perched on his knee, her blond hair blowing back over her shoulders, her feet in flowery Wellingtons and her hands clamped on to the handlebars beside his.

Morag, after a few seconds' immobile amazement, had snapped into action.

Making a noise that was half exclamation, half snort, she strode over to the tractor. Her lips were drawn back over her prominent teeth and her eyes bulged with fury. 'What the hell do you think you are doing?' she yelled.

'Excuse me?' Benny shouted cheerfully back, cupping his ear. 'Can't hear a thing for this goddam engine. Gimme five while I find the off button.'

The roaring ceased. Morag resumed her attack. 'Just what,' she demanded, 'do you think you're doing here with that . . .' her eyes narrowed, '. . . that *thing*?'

'It's our tractor,' Benny said cheerfully, patting the shining scarlet bonnet of the machine. 'We've just bought it. We're going to plough our patch with it. It struck us as the easiest way—'

'Easiest?' Morag interrupted furiously. 'Allotments are not supposed to be easy. They're all to do with communing with the soil, feeling the rhythm of nature . . .'

'Oh sure,' Beth replied blithely. 'But we haven't got time

for all of that stuff. We're only here at the weekends because we live in London during the week.'

'Well if you think you're going to use that thing here on your allotment you've got another think coming,' Morag shouted.

'Hey, not just on *our* allotment,' Benny replied. Now he had given up trying to charm her, he was rather enjoying winding up this ghastly woman. 'We're very happy to go over anyone else's if they want to save themselves a job. It seemed to us that the ground was pretty stony and it would be hard going digging it all up by hand.'

There were a number of interested murmurs at this. From where they were working, people started to straighten up and try to catch Benny's eye.

Morag held up a hand. 'No tractors on these allotments,' she said sharply. 'No pesticides. Nothing unnatural.'

'There's no rules against tractors,' Benny stoutly pointed out. 'I checked with the guy in charge.'

'Saint John,' supplied Beth, with a giggle. 'Dear old poppet,' she added fondly.

Morag's nostrils flared. She planted her hands on her hips. 'Allow me to inform you,' she said shrilly, 'that St John Goodenough does *not* run it all. *I* am Vice President of the Allsop Allotments Association.'

Benny shrugged. 'Sure you are. But I can still do what I like on my own allotment. Bury nuclear waste if I want to ... Hey, *joke*,' he stressed hurriedly as a murderous look entered Morag's eye.

The smile that lingered on Catherine's lips now abruptly vanished as the vicar, clearly taking her expression as encouragement, asked her for her views on sisal. The vicarage floor was currently aswirl with a particularly assertive red and yellow Axminster, and whenever he read from Revelation, the scenes of chaos never failed to bring this pattern before his eyes.

Catherine privately thought that the vicar should spend less time chatting and more time working his allotment. For all that he was, presumably, a deeply conscientious and hard-working man of the Church, his plot showed the least improvement of anyone's. It was a stony, weedy patch in which he had made few successful incursions. One would somehow imagine a vicar to have green fingers. All that in the Bible about ploughing the fields and scattering, the lilies of the field and so on. Yet nothing the Reverend Tribble had planted appeared to have taken root.

'Would you like some of my spare carrot seeds?' Catherine suggested, hoping that this would get rid of him. It was a hint wrapped in a kind and sympathetic gesture, which she had always found to be the best way to persuade naughty or recalcitrant children.

'Mm, thanks,' said Reverend Tribble, taking the packet she proffered. But instead of walking away he continued to look at her, his long face creased with preoccupation.

'What's the matter?' Catherine asked, feeling instinctively that something was. He was staring at her in a very strange and intense manner.

To her mild horror, the Reverend now dropped to his hunkers beside her. A scent stole across her nose, something musty and redolent of damp vestries. Or perhaps damp vests. 'Do you mind, Miss Brooke,' he breathed, 'if I ask you a question?'

Catherine's fingers busied in panic about her carrot seeds. Not another curtain query, she hoped. Or, worse, during the last conversation the vicar had shown signs of moving on to roller blinds, having, as he said, been unable to help noticing she had them fitted to the windows of her own cottage. A process which had been so painfully boring and yet fiddly that Catherine had promised herself never to speak another word about roller blinds for the entire remainder of her life.

'I was wondering,' the vicar mused, 'whether we might plant seeds of a rather different kind together, Miss Brooke.'

Catherine swallowed. Her grey eyes widened with fear. What was the vicar about to propose?

'Basically,' the vicar murmured, 'I'm trying to hit on a way to get more children into the church – as regulars, you understand – and I thought perhaps you could help me.'

Catherine started. 'Er . . .' Her mind reeled. This was not part of her remit as head teacher.

A smile now ruched the vicar's thin mouth. His eyes seemed to kindle with some understanding. 'Ah. Do we have a problem here? I must admit I have wondered . . .'

'Wondered about what?' Catherine asked indignantly. She resented the word 'problem'. The term 'regulars' had left an odd echo, too, as if the vicar thought of his flock as a landlord thought of his drinkers.

The vicar's face suddenly seemed very close to hers. 'Are you,' the Reverend Tribble breathed, 'a Believer, Miss Brooke?'

Catherine jumped slightly. Although it was in theory a logical enough question coming from a vicar, it was the last she expected. Most vicars of her experience determinedly dodged this particular issue, in silent acknowledgement of the potential embarrassment a likely negative could result in.

'A Believer,' Catherine repeated, sticking her fingers hard in the earth and playing for time.

'Yes, Miss Brooke. Do you believe in Our Lord Jesus Christ?'

She looked into his eyes, which were suddenly wide and clear and brimming with sincerity, with perhaps a hint of moisture caused by the gathering breeze, and felt her face glow hot and crimson. She gazed at him desperately. 'Well, it's not that I *don't* believe, Vicar,' she muttered, twisting her fingers.

He nodded sympathetically, a few strands of thin hair lifting lightly in the wind. She noticed, irrationally, that he had both a short forehead and a long upper lip and it might have been better for his face if these proportions had been reversed.

'It's just that, well, to be perfectly honest, I'm not sure that I *do* believe either,' Catherine muttered, staring at the ground. It was, she knew, an inadequate response, both to the vicar and to herself. It suddenly seemed to her that someone in charge of children's education, a headmistress, to boot, should have this burning universal question rather more worked out in her mind. Not least in case one of the children asked the same thing, although so far none had.

'Yoo hoo! Miss Brooke!' a voice suddenly interrupted them.

Catherine paused, recognising the tone only too well and caught between a rock and a hard place. Did she want to talk to Morag Archbutt-Pesk even less than she wanted to stay with the Reverend Tribble? It was a close call. But at least Morag was unlikely to interrogate her over her relationship with the Lord.

'Come on over,' Morag ordered, from above Catherine in the part of the allotment field where the land seemed smoother, richer and less stony than that below.

'Do excuse me,' Catherine muttered to the Reverend Tribble.

Morag, who was grubbing in the ground, revolved in an unattractive squat-walk as Catherine approached and pointed a sinewy, tattooed arm at a large roughed-up area with no apparent order to it. Was it, Catherine wondered, a compost heap?

'My random vegetable patch!'

'Your what?'

'None of those unnatural rows for me!' Morag declared. 'I'm going back to nature and the dawn of cultivation – scattering the seeds everywhere and seeing what grows where.'

'I see,' Catherine said tactfully, thinking what a waste of time that seemed. Surely the point of an allotment was to cram every available inch with the reliably produce-yielding plants that had been developed over centuries to lighten the vegetable-grower's load? Morag's method seemed both wasteful and wilfully ignorant. 'Is that the best use of an allotment?' she ventured, thinking of all the disappointed would-be vegetable growers who had failed to secure one at the village hall meeting.

Morag looked impatient. 'I'm trying to give you some help. You should do the random vegetable planting on yours. Let's face it, your rows don't seem to be doing all that well.'

'Er . . .'

'And of course,' Morag interrupted, answering her own conjecture, 'you'll want a good vegetable yield so you can improve the organic content of school lunches. Which could do with improving, let's face it.'

Catherine clenched her fists. But then, suddenly, spectacularly, her attention was arrested by something on the neighbouring plot. She stared. She frowned. No. It was impossible.

Morag's gleeful voice interrupted. '*A-ha*. So you've noticed.'

'Er, yes,' Catherine said doubtfully. 'Is it what I think it is?'

The large shape that was roughed out in the centre of the adjoining allotment using some sort of white marker was certainly a very distinctive one.

'Dweeb and Vicky have had a lot of trouble conceiving,' Morag informed her – and anyone else who might be listening – loudly.

'Er . . .'

'So they decided to dedicate part of their earth resource to a Conception Garden. That penis shape has been planted with chamomile and other plants traditionally associated with fertility.'

Catherine swallowed. 'I see. And they'll pick the plants, will they? Put them in a drink or something . . . ?' Her voice faded as Morag's face split in a triumphant grin and she wagged her finger.

'Not quite. They plan to make love on it whenever there's a full moon.'

Catherine's eyes widened in horror. 'But what about everybody else? The vicar, for instance.' She cast an apprehensive glance over towards the Reverend's plot and was relieved to see that he had gone.

Morag tossed her hennaed head. 'Oh, Vicky and Dweeb are cool about that. Anyone else is welcome to use the sex garden when they're not using it themselves. The vicar as well if he likes. We thought it would be a great resource for the village.'

Catherine could not think of anything to say to this. 'Well, I'd better be getting back . . .' she muttered, stumbling in her haste to escape from the sex garden. Where, she wondered, were Beth, Benny and their tractor when you really needed them?

Chapter 32

'Wow!' exclaimed Beth, ushering Mary into Bijou Cottage and staring at her skirt. 'Is that new?'

Mary's heart sank. The skirt, which featured large yellow flowers on a cyan blue background, was indeed new. New to her, that was, but not to Mrs Shuffle, to whom it had apparently belonged since the early seventies.

It had been much too large originally but Mrs Shuffle, in honour of what she kept referring to as Mary's 'big night out', had taken it away and returned it almost cut in half. Mary had no doubt that it looked hideous, but everything else she owned were trousers that were out at the knees, and as all the mirrors in Underpants were either clouded and moulded with age or only showed anyone to torso level, it was impossible to see for herself the full appalling effect. Judging from Beth's reaction, however, appalling it obviously was.

'Don't tell me,' Beth squealed.

There was nothing Mary wanted to do less.

'It's Prada, isn't it?'

Mary's mouth dropped open. She searched for a reply, but

Beth was already pushing her forward into the small, pretty, low-ceilinged sitting room, twittering hospitably all the while.

But it was Mary's turn to stare now. Outside of an interiors magazine, she had never seen anything like the Ferraros' cottage. Everything was neat, clean and new. Everything hard was painted distressed white and everything soft was covered in pretty patterned fabrics, mostly rose-print. There really was an enormous amount of rose-print, Mary saw. But how comfortable and welcoming it looked compared to the gloomy damp of Underpants. Even if it did have an utterly ridiculous name. Bijou Cottage. She and Monty had had to hurriedly straighten their faces when Beth opened the front door.

But Mary did not feel like smiling now. She felt simply envious.

There were plump seats and sofas everywhere. The polished floorboards shone in the light of lamps on low antique tables in the corners. Logs were piled neatly in the ancient stone hearth. Summer flowers – roses, hydrangeas – foamed out of rustic china jugs set everywhere from the deep-silled window to the mantelpiece, over which a gold-rimmed mirror reflected the candles on the table.

'It's beautiful,' Mary breathed.

'Do you think so! We've gone for shabby chic,' Beth exclaimed, gratified.

Mary didn't know whether to laugh or burst into tears. Instead, her eyes roved the unstained, crackless ceilings in wonder, admired the shining, unbroken panes of the windows, felt the floorboards reassuringly solid beneath her.

As Benny handed Mary a glass of champagne she looked

at it, trying to remember the last time she had had some. She concluded with a pang that it must have been her wedding.

'It's only Veuve Clicquot,' Beth apologised. 'I guess you're used to Krug. You probably bathe in it,' she tittered.

Monty burst out laughing and then, as Beth looked at him strangely, tried to pretend he was sneezing in his handkerchief. Mary, meanwhile, realised with no small amazement that Beth absolutely was not joking. She really thought they lived in the lap of luxury with footmen and sedan chairs. What should she do? It seemed rude to disabuse her hostess of her fantasies about them, particularly as they were fantasies Mary herself wished were true. On the other hand, they could hardly lie.

'Your place looks incredible,' Beth enthused. 'Is it as incredible as it looks?'

Mary paused. 'Probably a bit more incredible than it looks,' she confessed, trying not to catch Monty's eye. It would never do to laugh.

'It's Monty's ancestral home, isn't it?' Beth enquired brightly, looking at him.

Monty nodded. 'Yes,' he smiled, 'I'm the last survivor of the Longshott line, holders of the ancient estate of Weston Underwood, one hundred and forty-four acres, two fishing lakes, and mansion house comprising Georgian portico, medieval great hall, Tudor wings and chapel, ancestral home of the Longshotts for over five hundred years!'

'You don't say!' breathed Beth in ecstasy.

Mary felt her heart well with love. Her husband was doing his best to oblige, to give the Ferraros what they wanted, while keeping on the side of accuracy. The last survivor bit was probably too much information, however; their childlessness was their own business and one into which she did not wish the Ferraros to pry. Especially as there was no explanation for it; never, it seemed to Mary, had she and Monty made love as passionately as they had recently, with the imminent parting hanging over them.

As Monty, encouraged both by Beth and the alcohol, which he drank only rarely, began another speech in praise of his home and lineage, Mary stepped in. Laying a gentle hand on her husband's arm she smiled apologetically at Beth. 'Monty's obsessed with Underpants, I'm afraid.'

There was a silence. 'Excuse me?' Beth asked, startled. 'It must be my ears, still full of bubble bath.' She tapped her pretty, flat ears and shook her fair head charmingly. 'But I thought I heard you say Monty was obsessed with . . . underpants?'

As Monty hastened to explain it was the traditional nickname for the house, Beth, remembering that nicknames were terribly smart and that the British upper classes gave them to everything, clapped her hands. 'How hilarious!'

Benny, from the fireplace, eyed Monty. Was it his tired eyes or did that dinner jacket really have a green tinge? British aristocrats, he knew, famously prided themselves on their battered clothing, but there was battered and there was downright bludgeoned. The wife was great, though. Polite and restrained, not too excitable and adorably pretty in that rather windswept way that English women carried off so well. He loved her wide eyes and highly kissable tip-tilted nose in particular. He was surprised that crazy outfit was high fashion, as Beth insisted it was, but he'd long since ceased to understand clothes.

For all his appreciation of Mary's charms, Benny was exhausted. It had been a hell of a week and the last thing on earth he wanted on finally reaching Bijou Cottage was to entertain people. He forced himself to remember that it was a worthwhile effort; that they needed to make friends and influence people, and here they were, doing just that. Besides, nothing much was required of him at the moment apart from opening bottles of wine, which Monty, it had to be said, was doing full justice to. Beth, meanwhile, for reasons Benny couldn't fathom in summer, was currently wittering on about skiing.

'You've never been to Gstaad? You should, you really should,' she was urging Mary in what Benny had come to think of as her Best Patrician Brit. 'Gstaad is just marvellous. Last winter was divine. Simply divine. Great – I mean marvellous – snow. And we spotted Wills and Harry!'

As Mary tried to look enthused, Monty took the conversational baton in delight. 'Well of course I'm a great fan of snow, ha ha. Being an explorer.' This provoked a storm of clueless, breathy questions from Beth about his expedition.

'You're joking!' she exclaimed, her eyes and mouth wide with amazement. 'You've got to rub your naked body every day with handfuls of snow to slough off dead skin cells? And pee out of a suit that zips open from front to back underneath?'

Monty, hungrily munching on the vegetable crisps Beth was passing round in a dish from her collection of vintage china, nodded.

'And you'll be in minus forty degree temperatures with the dangers of ice cracking beneath you at any moment?' Beth gasped.

'Yes, but . . .' Monty looked uncertainly at his wife, who appeared pale and tense. 'I'm having full training. Emergency first aid, underwater swimming, shooting, even basic dental repairs. The sponsors are making sure of that. I'm going to

London next week to start it, as I believe I mentioned.'

'Oh yes.' Beth nodded, her hand holding an aubergine crisp arrested halfway towards her mouth. 'Where will you be training?'

'Some army camp in Hendon,' Monty said vaguely.

'Yes, but where will you be staying?'

'Oh. Er. Well, a bed and breakfast somewhere near it, I suppose,' Monty confessed reluctantly without looking at his wife. The fact that two weeks in a bed and breakfast would cost money they didn't have was a sore subject. Monty had promised to find the cheapest possible room in Hendon, which seemed to Mary a fate almost worse than the Arctic itself.

Beth screwed up her delicate nose. 'Ugh. Sounds horrid.' Her face smoothed out suddenly and she beamed. 'Hey. I've just had a great idea. Why not come and stay with us while you're training? Benny and I have got a great big house in Notting Hill that's empty apart from us. Why don't you come and keep us company before you go off? We'd love to have you.'

'Er . . .' Monty rubbed a large thin hand through his pale hair in surprise. He looked cluelessly at Mary, who threw the question back at him by shrugging nervously, then stared back at Beth, an uncertain smile rushing and retreating across his face. 'I mean, that's awfully kind of you,' Monty muttered, 'but I couldn't possibly intrude . . .'

'You wouldn't be.' Benny detached himself from the prop of the fireplace where the three of them stood in a group with their glasses. 'It's a good idea. We'd love it. You'd be company for Beth when I'm at, erm, work. Sometimes I have to work a little late,' he added guiltily.

Mary looked uncertainly at her husband. Of course, it

would save them money and was, in fact, a godsend, but was it polite to accept? They hardly knew the Ferraros and were in no position to repay hospitality and kindness such as this. Monty, however, was all smiles and eagerness. 'Well, if you're sure, that's very kind. Incredibly kind. Thank you.'

Chapter 33

They sat down. Mary gazed in wonder at the flower-patterned plates and the brilliantly new knives and forks whose handles were each one a different pastel colour. The glasses were faintly coloured too, in shades of pink, green and blue, and all the very colourful napkins were patterned differently. They were all new and obviously fashionable and expensive. But Mary couldn't quite shake off the idea of being at a child's tea party and that any minute Benny was going to blow up some balloons.

What Benny actually did was continue to open wine which Monty, Mary worriedly felt, was consuming at a startling rate. She hoped the food would soak it up.

Finally, Beth placed another flowered china serving plate from her vintage collection on the table. Mary leant forward, eager to see what the latest dinner-party sensation among London's leaders of fashion was. It was small, certainly. On a tiny pile of couscous, eight minuscule lamb chops were neatly arranged.

'All from Borough Market this morning,' Beth beamed, pronouncing it Bowruff.

'Delicious,' said Monty, helping himself to most of the vegetable sauce from the small bowl on the table.

'Oh, sorry. That's for everyone, is it?' he added a few seconds later, as Mary emptied a teaspoonful from the same bowl over her tiny pile of grains.

Benny sighed. The fact that his wife didn't believe in second helpings, or first helpings of any substance, could be a challenge. It was one he overcame in the working week by supplementing his diet with bagels, but secret stashes of carbohydrate were a less simple matter in the country.

Beth, having served herself a teaspoon of couscous, turned conversationally to Mary. 'So you gave up work?' she smiled. 'Me too. I used to work for an interior design firm but I stopped when I met Benny.' She beamed at her husband. 'And now I just spend his money, don't I, honey?'

'You certainly do, honey.'

'Gave up work?' Mary repeated, thrown. What else did she do *but* work? 'Oh, I see what you mean. Office work. Yes, I suppose so. I used to work at Sotheby's, though. In the eighteenth-century art department.'

'It sounds wonderful,' Beth said vaguely, looking up from her covert examination of Mary's – surprisingly, for a mansion-dweller – split nails, under which an even more surprising thin line of dirt remained. But aristos – true aristos – were always a little ragged around the edges. It was a sign of authenticity. 'Hey, have you got a wardrobe full of evening dresses?' she asked suddenly. 'A ballroom?'

Mary shook her head. Wanting to get off the subject of Underpants, she introduced that of the allotments.

'What are you planting?' Beth asked.

'Oh, the usual. Potatoes. Onions. Carrots.'

Beth looked disappointed. 'But you can get all that from Sainsbury's, surely.'

'Er . . .' Mary blinked. Where exactly did she start with this one? That she, personally, couldn't get them from Sainsbury's as it was out of her price range? Or that the whole point of growing your own was no longer needing to go to the big chains?

'I'm not bothering with the basics. I'm going for exotica,' Beth explained airily. 'I'm putting in cardoons, blue peas, red aubergines, Peking sprouts and Zanzibar feather artichokes to begin with.'

Benny raised his eyebrows at this, but not too high. He was accustomed to indulging his wife's flights of fancy. The wine was starting to revive him slightly, reminding him that he had an agenda for this evening, which was to find out the extent of Mary and Monty's social contacts, and how they could be pressed into the service of the Ferraros.

'Must be pretty sociable,' he muttered to Mary. 'Guess you know a lot of people.'

As this was the first remark Benny had made to her, ground out in his thick American accent, Mary was startled and as a result misunderstood and thought he was talking about the allotments.

'Oh yes. There's Mr Peaseblossom, who has the plot opposite mine,' she enthused. 'He's about ninety and very helpful. He seems to know everything there is to know about carrots.'

Benny's face fell slightly. While he wanted to be accepted in the village, ninety-year-old carrot experts were not necessarily his target audience. Benny's faith in the allotments' ability to deliver the social solution he sought was now wavering after the several visits he had made. None of the people up there seemed particularly sparky, and Morag Archbutt-Pesk wielded unnatural influence over the whole shebang, which was bad news. He had hoped the Longshotts could point him elsewhere.

'He's a real character,' Mary continued happily, letting champagne and enthusiasm launch her into a description of Ernest Peaseblossom, white shirtsleeves rolled up, braces hoisting baggy greenish trousers, brown flat cap perched above his large and flappy but nonetheless failing ears. The old man's partial deafness meant he shouted rather than spoke; his peremptory roars had taken Mary by surprise at first.

Her lack of horticultural knowledge, on the other hand, had surprised Ernest equally. He had seemed shocked by how little she knew.

'ARE YOU GOING TO EXPOSE 'EM TO PLENTY OF SUNSHINE?' he bellowed at Mary, seeing her opening a packet of cabbage seeds.

She had nodded.

Ernest had shaken his head disapprovingly. 'YOU'RE GOING TO HAVE PROBLEMS, THEN. DON'T LIKE TOO MUCH SUN, CABBAGES DON'T.'

'Oh, right,' Mary said, hurriedly reassessing the position of the crop on her plot.

The next time she had arrived, with onion sets, Ernest had ambled over again. 'YOU GOING TO GIVE THEM LOTS OF WATER?'

Mary had confirmed eagerly that she was.

Ernest had sucked in his teeth. 'OH DEAR. DON'T LIKE TOO MUCH WATER, ONIONS DON'T.'

On the third occasion Ernest's red ears and white shirt loomed into view, Mary had been ready.

'YOU GOING TO PUT PLENTY OF MANURE ON THEM?' he had boomed, nodding at the nasturtium seedlings she was positioning. Nasturtiums, Mary had decided, would brighten up the allotment. You could eat them too, of course.

Familiar by now with Ernest's reverse-thrust methods of gardening advice, Mary had shaken her head. 'No. I don't think so.'

Ernest had clicked his tongue disapprovingly. 'WELL YOU SHOULD,' he had opined loudly. 'I ALLUS PUT PLENTY MANURE ON NASTURTIUMS MESELF.'

Having completed the anecdote, Mary, feeling suddenly shy again, smiled around awkwardly. Monty was laughing heartily and Benny was smiling, but Beth looked blank.

'Dessert – I mean pudding – anyone?' she sang. 'I got some goat's cheese ice-cream from Bowruff.'

Pudding time, Benny registered. Getting towards coffee time, traditionally the business section of a meal. Time, Benny thought, to find out exactly what use the Longshotts could be in helping himself and Beth gain acceptance within the local community.

He laced his fingers together in relaxed and confident fashion, leant forward and smiled encouragingly at Monty. 'You must have lots of friends in Allsop,' he began, as cheerfully as his exhausted and somewhat inebriated spirits would allow.

He watched as the handsome face opposite split into an apologetic grin. 'Not really. I'm afraid we've always rather avoided the village.'

Benny's eyes bulged. He groped for the stem of his wineglass and emptied the rest of his claret into his mouth.

Beth and Mary had by now disappeared into the kitchen,

ostensibly to load the state-of-the-art dishwasher. 'I expect you'll miss Monty terribly when he's gone,' Beth said, looking at her questioningly.

She was, Mary saw, obviously fishing for confidences. But Mary was not in the habit of opening her heart to people she had only just met, or even people she had known for years, like Mrs Shuffle. In the secret core where she kept her inmost thoughts she did not really expect anyone else to be interested in her problems and felt, besides, that she had rather made her bed in respect of Monty's expedition. He had never, even before they had married, made any attempt to disguise his passion for exploring. 'I expect I will,' she said breezily to Beth. 'But I plan to keep busy.'

Beth's reaction was unexpected. An expression of despair flashed across her bright, pretty face. 'I try to keep busy,' she said in a low voice. 'Benny leaves me alone a lot. I mean,' she added, raising her eyebrows and sighing, 'he's not at the North Pole, for sure. But sometimes I think he might as well be.'

Mary tried to look sympathetic but felt even more uncomfortable. She did not wish to be Beth's confidante, partly because she hardly knew her and partly because of what Beth might want to know about her in return. She had no idea what to say. She supposed long and late hours went with the territory of making as much money as Benny evidently did. As the main beneficiary, Beth couldn't have it both ways. She looked helplessly back at her hostess.

Beth's grin had quite returned to her face, however. 'That's why it'll be so nice to have Monty about, even if he's spending the day learning to shoot polar bears and performing extractions of his own molars.'

*

Mary and Monty walked home from Bijou Cottage. It was a warm evening and a taxi, even if it could have been persuaded out from Mineford, was financially out of the question.

They exchanged a few words about the evening. Monty had enjoyed it. Yet the chic cottage, which had struck Mary with the force of a juggernaut, hardly seemed to have made an impression on him at all. Mary smiled to herself, obscurely relieved, though unsure exactly why.

They were both tired, and conversation soon gave way to companionable silence. Mary held Monty's hand tightly and snuggled into his arm as they walked along. The village was empty and silent – apart, that was, from an extraordinarily loud television which seemed to be coming from the cottage at the very bottom of Beth and Benny's lane. As the two of them went past, a gale of mocking studio mirth boomed out at some occurrence on the screen. Mary clutched her husband's hand. The noise was sharp, unpleasant, ugly. She felt, suddenly and irrationally, as if the laughter were directed at her.

Perhaps the wine had heightened her senses. There was a slight spinning in her head, a mist in her brain and drama in everything she saw. The pure white light of a crescent moon shone above the churchyard, glinting on the weathercock and glancing off the carved marble of those monuments high enough to be seen above the wall: urns, angels, an obelisk. Mary averted her eyes. Even death looked beautiful in this moonlight, but it was still death, and not something she wanted to dwell on.

They walked slowly down the village high street and Mary felt her jagged mood smooth out with the peace and the summer scents wafting from every garden. There was still day enough to see, by some of the cottage doors, roses growing up the wall. In the limited light, the red ones smouldered and the corals glowed deep orange pink. Was there, Mary wondered, anything quite so pretty as old stone and roses together? The one ancient, hard-wearing, plain, rough and grey, the other delicate, transient, beautiful, soft and bright. The purely functionary set against the purely decorative. The contrast was exquisite.

On another cottage, an impressive wisteria in full flower spread across the front. Mary, who had an idea of how long these things took to grow, slowed down to admire it as she passed, noting in the dim light the silvery, twisted branches holding the heavy, bell-like blooms, each emitting a faint scent and sporting a range of colours from resounding violet to palest blue.

While it seemed to Mary that everyone should be out in this soft, velvety, perfumed air, she was glad that they were not, and that she and Monty were alone. There were, after all, few evenings left together. Each one must be special, memorable, beautiful.

They walked out of the village, on the road that led up to the moor. It was darker now and the colours were fading completely; the bright green and white of the hedgerows, even the red of the occasional spattering of poppies, now showed in shades of grey. Cows stood or lay in the fields they passed, nudging each other, murmuring and exclaiming. Birds settling down for the night chirruped in the bushes, and now and then, soft and low, an owl could be heard amid other, less identifiable squawks and squeals; foxes, Mary imagined. Or cats. One never really knew. But the countryside at night was never silent.

Above the cows and the squalling birds spread the deep blue of the evening sky against which the stars lay back and shimmered. The Plough was visible, glittering over the trees and fields.

She slid a glance at her husband; his profile was creased in thought. He was, she knew, somewhere around the North Pole. Would Monty think of all this when he was out amid the snow wastes? Or even when he was in Notting Hill? It had been a kind offer, but something about it nagged at Mary. Should he really have said yes?

She found herself dwelling on Beth. What must it be like to be her? It wasn't so much her new and pretty clothes, fashionable house or obviously high level of grooming that provoked Mary's envy, but the simple things, the amazing feeling it must be to get in a car and know it would work. Or turn on a bath tap and know water would come out. Hot water at that. She parted with a longing sigh.

'What's the matter?' asked Monty, dragged from his thoughts and looking momentarily disorientated.

'I was just thinking about Beth,' Mary said, deciding not to go into the bath taps and car aspects. 'She's so pretty.'

'Is she?' Monty asked, surprised. 'I mean, of course she's very nice, asking me to stay and all that, but . . .' He stopped, flustered.

Mary tried to sound shocked, whilst inwardly rejoicing. 'Don't you think she's attractive?' Personally, she had been mesmerised by Beth's glowing oval face, her shining blond hair, her sparkling blue eyes, her clear-glossed lips out of which an endless stream of excited and approving sounds emerged. And which concealed some of those large, white, straight American teeth besides which Mary's own felt as crooked as the churchyard gravestones, even if they weren't.

'Not as nice as you,' Monty said, pausing. They were out of the village now, on the moor road.

'Beth's very beautiful,' Mary asserted, pausing beside him. 'Not as beautiful as you. Or as . . .'

As he turned to face her fully, she saw, in the limited light, that his eyes had narrowed. His long mouth twitched. She felt a tingle of answering excitement in her breasts. He drew her to him, roughly for him, and at the contact with his chest her eyes flicked open and she gasped. Surely he didn't mean . . . now.

Mary giggled as her husband slid his long arms about her and hungrily kissed her neck. She could feel from the part of him pressed to her thigh that he really did mean now.

'Come on,' he murmured, pushing back her hair with his long hands and staring into her eyes. 'I'll be gone by this time next week. We have to make the most of each other.'

The place where they now stood, devouring each other with kisses, was by a farm gate. Gasping, giggling, pulsing with wine and lust, they fell through the gateway into the field. As Monty held her close, Mary's cheek pressed against the soft, cold grass. The warm tears began to spill.

'Oh Monty,' she sobbed, clinging to him as if she would never let him go.

Chapter 34

'I can't believe what you're telling me,' Alexandra shouted down her state-of-the-art mobile so loudly that the teenage soap star and the daytime TV presenter having their toenails done next to her in Robby Trendy's VIP section leapt several inches out of their chairs with shock. 'What is these people's problem?'

'Prob*lems*,' Barrie Hemsworth, Deputy Chief Planning Officer for Mineford Town Council, gently corrected her. He was a stickler for grammar and felt himself and Lynne Truss to be fighting a losing battle against the rest of the world in this respect.

'I'm afraid there have been some objections to your planning proposals,' he informed Alexandra in the light, calm, detached voice that was his stock in trade. He swung his revolving office chair jauntily round as he spoke. People who thought that working in the council planning office was boring just had to be joking. It was a damn sight more interesting than Rubbish or Pest Control, that was for sure.

Of all the many aspects of his job he relished, Barrie particularly loved Objections. People got so het up when their cherished schemes were refused. Admittedly, most of the things refused were quite small beer; garages usually, the odd conservatory. Nothing on this scale, certainly. Alexandra Pigott's plans for the site of Betrothal Cottage, Allsop, were, it was safe to say, absolutely unprecedented.

'But what can they possibly object to?' Alexandra stormed, glaring, through her sunglasses, at her own face in the mirror as she waited for her highlights to take. 'All I'm doing is knocking down a shack and building a house with seven bedrooms with en suite bathrooms, panorama lounge, duplex dining room, library and billiard room, private cinema, wine cellar, indoor and outdoor pools, private gym and sauna, stable block, helicopter pad, indoor driving range and underground garaging for two sports cars, four four-wheel drives, a Mini Moke and a Winnebago. Plus a fifteen-foot-high security wall. Just what is wrong with my plans?'

Barrie cleared his throat. With the hand that was not holding the telephone he smoothed down his brown tie over his beige, short-sleeved epauletted shirt. Alexandra Pigott's question was a good one in that it was difficult to know how to start to answer it.

When the plans had come into the department, they had caused a sensation. The whole of Planning had crowded round the small table across which Alexandra's vision was spread.

Less surprising was the sight, shortly after Alexandra Pigott's plans had been shelved and ticketed, of Morag Archbutt-Pesk storming into the planning department.

Morag Archbutt-Pesk was a well-known figure in the Mineford planning department. No one in the entire council area had opposed as many plans as she had, and to planning department staff, the sight of the unmistakable mop of aubergine hair at public meetings was as familiar as the pub they routinely repaired to afterwards. Morag's reasons for opposing plans were often difficult to fathom; in general she seemed against any venture, however innocent.

'I demand my rights,' she had thundered in a voice that almost raised the artificially lowered roof, 'to see the plans proposed for the development of Betrothal Cottage, Allsop.'

Barrie had calmly got up from his revolving office chair and walked to the large beechwood cupboard where the thousands of plans currently under submission to the county council were stored. Instantly he drew out the folder marked with the number allotted to the Betrothal Cottage plan in the council's filing system. This astonishing speed was due less to Barrie's numerical memory than it was to the large red exclamation mark that some wit had drawn on Alexandra's plans underneath the council filing number. It was the only plan in the huge cupboard thus distinguished, and was therefore easy to spot.

Barrie opened the file and returned to his desk. He busied himself with various bits and pieces of administration, all the while keeping an eye on Morag poring over the plans. Secretly, he was surprised. He had expected more of a reaction; Morag had been known to explode over perfectly innocent garden sheds. Her calmness given the extraordinary nature of what she was looking at now was striking. She seemed to radiate satisfaction. Indeed, Barrie thought, squinting in order to make out her expression more clearly, Morag almost looked happy.

Alexandra, sitting in the salon, was anything but happy. This was disastrous news. 'But I got the hottest contemporary architects on the planet, Wak Wak Oops, to design everything,' she objected. 'They're Dutch and incredibly trendy.'

'Er, I'm not sure that's relevant,' Barrie murmured, pulling gently on his pepper-and-salt moustache. 'It's not the designers that are being objected to, it's the design.'

'So what's wrong with the design?' barked the Robby Trendy end of the line.

Barrie pulled towards him the first of many sheets of recycled A4 on which Morag's forty objections were scrawled in green ink. He cleared his throat as he tried to find one less damning than the rest to begin with.

'One objection was that there was no consultation with locals whatsoever, on the part of either the developer or their architect.'

One hundred and fifty miles south, in the VIP section of Robby Trendy's salon, Alexandra slammed her flute of complimentary champagne so hard against the arm of her purple-damask-covered boudoir chair that both glass and chair threatened to shatter. 'What do you mean, no consultation?' she snapped.

Barrie rubbed his eyes under his glasses. 'Well, that no one local spoke to anyone connected with the development. You know, when the architects were up there, taking measurements, assessing the land and so on. They must have been on several visits. The objector feels they should have been made available to explain their plans.'

Behind her oversized shades, Alexandra rolled her eyes. How could she explain to this hopeless yokel that the multi-award-winning Wak Wak Oops of Utrecht were far too cool, cutting edge and wildly expensive an architectural firm to do anything as hopelessly last century as actually visit a place where they planned to build a house. It was all done on

screen, using state-of-the-art simulated landscape programmes and bird's-eye-view digimaps. Allsop had been
surveyed and the house designed without the architect having
to leave his computer in Holland. She attempted to convey
this to Barrie.

Barrie's eyes widened as he tried to imagine how Morag
Archbutt-Pesk would react to this information. 'Er, even so,
there are objections to the proposed design,' he muttered.

Of the reflective black glass that was the proposed exterior
material for the entire building she had written, 'It's going to
look like an effing building society headquarters.' With such
force that the pen had at several points gone through the paper.
Barrie repeated this to Alexandra without referring to the effing
or the force.

'Building society!' Alexandra shrieked, making the
daytime TV presenter's pedicurist's brush slip in shock. The
daytime TV presenter glared at her. Bugger, thought
Alexandra, realising her chances of appearing as a guest on
that show were now over. 'It's not supposed to look the same
as everywhere else around it,' she roared at Barrie. 'It's what
Wak Wak Oops call . . . um . . .' she rummaged in her brain
for the term, '. . . creative contrast.'

Barrie's eyebrows shot up and came down again. That was
a new one on him. You thought you'd heard it all in this
game, but there was always something you hadn't. 'The
fifteen-foot-high security wall . . .' he muttered next,
referring to Morag's list.

'Wak Wak Oops say concrete with projecting glass shards
and barbed wire along the top is the best possible material,'
Alexandra stormed. 'Don't these idiots realise, John and I are
celebrities. We need protection. We're not like normal people.'

Barrie mopped his now moist balding head and reflected

on the undoubted truth of the last sentence. And possibly the one before, about them needing protection. Because Morag Archbutt-Pesk had left the planning office vowing, calmly but vehemently, that Betrothal Towers would get the go-ahead over her dead body. An outcome which, as more than one of Planning remarked afterwards, was almost worth contravening conservation area regulations for.

Barrie ploughed on, squinting to make out Morag's increasingly agitated scrawl. She had obviously become more furious as her list went on. 'Another objection cites the needs of first-time rural home-buyers who have fallen off the housing ladder.'

Alexandra blinked. She had not the faintest idea what Barrie was talking about. Something about people falling off ladders. 'All our builders will be fully insured,' she snapped. 'Or Polish.'

Barrie decided to wind the conversation up. It was approaching lunchtime.

'There will be a public meeting where everyone can come and state their objections,' he now told Alexandra. He named a date within the next month.

In the salon, Alexandra whipped out her BlackBerry. 'I can't come then,' she snapped. 'I'm down to the last three for a part on *Midsomer Murders*.' She huffed as she shoved the BlackBerry away. That *The Clink*, the celebrity reality prison show to which she had pinned all her hopes for super-stardom, was not now, after all, going to happen had been the other hefty blow she had sustained recently. Max had called only yesterday with the news that the idea had been pulled after widespread objections that it trivialised the prison service. The offer of the *Midsomer Murders* audition had not been much compensation.

Barrie was impressed, however. He and his wife were big *Midsomer Murders* fans. 'What's the part?'

'A corpse, if you must know,' Alexandra muttered in a low voice. As Max had said, playing a corpse was a start. Or an end, depending on how you viewed it.

Barrie ran his stubby fingers through his thinning salt-and-pepper hair. 'These dates are immovable, I'm afraid, and if you're not around to defend your application there's little chance it will get approval.' Although, frankly, there was next to no chance anyway, so far as he could see. What exactly was a teppanyaki kitchen? And an underground driving range in Allsop seemed inadvisable, especially given the large network of caves that existed in the area. People might never see their golf balls again.

'Or you could always take evasive action,' Barrie suggested.

'Er . . .' said Alexandra hesitantly. What did evasive mean, exactly?

'Withdraw the application,' Barrie supplied, gallantly.

Alexandra shot upright so suddenly she felt something go in her side. 'Withdraw it?' she gasped, clutching her hip. 'Are you mad?'

Up the line, Barrie sniffed and spread his clean fingernails consideringly out on the desk in front of him. 'It is my considered opinion that to proceed with the development as it stands—'

'But it *doesn't* stand,' Alexandra cut in, her voice faint from the pain in her hip. 'That's the whole bloody point.'

'To proceed with the application as it currently is,' Barrie rephrased himself, 'would be most injudicious. The level of local opposition to your proposed development is such that defeat is inevitable.'

Alexandra gazed across the salon in miserable disbelief. Her lower lip trembled. Then, from a hundred and fifty miles north, she heard the reedy voice of Barrie again.

'You could always resubmit it,' he suggested.

Hope flashed through Alexandra. 'What, the same one? Great. I'll do that then.'

Barrie sighed. This was all rather more difficult than he had anticipated. He straightened his oatmeal tie and stared fixedly at the set of his flat gold watch – for twenty-five years' service – amid the greying hair of the forearm exposed by his beige short-sleeved summer shirt. The queue for lunch would have formed by now.

'Not as it is, no. My advice would be to submit something completely different. Start afresh.'

Alexandra thought of the bills from Wak Wak Oops. 'But I've spent a fortune on a cutting-edge design.'

'I'd advise something more vernacular,' Barrie advised.

Alexandra frowned again. Weren't vernaculars something you got on the soles of your feet?

'By which I mean more villagey, more in tune with the buildings around. More traditional, smaller, less eye-catching . . .'

'More like the bloody shack that's there at the moment, you mean,' Alexandra fumed.

'Precisely,' Barrie said lightly. 'My advice to you, Miss Pigott, is to withdraw the current application and submit another in due course which involves only necessary restructuring and rebuilding of the present building, Betrothal Cottage, in order to render it habitable again.'

Alexandra gasped. Could it be true? The planning officer was advising her – nay, implying that her only chance was to rebuild the filthy, rotting, rusting pile next to the betrothal stone?

'But it's a fucking matchbox,' Alexandra howled. 'It's got four bedrooms at the absolute most.'

Barrie, whose own home boasted only three, frowned at this. 'It's up to you, Miss Pigott,' he remarked smoothly. His eye caught the office clock. Ten to twelve, and he happened to know corned beef hash was on the canteen menu today. There'd be a stampede; the hash made by Elaine, the canteen manager, was famed throughout the county offices and people had been known to come to blows.

'If you wish to proceed down my recommended route,' he informed Alexandra briskly, 'I can furnish you with the details of several local architects who specialise in the sympathetic restoration of historic and village properties. I'm afraid I must go, Miss Pigott, so can I take it that the application as it currently stands – sorry, exists – is withdrawn?'

'I just can't believe it,' Alexandra wailed, clutching in anguish at the foils on her head. Robby Trendy, terror in his eyes, immediately dashed over and inspected them.

Chapter 35

It was a hot, quiet afternoon on the allotments. Mary was planting leeks and trying not to worry about Monty, who had been in London on his training course for several days now. He had called her daily, but finances inhibited lengthy calls, even if Beth could be heard in the background loudly encouraging Monty to stay on the phone as long as he liked. But because Beth was in the background, Mary was unable to ask Monty what the Ferraro house in Notting Hill was like. 'It's, erm, very nice' didn't paint the fullest of pictures. But Monty was a man of few words at the best of times and she doubted, even had he been alone in the house, that she would have found out much more.

About his training he was more forthcoming. 'They're feeding me up, Mary!' he told her. 'Got to put on about two stone for the expedition.'

She had felt a pang at this. The times that she, with her love of cooking, had tried to feed Monty up too. But he had never been interested.

'They're making me run around with three tyres attached to my back,' he had added.

'Why?'

'Because it's the same weight as the sled I'll be pulling with all my things on it.'

Mary felt she was pulling the weight of three tyres around inside her heavy heart.

Still, at least one of them was happy. And hopefully Beth and Benny, when they came up this weekend, would be able to give her more details.

Mary glanced over at the Ferraros' allotment. Given that the Americans had had theirs a mere few weeks, as she herself had, and also given the fact that they spent all week in London, the amount they had achieved was, Mary considered, remarkable. The amount they had bought, even more so. The Ferraro plot bristled with expensive equipment. There were pastel-painted pots; lengths of polytunnel; terracotta forcing jars; chairs, a table, a wrought-iron pergola and a covered area beneath which the tractor and rotivator were parked. A shining battalion of chrome royal-warrant-stamped forks, rakes, spades and trowels, all with turned mahogany handles, were stored in a doll's-house-like shed that was painted a muted sage and with rose-printed curtains at the square window. It had arrived in one piece on the back of a lorry; the driver, to Beth's disgust, had refused point blank to carry it up the stepped path and in the end it had been dismantled and dragged into position by a grunting, sweating Benny.

Inside it, as well as the forks, Beth and Benny had installed a battery-operated cappuccino machine. 'Why don't you just set up a McDonald's on the allotments and have done with it?' Mary once heard Morag snarl at them.

On Mary's own plot, by contrast, there was little to see apart from turned brown earth punctuated with rows of

string to mark the places neatly and gradually planted out
with suitable vegetables whose seeds or plants she bought
whenever she saw any cheap enough. Mary trawled the
garden centres and DIY shops, looking for bargains, as well as
Mineford's one remaining greengrocer, who sometimes had
seeds too, as did the supermarket.

The potatoes were showing the tiniest of shoots already,
which was particularly pleasing. Mary had been delighted to
discover from Ernest Peaseblossom that small, greenish
potatoes that had started to sprout were eminently suitable
for the purposes of propagation. She had, a mere few days
ago, discovered a cache of just such potatoes under one of
Monty's many maps that were still, notwithstanding his
departure, spread about the kitchen, and, being made of old,
thick, oilcloth-like material, tended to frustrate all efforts to
fold them up neatly, or fold them at all.

She took a deep breath of satisfaction, savouring the
feeling of calm that was the most unexpected of the benefits
of her allotment. The whole venture had originally been
about producing good food cheaply, and perhaps meeting a
few people while doing so. But it had turned out to be so
much more. She had found she loved the feeling of earth
beneath her fingertips, the satisfying turn of the spade or hoe
to the interest of the ever-present robin who hopped about
the borders hopeful for a chance and juicy worm.

Admittedly, the first couple of visits had been hard and
dull; picking, with her bare hands, the many stones and
other rubbish out of the earth. But then she had invested in
the cheapest possible bargain-basement set of tools from the
Mineford pound shop and found this transformed everything. Never could £3.99 have been better spent, Mary had
thought, turning over the chunks of wet earth with her

plastic-handled spade and hoe and enjoying their chocolate hue and cold metallic smell. With the help of proper implements – well, proper-ish – it all looked so different so quickly; from neglected rough patch to rich potential seedbed.

She enjoyed the planning of her patch, loved standing up every now and then and admiring the view from the hill over the sun-soaked village below. It was hard work, but cathartically so. Mary dug away her frustrations, fears and worries about Monty, and the exercise, she found, had improved her sleep. While even the clouded mirrors of Underpants were incapable of obscuring the fresher, rosier look that sunshine and fresh air had already brought to her skin.

She looked over to where, several patches away, laboured the bent and ancient frame of the only other person on the allotments this afternoon, eighty-something Ernest. Mary had grown fond of the dignified old man who worked almost as long on his allotment as she did on hers.

The air was so sweet and still that Mary could hear Ernest grunting and panting now, even from where she knelt in the earth some distance away, trowel in hand.

Ernest, too, was doggedly planting out something. The warm afternoon sun winked on the metal fastenings of his braces and glittered in the drip permanently at the end of his large and red-veined nose. Mary thought she had never seen anyone with nostrils quite as large as those of Mr Peaseblossom.

He put them to good use, however. The first time Mary saw him bend, scoop up a handful of earth and press it to his nose, she had thought he was, after some ancient and rustic fashion, wiping it. But after seeing him repeat the action a number of times she had plucked up the courage to ask him what he was doing. Ernest Peaseblossom had explained in a stentorian bellow that sniffing the earth you intended to put vegetables in was very important. He could, he shouted, detect certain nutrients through smell alone and that helped him decide what to grow where. 'THE ANSWER,' he yelled, turning small, bright, amphibian eyes on Mary, 'LIES IN THE SOIL.'

Mary had been impressed. Ernest Peaseblossom was clearly the vegetable-growing equivalent of those great Noses who dictated the fortunes of the famous perfume houses. And Ernest's past was, accordingly, not without its glamour. He had, she discovered, once been a professional gardener on a big estate somewhere in the county. To her disappointment, this had not been Underpants, although, fascinatingly, Ernest had known the last gardener at Weston Underwood and was puzzled to hear about the lead poisoning. The land had been fine when he had known about it.

'No longer,' said Mary.

'A POOR DO, THAT,' Ernest remarked, shaking his head sorrowfully.

Mary had been excited at this tangible connection with Weston Underwood in its glory days until Mr Peaseblossom had shouted, with a dismissive sniff, that the last gardener 'WERE A FUNNY FELLER AND 'E DRANK AN' ALL.'

Ernest's own horticultural glory days, Mary heard, had ended with the death of the estate owner and the parcelling up and selling of the land to descendants who had in turn sold it to property speculators. 'AYE, THERE'S HEXECUTIVE HAPARTMENTS NOW OVER WHERE I USED TO GROW ME PRIZE DAHLIAS,' he bawled at Mary. Ernest was now in sheltered accommodation in Allsop which, 'ALREET' though it was, was surrounded by concrete flagstones and thus lacked horticultural opportunities. A widower, but without children or grandchildren, he missed his garden and had leapt – as much as an octogenarian could leap – at the opportunity to have some land of his own at the allotments meeting.

Mary bent back down to work, to lose herself in contemplation of her beloved green tips, each already well known to her and whose individual development she was hovering over like an anxious mother does a child.

And very possibly, she was aware, instead of a child. Let alone a husband. But, ridiculous though it was, she knew, the potatoes she had planted, that had sheltered beneath his maps, felt like a connection with Monty. As long as the potatoes flourished, Mary felt sure, Monty would be fine.

'I won't ask,' said Mrs St John Goodenough, seeing her husband's face as he put the telephone down.

'No, don't,' he replied in a voice that sent her eyes firmly downwards to the onion she was stitching on the cod-Elizabethan herbal sampler intended for her daughter-in-law's Christmas present.

At the sharp sound of the unscrewing of the whisky bottle, Veronica looked up again. St John was splashing great slugs of Lagavulin into a tumbler. 'But you're not a whisky drinker,' she said faintly.

'I *wasn't*,' St John corrected.

The world where he had drunk socially, moderately with dinner or as a pleasant late-night nip to send him off to slumberland was now gone. That was the world before Morag Archbutt-Pesk had joined him at the helm of the Allsop Allotment Association. The hell in which he now existed required relief through large quantities of powerful alcohol administered regularly.

After the whisky had glowed in his veins for a few moments, he felt calmer and more capable of rational enquiry.

Oh, why had he done it? Why had he made her vice president? But what choice had he had? He might control the allotments in theory, but in practice, as he had failed to secure one himself, his foothold was more slippery than Allsop high street in a downpour.

Nor was this the only way in which Morag had disturbed his peace. She had seized control ultimately by suggesting that he, as president, had serious and direct responsibilities for the allotments, despite the fact he didn't have one himself. These ranged from health and safety directives to potential legal liability should someone's annual vegetable yield fall below their expectations. Had he, she demanded, taken out personal insurance?

After a few sleepless nights St John had decided that, far from being a pleasant and public-spirited diversion, the allotments were a potential legislative timebomb in which carrot blight could see him and Veronica living the rest of their lives in penury. He needed, as Morag said, to share the responsibility. He gave in and gave her a role. He had lived to regret it. But would he, St John wondered, live much longer?

'She's demanding that we cultivate the allotments with a horse and plough,' St John whispered to his wife.

Chapter 36

Allsop looked very chocolate-boxy tonight, Philip thought as, home from work, he hurried up the village street to his own front door. In the ochreous evening light, the textured fronts of the old stone cottages seemed to glow, their windows gleaming and the geraniums on their sills positively aflame. Philip stopped short to absorb a sun-warmed mullion here, a rich burst of green garden there, admiring as he rarely did the differing angles of the cottages, the up-and-down line of the roofs, grouped in a harmony all the more striking for being the result of accident; simple need and circumstance rather than any particular desire to please the eye.

He decided to go up to his vegetable plot. After a day wrestling with the finer points of conveyancing and setting up sheltering trust funds, it would, he imagined, be rather relaxing to plunge his spade into the earth and simply dig. It was time he gave the allotment some proper attention. He'd only been there once since he was allotted it, after all.

It was a warm evening. Even the cottage's shadowy upstairs bedroom felt stuffier than usual. Philip laid his dark suit across the bed and looked in the wardrobe for something suitable to work the land in. Here was an old blue T-shirt, here some creased but serviceable chinos. He was not, Philip had discovered, particularly talented with the iron and in the end had succumbed to the invitation of the local launderette to stuff his clean, dry washing in a bin bag and give it to them. He did this every Monday, and every Friday he picked up a large armful of pressed clothes, each on their individual wire hanger. It was some comfort, although not much.

Philip went to the deeply recessed window and looked out, trying to assess the weather. Would it get cold later? The sunlight on the neighbour's garden across the lane was still rich and bright, but one never knew. He remembered a light jacket somewhere; shabby but comfortable, bought off a second-hand clothes stall when he was a student. That would be just the thing.

He rummaged in the wardrobe for it. It was not hanging up, not even at the back. Nor had it fallen down. It was not in a creased heap behind the shoes, spare pillows, additional blankets and other general detritus. Strange. Perhaps it had been lost at the dry cleaner's.

This grey sweatshirt would do instead. Philip pulled it out, closed the wardrobe door – and then remembered.

The jacket. The jacket he had been looking for. It was the jacket he had been wearing. That night.

The sledgehammer of memory socked him in the guts. Doubled up, gasping, Philip scrambled on to the bed and lay there panting, his knees in his chest, his eyes painfully tightly shut. But not tightly enough to stop, behind his eyelids, images flaring and flickering.

He was standing on the hard shoulder of a dark motorway. He was struggling with someone – a big, powerful man – in a green fluorescent coat. 'Leave me alone!' Philip heard himself yelling, straining to look back over his shoulder at the heap of buckled and twisted metal under which was his wife.

He had to get to her. Get all that stuff off her. But all the wrenching and pulling he was capable of was unequal to the grip of the man in the fluorescent jacket. 'Let me go!' Philip now heard himself screaming.

'Let me go,' he sobbed now, opening his eyes and finding not the hellish scene of Emily's death, but the white bedroom ceiling and the bare bulb he had not yet bought a shade for. It was over. He was alive. It was a miracle. Yet was it, really? It seemed to him that those blurred, confused, semi-concussed hours in the motorway darkness as the ambulance sirens blared and the traffic screamed by, when he, all unknown to himself, had several broken ribs and a badly cut face, were a state of comparative bliss. He had not known, then, that it was all over.

Philip strode quickly to the bathroom and splashed his face with cold water. He walked shakily around the house for a few minutes, breathing deeply, before pulling open the front door. The rich blaze of evening colour, warmth and scent sprang on him like a cat.

He walked down the high street, slowly at first, then faster, as strength and purpose returned to his limbs. Eventually, feeling almost cheerful, he twirled the first Mr Palfrey's spade over his shoulder.

'Hi ho, hi ho, it's off to work we go,' someone shouted mockingly after him as he strode through the centre of the village.

Philip turned round in surprise. People did not normally shout discouraging remarks at each other in Allsop, although no doubt they made enough of them behind closed doors. He looked around for the shouter.

Sitting on the base of the ancient market cross outside the equally ancient pub was a thin, dark-haired boy. He looked, Philip thought, about eight although it was difficult to be sure with that hooded top pulled over his face. What he was sure of was that the figure radiated hostility. 'Hi ho,' the boy shouted again for good measure. Philip flicked him a disapproving glance – unpleasant little swine – and continued on his way.

As he heaved up the steep-stepped lane towards the allotment field, Philip could see that a number of people were on site. As he ascended further, his breath coming in short, painful pulls as the gradient increased, his stomach knotted with apprehension at the prospect of having to socialise. Meeting new people was not his favourite thing. That had been one of Emily's talents. At the thought of her, he felt panic rise. The jacket had been a tremendous shock. He had still not recovered. But he was out in public and he must seem to be in control.

It was difficult not to think of her again, however, as he entered the farm gate into the allotment field. Emily would, Philip knew, have read up on allotments copiously and had the whole plot planned out by now.

He gripped the handle of his spade determinedly and looked around. The air seemed to shake with activity. There were shouts, agitation. What was going on?

At the top end of the field, just where the flat bit started to slope, some people were trying to persuade a large grey horse to leave. It had, Philip imagined, got in by accident and was stamping about, obviously reluctant to co-operate with the evacuation programme.

'Come on, boy,' shouted a strident voice he recognised. It was that of the domineering woman with the purple trousers.

Her ineffectual partner was there too, Philip saw without pleasure, and the idiot with the blue velvet top hat. Considering there were three of them and only one horse, they seemed to be making little progress in persuading it off the land. One would have thought, in common with any other sensible mammal, that it could not get away from them fast enough.

There was something strange about the horse's position. Just to make sure, Philip scrabbled in his pocket for the plan he had been sent by the Allsop Allotments Association. His plot, he knew, was one of those furthest from the gate, towards the corner of the field where the flat bit sloped. Somewhere near where the horse was.

As Philip approached, he saw that his plot was not only near where the horse was. It actually was where the horse was. The horse was on his allotment.

Morag, busy with the animal's back end, had not noticed the solicitor enter the allotment field. She was unpleasantly surprised when the tall, sober figure, unfamiliarly dressed in chinos and an old grey sweatshirt, loomed into view. 'What's that horse doing there?' Philip asked mildly but firmly, eyeing the large and frightening animal which, he now saw, appeared to have something strapped to its back end.

'Facilitating a non-fossil-fuel-guzzling, non-ozone-layer-damaging, tradition-lifestyle-respecting bio-ethical organic means of land cultivation,' Morag shot back immediately.

'Sorry?'

'Ploughing,' Morag snapped. What did it look like? The horse had a plough attached to it, did it not? Was the man an idiot?

'*Ploughing?*' Philip repeated. He stood silently for a few seconds, computing the situation. He looked at it from several ways, not one of which made sense.

The horse was not ploughing, for a start. It obviously hated and feared the machinery strapped to its bottom and equally obviously had no idea what to do with it. The result was that it was turning in a tight circle whose centre was molten mud, while the outside remained tough and tufty grass. The molten mud, moreover, was Philip's own.

'There appears to be a misunderstanding,' Philip concluded eventually. 'This is my allotment and you are, er, ploughing it with a horse. I don't recall either asking you to or giving you permission.'

Gid, behind his partner, experienced a tremor of apprehension. He had been less than certain about putting this particular part of her Vision into practice. But Morag had been determined and you could see from her expression that she still was. You had to admire her, and he did. He had no other choice.

Morag, meanwhile, had placed her hands on her hips and was staring challengingly at Philip. 'These allotments are part of a traditional village settlement,' she announced. 'They should be cultivated in a traditional organic way respecting the earth and the methods of our forefathers.'

'These allotments,' Philip replied, 'are the property of the individuals to whom they have been assigned. It is up to them how they cultivate them, no rules having been established in that respect.'

In the background, Gid listened worriedly. He was starting to wonder whether the ploughing idea had been such a great one after all.

It had been fine in theory, but as soon as they had arrived at the actual allotment with an actual horse – borrowed from someone Dweeb knew – and a plough – borrowed too, albeit without her knowing, from Gid's mother's garden where it had served as a charmingly rustic curiosity – things hadn't gone to plan.

The horse had failed to go on to Morag and Gid's allotment, for a start. It had gone straight to Philip's patch and stayed there; the patch contained, it appeared, some sort of grass of which it was fond. It was at this point that Morag decided on her most audacious plan of action yet. Why not? she argued. The know-all solicitor had only been to the allotments once. He was obviously not interested and they should therefore claim squatter's rights on his land and simply plough that first.

Only now Philip had turned up, and that rather changed things. For all her fighting talk, determination to appear in command and general bristling aggression, Morag felt less so than usual. Even she had to accept that the ploughing initiative had not been a success. She had been outraged to discover it was nowhere near as easy as it looked in medieval illustrations.

Philip, meanwhile, was looking at the horse, which looked as fed up as he was. He felt sorry for it. Whoever's fault all this was, it wasn't the horse's. 'Now will you please get your horse off and let me get on my land,' he instructed Morag.

But Morag was not giving up that easily. 'Whether or not this is still your land is open to question,' she stated, her solid boots, soled in yellow rubber with uppers of rainbow-coloured leather, unmoving in the earth. 'You hardly ever come here. It was therefore decided that the neighbouring plots could establish squatter's rights.'

'Haven't we just been through this?' Philip asked, catching the eye of Gid, who snatched his gaze away in terror.

'Not with regard to neighbouring plots and their rights over untended neighbouring plots,' Morag snapped.

'I see,' Philip said calmly. 'And who owns the neighbouring plots to mine?'

'Gid and me, Dweeb and Vicky and Gudrun and Tecwen.'

'Ah.' Rather as Philip had thought. The woman's audacity was astounding. 'Allow me, as a law practitioner, to give you a free piece of legal advice,' he addressed Morag. 'Squatter's rights, in as much as they apply anywhere, certainly don't apply to this situation. Now will you please get off my land and on to yours.'

'And leave it to your ruinous, tradition-disrespecting methods of cultivation, I suppose,' Morag snarled, realising, if not quite accepting, that she was defeated.

'If that's what you call this,' Philip sighed, holding up Mrs Palfrey's old spade. Enough time, as he saw it, had been wasted. 'Look, I'd quite like that animal removed, actually. It's preventing me from getting on with my digging.'

Neither Morag, Dweeb nor Gid made any move. The latter two especially.

'Will you please get that horse off my plot?' Philip repeated.

Morag mumbled something sulky. Philip did not quite catch it. 'I'm sorry?'

'I can't,' Morag muttered tersely. 'It won't move. I can't make it.'

Philip frowned. 'But it's yours, isn't it?'

Morag's aubergine hair whirled in a negative.

'Then,' Philip enquired patiently, 'who does it belong to?'

'It's not ours,' Dweeb said hurriedly.

'It's dangerous,' Gid said feebly.

'It doesn't like men,' said Dweeb.

'And who can blame it?' snarled Morag.

The horse's eyes were rolling and one vast hoof was pawing at the muddy ground. Its big, wide body jittered, as if it might do anything at any moment.

'Can I help?' asked a voice.

The company turned to see the headmistress in her jeans and white T-shirt striding towards the horse with the confidence of one who had dealt with such situations all her life. 'I used to ride as a child,' Catherine explained as she approached the pawing, snorting animal. 'C'm'n, boy,' she murmured, stretching out one slim hand.

Her fingers moved closer to the horse and patted its snorting, jerking nose. Immediately the animal seemed calmer and was soon soothed enough for Catherine to capture its bridle.

'Well done,' said Philip, enthusiastically. He felt surprise, as well as a stirring of admiration. The headmistress clearly had hidden depths. That was a brave thing she had done. He certainly would never have risked it.

Catherine's attention, however, was entirely on the horse, to whom she was murmuring soothingly. 'What's all this?' she asked, examining the contraption behind it. 'It looks like one of those ornamental ploughs you get in gardens.' She stared at the small group incredulously, especially the solicitor. What was he doing here? She had imagined him a sensible, intelligent person.

Philip, while gratified to see Morag redden, felt suddenly anxious to distance himself from the others. He did not want Catherine to think he was in any way involved. 'It would be great,' he said to the headmistress, 'if you could just take it to the gate and tie it up. And then perhaps,' he added to Morag, 'you could arrange for whoever owns the unfortunate creature to come and fetch it.'

As Catherine led the animal fearlessly away, Philip found himself staring after her for some seconds. Then, turning back to his allotment, he saw that the horse had deposited a large and very useful heap of manure right in the middle of his patch. He glanced at Morag, half expecting her to claim squatter's rights over the horse dung. But for once she remained silent.

Chapter 37

Everything imaginable was going wrong, Alexandra thought furiously. She hated the people in charge of the new, revised plans for Betrothal Cottage.

Roger Hassock and Mark Hemp of Hassock & Hemp, Architects, had come down from the Midlands to the Knightsbridge apartment for a meeting with Alexandra. They were both short and softly spoken, with humpy shoulders, long, grey-streaked fringes and big, brown, mealy, woolly-collared cardigans that did up with big granite-coloured buttons. There was something troglyditic about them which Alexandra, who liked her men glossy, did not respond to.

Nor did she like the air of suppressed mirth with which the architects had emerged, copies of the *Guardian* clamped under their arms, from the leopardskin-lined private lift with baroque mirror into the marbled lobby of the penthouse. Mark Hemp had even gone so far as to say that vernacular reconstruction of the type they were proposing for the cottage – interior stone walls, reclaimed timber floors – didn't seem particularly in tune with her tastes.

They were dead right, Alexandra thought, looking at the

plans as Hemp and Hassock undid folders with the texture of wholemeal crackers and spread them out on the black lacquered dining-room table. One bathroom! One kitchen with no preparation area? Where would the hired staff go when she gave dinner parties? A tiny sitting room with a fireplace at the end, not a glass pillar in the middle over a statement gas-powered brazier? A bedroom on just one level, not the duplex she had planned, and completely lacking a balcony and floor-to-ceiling plate-glass windows?

Compared to Wak Wak Oops's designs, the new plans were dull and unadventurous beyond belief. Hemp and Hassock, lumpen and woolly against the hand-painted silver wallpaper of the dining room, even more so.

She looked up at the architects, who were watching her with what she felt certain was amusement. The certainty made her cross.

'The underground garage seems to have gone,' Alexandra said huffily.

Roger Hassock leant forward. 'Planning permission would have been very difficult,' he explained in his low, rumbling voice. 'And it would have been nearly impossible to build it, given the conditions on the site.'

Alexandra's sunglasses flashed challengingly. 'My Dutch architects managed to find a place to put it.'

At this, Mark Hemp smiled and cleared his throat. 'Ah, yes. The Utrecht firm. They didn't actually survey the site, I understand.'

Alexandra glared. 'They didn't need to. They had cutting-edge technology. They had digimaps and virtual site programmes and . . .' She paused, frowning, trying to remember the rest of the science the firm had blinded her with.

Roger Hassock's thick fingers, with his square nails and thick wedding ring, danced on the edge of the lacquer table. 'Ye-es. Quite. But sometimes even the finest, ahem, cutting-edge technology is no substitute for actually being there.'

Mark Hemp leant forward now, an understanding smile widening his wide face yet further. 'Yes, they unfortunately failed to notice the large mineshaft directly beneath the house. This limits, as I am sure you appreciate, what can be built downwards. We need to secure the house's position, not make it more vulnerable.'

As they went on in this vein, Alexandra felt impatient. All Hassock and Hemp ever talked about was problems.

Then a thought struck her. 'Hey. That's not the only land I've got in that village.'

Roger Hassock pushed out his pale, fleshy lips. He had, Alexandra noticed with distaste, pores so big they looked as if each had been dotted on his face with felt-tip. 'How do you mean, not the only land? You mean there's somewhere else we can build?'

Alexandra's hair whirled in excitement as she nodded. 'Yeah. I've got this allotment as well. Hang on a minute, I'll show you. They sent me a map of where it was.'

But Hassock and Hemp were already exchanging glances. 'I don't think that will be necessary,' Mark Hemp was saying, crushingly.

'Why not?' Alexandra, on her feet in a tight silver mini-dress, stared at them accusingly. 'They're big, aren't they?'

'Big, yes,' Roger Hassock was saying, his large, light eyes dwelling on Alexandra's hips and bosom. 'Because, because . . .' He frowned and looked at his colleague. 'What was I saying?'

'That it won't be possible to build on an allotment site,'

Mark Hemp supplied, somewhat impatiently. 'It's communal, possibly green belt, all that.'

Alexandra slumped back down at the table again. Her idea had seemed a stroke of genius, but it was a big no again. The question was, what the hell was she going to do with that allotment? Getting one had seemed such a good idea at the time, especially as it had annoyed that horrible woman. But at this rate, if she didn't find something to do with it soon she'd have to go and bloody plant things in it.

While, somewhat miraculously given their general pessimism, Hassock and Hemp seemed confident that their new, vernacular vision would overcome any possible objection from the locals, they were deeply doubtful that any workmen would be found in order to start building it any time soon.

'It's what we call the Mineford Fortnight,' explained Roger Hassock.

'The *what*?' Alexandra pulled a face. 'Is that some sort of carnival?' Of course, in the sticks, they got up to that sort of thing in the summer. She'd seen it on *Emmerdale*. Waving flags, throwing wellies and clog-dancing. Presumably it kept them from dying of boredom altogether.

'The Mineford Fortnight,' Roger smiled, 'means that whatever schedule you've got for anything, particularly building, you need to add another two weeks on to the start date. At least.'

'Why?'

'Because that's how Mineford works,' Roger Hassock said simply, opening his hands to underscore his point.

Alexandra clenched her tanned fists and rolled her eyes to the penthouse's chandeliered heavens. This was turning out to be a bad morning. An invitation to the wedding of one of

John's England team-mates had come in the post, which immediately fired her jealousy. But John's reaction had been even harder to bear.

'Let's not go,' he had pleaded, placing the invitation, personalised in gold letters on pearlised card, back on the hall table after the most cursory of glances.

'Not go!' Alexandra exclaimed, clutching her embroidered Matthew Williamson robe in horror. In her pink marabou-trimmed Jimmy Choo mules, her feet had shaken. 'But,' she had objected in a devastated croak, '*OK!*'s taking the pictures, it's at Blenheim Palace and they're having Enrique Iglesias and a honeymoon on the Galapagos islands.'

John had sighed. 'Exactly. I can't stand that sort of do. Chocolate fountains and ice sculptures of Las Vegas . . . ugh.' He had shuddered, picked up his sports bag and come to kiss her goodbye. 'I'm off to training. See you later.'

Alexandra's mouth, with its customary frosting of Iced Skinny Latte, had opened and closed in silent panic. John could not mean this. As the gold doors of the lift had slid together behind him, she had gripped the faux-marble surface of the invitation-bearing sidetable and let out a wail of sheer despair.

But, had she but known it, this was just the start of her morning's troubles. Soon after she showed a smirking Hassock and Hemp back into the leopardskin-lined lift, Max had called. She had not got the *Midsomer Murders* corpse part, after all. 'Stiff competition, baby,' Max had said breezily.

'As it were,' he added with a cackle.

Her career as an A-list celebrity, Alexandra fumed, was in danger of slipping into the B zone.

Chapter 38

Panting slightly at the steep ascent, Catherine climbed the stepped path to the field of plots in her allotment jeans but a clean, new white T-shirt. She had dressed more carefully than usual and, while make-up had seemed a step too far, she had brushed her chestnut bob before setting out. She resisted admitting directly to herself that this was all because the solicitor might be there.

She had never been up as close to and facing Philip Protheroe as during the horse incident, and he was much more attractive than he seemed from a distance. Long-lashed eyes behind his glasses and a really very nice mouth. And all that thick black floppy hair.

But of course, her interest was mere friendship – she was far too busy for relationships other than those with five to eleven year olds and their parents these days. Or with varieties of potato. And she'd always gone for exuberant blond men anyway, not dark and self-possessed ones with glasses. Widowers too; like everyone else in the village Catherine had heard the tragic story of the car crash that had killed Philip's wife. It was a story that made her tender heart churn with pity. But of course, with all that behind him, he would be a man with baggage. Even if he was interested in her, which of course he was not.

She forced her thoughts elsewhere. Would Mary be on her plot? she wondered. Their allotments faced each other yet they had said little to each other at first. Catherine had been rather intimidated both by Mary's beauty, all the more striking for its obvious effortlessness – no Julia Cooke syndrome here – and also by the apparent professionalism with which the other woman had dug her soil over. Catherine was aiming at a successful potato and perhaps an acceptable onion.

She was aware that while the progress of her own embarrassingly new spade and hoe was slow and constantly impeded by bricks, stones and compacted lumps featuring both, Mary dug as keenly as if she had been doing it all her life; her long, athletic limbs moving easily beneath her baggy shirt and torn jeans, her dark hair drawn back from her thin, pale, yet lively face.

Mary put in more hours even than Catherine did herself and already had a display that, Catherine could see, showed promise of magnificence. Her rhubarb looked good already; thick, thrusting and healthy stalks in the most wonderful shades of pink. Colour, in fact, was a hallmark of Mary's patch; she had also planted some chard which even now, at this early stage, showed glossy, curling leaves and stems the most arresting red or yellow.

But then a chance exchange revealed that Mary, like Catherine, had never had a vegetable plot of her own before either and had acquired all her tips from library books.

'Oh, and Ernest of course,' she had added, waving towards the next allotment, which seemed to Catherine to have developed with amazing speed. Ernest Peaseblossom, for all his advanced years, had planted several neat rows, installed a polytunnel and introduced an upturned bucket to sit on all in the time it had taken her to work out how to bed in a leek.

The women had soon become friends. Mary had been gratifyingly interested in Catherine being the headmistress of the school. 'What a fascinating job,' she had exclaimed. 'It must be lovely to work with children.'

Catherine, her thoughts flying instantly to Sam Binns, had tried not to pull a rueful face. It had been even harder to resist the temptation to pour all her sorrows on the boy's account into this woman's sympathetic ear, but resist Catherine did. Confidentiality was crucial in her profession; one had to be careful who one spoke to.

For her part she was intrigued to find that Mary lived in the huge house on the moor, Weston Underwood. Alone. Her husband, who Catherine vaguely remembered seeing at the allotments meeting in the village hall, was away from home at the moment, training to make an expedition to the North Pole. When Catherine had recovered from the unexpectedness of this, she was delighted. 'How glamorous!' she had exclaimed. It seemed to her that Mary's glowing face had suddenly lost some of its light, but she smiled and nodded brightly. Catherine guessed that she missed her husband. 'He'll soon be back,' she ventured, sympathetically.

'Well, he's not gone yet,' Mary confessed. 'He's still in London, training. He's staying with the Ferraros, in fact.' She gestured towards the green hut with the rose-printed curtains and the red tractor beneath its shelter.

'Oh.' Catherine was surprised. She hadn't realised the two couples were so close. But there was a lot she didn't realise about Allsop, admittedly. The Ferraros, anyway, hardly seemed to be around; after the first excitement of their allotment, they rather seemed to have lost interest. So it was difficult to keep tracks on who they were seeing socially.

The exchange had been the first stage of a lively mutual regard between the two women. They were still not quite at the point of familiarity where they arranged to garden together, but their sessions seemed increasingly to coincide. Possibly because, Catherine conceded as, tonight, she mounted the long, flat, grey stone steps leading to the allotment, both she and Mary were at their plots most evenings.

Catherine entered the allotment fields to see Mary rhythmically digging in the sunshine, dressed in her usual navy baggy trousers and T-shirt that was so huge on her it must once have belonged to her husband. It was the husband that Catherine wanted, in fact, to talk to Mary about.

She paced over the uneven grass, past plots in various stages of development, the evening sun surprisingly strong in her face. 'Hello!' she called to Mary as she approached.

Mary, squatting on her hunkers with her trowel, looked up, grinning in welcome, flicking back a tendril of dark hair and putting one long hand along her brows for shade.

'I've got an idea about your husband!' Catherine announced.

At the mention of Monty, Mary's smile broadened. In the rich light, with her dark hair, she looked, Catherine thought, positively beatific. She obviously loved this man now away in London, Catherine realised. The headmistress felt, not for the first time with Mary, a pang of envy. To feel so strongly about someone, someone one was married to, even more!

Catherine excitedly shared the idea. 'I've been talking to the children about him. Told them about what he was doing, hope you don't mind. They were really interested. So it struck me that a really great thing to do would be to track his expedition.'

With a sudden movement that frightened a couple of cabbage whites investigating some just-planted leeks, Mary clapped her hands. 'What a good idea,' she beamed.

Catherine was delighted. 'They were thrilled about him being in minus forty degree temperatures, facing polar bears, blizzards, the dangers of ice cracking beneath him at any moment and all that . . . oh sorry, you probably don't want to think about that,' she added, seeing Mary's face fall.

'Er, not really,' Mary admitted, attempting a shaky smile.

Catherine decided not to add that, of all the other gory details Mary had mentioned and which she had repeated to the children, the one that had captured their imagination most was Monty having to rub his naked body every day with handfuls of snow to slough off dead skin cells and pee out of a suit that zipped open from front to back underneath for this express purpose.

Catherine ploughed on with her idea. 'We thought we'd get maps up on the wall and chart his progress. I can call you every day and you could tell me where he is and we could show it on our map. It'll be fantastic for them to get practice in co-ordinates, mapmaking, geography . . .' Happily she ticked the units off on her fingers.

'Oh yes!' Mary exclaimed.

Her face fell again for a moment, and to Catherine the lovely, gentle face suddenly looked terribly worried and vulnerable.

'I expect it's rather scary,' the headmistress said gently. 'Him going away like that.'

Immediately Mary rallied, flashed a big smile and straightened up. 'But I'm sure it'll be all right. It's so nice he's staying with the Ferraros anyway. A comfortable start to everything.'

'Yes, they can tell you how he is,' Catherine agreed. 'When you see them.'

Mary nodded hard to shake off her face the expression of frustration that the Ferraros had not appeared since Monty went to stay with them and she hadn't liked to keep ringing the Notting Hill house. Monty, meanwhile, though he called frequently, never called for long, and as a consequence her idea of what he was doing was sketchy. The dental course had been nasty, she gathered, but that was no surprise.

The two women smiled at each other, parted by mutual silent agreement and, for the next half-hour, until Mary left, worked their allotments in companionable silence.

After she had gone, Catherine cursed herself for not asking Mary's advice about sweet peas. She had installed several rows a week earlier, but they did not seem to have stirred, and lay defeatedly on the ground around the base of their plant stake. All the books had assured her they were easy to grow, and yet it seemed impossible that these weedy, insubstantial wisps would rise and climb into that sight so redolent of summer, a thick, scented wall of rioting pink, white, red, blue and dark purply black against a frame of twisting green.

As she was pondering what to do, Catherine sensed the tread of someone approaching and, not wanting to raise her eyes, found herself staring at a horribly familiar pair of black lace-up leather shoes.

'Good evening, Miss Brooke!' the vicar's voice boomed. 'And good evening to you, young man,' it added, un-expectedly.

Catherine looked up. To her surprise Sam Binns stood,

eyes slitty and hostile beneath his hoodie, trainered feet planted apart, his entire, skinny, black-clad body radiating defiance, on the grass at the edge of her plot. How long had he been there?

'Hello, Sam,' Catherine said, welcoming yet wary.

Sam was not looking at her, however. He was frowning at Reverend Tribble, who beamed back at him.

The vicar, seemingly realising that his campaign to get more children's bottoms on pews had hardly got off to a flying start here, straightened himself up, staggering slightly on the soft earth. He flicked some smudges of dirt from his cassock.

'Not very good to garden in,' Sam remarked.

The vicar put his head on one side and gave an understanding beam. 'I beg your pardon?'

'That dress of yours,' Sam said loudly. 'Not very good to garden in.' Catherine silently agreed. It didn't look very comfortable either, especially now the weather was so warm. Perhaps if he wore a pair of trousers and a T-shirt the vicar might find he had more success with his vegetables.

The vicar's smile disappeared. 'I personally find it a suitable garment for any work the Lord sees fit to put my way,' he said stiffly.

Catherine and Sam watched him go, his cassock flapping. He presented, Catherine thought, a strangely traditional picture as he descended the long stone steps into the village. Beneath a glorious blue evening sky Allsop was looking both lovely and ancient, the rich late sunshine glowing on the higgledy-piggledy roofs and random stone of the cottages and picking out the golden weathercock on the top of the medieval church. It looked as it probably had hundreds of years ago, and its vicar did too.

Catherine turned her attention to her most difficult pupil. 'What can I do for you, Sam?' she asked.

The boy shrugged. As usual outside school, his thin, pale, pinched face was hidden in the shadowy depths of his hoodie. He lingered.

'Shouldn't you be having your supper?'

Still the boy did not reply. The headmistress suppressed a sigh at his routine rudeness and bent back to her work on the ground. No doubt Sam was here to silently sneer at her evening efforts just as he did at her daytime ones, although thankfully less obviously these days.

Well, let him, thought Catherine. Personally, she was proud of what she had achieved on her plot, not to mention her school, in a relatively short time. Things were, the cautiously optimistic Catherine felt, improving all round at Allsop Primary; while Olivia Cooke had defected as threatened, none of the other mothers murmuring about doing the same actually had. The school's headlong hurtle towards Special Measures had certainly been halted and it was now heading, slowly but surely, in the reverse direction.

As for the allotment, several evenings' and weekends' concentrated effort had resulted in earth almost cleared of all weeds and stones and beginning to look really quite allotment-like. She contemplated with satisfaction the large oblong of turned, rich, dark soil she had wrested from the stones and weeds and it seemed to her to be full of potential. It was just a shame about the sweet peas, that was all.

She was quite lost in contemplation when she heard Sam Binns say something. She looked up, surprised he was still there.

'Sorry, Sam? I was miles away.'

'I said, what have you planted?' the boy repeated, sullenly. 'What're you growing on your allotment?'

Catherine looked at him in amazement. She realised both that she had never heard him ask a question before and that this was the last question she would have expected. He stared back at her challengingly, yet with a hint of defensiveness, as if asking something represented, for him, an enormous personal risk.

'Er, oh well, the usual things I suppose,' Catherine said hurriedly, still not certain this wasn't some kind of joke. 'Potatoes, carrots, onions. That sort of thing.'

Sam nodded. 'Best be careful with the onions. Really difficult things to grow, onions are.'

Catherine blinked. Had Sam Binns just said what she thought he had said? Had he really offered an opinion about the cultivation of onions? '*Are* they?'

'Me grandad used to grow vegetables,' Sam now muttered from the depths of his hood. 'I used to help him a bit.'

'Did you?'

'He used to say water could make or break an onion crop,' Sam said, his head almost appearing in the light at the end of his hoodie tunnel.

Delighted and astonished at this unexpected opening-up, Catherine caught at the explanation. '*Did* he? *Really?* How *fascinating*!'

Even to her own ears this sounded hopelessly over the top. She sounded over-bright, forced. She saw at once that she had overreacted. Sam immediately shrank back into his hoodie and loped off.

Catherine worked for another hour, trying to erect a row of beanpoles. It was not as easy as it looked in Monty Don, who was spread out on the earth beside her and resolutely refusing to stay open at the right page.

Struggling with the canes, she thought about Sam Binns and his grandad. It was the first time she had ever heard the boy volunteer anything about his past; anything positive ever. And had she capitalised on it, recognised it for the valuable opportunity it was? No, she'd scared him off, possibly for ever, by shrieking in that patronising way.

Chapter 39

St John crashed the phone violently back into its cradle. His hands shook as he reached for the Lagavulin. Veronica looked up in concern from her sampler on which she was now finishing a carrot. 'That Archbutt-Pesk woman again?' she asked sympathetically.

The cut crystal clattered against St John's teeth as he lifted the drink to his lips. 'She's really done it now,' he muttered. His eyes as he looked at his wife were wild.

'Why, what's happened?' Veronica murmured soothingly as she put the final stitch into a feathery green frond. St John had once laughed at her fondness for embroidering vegetables, claiming it was not half so much fun as growing the real thing. But four weeks into the Allsop Allotments project Veronica considered her method of vegetable production to be the only safe one. Her carrots may not be edible, but they were satisfactory in their own way and they caused her infinitely less mental anguish than the ones on the allotments – and the allotments in general – cost her husband.

'She wants to have a communal earth closet,' the chairman

of the parish council shuddered, splashing more whisky into his tumbler. Veronica looked up.

'What's wrong with that?' she asked brightly. 'Sounds like a good idea to me.'

A kind of loud, spattery roar now came from her husband. This was the last reaction he had expected. 'An earth closet a good idea?' he gasped. Veronica was so obsessive about lavatorial hygiene that she insisted on different loos being used for number ones and number twos.

Veronica blinked faded blue eyes over her bifocals. 'Well, isn't it some sort of compost heap?'

St John shook his head so hard his jowls wobbled in the slipstream. His moustache dripped with whisky. 'No it certainly isn't,' he ground out, proceeding to spell out for Veronica's benefit exactly what it was. She turned white.

'How utterly disgusting,' she whispered after she had taken a second or two to collect herself. 'Can't you stop her?'

'In the sense that the Allies could stop the Germans after Dunkirk,' St John said bitterly.

Veronica shook her head sorrowfully and turned her eyes back to her embroidery. She was preparing mentally to start a cabbage and could have done without such dramatic distractions. 'It doesn't bear thinking about,' she murmured.

'Thinking about it's the easy bit,' St John said darkly.

Mary, on her knees in the soil, trowel in hand, was thinking about Monty as usual. It wasn't his fault, she knew. She should not get too annoyed at the fact that he was unforthcoming on the telephone. They had never been apart before; he had hardly had much practice at long and descriptive calls.

And now, soon, they were going to be apart for the

longest time they ever had. The sponsors seemed to keep changing the departure date, but sometime soon, Mary knew, Monty would be setting off for Canada, from whose northern tip he would begin his journey, walking, skiing, climbing and swimming over four hundred miles of frozen Arctic ocean to the geographic North Pole. Monty, her beloved Monty, alone with a moving and unstable ice pack beneath his boots, at the mercy of ocean currents below and winds above. With only a compass to guide him. At night, alone in the dark, cold wastes of Underpants, she was gripped with terror at the thought of her husband, his guileless blue eyes despairing, his golden lashes weighted with frost, alone in the cold wastes of the Arctic Ocean – but light cold wastes, as the area, Monty had explained, got six months of continuous daylight at this time of year.

During the day, thank God, she had the allotment.

During the few weeks that had passed since she acquired it, she had, Mary recognised, come utterly to depend on that small patch of earth. In his gnawing absence, it had almost taken over from Monty as a source of comfort and cheer and a repository of love. Since it had become hers she had visited almost every day and now knew the site and size of each emerging vegetable rather better than she knew the rooms at Underpants, some of which, in the furthest depths of the house, she was only vaguely aware of. There were rooms near the Gentlemen's Wing, Mary knew, that she had seen perhaps once in her entire time here.

'NAY, MARY, LET ME SHOW YER.'

The incredibly loud voice, interrupting her reverie, made Mary almost jump twenty feet into the air with shock. She looked up, and there stood Ernest, shaking his wizened head. He stepped forward in his muddy boots and greenish-brown trousers and carefully lowered himself down. 'YER PUT 'EM THIS FAR APART, LIKE THIS . . .' With an energy unexpected in one so old, Ernest Peaseblossom seized the radishes she was about to plant in his big gnarled hands.

'But it says in Alan Titchmarsh . . .' Mary objected faintly.

'AYE, I DARESAY.' Ernest squinted down at her. 'BUT YON TITCHMARSH FELLER 'ASN'T SEEN THE PLOT YE'RE WORKIN' IN, MARY. YER'VE GOT TER ADAPT YER PLANTS TO THE CONDITIONS. THE ANSWER . . .'

Mary smiled up at him. 'Lies in the soil.'

'Ah! I'm glad to hear you talking about the soil,' now interrupted a harsh and aggressive voice from behind.

As Ernest, apparently not hearing, continued to space the radishes, Mary twisted round to look at Morag Archbutt-Pesk. 'Yes,' she agreed, wanting to add that the soil seemed a natural enough subject, given their location, but could not bring herself to be rude, even to Morag.

'Well the soil is going to be a major beneficiary of the latest exciting innovation on the allotments,' Morag announced.

Mary squinted suspiciously up at her. She knew all about Morag's innovations. The horse episode had been the talk of the plots. 'What is it?' she asked cautiously, as Ernest's papery yellow arms continued to work busily away with her trowel.

'The ultimate recycling system!' Morag announced, slipping easily into her patter. 'Reaffirming our commitment to the environment.'

'Is it something to do with solar panels?' Mary hazarded.

'No!' exclaimed Morag. 'Much more exciting than that! An earth closet!' She looked at Mary, triumphant and beadily expectant.

Mary had immediately imagined some sort of large wardrobe full of dirt. What use would that be?

'An earth closet!' Morag's eyes were gleaming. 'You know. A loo. An all-natural toilet.'

'Er, great,' Mary muttered. 'I'm sure you and Gid will find it very useful . . .'

But Morag was shaking her head. 'Oh no no no. It's not just for me and Gid.'

'It isn't?'

Morag's purplish, patchy hennaed hair flew about in an emphatic negative. 'Oh no. That would be selfish.'

'Are you sure?'

'Yes. It's a *communal* earth closet I'm talking about. For *everyone* to use. And everyone *must* use it, in order to keep up the turnover . . .'

There was a strangled sort of noise from behind. From Ernest.

'I've never, ah, seen an earth closet,' Mary muttered. 'What does it look like?'

'Sort of a bucket filled with dirt,' Morag explained jauntily. 'You do your business and then add more earth on the top. As does the next person. And when the bucket is full it gets emptied out. Natural fertiliser! What could be better?'

Mary blinked. The beauty of the afternoon now seemed dimmed. The air had been fresh and stimulating – or rather it had been to Mary until a few moments ago. Morag's suggestion, however, seemed to her to propose the creation of a very different sort of atmosphere.

'I *know*!' Morag said jubilantly. 'I quite understand your amazement. It is *such* a wonderful idea. And of course, while you know me as a modest person,' she paused and prinked, 'I must say that I am delighted and not a little proud to be the one who thought of it.' She gave a little happy sigh, then her eyes, rolling watchfully about as ever, suddenly narrowed and hardened. 'Oooh! I see that the arch-capitalist running dogs are honouring the allotment with one of their rare visits.' Her voice was brutal with sarcasm.

Realising she meant Beth and Benny, Mary, knocked off course from contemplation of Morag's wonderful idea, glanced over to where a blonde woman in a flowered dress and rose-printed wellies was coming through the gate. Her heart leapt with excitement. Beth, who, that very morning presumably, had left the house where her own beloved Monty was. She half scrambled to her feet, but Morag was quicker.

'I must break the great news about the earth closet to them,' Morag exclaimed. She bounced off, radiating self-satisfaction.

Mary sank back down. She would have to wait until later. She noticed that Ernest seemed agitated. His wrinkled visage, normally red, now purple with indignation, his toothless jaws clamping agitatedly together. 'I FOUGHT HITLER,' he expostulated foamily. 'I'M NOT GOING TO SHIT IN A BUCKET NOW.'

Mary nodded. She was relieved, if surprised, that he had heard everything, as telling him seemed the first of the many difficulties obviously ahead. She wondered too how keen Ernest would be to sniff the soil after this.

'Gross!' shrieked Beth, five minutes later, staring at Morag in horror. 'You gotta be kidding.'

'I assure you I am not kidding,' Morag snapped back. 'I would never joke about matters as important as eco-responsible stewardship of the land.'

'Or about anything else,' Beth muttered.

'Well it's obviously a joke to you,' returned Morag rudely. 'You two are environmental disaster areas. Two houses, a massive four-wheel drive, one tractor . . .'

'It's just so unhygienic,' Beth cut in, stamping her rose-printed wellies on the ground in childlike disgust. 'Ew!'

Morag tossed her head. 'You Yanks. You've got an unhealthy obsession with cleanliness.'

'Not as unhealthy as what you're suggesting,' Beth hit back.

'I take it then,' Morag said sneerily, 'that if you are unwilling to participate in the creation of this great environmental opportunity you are also willing to forgo its benefits.'

Beth looked blank. 'Benefits?'

'Free fertiliser mean anything to you?'

'Er, no. No thank you,' Beth said swiftly, her face, initially blank, now registering nauseous comprehension. 'You keep it. I'll stick to Fisons if it's all the same to you.'

Which of course it wasn't, but Morag was uninclined, for once, to stay and argue the toss. Philip Protheroe had just come on to the allotments and she had yet to sign him up to her wonderful idea.

Mary lost no time in scooting over to Beth, who greeted her with warmth.

'No Benny?' Mary asked, delaying, for politeness's sake, the questions she was desperate to ask.

Beth groaned and raised her eyebrows. '*Work*. You know.'

'And . . . Monty?'

This provoked a much more positive response. 'He's fine,' Beth beamed, her white teeth shining in the sun as she shook back her shimmering hair. 'They seem to be working him hard at the army base, but I think he's enjoying it, apart from that dental course.' She grimaced.

Mary smiled. 'I heard about that.'

'Yeah, he's happily parked in our guest suite,' Beth added, flicking an interested insect off her neat flowered bosom. 'He's very polite about it, always saying how great it is. Which is praise indeed from someone who lives in, like, a mansion!' Beth's eyes rolled comically and she giggled.

Mary tried to look as if she knew what Beth was talking about. Guest suite? Monty had said his bedroom was nice, that was all.

'Hey, and what about *that*?' Beth exclaimed with a tinkle of disbelieving laughter, rolling her eyes towards where Morag, in the distance, was now obviously informing Philip Protheroe of the prospective innovation. From the way he was standing, arms tightly folded, back rigid, he was taking some persuading of its merits. 'An earth closet!' Beth's pretty rose mouth, slicked as always with a layer of gloss, screwed up in disgust.

Mary, while she agreed about the overall unpleasantness of the idea, was aware that she did not have the same lavatorial frame of reference as Beth, whose warm, new upstairs bathroom in Bijou Cottage boasted what was possibly Allsop's only bidet. And certainly its biggest bathroom cabinet and probably fifty per cent of its towels. Whereas, certainly in terms of discomfort and primitiveness, the closet was not an enormous distance from some of the loos at Underpants.

'Like, pee in a pail!' Beth shook her shining head. 'No way. *No way*. She's gotta be kidding.'

Chapter 40

Philip was putting in some potatoes. They had struck him as an unfussy kind of plant it might be relatively simple to grow. As he started to dig, he tried not to look at the nearby plot belonging to Dweeb and Vicky. It wasn't so much the penis-shaped flowerbed that bothered him – that was at least low level. But the various Buddhist flags and revolving rainbow wheels were just messy.

He also deplored the fact that Dweeb and Vicky had planted a large swathe of their patch with hemp and flax; the latter supposedly to make oil from and the former rope. He doubted Dweeb knew much about oil production despite manufacturing prodigious quantities of it down the centre of his hair.

There was also the matter of those drooping green shoots in the corner that reminded Philip unavoidably of the cannabis factory he had once had to inspect in, of all places, an old lady's attic. Her grandson, who had been very much of the Dweeb persuasion, had told her he was growing geraniums.

The pointless self-indulgence of Vicky and Dweeb's plot

irritated Philip but he turned his back on it and tried not to think about it. He was well practised at not thinking about the things that upset him and slowly the rhythm of his digging, the smell of turning earth, the grassy gusts of soft wind and the clear evening sky spread out like a blue sail above the sunlit village all conspired to make him feel, if not ebullient exactly, at least at peace with the world. As he worked, he became warm, and peeled off the grey fleece top he habitually wore to the allotments to reveal a bright red T-shirt.

Strong colours were not normally his preference, but the shirt had been in a special offer two-pack at the supermarket and he had thrown it in the trolley thinking that they would do for the allotments. These days, he did not spend much time thinking about clothes. Emily had always picked his out for him, taking particular delight in updating and enlivening his wardrobe with trendy pieces she found on trips to London to see her publisher. But the vintage-print Tintin pullover and pink checked shirt, her last gifts in this respect, had not emerged from the back of the wardrobe since her death. He had not even unwrapped them.

He felt his self-possession wobble slightly at this thought. Then, as a pair of rainbow leather boots planted themselves right in his eyeline, he felt it wobble further. What did the ghastly Archbutt-Pesk woman want now?

'An earth closet?' he echoed in amazement, a few moments later.

He stared up into Morag's implacable gaze. Her hennaed bob flew up and down in confirmation. 'There's no need to look quite so surprised,' she said sternly. 'It's what our forefathers used. What everyone used up until reasonably recently.'

'Not necessarily,' Philip remarked, his dark brows drawn in contradiction. 'The Romans had running water. Flushing loos, in fact.'

Morag pursed her lips, as if this confirmed everything she had always suspected about the Romans. 'Gid and I,' she remarked, 'are moving towards a lifestyle completely free of the need for running water.'

'Bully for you,' Philip almost said, but didn't. He disliked this woman but could not quite bring himself to be rude to her. Rudeness had never been one of his strengths, if strength one could call it.

'The earth closet,' Morag continued, 'is our gift to the village, to help it towards a realisation of how unnecessary some of the modern conveniences we take for granted are. As well as,' her eyes gleamed, 'generating a source of excellent free fertiliser.'

Philip thought of the horse. Morag had supplied him with a reasonable amount of free fertiliser already.

'So can I count you in?' she pressed, bouncing slightly on the heels of her rainbow boots.

'Is everyone else using it?' asked Philip, standing his ground firmly in his battered trainers.

Morag nodded. 'Vicky and Dweeb, Gudrun and Tecwen . . .' She counted off the names on her fingers, bending the digits emphatically back in a way that made Philip cringe. 'I haven't asked the headmistress yet,' Morag added meaningfully, as, at a flash of pink, Philip's eyes darted over to the gate. Catherine was entering, looking flushed and pretty in a rather clinging rose-pink T-shirt.

It struck Philip now that a conversation about the toilet habits of their co-allotmenteers was distasteful. He also wished to get rid of this bullying termagant. 'I'll think about it,' he said, not intending to do anything of the sort. He realised he felt disgusted, less at the earth closet than at Morag. It was horrible of this unpleasant woman to ride roughshod over the planting peace with her bullying ways. She harried everyone constantly; everyone had to obey. Philip didn't believe for a second that she was an eco-enthusiast. He thought she was a megalomaniac.

'We must act collectively,' Morag warned him sternly as she wandered, at last, over to her own plot. From under his brows he watched her go and returned to his potatoes.

'Is that true?' a voice suddenly said.

Philip raised his dark head. A lock of hair flopped into one eye and he shook it impatiently out. Was he to have no peace this evening? 'What?' he said.

He found himself looking into the thin face of a lanky boy of about eight. It was, the solicitor recognised, the same boy who had mockingly likened him to Snow White's seven dwarfs at the village cross a week or so before. Philip's eyes narrowed with suspicion.

'Is that true?' the boy repeated. He spoke with a forced and slightly hostile quality, as if he feared Philip's reaction.

'Is what true?'

'About the Romans? About them having flushing bogs?' An eagerness had entered the apprehensive voice. Philip recognised it and was intrigued despite himself. He straightened up and looked down at the boy, who lounged against the dry-stone wall at the side of his plot. The sinking sun had plunged it into shadow and Philip wondered how long the boy had been there. Long enough to have heard about the earth closet, obviously.

'Yes, as a matter of fact it is true,' Philip said, staring at the thin white face glowing in the depths of the hooded top like a skull. He waited a few beats before adding, 'Are you interested in the Romans?'

The boy nodded. 'They're all right. I like 'em better than all this stuff she's teaching us.' He poked his close-cropped mousey head out of his hood and nodded it at the far side of the field, where Catherine was patiently working away. 'All about sweaty feet and giants' brains turning into clouds and that.'

'Is that what she teaches you?' Philip said, his gaze lingering wonderingly on Catherine's pink-clad torso. Flitting across his mind came the thought that no one remotely so attractive had ever taught him at school and that Sam was very lucky.

Although he seemed, for the moment, unaware of his good fortune in this respect. 'It's daft, all that cloud stuff,' the boy said. 'Not real like the Romans, any road.'

Philip raised his dark brows. 'No, the Romans certainly weren't daft.' He felt a wave of warmth. The Romans had always been his favourite period of history. He had at one stage thought about studying it professionally, becoming a historian. Perhaps he still could. Anything was possible now that everything he had ever wanted had been taken from him. It was ironic, really.

He turned his attention back to the boy. He was surprised to find fellow feeling, an interest in the Romans, in this child who had, in their brief acquaintance, struck him as the sort who graffitied bus stops and later gravitated to more serious crime. He had seen many such youths in his office. But this was the first potential young offender who had ever wanted to talk about pre-Christian ablutionary arrangements.

Nonetheless, he had come up to his allotment to garden and not to talk to strange boys with a history of rudeness.

Philip bent over his patch again and started to fork up earth.

'Them potatoes?' asked the boy.

Philip looked up. 'You still there?'

The boy shrugged. 'What sort are they?' he persisted.

Philip leant on his fork. 'Belle de Fontenay, if you must know.' His tone was sardonic; he expected this information to have less than zero impact on the child. To his surprise, the boy nodded sagely.

'Good flavour and delicate texture. Prone to slug damage though, and you can have a problem with wireworm tunnelling.'

Philip blinked. 'You're very well informed.'

The boy acknowledged the grudging phrase by shoving his head slightly further out of its black fleece tunnel. 'I should be. My grandad were a champion veg grower. I used to help him a bit.'

'I see,' Philip said, obscurely touched by the information. 'And he used to grow potatoes, did he?' He sensed that with the information about the grandfather, something precious and delicate was being offered and he had to acknowledge it in some way.

The boy shrugged. 'Potatoes. Leeks. Carrots. Beetroot. Parsnips. You should have seen his garden. He used to plant everything in different containers like, not just stick 'em in the dirt. Used to grow parsnips in drainpipes filled with compost, carrots in a big wheelie bin, potatoes in black bin bags. Even used to cover his leeks with bubble wrap.' The words, hesitant at first, were tumbling over themselves by the end of the speech. The boy's eyes shone.

'That's amazing,' Philip said. He had no idea people went to such lengths.

The boy looked fully at Philip, his face radiating

remembered pride and wonder. 'He loved 'em, you see. And every specimen came out championship level. Always won top prize in every show.'

Philip nodded. 'And he still grows vegetables, does he?'

The boy's face shut like a slammed cupboard door. His head retreated back into his hoodie. 'He's dead now,' he muttered.

'I'm sorry,' Philip said shortly, feeling even more uncomfortable than he would have imagined.

The boy shrugged. 'Don't be. They're all dead. Me mum's dead, too.'

Philip shut his eyes briefly at this brilliant flash of raw pain. Neither of them spoke for a few moments. Then suddenly he found himself saying, in a low voice, 'My wife is dead as well.'

He did not know what he was expecting the boy to say. But the response – no words, just a steady gaze from within the hoodie – seemed adequate. He returned to his digging feeling profoundly shaken. The death of Emily was the one subject he never referred to in public.

And yet here he was, airing it to some skinny, ill-mannered kid. What was the matter with him?

When Philip looked up again, the boy had gone.

Chapter 41

'Alexandra Pigott on the line.' The flat voice of the fish-eyed twenty-something who manned the reception desk of the To The Max agency floated through the intercom into Max's office.

The head of the firm scowled tetchily at the Rolex on his spray-tanned wrist. He was going to spend five minutes on this call; no more, and a good deal less if possible. There was no money in long conversations with B-list clients, and B-list was most definitely what Alexandra Pigott was these days. There'd been a glimmer of A-list once, when she'd been all set for *The Clink*, but that had never seen the light of day for various stupid reasons. None of which would matter in the least if Alexandra had managed to land a starring role in her own big fat footballer's wedding, the sort he could flog to the celeb mags for a couple of million. But she hadn't even managed to do that yet. She was a blonde wannabe, just like so many others. So many others on his books, too, which was becoming a problem.

'Put her through,' he said reluctantly. Then, at the crackle of transfer, his face lit up and his voice was suddenly all smiles. 'Hey, Alexandra babe. Great to hear from ya! How you doing?' Although he rarely stirred outside of Soho and had been born in Basildon, Max liked to sound as American as possible.

'I've got it!' Alexandra shrieked, dispensing with the preliminaries.

On the other end of the line, the agent shifted his salmon-pink-suited bottom restlessly on the black leather of his oversized and throne-like revolving office chair. 'Got what?' he asked, looking at his watch.

'IT!' Alexandra shouted down the other end of the phone in the evident belief her agent could not hear her.

'It?' Max tried to stifle a yawn.

'I've just had a great idea and I wanted to run it by you,' Alexandra yelped.

Yeah, yeah. Sure she had. Max slid an eye towards the Rolex. She had three minutes left. Enough time for this idea to run by him and off into the distance, never to be seen again.

Alexandra, at her end, took a deep breath. She had a tendency to gabble when she was excited, she knew, and she wanted to sound as sensible as possible.

'Come on, babe,' Max muttered, 'I gotta be leaving for a meeting in a minute. What is it you want to talk to me about?'

'Allotments,' said Alexandra.

The agent closed his eyes hard and opened them again. He had been out late the night before at the launch of a new top-shelf magazine, *Supermarket Babes*, in which scantily clad women did outrageous things with mass-market produce. He had not slept well afterwards. One particular shot with a wholemeal baguette had stalked his dreams.

'Allotments?' he repeated, bewildered. 'You want to talk to me – to me – about . . .'

'Allotments, yes,' confirmed Alexandra triumphantly. 'I've been racking my brains for a new fly-on-the-wall idea. Something I can star in myself, that would be about me.'

'Naturally,' murmured Max, wearily.

'And then I just thought, hey, I've got this allotment in the village where the house is.'

'You have?' Max was astonished. He didn't think Alexandra knew one end of a carrot from the other, which was certainly not the case with some of the Supermarket Babes. He swallowed.

'Well I have, but I haven't been there yet. You know me, Maxie,' Alexandra cackled. 'I don't know one end of a carrot from the other. And, you know,' her voice rose steeply with excitement, 'I thought that was what the series could be about. Me, trying to grow things on an allotment. Sort of like Alan Titchmarsh meets Victoria Beckham.'

In your dreams, thought Max sardonically. He raised his eyebrows and rubbed his nose, which was fizzing slightly at the end as it always did if an idea had legs. The legs on this one were, admittedly, short. But they were there.

Of course, there were more fly-on-the-wall programmes these days than there were actual flies on the wall, but hadn't just one such fashionista-meets-farmyard effort, *The Simple Life*, launched Paris Hilton's career?

'Don't you think it's brilliant?' Alexandra demanded. 'Can't you see it being a massive hit?'

Max sniffed. 'I just can't see you in an allotment, somehow.'

'Why not? Actually, Max, this may surprise you, but I think I've got an affinity with vegetables.'

Actually, Max thought, that did not surprise him in the least.

The second hand on his Rolex was about to reach sixty. Her five minutes were almost up. He drummed his fingers on the table. As an agent, he had to show he was doing things for his client and he really hadn't done much for Alexandra lately. It could be worth a press release at least. A photocall with Alexandra digging over her plot would be easy enough to set up. Then they could take it from there – or just leave it there, depending on what interest there was.

'Um, great idea, babe. Yeah. Why not? Whatever. Let's give it a go.'

Chapter 42

It had been a perfect hot, blue and gold day and now the sun was sinking slowly into the pillowing hills in a blaze of pink and yellow. With the glowing clouds framing the magnificent corals, roses and daffodils, with here and there a touch of Tiffany blue, it looked, an admiring Catherine thought, like a stately home ceiling. All that was missing were the cherubs.

'My goodness, Miss Brooke,' the vicar beamed, planting his tightly laced black shoes at the edge of Catherine's allotment. 'The Lord really *has* provided.'

Catherine, starting from her contemplation, thought at first he was talking about the sunset. And he had a point, certainly. The most hardened atheist could not deny that there was something celestial in its beauty. But the Reverend had his back to the magnificent display in the sky and was staring at her parsnips. He seemed to be more impressed with her allotment than the trumpet blast of colour behind him.

Realising this, Catherine tried to look pleased at the compliment, although she felt rather short-changed by it. As the Reverend, who regularly witnessed her endeavours, well knew, it was less the Lord than her own back-breaking effort that had produced a plot of such abundance as hers now promised. She looked at it proudly. Leeks, potatoes, onions and carrots were burgeoning in neat rows. Her lettuce patch was a froth of frilly green and red leaves, and in the tiny plastic greenhouse, tinged gold and copper by the setting sun, her Moneymaker tomatoes were displaying their first yellow flowers.

Conscious that politeness demanded she say something positive in return, she looked over at the Reverend Tribble's patch. 'How are your lettuces?' she asked after a few considering seconds.

'Doing nicely, thank you,' beamed the Reverend, waving his hand at a row of flourishing green heads.

And actually, Catherine thought, it *is* thanks to me. She had grown so sorry for the line of barely visible and obviously parched vegetation, whose failure to develop the vicar treated as a sort of unfortunate accident rather than the result of his own neglect, that she had started to water and feed it herself, when the vicar was not there. She chose not to tell the Reverend Tribble about this. He might construe it as encouragement towards the closer friendship he was still obviously determined to establish.

It was a relief to see, a few minutes later, the Reverend hurrying down the hill with his gown flapping. His mobile had just rung; one of his flock, an old lady nearing the end, was apparently asking to see him. Catherine felt a rush of pity, both for anyone dying on such a wonderful evening and also for the idea of the Reverend Tribble's face being one of the last one saw. She chided herself for such an uncharitable thought. It was just that it was easier, somehow, to believe in the existence of an Almighty whilst looking upon the magnificent sunset than it was whilst looking upon the Reverend Tribble.

She turned back to her sweet peas and was again reflecting with pleasure on how well they seemed to be coming on. But of course the improvement in her plot was not entirely due to herself alone. Sam Binns had played a part too. More than that: the troubled eight-year-old boy was the presiding genius over the cornucopia now before her.

And yet his troubledness was less evident these days. The aggression that had marked his first few weeks appeared, apart from occasional flashes, largely a thing of the past. He was rarely rude in class, seemed stimulated by the lessons, interacted more effectively with his peers. Smiles flashed across that serious, thin, pale face, if not regularly, then at least occasionally. While, obviously, rehabilitation was far from complete; had probably only started, there was no doubt that Sam Binns had come on in leaps and bounds.

Even Miss Hanscombe and Mrs Watkins, while possibly buoyed by the approaching end of term, had admitted he had improved, although they harboured reservations as to whether this would last until the new term started in September. Mrs Newton, however, seemed to have no such doubts. She had popped into the school several times to communicate damp-eyed delight at how much happier her foster son seemed to be. 'It's a miracle, Miss Brooke. He eats with us and everything. We even managed a game of Scrabble the other night; he won as well!'

Whilst credit for the transformation clearly belonged to everyone, not least Sam himself, and Catherine lavished praise and encouragement on all involved, she wondered privately whether Sam's behaviour hadn't started steadily to pick up around the time he had first got involved with her allotment. Certainly, it had improved since as steadily as the health and variety of the vegetables on her plot. For which he was, in fact, largely responsible.

Sam it was who had encouraged a more wide-ranging programme of planting – herbs as well as vegetables, plus sweetcorn and beetroot too – than Catherine, left to her own devices, would ever have entertained. The results were impressive, especially when one considered the astonishing number of stones that had choked the earth originally. Stones which Sam had helped dry-stone build into various useful little growing areas here and there, providing added shelter for young plants.

Yes, Catherine thought, hands on her hips, looking about her in satisfaction. The allotment was a triumph. Even St John Goodenough had remarked recently that her burgeoning Brussels looked almost good enough for Chelsea.

She noticed now, at the other end of the field, the figure of Philip Protheroe, the solicitor, working industriously. His long body was outlined with brilliant gold by the setting sun. The last rays flashed on his glasses and the points of his gardening fork busily turning the amber-lit earth. Poor man, losing his wife like that. Losing his wife at all. Briefly, Catherine wondered what it was like to be married. Married to Philip Protheroe.

Philip straightened suddenly, and unexpectedly looked over at her. With a thrill of alarm that both surprised and shocked her, Catherine ripped her eyes away.

Then, as a pair of familiar rainbow-coloured boots planted themselves in her downcast eyeline, she received another shock. She tried guiltily to conceal her slug pellets.

'Is that *chemical* weedkiller?' The acid voice cut through the sweet summer air. Morag had spotted another incriminating substance altogether. *Damn*, Catherine thought. Caught red-handed.

'Hello, Morag, well, it's only Tumbleweed, nothing nasty.'

'It's *all* nasty,' Morag said damningly.

Catherine bridled, stung by the unfairness. Morag seemed to have no grasp of the degree of things. Everything was black or white to her. Catherine was tempted to point out that Tumbleweed was nowhere near as nasty as what Beth and Benny put on their plot. They sprayed as much chemical as they liked whenever they liked, and seemed to take particular delight in doing so when Morag was around.

'Is there something you want, Morag?' Catherine asked, deciding that getting rid of her as soon as possible was more important than arguing about pesticides.

The other woman nodded eagerly. 'I've come to share some very exciting news. Ground-breaking stuff.'

Catherine raised an eyebrow. Digging the allotment had been ground-breaking stuff. And back-breaking, until Benny and Beth had stepped in with their tractor.

As Morag explained about the earth closet, Catherine felt her apprehension had been more than justified. Was there no end to it? First Vicky and Dweeb's sex garden – which thankfully the vicar did not seem to have noticed – and now this. Was there any escape on the Allsop allotments from mankind's more basic functions? It was enough to put one off one's vegetables before one had even grown them.

'Just think how convenient it will be!' Morag enthused. 'We can go on site now instead of having to hold it in. And it can be put to use. What could be better?'

'Er . . .' Catherine interrupted. 'But where would it be? I mean, there isn't room on anyone's plot.' She was determined to avoid any possibility of Morag putting it on hers. As one of the end ones, she sensed it was vulnerable. Her eyes flicked nervously at her freshly dug borders.

Morag was pacing menacingly up and down the strip of grass between the edge of her plot and the empty one behind it belonging to Alexandra Pigott. 'Here,' Morag announced.

'Right next to my plot?' Catherine challenged, her voice shaky.

'No. On hers.' Morag gestured towards Alexandra's weed-covered, stone-studded and generally untended space. 'Why not? She's never been here.'

'Yes, but you can't just take it over and do whatever you like—' Catherine began.

'I'm not just doing what I like,' Morag cut in rudely. 'I'm proposing to install a community facility on land that is currently criminally underutilised.'

'But . . .' Catherine felt her heart rate step up and her face warm with the consciousness that injustice was being done. 'You have no idea what Alexandra is planning. Yes, okay, she hasn't been here yet – so far as we know – but she could turn up at any moment.'

Morag, hands on hips, glared back at Catherine. It was, she felt, completely typical of the schoolteacher to take the part of the ludicrous tart with the hair extensions. She felt murderous. 'Turn up? I don't think so.'

'Yes, but she might.' Catherine stood her ground or, rather, Alexandra's.

'After I single-handedly defeated her planning application?' Morag planted her hands on her hips in satisfaction. 'I don't think so.'

Catherine had heard something about this. There had been some unsuitable building mooted for the top of the lane leading from the church. But then the plan had gone as soon as it had come, so it had seemed. 'I thought she withdrew the application,' Catherine said doubtfully.

Morag's purple shaggy bob jerked up and down affirmatively. 'Yes, because of my objections. She's putting in another, but I'll see that off too.' She sniffed and looked around decisively. 'She'll not be moving here, don't worry.'

'All the same,' Catherine said. 'I really don't think it's for you to decide what happens to her plot.' The two women stood glaring at each other over Catherine's sweet peas which, since Sam Binns had advised her to water them sparingly, had taken off satisfactorily after all.

'I just don't think you should . . . you know . . . Oh, hang on,' the headteacher exclaimed suddenly. She looked over at the red T-shirted figure in the distance. 'There's Mr Protheroe. He's a solicitor. Let's ask him about it. He'll know what the position is.'

She waved wildly at him, hoping to catch his eye. The urge to see him up close again, plus that to get rid of Morag, made her bold. She found herself wondering if Philip had agreed to use the earth closet and found it unlikely.

As the solicitor noticed her gestures, raised a hand in acknowledgement, and approached, his long legs striding easily and, it seemed, eagerly over the bumpy field, Catherine swallowed and felt her face redden again.

'We can't just do what we like on other people's allotments, whether they've used them or not. Can we?' she called as Philip came up and gave her a wide, easy smile that provoked a clutch in her stomach. She hadn't realised what nice arms he had. Long, lean, yet muscled and strong-looking. The split-second thought of being held in them shot like an arrow through her mind.

'We're *liberating* this one,' Morag was saying in her loud, harsh voice as Catherine rejoined the here and now. Her tattooed arms were folded and she looked challengingly at Philip.

'We perhaps should ask St John Goodenough. He's the president, after all,' Catherine panted, her heart beating rapidly. She wished to show Philip Protheroe that she was no walk-over for Morag.

'That's correct,' Philip, to her gratification, agreed. 'He should be consulted on all disciplinary matters pertaining to the allotments.'

'Yes,' snarled Morag. 'Except that he hasn't got an allotment.'

'That's irrelevant. As the president, he is technically in charge.'

Morag cast a look of loathing at Philip. She wished he was irrelevant too, although she had a sinking feeling he wasn't.

Chapter 43

Mary stood in the huge and echoing entrance hall at Underpants. She felt lost and disorientated, and while this was not unusual given her ever-present worries about her husband, it was not entirely because of this.

It was raining; and while a light drizzle would not prevent her from going to her allotment, this was a downpour of a severity to render any horticultural undertaking impossible.

She walked to the window and looked out. Outside was green and glowing, but irredeemably soggy. The distant hills which showed purple in good weather were now barely visible, masked beneath veils of grey. On the moor beyond the park gates rain poured down on the larks and the tattered cowslips on the old spoil heaps. In the park itself, the luminous green of uninhibited, uncut grassland fizzed and shone in the wet. Mary imagined the land drinking up the water thirstily, in relief, after so many weeks of good weather. But it made her feel compressed and shut in.

Her fingers itched for her trowel. Her plans for today had been thwarted. The Mineford hardware shop had had an offer on some rocket seeds, but circumstances had conspired against her planting them. She could almost taste the rocket in her mouth: peppery, strong, chewy and, thanks to Ernest's advice, saved entirely from the rocket-munching flea beetle.

Her gloomy thoughts lifted. She was aware, as she looked up into the great shadowed vault of the hall above her, of feeling less defeated by Underpants than was usual. Perhaps it was the darkness of the rainstorm; the rotting plasterwork and detaching flaps of wallpaper were not quite so visible as they were when it was sunny outside. Perhaps she had slept particularly well; certainly, the regular exercise on her plot had made the insomnia she had occasionally suffered from a thing of the past. For whatever reason, for the first time in many years she felt the urge to have a proper look around the house.

She set off. As she walked, her impression grew that the place looked subtly different. She could not think why; nothing, after all, had changed for the better. In fact, it all looked slightly worse with the gloom, the dark, the rain spattering against the many-cracked windows and the drips from the ceiling that, slow, light and occasional at first, were now becoming steadier and heavier.

Something was different, nonetheless. And it now dawned on Mary that that something was her, rather than the house. Looking, on the walls of the salon, at the dirty oblongs of darker silk where pictures once had hung, Mary realised she felt sobered, but for once, not sick. The sight did not tug at her innards. She no longer felt, as she had done, personally to blame for the state of the place, as if somehow she should have fixed it and hadn't. Now, with several weeks' distraction, hardly giving the place a thought because of her enthusiasm for her vegetables, Mary realised she felt differently about Underpants. Less intimidated. More energetic. She cast a glance upwards. Even the fact that Lady Amelia was no longer *in situ* didn't depress her as it had.

She thought hard. Could such a tiny plot really be responsible for such a substantial change? On the other hand, while her allotment was about a millionth of the size of Weston Underwood, what it represented was success. Or, at least, progress. It was triumph over adversity; physical proof that she, Mary Longshott, could take a scruffy piece of stony land and make it into something not only productive but even, in its utilitarian way, beautiful.

It was also hers. A project all her own. Whereas Underpants, even if she had been able to restore to original perfection every last inch of it, would never be. Monty occasionally reminded her how they held it in trust for the next generation. But of course, Mary thought sadly, there was no next generation and it was obvious now there never would be. With an effort, she forced the thought away. There was no point crying over spilt milk; baby milk that never would be spilt even less.

She returned her thoughts to the more cheerful one of her flourishing allotment. She had made something out of nothing there; rescued something useless, brought life and order where there had been moribund mess. Were there any lessons she could turn to the house?

Of course, the pulling off of anything resembling, even in the smallest way, the same trick at Underpants would be dogged with problems; nonetheless, Mary was, for the first time, thinking of the huge old place in terms of its possibilities, maybe in certain small areas, rather than the utter impossibility of the whole sodden, rotting pile. She had nothing in mind, no solutions at all, but felt instinctively that the new spark of willingness and adventure, sprung up even as the shoots on her plot had sprung up, was actually more important.

The first stage in conquering her fear, she now saw clearly, was familiarising herself with the scale of the problem. She must take advantage of Monty's absence to do something he would never have been capable of. Of looking round the rotting mansion and estimating, with calm, rationality and above all, distance, just how bad things were. Only then could she do anything about it, if anything could be done.

There seemed no time like the present. It was raining; she couldn't go out, and there was no one else in the house to distract her. It was not Mrs Shuffle's day and Monty was charging around Hendon with tyres attached to him. Or something of the sort.

It struck Mary now, as she headed out of the back of the hall, that she too was embarking on a bold and dangerous expedition. Out there, in the vast mansion were uncharted territories, unnavigable passages, possibly ice-floes in some of the damper, colder bits and possibly, around the level of the attics, some of the other last wildernesses in Europe.

The sitting room led through a smaller and even more wrecked chamber out into another hall from which a huge, grey-stone, shallow-stepped staircase billowed into the chill gloom of the upper floors. Normally this was where Mary quit the ground floor for upstairs; it was the route to their bedroom. But instead of climbing the stairs she pressed on, going to the left of them, into the passage which always seemed to yawn dark and uninviting and down which she had never gone far.

It was, she now discovered, going down it, every bit as dark and uninviting as the last time she had bearded it. Intimidating too, lined as it was with murky and near-invisible portraits, huge in their dim gold frames. Here and there, some skull-like ivory forehead could be detected through the darkness.

At the end were some stairs she was unsure of ever having seen before. Given the prevailing gloom, she could not see them particularly well now and ascended stumbling. At the top, she leapt back with an exclamation of horror. She had rounded a corner and now rising before her was a fully armed knight, huge and black against the dim back-light from a latticed mullioned window, his arm, holding a vicious-looking sword, raised terrifyingly as he advanced. She realised a split second later that it was a suit of armour.

It took a few minutes to recover from the shock. By the time she had, Mary stood before a door of smaller size and greater age than those she had passed through so far. Dimly she remembered that it led to the older part of the house and pushed at it.

It opened into lashing rain and wind. Mary, terrified, shrank back before her feet, balanced on the rotting threshold, could topple her into a sheer drop. She had forgotten there was no building beyond; not for the last few hundred years, anyway. She swayed dangerously on the edge of a precipice. Whatever corridor the door had once led to was now a heap of stones which lay more than twenty feet below in the weeds and grass.

Mary closed the door, her heart hammering and her forehead damp. Perhaps, her timorous old self suggested, she had now seen enough. Better to go back into the part of the house that, while hardly rock-solid, was at least not quite this dangerous. But her new, resolved, braver self resisted. She'd got this far. She would complete the job. Get the big picture. The big, very broken picture.

Up and down a labyrinth of dark brown corridors Mary now went, moving swiftly in case the thin, creaking, unsteady floor, as in parts it threatened to, suddenly gave way beneath her feet. As she passed into rooms she was certain she had never seen before, the thought struck her that it was rather like exploring Sleeping Beauty's castle. Certain rooms had the air of not having been entered for a hundred years at least. Mary could easily imagine an evil old woman with a spindle somewhere. But would Underpants ever come back to life again, like the castle in the fairy tale had? And who was she in the drama anyway – the prince with the life-giving kiss, or the dormant princess, oblivious to reality? Or was the house itself the Sleeping Beauty?

She had, she realised, stumbled back into a part of the house she recognised now. Here was the nursery, with its high windows covered in what looked like brown paper, casting a yellowish light over the woodwormed rocking horse, the small chairs, the big, all-purpose wooden table whose surface was covered with cardboard boxes, the dusty wooden floor.

She imagined it immediately as it must have been once, full of noise, the shouts, the laughter of the children, the wails of babies, the implorings and stern instructions of the nursemaids. She looked round the screened, high-ceilinged and dusty chamber, her throat full. Monty had played here as a child, he had told her, an only boy with his nanny in the cavernous room. Listening, she had silently vowed to fill the room up with their own children; a mixture of white-blond and dark heads, both male and female. Never had she imagined then, in the first flush of marriage, that they would have no children at all.

About to leave the room, Mary lingered over the mantelpiece by the door. Beneath the large mirror, in which so many junior nursemaids must have once admired or sighed over themselves, the high, narrow marble shelf held, besides a great deal of dust, a number of random jigsaw pieces and a few playing cards. Looking closer in the yellow light, Mary noticed that the jigsaw pieces seemed to be part of a snow scene. There was what looked like a jagged edge of ice; pale blue sky beyond. And here was what looked like a bit of a polar bear. Had this jigsaw once belonged to Monty? Mary pictured, in a flash, the small, very fair head of her future husband, bent over a table, no doubt that one over there, diligently and presciently piecing together a scene of the very place he was about to visit, now, so many years later.

Alone in the dusty old nursery, Mary felt the pain of childlessness return with renewed force. Her success with vegetable-raising made it worse. She could breed carrots, but not people. Had the poisoned land round the house somehow crept into the fabric of it? Into her?

A wave of doubt swept sickeningly through her stomach. Fingering a damp playing card on the nursery mantelpiece, Mary wondered why she was even thinking about keeping Underpants going. With no one to hand it to, what was the point?

Sighing, she turned over the card, and suddenly laughed aloud. The card was an ace. And of spades. What else?

Feeling more cheerful, she pressed on. The more familiar territory continued. Here was the billiard room, built for recreation after those enormous lengthy dinners comprising endless courses that the Edwardian era was famous for. And which most certainly must have taken place at Underpants, although no books containing details of the lobster thermidor and turtle soup of a bygone era seemed to have survived.

Mary remembered that when she had first come to

Underpants she had been puzzled by the apparent lack of a library. But as time had gone on she had ceased to wonder. Probably there wasn't one. Monty rarely read anything but maps, and possibly his forebears were the same.

She could see through one of the many holes in the papery brown blinds that the rain had stopped. The grey clouds had cleared to expose a sky of improbably beatific duck-egg blue. She could go to the allotment if she wanted. And perhaps she should get back to the part of the house she knew.

Because, once again, she seemed to have strayed off course. The straight-line formality of the house's Georgian frontage, the part with which she was most familiar, had given way to a series of bendy corridors, thick with dust, with uneven floors and windows of all sizes and periods. The view out of them was not across the drive and the park any more, but over the vegetable gardens at the back of the house. Mary gazed at them with a morbid interest. They looked even more shattered now than when she had first looked at them, so many years earlier.

As before, beneath the rubbish, a number of large, sloping beds could vaguely be discerned. That shattered heap of glass, formerly the greenhouse, was still there. Mary stared at it, remembering what Ernest Peaseblossom had told her about the melons, figs and grapes that once had been grown there.

She turned away with a sigh. Nothing she could do about that. But if she got a move on, she could get to her own vegetable patch in Allsop and plant the rocket.

She looked up and down the corridor, unsure which way would be fastest. Some of the Underpants corridors had a habit of going on for some time without either turning or staircase. At the foot of this particular corridor was a pair of big double doors. Perhaps they would lead somewhere. She walked rapidly down and tried the handles; they were stiff, locked. She rattled them and eventually, rotted and rusting, one snapped off. Mary gasped and stepped backwards, appalled at her vandalism. The doors, listing slightly on their hinges as gravity pushed aside their bolts, creaked drunkenly, slowly inward.

Heart hammering, Mary stared into the room now revealed. How many centuries had passed since last these doors were opened? She was staring into a long chamber where the same rotting shades as everywhere else covered the windows. Everything looked brown in the yellowish gloom, and indeed was, made as it mostly seemed to be of wood and leather. There were long brown leather sofas in the spaces between the windows, oak tables and chairs up the centre and, stretching away into the gloomy distance on either side, miles and miles of books. There was a strong smell of paper in the air, albeit a close, rotting, damp smell that did not augur well. Mary realised she had finally found the library.

She felt a rush of mixed excitement and apprehension. It was impossible to be a civilised, educated person and not be fired by the discovery of books. And books in such abundance. She could see even from this distance that some of the volumes were very old, and her fingers lifted and twitched with the urge to examine them. She paced to the nearest shelf with a rising sense of excitement. Could a few be sold to get a restoration project off the ground?

These hopes were dashed, however, when she saw the state the books were in. White tidemarks of damp across their leather spines, their leaves soggy and blackened. Who knew how long they had been like this?

An entire huge room lined with rotting, unreadable volumes was peculiar and powerfully horrible. There must be at least one legible book. She scoured the shelves, but the wet had started at the bottom and was almost at the top; the books had swelled like corks and many were rotten and green. Only a couple of shelves at the far end, Mary squintingly assessed, above the last window, seemed less badly affected than the rest. Might there be anything valuable or interesting up there?

Balancing on a rotting sofa arm and stretching up as far as sinew would permit, Mary reached for the tall, faded spines bound with orange cloth. She caught the top of one with a finger and pulled it down, blinking and sneezing in the cloud of dust that resulted, and staggered under the weight of the unexpectedly heavy volume before lowering herself carefully down and putting the book gently on the nearest table. She opened it and squinted in the dim light.

'Recipe for Onion Tart' she saw in a flowing, beautiful but clearly legible hand. 'By Lady Amelia Longshott'.

A recipe book. Not a first-edition Dickens, Austen or Shakespeare after all. Lady Amelia Longshott and her onion tart were hardly going to save Weston Underwood. Were they?

Chapter 44

'Honestly, it's ridiculous,' Beth hissed to Benny. It was Saturday morning and, after a leisurely breakfast, they had arrived at their allotment.

Benny, his thighs straining uncomfortably as he squatted below his wife, looked up defensively. Had she worked out from his uncertain hand gestures that he really had no idea which way up to plant the artichokes? Beth was not, however, looking at him. She was glaring at the back view of Dweeb as he loped towards the earth closet, his velvet top hat nodding with the movement. Beth and Benny watched as he had to bob deeply down – almost curtsy in fact – to fit his headgear in.

'The way they're always rushing to use that gross thing,' Beth added. 'They're obviously making a point. They use it more or less all the time.'

Benny nodded. He was guiltily aware of not having been on the allotments – or in Allsop at all, or even in Great Britain, thanks to a sudden surge at work – since the earth closet had gone up, but he had heard about it at some length over the telephone. 'It's so unaesthetic,' Beth had heatedly complained. 'I mean, what's the point of us working away making our plot look good when some great rusting john is plonked just across the way from it?'

He could sympathise with her outrage. Beth had worked hard on the allotment, when she was there, that was, and even if her adventures into the more recherché end of the plant spectrum were not always blessed with success. It was unlikely, for example, that they would be drinking Château Ferraro from the vines on the pergola for some considerable time yet. Even given global warming. But it was unsurprising she felt furious about the earth closet.

Conscious of his recent, frequent absences – more frequent even than usual, that was – Benny was eager to agree with his wife on any topic she chose. Although, rather to his surprise, Beth had not been as angry about the absences as he had expected. She had raged in the past about the long hours he worked, branding him selfish and neglectful. But over the last fortnight barely a complaining word had escaped her lips. He hadn't, admittedly, seen much of her lips, or the rest of her come to that.

Benny was enormously relieved. It was possible that Beth, at last, had made the connection between the large amount of time he put in at work and the large amount of money there was for her to spend.

And now he was finally here, looking at the facility himself, he found he did not have to force himself to agree with her about the earth closet. It was about the size of a roomy telephone box and had been built on Alexandra's allotment by Gid and Dweeb under Morag's direction. Fait accompli speed, rather than modesty and efficacy, had been her priority.

It consisted of a rickety frame whose upward struts were

various lengths and apparently obtained from several sources. On top of this frame were nailed four different-sized sheets of battered corrugated iron which did not quite provide full cover but at least ensured that only shoes could be seen. Benny had no idea what was inside the earth closet. He had not yet looked in it. He did not intend to.

It really was very unattractive. As was the regularity with which Dweeb, Vicky, Gudrun, Tecwen and of course Morag and Gid went about their even more unattractive business with it. They paced backwards and forwards to the biodegradable lavatory with such frequency that there was quite a path now worn in the grass bordering his and Beth's allotment. He also shared Beth's annoyance at the superior way they bounced past, looking as self-righteous as anyone could considering they were about to crap in a bucket.

Benny edged away slightly. A gust of wind laden with scent had brushed his nostrils. They had both learnt the folly of standing downwind of the closet when it was occupied. And increasingly when it was not occupied too. The bucket, or whatever was inside, was evidently filling up.

Beth looked at the ramshackle erection with loathing. 'I can't stand having that gross thing right next to us,' she declared suddenly.

'Me too,' Benny agreed.

'No one ever consulted us about putting it there,' Beth added crossly.

'No. They did not.' Benny frowned.

'Still less asked that Alexandra person. They stuck it on her allotment, even though the solicitor said they shouldn't. But Morag bullied poor old St John into agreeing,' Beth complained.

She narrowed her eyes and stared at the hated edifice, as if,

Benny thought, it would spontaneously combust with the force of her dislike. He hoped not. That might be messy.

'St John hates it as well,' Beth maintained now.

St John had not only allowed Morag to bully him into agreeing to the erection on Alexandra's allotment. He had made a token visit too. He had feared the consequences – legal, psychological, telecommunicational – if he didn't. A broken man, he now endlessly rued the results of having let Morag in a half-open door and allowed her to take the kingdom. He had emerged from the earth closet looking shaken.

'And Ernest.'

'Who's Ernest?' asked Benny, suspiciously. Hopefully not some footloose single man who might be attracted to his wife.

Guessing something of his thoughts, Beth trilled with laughter. 'Oh honey! Ernest's about a million. That old guy who has the plot next to Mary.'

The corrugated-iron partition – it could not be called a door – now juddered and scraped open to release Dweeb, who bounced past looking very pleased with himself. Beth watched him with loathing. 'We've got to get rid of it,' she hissed when he was out of range. 'We've got to think of something.'

'Still on the Norsemen?' beamed the vicar.

Catherine fought a sharp reply. She had earmarked this Saturday morning to get on with the pressing business of deciding how far apart her carrots should go. Sam Binns, watching her the previous night, had warned of the dangers of crowding which apparently made the roots split into horrible little orange hands which were no use to anyone.

Catherine shook her head. 'Actually, we've moved on to the Romans. More pagans, I'm afraid.'

The vicar raised his rather straggly eyebrows. 'I see.'

'By popular demand,' Catherine added. 'The children really wanted to know about them.' She had been surprised and pleased when the children proposed their own subject, and amazed and delighted when Sam Binns emerged as one of the most vociferous in its support. He seemed to be finally coming out of his shell, albeit cautiously and still reserving the right to be disruptive, especially in classes run by Miss Hanscombe and Mrs Watkins. But in Catherine's lessons, for the moment at least, he was largely behaving himself.

'They became Christians in the end, of course,' Catherine reminded the vicar. She hoped this would close the conversation. But the Reverend Tribble seemed about to say something else when they were suddenly interrupted.

'I've brought you these, miss,' said the voice of Sam Binns. He seemed to Catherine to be speaking with unusual force. She looked up, searching for his face within the concealed depths of his hoodie. But Sam was not wearing his hoodie. His small, skinny, short-haired head stood bathed in bright morning sunshine, looking pale, fragile and fierce. His slanting eyes were narrowed, either against the light or in self-protection. He was swinging a plastic bag to and fro like a metronome.

Catherine leapt at the interruption. 'Sam! How nice to see you! What have you brought me?'

'Good morning, young man,' intoned the vicar. Sam flung him a glance and a brief nod before returning his attention to Catherine.

He rattled his bag. 'Potatoes. It's best to plant them from

real potatoes. Mrs N had some at the back of her veg store that were going a bit off, like, and sprouting a bit so I got her to give them to me.'

Catherine nodded, glad to hear this evidence that Sam and his kindly foster mother were finally interacting on some level, even if it was only that of rotting vegetables. Gazing determinedly in the depths of Sam's bag, she was relieved to see, out of the corner of her eye, the vicar's black lace-ups move away.

'I'll leave you to it, Miss Brooke.' His voice held a hint of annoyance.

'Goodbye, Vicar.'

She exchanged a conspiratorial smile with Sam. The boy had plunged a skinny arm in his bag and now produced a fistful of new potatoes from which thin roots emerged. 'You just need to plant 'em like this . . . here, I'll show you.'

'Oh, I see,' said Catherine, after a few minutes.

Ten minutes later they were still working absorbedly. Sam, Catherine found, was a much neater and more precise worker on her allotment than he ever had been in her school.

'Helloo there!'

Oh God, thought Catherine in frustration. Was there no end to the interruptions?

'It's like bloomin' Piccadilly Circus here,' grumbled Sam, for all the world, Catherine thought with a pang, as if he had been there.

She looked resignedly up to see Gid standing there in a silly red beret, the mirrors on his waistcoat flashing in the sun. 'Just off to use the new facilities!' he grinned meaningfully as he approached the door of the earth closet.

Catherine nodded. Her first hope was that Sam would not shout something rude. Then she found she rather wished he would. But he merely looked up contemptuously before returning his concentration to the tubers.

Catherine could not help noticing that Gid was inside the earth closet a long time. From time to time she stole a glance at his feet, but the pair of purple leather boots patterned with yellow moons and stars never moved from their position beneath the corrugated iron. The wind, rather unfortuitously, had dropped and all was still, meaning that any movements Gid eventually started to make could clearly be heard. Catherine looked away as the feet moved and there came the faint sounds of scrabbling. Gid emerged looking very pleased with himself.

'Tried it yet?' he asked Catherine in the jaunty, bouncy way he had which irritated her despite herself. Gid in general was irritating. He was soft and smelly looking, like a Camembert, she thought.

'Er, not yet,' Catherine confessed, as a strange sound came from Sam's direction.

'Well you need to,' Gid warned. 'We've got to get that bucket filled and emptied regularly.'

Catherine swallowed. She did not wish to think about either process. It now, troublingly, occurred to her to wonder whose job the emptying would be, and where.

The strange noise was still coming from Sam. Only as Gid bounced off back towards his own allotment did Catherine realise that he was laughing. She had never seen or heard him do this before.

'You shouldn't laugh,' she chided. 'I'm sure they think they're doing something very worthwhile.'

Then she caught his eye and giggled as well.

*

Philip, working at his cabbage rows, was aware of a looming presence. He had, however, by now developed the skill, crucial on the Allsop allotments, of not looking up and thereby committing to time-wasting conversation with someone he did not wish to talk to. Unfortunately, it seemed, the looming presence had developed the compensatory knack of lingering until it was acknowledged. After a few moments of seeing who blinked first, the betraying urge to be polite overcame Philip. Resignedly, he raised his eyes.

It was Gid, trowel in hand, positively radiating his own brand of unfocused eagerness. 'Hi, man,' he addressed the solicitor jauntily.

'Hello,' Philip muttered, noting with distaste the other's claret beret and felt jacket embroidered with red thread and Indian mirrors. Why must the man always dress as a circus act?

'How's it going?' Gid added.

'Fine.' Philip wondered what all this was leading up to.

'See my new bush?' Gid gestured at a straggly shrub wilting by his moon-and-star covered boot.

'Great.'

'It's a raspberry bush.'

'Oh.'

'I'm growing fruit for production,' Gid told him. 'I'm getting out of the rat race and joining the jam race.'

'Oh, right.' Philip wondered exactly what sort of rat race Gid thought he was involved in.

'This bush,' Gid added proudly, 'represents a giant step for ethical organics versus corporate greed.'

Philip eyed the wilting plant. It did not look to him like something that might one day challenge the mighty empires of Tiptree and Bonne Maman. 'Don't you think you might need more than one raspberry cane?' he was unable to help asking. 'And what about a fruit cage?'

Gid looked shocked. 'I'm not caging anything on my earth resource, okay?' he stated. 'Everything on it's born free and unterrorised by chemicals.'

'It just helps keep the birds off, that's all,' Philip muttered, turning back to his cabbages and wishing Gid would shut up and go away. Instead of which, the other man merely attempted a new conversational gambit.

'Warm, isn't it?' Gid said, squinting at the sky.

'It's very nice, yes,' Philip said shortly.

'I didn't say it was *nice*,' Gid looked at him accusingly. 'I said it was *warm*. Very warm for this time of year.'

'I'd say it was quite normal for July.'

'*Very* warm,' Gid repeated emphatically. 'It's because of the ozone layer, of course. Or lack of it. Global environmental policies – if you can call them that,' he added contemptuously, 'have been a disaster.'

Philip passed a weary hand over his forehead. While he agreed that the government could absolutely have gone further in this respect, he did not want to discuss it now. He did not want to discuss anything with Gid. Ever.

'We gave the government every chance,' Gid was saying ruefully now.

Philip gave an irritated snort. Gid's assumption of his political allegiances were presumptuous, he felt. But it turned out that Gid's 'we' was not general, but particular. Very particular.

'We gave them every chance,' he repeated. 'Morag wrote to Gordon Brown offering him the chance to come and justify his policies before a hand-picked audience of Morag, me and several like-minded friends. But he never turned up.'

'You don't say,' Philip murmured drily. Deciding that enough time had been wasted, he resolved to get rid of the man.

'I mean,' Gid mused, 'whatever Labour say about Kyoto, you're never going to see a windmill on the roof of Number Ten, are you?'

'Er . . .'

'Or Gordon Brown on an ethically sourced Fairtrade trike.'

Philip rolled his eyes. 'Look, I don't want to be rude . . .'

Gid nodded. Inside, however, he was panicking slightly. The mission with which Morag had charged him did not seem any nearer completion. He had been instructed to charm Philip over to the side of the earth-closet users; his addition to the ranks, Morag had pronounced, would be a valuable propaganda victory. She had persuaded exactly fifty per cent of available users into the closet, but the other half, Philip included, remained firmly out of it. And Morag wanted total compliance.

For all her personal dislike of him, Morag had reluctantly realised that the solicitor was an opinion-former on the plots. People respected him and would follow his lead if he could be persuaded to come down on the side of the earth closet. Or better still, actually in it. 'Where he goes, others will go,' Morag proclaimed.

Gid now decided to cut to the chase. The guy was obviously about to lose it. Time for some subtle persuasion.

'Look, man,' he said, summoning his best reasonable tone. 'You don't have to be shy, you know. Or embarrassed. There's nothing to be ashamed of. We'll all support you.'

Philip's eyes narrowed with suspicion. What was this idiot talking about now? His intestines clenched. If this was about Emily . . .

'No need to hold it in,' Gid was now adding brightly. 'If you want to let it all go now, you can. Any time.'

As the rage mounted within him, Philip's hand tightened round his fork. It was becoming increasingly difficult to restrain the urge to bring it crashing down over Gid's claret beret.

'It's all natural,' Gid was adding brightly. 'You just need to loosen up. It's the ultimate recycling, let's face it.'

This was more than even a mild-mannered solicitor could bear. 'Go away,' Philip snarled, his eyes burning into Gid's.

Catherine and Sam had just finished bedding in the potatoes and had replanted her carrots according to his grandfather's exacting standards. Sensing a kerfuffle on the other side of the plots, she looked up. To her great surprise she saw Gid backing away in front of an advancing and clearly angry Philip, who was holding a fork threateningly in his hand.

'Wow,' Sam said, his voice containing a rare, impressed note. 'Phil looks well pissed off.'

'Yes, he does rather,' Catherine concurred. She looked at her companion in surprise. 'Phil? I didn't realise you knew him.'

Sam nodded. 'Yeah, he's all right, Phil is. He knows a lot about Romans. But not much about vegetables,' he added with a chuckle. 'I've been down to help him a couple o' nights, get him started, like.'

Catherine raised her eyebrows. That Philip, like her, was taking an interest in the unfortunate Sam Binns made her warm to him further. Was there anything more attractive than a kind man?

'He's a widow, he is,' Sam remarked.

'Widower,' Catherine corrected gently, remembering the information unwillingly gleaned from Morag. She was surprised that the solicitor should have confided in Sam about it.

Sam looked thoughtful. 'I reckon he thought he could tell me 'cos I know what it's like. With me mum and that . . .' The candid face he turned to Catherine wrenched her heart.

'Yes,' she struggled through her suddenly full throat.

'I know what it's like to be by meself,' Sam said quietly, staring at the ground.

'But you're not really on your own, Sam,' Catherine said softly. 'You've got the Newtons looking after you.' Obviously it wasn't the same as a real mother. And Catherine would not even have mentioned it had she not gathered from Mrs Newton, who had popped into the school a few days before, that the situation with their latest and most difficult foster child was definitely improving.

Sam shrugged. He looked at her. 'You're by yourself as well, aren't you, Miss B?'

'Well, yes,' Catherine said quickly, 'but that's largely my choice, Sam.' She was anxious to avoid self-dramatisation, to avoid claiming a part in all this very real pain.

'But you'd rather not be?' Sam pressed, his wide-apart dark eyes unflinching. 'You'd rather have a bloke than not, wouldn't you, miss?'

It was hard not to smile at the boy's audacity. 'Relationships just haven't worked out for me, Sam, that's all. Now,' she added briskly, 'do you think there's time to do these turnips before we go home?'

Chapter 45

In Weston Underwood's vast kitchen, under the light of the one lamp – as usual all the others were out for reasons of economy – the huge shadow of Mary's hand capered wildly across the opposite wall as she turned the big yellow pages covered with a clear, flowing hand. *Lady Amelia's Recipes* was proving an unexpectedly interesting read. There was something rather awe-inspiring, as well as sad, Mary thought, suddenly looking up, to be sitting in the very kitchen where all these recipes had presumably been developed.

The place was so dark, still, silent and empty now. It was almost impossible to imagine it as it must once have been, the stone floor covered with moving people and the occasional dropped piece of copper or pewter, the entire space hot, noisy and bustling with life; pastrycooks, butchers, still-room maids, spit-boys, dairymaids, potmen, butlers and the rest of it, all going about their separate and yet connected businesses, labouring, sweating, chatting, shouting, cursing and laughing under the lofty ceiling.

And certainly, on occasion, there would be Lady Amelia herself who, from the evidence of her cookbook, was every bit the sophisticated creature she appeared on her ceiling portrait.

Having leafed several times through Her Ladyship's book, Mary felt that her sense of the former chatelaine was growing. Lady Amelia was clearly a woman who concerned herself intimately with what was eaten under her roof, and she seemed to have surprisingly contemporary ideas on the subject.

The instructions were clear and uncomplicated despite the period – late eighteenth century; some of the recipes had dates on them – and the dishes were described with an almost modern emphasis on freshness and flavour. Reading about the onion tart had made Mary's mouth water. It sounded, she thought, really quite simple. She felt her old interest in cooking stir. It might be fun to try the tart recipe out, had she any of the ingredients. She was of course growing onions on the allotment, but they wouldn't be ready until the autumn.

She felt, Mary realised, rather inspired. Who would not be? Here, after all, was the very kitchen in which the tart was originally prepared. And she the present-day holder of Lady Amelia's former post. What was more, her husband, as Lady Amelia's often had been too, was far away. The thought now struck Mary that Lady Amelia, so similarly abandoned, might have started her recipe book for something to do during long, lonely nights such as this one. The idea was comforting and companionable.

She read on. Here was a recipe for roast lamb. With a stinging saliva rush to the mouth, Mary remembered how much she had once loved this particular meat. And here was another for creamed potatoes, another vegetable she was growing, of course.

She felt a wave of envy for Lady Amelia. Not only because,

in her time, Underpants would have been entirely habitable, but because, judging from the variety of fresh produce she was cooking with, Lady Amelia clearly had a huge and abundant supply of vegetables. From her own, now-vanished, kitchen garden, presumably.

It was so sad, Mary thought. What had happened to the vegetable garden seemed almost worse than what had happened to the house. At least the house, even in its current rotting state, held an echo of what its prime had been like. One could imagine the colours, the scenes, the inhabitants. But no echo remained of the vegetable garden – apart from stones, smashed glass and this book. Mary ran a contemplative hand across the cover that Lady Amelia herself may well have been the last to close. She thought of the lead poisoning. Even if a miracle appeared to rescue the house, vegetables would never be grown at Weston Underwood again.

On the other hand, she was growing her own onions, albeit some distance away. So there was some continuity there. Mary turned back to the onion tart. It really did look very simple. She needed some flour, a bit of butter, some soured cream. And onions of course. Well, all that was easy enough – and cheap. She would be going into Mineford tomorrow to do what denuded shopping she required now Monty was gone. She could pick it all up then.

Chapter 46

It had taken Max more than a week to arrange the photocall on the allotments. Alexandra had chafed at the delay. But finally the appointed morning had dawned.

Petra agreed with her boss that tiny gold hotpants would be just the thing. Practical yet stylish, as Alexandra said. Whatever Alexandra said, in fact. It was not in the stylist's interests to disagree. Who else would pay her such a colossal salary for a job which essentially involved trailing after Alexandra into shops and offering fulsomely flattering opinions by the mirror whenever she tried things on?

'A bit of bling,' Alexandra announced, slipping the tiny shorts on.

With the deference of one placing the triple crown on the Pope, Petra added a tartan scarf to the ensemble. 'That'll go down well in Scotland,' she remarked.

'It's not Scotland. It's the Midlands,' Alexandra snapped.

Petra shrugged. It was the same difference as far as she was concerned. They took the leopardskin lift down to the basement garage. Alexandra pointed her pink pearlised battle wagon north and set off for Allsop and, she was confident, stardom.

Those on the Allsop allotments that morning were too absorbed in their various tasks to notice the large pink car arrive in the village below them. Philip Protheroe was mulching and Catherine, aware of his presence, was weeding between her bean rows while Sam thinned out some turnips. The vicar, aware of Catherine's presence, was pretending to attend to his lettuces. Ernest Peaseblossom was planting calendula beside his tomatoes, to tempt away the bugs on his Moneymakers. Dweeb and Vicky were mending their Buddhist flags, victims of unruly wind. Beth and Benny were absent, as was Mary, who was poring over her recipe book at Underpants. Morag, however, was striding about the plots as usual, rolling a bossy eye over the efforts of the others. It was hard, Philip felt, under this unwelcome scrutiny, not to feel like a convict in the prison garden.

He looked up, suddenly aware of something else besides Morag. The air, which had been peaceful, now seemed rowdy, full of approaching noise, clanks, exclamations and sharp bursts of laughter. The voices of men. It sounded as if an enormous crowd were coming.

Sam and Catherine stared up in shock from their bean rows and turnips. On the allotment just in front of them, a mere thirty feet or so away from where they worked, an extraordinary scene was unfolding.

A clutch of hard-boiled-looking men in jeans and black leather jackets were crowding on to Alexandra Pigott's unworked and overgrown allotment. Some had the fat black and silver lenses of professional-looking cameras protruding from their torsos. Others carried great black foam sausages aloft on poles above colleagues with film cameras on their shoulders. Some were muttering into mobiles, others held out microphones. Some knelt. All looked tense.

'What's all this about?' muttered Sam.

As the film crews and photographers arranged themselves down one side of the plot, his question was answered.

'Alexandra!' breathed Catherine.

Two women now detached themselves from the gaggle. One, whose blond hair tumbled roughly about her shoulders, wore a white fringed kaftan, wedge-heeled white espadrilles and large sunglasses with white frames. She was very thin and was fussing conspicuously over the other, whose bright, white-blond hair was drawn back into a high, smooth, bouffant ponytail.

Huge black sunglasses almost entirely covered what, even so, was obviously a thickly made-up face. Beneath tiny gold shorts, the woman's long brown legs were exposed to knee level, from where a pair of high-heeled pink Wellingtons sporting the interlocked letters of a famous designer logo took over. Straining over the blonde's buoyant breasts was a tight black T-shirt with the words 'Earth Mother' flowing across it in sparkling diamante script.

'The perfect gardening top!' Alexandra had exclaimed to Petra in Selfridges the day before, on spotting the Swarovski crystal and cashmere top. It was here, too, that she had spotted the perfect finishing touch, a brilliantly new silver spade, the spade part emblazoned with the same designer logo as the boots. She gripped it now in her freshly manicured fingers.

As Catherine and Sam watched, open mouthed, Alexandra flashed a brilliant white smile at the film crew and proceeded in rickety fashion over the stony, weed-sprouting earth of her patch.

The loitering mob beside her instantly sprang to attention. 'A-a-a-nd action!' called someone. The air was filled with the sound of whirring camera motors and zooming lenses. The photographers and camera crews, Catherine now saw, had been supplemented by those working on the allotments. She met, momentarily and thrillingly, the level gaze of Philip Protheroe. Less rewarding was the sight of the Reverend Tribble, panting up to see what all the fuss was about. And now the flashing mirrors of Gid's waistcoat had joined the throng, along with a clearly fascinated Merlin, Dweeb's lolling velvet hat, Gudrun's shining nose and Morag's aubergine bob. Morag, Catherine noticed, wore a look of unabashed hostility.

Alexandra beamed at the arriving crowd, waved a jewelled hand and croaked, 'Hi, guys!' in a throaty Cockney voice. 'Hey, thanks for coming.'

'We were here anyway,' barked Morag.

Alexandra ignored her. She made her way slowly and unsteadily in her high rubber heels over the heaps of stones. As one heel slipped into a soggy patch, her pearlised lipsticked mouth contorted with disgust.

'What you growin' there, Alex?' called out a short, red-faced man brandishing a microphone. 'Bricks, is it?'

Beneath her sunglasses, Alexandra frowned. She paused, pulled a mobile from her gold shorts and flicked it open. 'I've got Alan Titchmarsh here on speed dial!' she announced to her audience. 'He's going to tell me where I should put my broccoli.'

'I'll tell you if you like!' roared the short man, to gales of laughter.

Alexandra contemptuously tossed her platinum ponytail. 'And Petra here,' she added, gesturing at her companion, 'my personal stylist, is on hand to advise on the most aesthetic combinations.'

'Didn't realise you had any on!' bellowed the short man.

Alexandra paused, lifted her spade slightly and flashed a huge grin. Catherine guessed that a set-piece picture was about to be taken.

Her fingers gripping the designer spade, Alexandra, a crazed beam stretching her face, prepared to plunge it into the earth to create the shot that would front whatever TV series might eventually be made. An iconic image, Max had assured the photo agencies and freelance film crews who were all, in the end, he had been able to round up for the latest phase in Alexandra's celebrity career.

But even as she raised the spade, flicked back her hair, stretched her smile and prepared to dig, something stopped Alexandra in her tracks. Something was not quite right.

She paused. She frowned. The mobile with Alan Titchmarsh was passed to Petra in her increasingly muddy white espadrilles. As the crowd watched, the cameras poised for action, Alexandra took a hunched, unsteady, suspicious step forward. The spade with its designer logo flashed in the morning sunshine as she raised it straight in front of her.

'What the hell,' growled Alexandra, stabbing in the direction of the vertical rusting box in the middle of her allotment, 'is *that*?'

There was a silence. A few titters from the film crew.

'And what,' Alexandra bellowed, having inhaled a series of increasingly deep and increasingly suspicious breaths, 'is that goddam awful *smell*?'

Morag now stepped forward. She strode on to the

allotment with the air of one gladiator about to face another, and stood protectively in front of the earth closet, as if to shield it from Alexandra's molten gaze. '*That*, as you call it,' she declared, mocking Alexandra's outraged tones, 'is an eco-friendly ablutionary solution system. The aroma you refer to is that of natural waste products decomposing in an entirely natural way.'

'*What?*' shrieked Alexandra. She tried to take a step forward. Her heels stuck, however, and she almost fell over. '*Shit*,' she growled.

'If you want to put it like that,' Morag snapped.

The air was now filled with noise. The cameras were snapping and whirring and the sound recorders jabbing in Alexandra's direction. 'TV gold, this is,' one of the cameramen could be heard saying to another as Alexandra finally lost her balance and fell over, exposing a silver thong to the delighted multitude.

Petra drove her employer home. Alexandra herself was too furious to do anything but totter out in her gold shorts to buy champagne from the first shop that sold some and afterwards sit in the back of the car drinking it from the bottle and glaring burningly out of the windows. All the way back down the M1 she had stared, unseeing, through her black sunglasses and the heavily tinted glass beyond, asking herself the same question.

How had it happened that she, with beauty, wealth, fame, style, Max, Petra, London's best spray-tanner, Robby Trendy and a crack team of waxers to her name, could not manage to completely annihilate some aubergine-haired, bug-eyed, moustachioed and tattooed nobody?

Besides being, Alexandra now suddenly suspected, the force behind the objections to Betrothal Cottage in its former incarnation, Morag had now stuck her hideous rainbow-leather boot into Alexandra's career as well. Her appearance on the Allsop allotments, which had seemed to promise so much, had been an unmitigated disaster.

The projected reality show had turned out to be a rather different sort of reality, Alexandra thought crossly. The knowledge that she had looked a fool gnawed at her. And all because Morag Archbutt-Pesk had stuck a bucket of shit in a rusting box right in the middle of her plot. Without even asking.

But Alexandra was determined to fight back. She always did and she always would; no Pigott took things lying down, unless that thing was John and that was obviously different. And so it was that by the time Petra was struggling through Swiss Cottage, Alexandra had called her agent and instructed Max in no uncertain terms to suppress any existing footage at all costs and reschedule the shoot. He was not especially willing to do this.

'Tell them I'll do it again in a bikini,' Alexandra ordered.

Max conceded this might attract interest. 'When?' he asked her.

'As soon as possible,' Alexandra vowed. Or, she added to herself, as soon as I've got that bloody crap bucket off my vegetable patch. How this was to be achieved was the next big question.

Her instinct – and stink was the word, from what she remembered – was to simply have the place knocked down. Have it removed altogether. But Morag Archbutt-Pesk would obviously resist this – probably chain herself to it or something – and more bad publicity would be created. No, she would have to think of something more subtle, Alexandra concluded. Whatever was to be done had to be done by stealth.

Chapter 47

The next Saturday morning, Benny went to the solicitor's. A paper concerning a deal he was involved with had been sent overnight to Bijou Cottage. It needed his signature and that of a witness, and as Beth was too closely related to oblige, and none of the crazies in his street were going to know his business, least of all Morag Archbutt-Pesk, Benny had decided to cut to the chase and go see a lawyer first thing Saturday morning.

The nearest lawyer turned out to be in Mineford, which Benny knew as a dark sprawl full of shouting, drunken people whenever he went through it, as he had done last night, in the car on the way up from London. It was the last habitation before Allsop, although it always looked so godawful he would never have dreamt of visiting it unless he had to, as now.

The lawyer was a surprise. Benny had been expecting some bibulous Dickensian hayseed in kneebreeches and pince-nez. And the office he was shown into by the receptionist – a woman in scary glasses – was certainly suggestive of such a character; pretty goddam Victorian, Benny thought, with its plug-in oil heater, dial rather than push-button telephone and one wall completely full of ancient ledgers. Yet the serious, dark-suited solicitor sitting behind the unexpectedly upscale polished mahogany desk was not only youngish and alert, but surprisingly refined-looking.

For all his desire to be popular in his own village, Benny was far more interested in business than he was in other people. He did not immediately make the connection between the tall dark man he had occasionally spotted on the allotments and the tall dark man sitting before him now.

Philip Protheroe, on the other hand, knew exactly who Benny was, both from the allotment and business points of view. He studied the financial pages for his clients' benefit as much as his own. Little old ladies frequently pressed him for advice about money, and it was beyond his conscience to deliver them into the hands of the financial services sharks. He knew exactly who Benny was, and quite a lot about his firm too.

Although there was little general chit-chat at the meeting, the incurious American soon divined, to his absolute amazement, that the young man opposite him had an impressive grasp of City affairs. And not only that, he seemed as efficient and smart a lawyer as Benny had ever met in his life, and a good deal smarter than some. Most, even. After a while Benny realised he had seen him before, and by the time the business was done and they stood up to shake hands in farewell, he finally remembered where it was.

'Hey,' he said to Philip. 'You're the guy won't crap in that bucket either.'

A sudden explosion from outside the door greeted this remark. Mrs Sheen did her best to make it sound like a sneeze. Philip remained expressionless. While it was true that he had so far resisted Morag's attempts to force him through the corrugated-iron door, it was not, he felt, a subject suitable for discussion at the office. Or at least not when Mrs Sheen was listening to his every word through the intercom.

'Well good for you, Joe,' Benny grinned. 'Beth and I are holding out as well. It's outrageous what that dame's trying to force us all to do. It's like Stalin never went away.'

Philip flicked the off switch on the intercom. He leant over the desk. 'Actually, she's given up trying to make me use the closet.'

'Lucky you.'

The solicitor raised an eyebrow. 'She's now trying to make me sign a contract saying I've renounced flushing.'

Outside the door, Mrs Sheen banged disconsolately about her desk.

Benny shook his head. 'Jesus. It's crazy. Beth and I are trying to think of something to get her off all of our backs. Or asses.'

Philip smiled. 'Good luck.'

'You don't seem too worried about it,' Benny observed. His own heartrate increased at the mere thought of Morag. 'Don't you think the whole damn business is a nightmare?'

'Well I agree it's annoying,' Philip said smoothly as he moved his tall, straight frame from behind his desk to show his client out. He had no intention of telling Benny that he knew what a real nightmare was. And that it was a good deal worse than people in purple trousers aiming at universal bowel control.

He talked loudly and thumped his feet emphatically on the floor as he accompanied Benny to the door. For all their sakes, Mrs Sheen needed to be given time to remove her ear from it.

*

Benny usually forgot people as soon as they had fulfilled his purpose, but he found Philip remained in his thoughts as he made his way back to the car park. He seemed a pretty smart guy for this town. Good-looking too. So what kept him in Meansford?

Benny walked on and Philip faded from his thoughts as the reality of his surroundings impinged. Jesus, this Moanford, Mingeford, whatever it was called. It looked bad enough from the safety of the car, but when you were actually walking through it, it was worse. A shithole, basically.

Apart from the honourable exception of Philip Protheroe, Benny thought, there was no enterprise here. No confidence, no can-do, no nothing. What this place needed was a Big Idea, but it was obvious no one round here ever had any small ones, medium-sized ones even.

Jesus, these shops were bad, Benny thought. The one he was just passing was the worst frigging supermarket he had ever seen in his life, and that was saying something. Nice Price, it was called. Were they being funny? he wondered. The only nice thing about that shop must be getting the hell out of it.

As he passed, a woman was doing just that. She bumped straight into Benny.

'Hey,' he said.

'Oh, I'm so sorry,' Mary gasped. She had completely failed to see him. Her entire concentration had been taken by the necessity of not missing the Allsop bus. The battered estate car in the courtyard at Underpants had flatly – in every sense – refused to start and the bus which ferried once an hour between the village and Mineford had been the only other option. Agonisingly aware that she was running close to missing it, Mary had shifted from foot to foot in the Nice Price checkout queue behind a myopic woman with obvious mental health issues who was slowly counting pennies into the palm of the grim-faced cashier.

Benny smiled when he realised it was Mary. He had hardly seen her since the dinner party apart from a few distant glimpses whenever he had made it to the allotments. Mary was always bent over her patch, working away.

A shame, really. Benny had always liked Mary, right from the beginning. She was so goddam pretty, for one thing, with those wide green eyes and all that soft hair, and that lovely body too, tall and slim, but curvy at the same time. Had he not been married to his own idea of the ultimate goddess, Benny thought, he might well have been tempted. How the hell Monty could leave Mary for months on end he could not imagine, but then, Benny reminded himself guiltily, he managed to leave Beth.

Chapter 48

'You in a rush?' he asked Mary, struck by her obvious purposefulness. Apart from the solicitor he had just met, it was a quality in short supply in Moanstick.

'For the bus,' Mary gasped, hesitating between the wish to be polite on the one hand and the wish to catch the bus on the other.

'The bus?' Benny echoed, realising after a few seconds that she meant public transport. 'Hey, I'm going your way. I'll give you a lift back.'

Sitting in the high-rise splendour of Beth and Benny's gleaming black four-wheel drive, Mary tried hard to remember why she had always disapproved of such vehicles. They guzzled petrol, they took up road space, they were frequently driven by people who shouldn't be in charge of a toy train set, but oh, thought Mary, settling blissfully back into the cream leather seats, they really were comfortable.

Mary was eager for news of Monty, although disappointed to find that Benny hardly saw him. 'I guess I leave the house pretty early,' he said apologetically. 'But we did take him out the other night. Did you know he'd never had sushi?' Benny shook his big dark head in amazement. 'We took him to Yo, he loved it, all those revolving belts with the food on.'

Mary felt a sudden, passionate longing to see the revolving belts with the food on as well. If only it had been her exploring London with Monty. But this was no time to be resentful, when she and Monty owed Benny and his wife so much.

'You're so kind, giving him somewhere to stay,' she said gratefully.

Benny shrugged. 'No problem. Actually, you're doing me a favour.'

'I am?' Mary's wide eyes widened further in puzzlement.

'Yeah. Beth's loving having him about. He's company for her while I'm not around. Things have been, um, a little busy at work,' Benny ruefully admitted.

Mary nodded. She remembered what Beth had said at the dinner party. Work was evidently an issue between the Ferraros. Perhaps Benny had better do something about it.

She changed the subject to the safer one of the allotments. Too late she realised this meant raking up – as it were – a subject that distressed Benny. On the subject of Morag, it turned out, he entertained violent views. Of course, Mary knew, no one liked the Vice President of the Allsop Allotments Association, herself included. But largely thanks, Mary guessed, to Ernest, who always contemptuously ignored Morag, she gave them a wide berth. Wider than the one she evidently gave Benny, it seemed.

'She's a goddam menace,' he spat. 'That earth closet's driving Beth crazy. She lies awake at night plotting how to get rid of it.'

As, in his agitation, he swerved wildly across the road,

Mary changed the subject again. She found herself telling him about Lady Amelia's recipe book, the ingredients for whose onion tart she had just bought.

She hadn't expected Benny to be even listening. She certainly was not expecting the look he cast her from the steering wheel beneath his heavy dark brows. It was bright and speculative. He was pressing a thoughtful smile about his lips. 'Hey,' he said. 'That's interesting.'

'Yes, isn't it?' Mary replied in surprise. She certainly thought it was herself, but failed to see why an old recipe book found in the rotting depths of a collapsing house might attract a busy financier's attention. She held up the bag of shopping. Benny eyed the Nice Price logo apprehensively.

'I'm going to try and cook something out of it tonight,' she told him proudly.

Benny nodded. 'Sounds good.' The business synapses in his brain were spurting and firing. There was an idea here, he just knew there was. He could feel it. His instinct, which had so far never let him down, was telling him that something about this book and this woman meant money.

'Wouldn't it be great,' he said, thinking aloud, 'if you could organise some sort of business cooking things from that book and market them under your house label. Kind of stately-home food for the masses. Ready meals . . .' The spurting in his brain had settled to a smooth roar. He was on a roll now. Talking ideas was one of the things he loved most.

Mary had leant forward and was staring at him in utter, round-eyed, open-mouthed shock. 'Wha-at?' she gasped.

Benny, at the wheel, smiled and shrugged. 'It'd be easy enough to finance. And the recipes sound suitable, sort of simple and light and vegetable based. Very contemporary.' He paused and tapped the leather-clad steering wheel consideringly with his big brown hand.

'Yeah. It's pretty easy really. All you need is good distribution, a kitchen, a coupla decent cooks, a fancy label with your house on. Lady Amelia's Kitchen, whatever. Aspirational food is where it's at at the moment, all those supermarket prestige brands and so on . . . Yeah, you know what, the more I think about this, the more it makes sense.' He slapped the wheel and chortled.

'But . . . but . . .' Mary gabbled, confused, panicking and instinctively trying to stop this juggernaut. She sensed that Benny was the sort of person who made things happen, and this was going far too fast for her. It sounded terrifying. Impossible. Out of the question.

'I mean,' she gasped, 'I'd never thought about any of this. I couldn't possibly. I haven't even cooked one single thing from the book yet.'

'But you can cook, right?' Benny eyed her from under his heavy brows again. She wished he would look at the road more.

'Well, yes. But I haven't got any money, I know nothing about distribution, I've never run a business and you should see my kitchen.' She stared pleadingly back at him.

Benny shook his big dark head, an expression of indulgent exasperation in his eyes. 'That's the problem with round here,' he said. 'No wonder it's in the state it is. People are just so goddam negative.'

It had been completely off the top of his head. Blue-sky thinking. A caprice, really, Benny thought as he lay in bed that night. A little five-finger exercise for the legendary powers of creative commercial thought which had got him where he was today. It had filled the time on the journey home and been pretty funny too, the way Mary had desperately tried to wriggle out of even considering the possibility. She had positively yelped in objection when he had finally hit on the name Lady Amelia's Pantry.

But after he had seen the house up close Benny had almost written the idea off. Jesus H Christ, it had been a ruin. A bombsite. He would never have believed it. Some of the windows actually had holes in them and there was grass sprouting out of the steps leading up to the front door. Was this why Monty was going off on his jaunt? To raise awareness, somehow? The house needed attention. The Longshotts were out of dough. They were skint. Distressed gentlefolk. Forget that – *traumatised* goddam gentlefolk. He had never seen anything like it. The Longshotts needed help. And he could give it to them.

The Lady Amelia's Pantry idea made more sense the more he thought about it. One of his clients was a successful head of a multinational who now wanted to invest in a new area. Heritage foodstuffs. As the client had put it, he fancied a bit of the Prince Charles Duchy Originals action. He would start a business from scratch if necessary. It just needed to be interesting. Unusual. A little bit different.

And Weston Underwood, Benny thought ruefully, was certainly different. Under the rose-print quilt, he clenched his fists. The answer was so obvious, it was ridiculous. Mary Longshott just had to get on board. She was full of objections, but it was a hell of a lot easier than crossing the Arctic Ocean. And, frankly, a great deal more likely to bring the money in as well.

*

A few miles away in the bedroom at Weston Underwood, Mary Longshott, tossing and turning on the lumpy pillows, was reaching the same conclusion. This was unexpected. She had wanted so much to bury Benny Ferraro's idea immediately. It was impossible in every way one cared to mention, and which, for that matter, she had mentioned to Benny. Lack of money, lack of commercial experience, lack of energy, lack of inclination to do anything but refuse.

The problem was that the idea had refused to be squashed. It flashed into her mind at unexpected times throughout the rest of the day, especially when she was in the kitchen. It popped up just as she went to sleep, when the best and worst scenarios would roll through her head like vast and runaway carriage wheels. She would get it under control, be about to dismiss it, and then she would remember the taste of the onion tart, which she had cooked for her supper, and which had been so easy and delicious.

And fun, most of all. All her old love of cooking had flooded back. It had been such a wonderful feeling, pressing pastry beneath her fingertips for the first time in what seemed years and possibly was. She and Monty had lived on pasta and pesto for ever, or at least that was what it felt like. To taste something real and fresh like the tart, warm, melting, full of the salty sweetness of onions, had been a profound treat and an amazing luxury. Lady Amelia's recipe was a sensation of taste and texture. She had certainly known her onions, in every sense.

And that was another incentive for her to investigate Benny's idea, Mary felt. Was it entirely an accident that she had come across the book in Monty's absence, in an hour of dark – in every sense – need? And then to bump into Benny and just happen to mention it to him. And, surrounding these events, the odds-against chance in acquiring the allotment itself. It wasn't too far-fetched to imagine that someone, somewhere, was orchestrating these apparently unrelated happenings. Could that someone, Mary wondered, be Lady Amelia, the former chatelaine reaching down the generations to help the new one?

Finally falling into an uneasy sleep, Mary dreamt about Benny's scheme. In her dream, she was putting her objections in the most vociferous terms to Lady Amelia, who sat opposite her on one of the salon's striped-silk sofas wearing the saffron-coloured Venus robe she had sported on the ceiling. 'Where am I going to get the money to launch a company from nothing?' Mary demanded boldly.

'Didn't Benny say he'd take care of all that?' Lady Amelia answered. Her face was calm and beautiful, her eyes large and blue in the Longshott way, and her lips very red. She had still, elegant, very white hands. Her voice was melodic, measured and held a hint of amusement.

Mary sighed. 'Well, yes. But I don't have any experience.'

'He has,' Lady Amelia replied immediately.

'But I don't know if I want to.' Mary remembered how, beside Benny at the steering wheel, alive with ideas, she had felt so old and tired.

Lady Amelia raised honey-coloured eyebrows. 'Well that's the important thing,' she said briskly. 'If you don't want to, you certainly should not.'

Mary nodded, satisfied. 'That's what I thought too. That's it, then. I won't.'

Lady Amelia's fine hands fluttered in her lap. 'Very well. But you should be sure that you won't regret this decision later.'

'Why would I? I'd be saving myself a lot of trouble.'

'But trouble is sometimes worth taking,' Lady Amelia replied softly. 'Anything really worth having requires effort and risk. You know that. You know it from living here.' She smiled wryly and lifted a hand into the gloom of the battered salon. Then she seemed to fade. Mary found herself staring at the worn red of the bedroom curtains, the former chatelaine's light, amused voice echoing faintly in her ears.

Anything really worth having requires effort and risk. You know that from living here. And she did, Mary thought. Life at Underpants involved effort and risk in daily abundance. And perhaps putting her efforts in other, new directions might be more effective than simply running around repositioning buckets below ceilings that threatened to collapse at any minute.

She wished she could talk to Monty about it. Talk to Monty about anything, come to that. But especially this. Her mood swung downwards and then, most unexpectedly, upwards again. A great burst of hope exploded suddenly within her. Why not develop the idea on her own? Surprise her husband on his return with what could be a solution to if not all their problems, at least some of them. In this most difficult of times, Mary now saw, she was being offered something positive to focus on. The can-do energy of Benny and his contacts. Only that could take her forward.

She felt a thrill of excitement of a sort never previously experienced. It was, she sensed, the thrill of risk, of launching off into the unknown and seeing what happened. Could this be me? Mary asked herself. Shy Mary Longshott, who never ventured much beyond the park gate? Where had this new confidence come from? Lady Amelia?

Or was it all, really, down to the allotment? Surely not. And yet, even given her husband's absence, the successful raising of vegetables there had encouraged her, energised her, given her confidence. What other untapped depths were there? Was the ability to run a food business – and food was what after all she was growing – one of them? Mary thought of Ernest Peaseblossom. Was he right, after all? Did the answer really lie in the soil?

Well, in the short term it lay with Benny Ferraro. She'd ring him first thing, Mary vowed.

Chapter 49

Benny, in Bijou Cottage, was still not asleep. His brain was, as always when he was excited, awhirr. He was rehearsing what he would say to his client, the one who was interested in the food business. He would tell him about this woman he knew, *great* cook, *incredible* house – well, *that* was no exaggeration – historic cookbook full of pretty modern-sounding recipes, it might all add up to something interesting. The client could not fail to be enthusiastic.

Of course, if Mary wasn't interested, there were plenty of small heritage producers kicking about who'd love an injection of serious money to expand. Although not all of them would have coupla-hundred-year-old recipe books. Could Mary not see the chance she was missing? He'd ring her first thing in the morning, Benny vowed, and try to persuade her again.

Suddenly, there was a commotion in the bed at Benny's side. Without warning, Beth rose like a geyser from the linen sheets and stared down at him, her eyes burning.

'I've got it!'

'Got what?'

'The answer!' He could vaguely see her blue eyes burning excitedly through the dark.

'Wow,' said Benny, uncertain what the question was.

'We can move it!' hissed Beth.

'Move . . . ?'

'The earth closet!'

Benny blinked. He realised that, despite being in Allsop and mere yards away from the loathed Morag, the earth closet had not crossed his mind for . . . well, whole hours. Mary Longshott and her recipe book had occupied every byte of his brain. But of course Beth had had no such relief and had thought of little else. 'Move it?' he echoed.

'We can dismantle it,' Beth said, sitting up in the bed excitedly. He could see her slender shape in its Cath Kidston pyjamas silhouetted against the curtains.

Alarm filled Benny. Much as he wanted to please his wife, this was a controversial suggestion. 'It might be heavy, though.'

Thinking about it, he doubted it was. The construction looked so flimsy it was amazing that a gust of wind – from outside or within – had not yet collapsed it. Unfortunate, too. It might have happened with Morag inside.

'Not sure, honey,' he murmured. 'The whole point of us taking an allotment was to make ourselves more popular in the village. They're not going to like it if . . .'

He thought of the undoubtedly brimming bucket inside. The steak he had had for supper lurched unpleasantly within his stomach.

'We don't have to touch it. We can always use the tractor,' Beth asserted, racing ahead.

'I'm not sure it's got an earth-closet-removing facility,' Benny pointed out.

He sensed her giving him another burning glance in the gloom.

'Okay, well, we don't have to move it altogether. Just to their side. They can hardly complain. They're the ones who use it most anyway. We'd save them a walk.'

'I guess so,' said Benny.

'Okay,' Beth said. 'So that's settled, then.'

'When do you think we should do it?' Benny asked.

Beth considered. 'Well, we need light. The next time there's a full moon, I guess.'

In London, beneath the lace-trimmed canopy of a four-poster bed in a Knightsbridge penthouse, a woman with long, tanned limbs lay spreadeagled beneath a handsome, athletic man. As John prepared to make love for the fourth consecutive time, Alexandra summoned the last of her strength and wound her long legs around his muscled back, now perspiring with the effort. She took her breasts in both hands, pushing them upwards, and did her best to sound in the throes of ecstasy. And then, as John groaned and collapsed on to her yet again, Alexandra bellowed with a triumph that was unmistakably genuine.

He propped himself up on his elbow, his handsome, eager, perspiring face glowing. 'Oh darling. That's fantastic! You came!'

From between fronds of tumbled platinum hair, Alexandra stared at her boyfriend in hastily summoned indignation. Even without her sunglasses, which she never wore for sex, she could see his face clearly enough to recognise his genuine delight. Was he joking? 'I *always* come,' she lied.

He grinned at her, then peeled himself off her body. As

always, it felt to Alexandra like removing a plaster. She winced, then, as the power shower in the bathroom shuddered into action, felt delight flow through her again as she remembered the real reason for her bellow of joy.

She'd got it at last. The answer to the problem. To Morag Archbutt-Pesk's earth closet. The solution was within her grasp. She'd have the thing removed at night. When no one could see her or suspect her of anything. Which they would not. In order to completely eradicate the risk of the story leaking out, she would not hire any heavies, any strangers who might tattle to the tabloids. She would take Petra and Imelda, the Filipino cleaner, and get them to move the thing instead. Imelda in particular would not turn a hair. She'd cleaned some unsightly messes in Alexandra's bathroom before now, particularly the morning after a big PR event.

There was only one thing to check out. The night would have to be light enough to work in. A full moon, in other words.

She sat up in bed. When was the next full moon?

John came out of the bathroom, a towel round his broad shoulders, to see his girlfriend sitting up in bed looking at him – or in his direction – with blazing eyes and an expression of unprecedented determination on her face. 'I need to know about the cycles of the moon,' she told him urgently. 'It's an emergency.'

John felt the colour drain from his face. All the feeling of relaxation and well-being that sex always produced in him vanished in a flash. His toes tingled with fear. It had happened, the very scenario his devout Baptist mother had warned him about. And it had happened too soon; he wasn't nearly ready for this degree of responsibility yet.

'You're not . . .' He swallowed. The fear rose now in his stomach. 'You're not . . . *pregnant*, are you?'

'God, *no*.' Alexandra met his appalled gaze with still yet greater horror. Pregnant? *Hello!* Where would babies fit in with her celebrity ambitions? Her high-maintenance lifestyle? Robby Trendy didn't have a crèche, did he?

Chapter 50

Mary was humming happily in the kitchen at Underpants. Lady Amelia's lemon cake had come out better than she had ever dared hope.

'Blimey,' remarked Mrs Shuffle, looking at the evenly cooked yellow circle from which the deliciously tangy warm scent was escaping. 'Looks good enough to eat, that does.'

'You must have some, Mrs Shuffle,' exclaimed Mary as she reached for a knife and cut into the cake's warm centre.

The cleaner looked gratified. 'Ooh, are you sure? It's not for a special occasion?'

Mary shook her head. 'I'm just working my way through Lady Amelia's recipes to see what works and what doesn't. Although I have to say, most of it works brilliantly.' Especially now Benny's advanced me a few hundred for the ingredients, she almost added, but resisted at the last minute. Money and Mrs Shuffle were traditionally difficult subjects; finding the one to give the other in particular.

Biting into the cake, Mrs Shuffle watched her employer busying about the kitchen. Despite the fact that Mr Monty was away, and she obviously missed him so much, Mary was a woman transformed; glowing with ambition and excitement. It was amazing the difference a purpose in life could make, Mrs Shuffle thought.

'Ooh, it's lovely, this is,' she said through a full mouth.

Mary blushed with pleasure. 'Thank you.'

Ah, bless, thought Mrs Shuffle. She's all excited. Looks prettier than ever, she does. 'So you're all set, are you?' the kindly cleaner prompted. 'It's all decided?'

'Quite a lot of it,' Mary nodded. Benny had been full of ideas, almost as many as her. The whole Lady Amelia concept had obviously captured him. Mary could see how Benny became obsessed by work and felt a twinge of guilt that she now was adding to the pile of concerns that kept him from Beth, who had been so kind. But her guilt was soon lost amid the excitement of new plans.

'Weston Underwood for the label, I think,' Benny had said when they had met for their first business discussion.

'Yes, and speaking of the label,' Mary added breathlessly, 'I've been thinking . . . there's a picture . . .' She started to tell him about the portrait of Lady Amelia on the ceiling. It would, Mary felt, look glorious on the packaging.

Benny was enthusiastic. 'That sounds great. These things are all about image, as you know. Speaking of which, we'll need some photographs for advance marketing. And a brochure.' Benny's eyes swept her outfit doubtfully. 'Got anything a little more occasion?'

Mary stared at him in surprise, then glanced down at her worn petrol-blue cord jeans, so old she couldn't even remember where they had come from. While the jumper, with its filigree gold buttons and riotous purple and white lattice pattern, could only be from the House of Shuffle.

'I mean, you're beautiful, of course. But you'd look even better with make-up.'

Blushing at the obviously genuine compliment – Benny didn't waste time – Mary realised she had not even thought about make-up for months. She had had some once, but had no idea where it was now.

'Well, I think we can shake on it so far, I'll get back to you when I've seen my client again. He'll probably want you to go and see him in London.'

London! Where Monty was. Should she, she wondered, pay him a surprise visit, before he left? She had the address of course. It would be wonderful to see him. She ached for a hug, a kiss, to see his face. To tell him about her new venture. He would be amazed. And, she was sure, delighted.

She had not yet mentioned the idea to Benny. He might tell Beth, who would tell Monty. Oh, let it be a surprise, Mary thought happily. Why should Monty have all the fun?

'So you're going to do it all here?' Mrs Shuffle looked round the great echoing kitchen doubtfully. 'With copper pots and mob caps and all that?'

Mary laughed. 'Not exactly. Can you imagine the health-and-safety issues?'

Mrs Shuffle couldn't. Neither health nor safety came to mind when she thought about Underpants. There had been times when she had seriously considered Hoovering in a hard hat.

'No, once we get the go-ahead there are plans to convert one of the outhouses into a special food production suite. It'll be very small scale at first, to see how it goes. The most obvious dishes to start with, and it'll all be marketed with Lady Amelia on the label plus the story of how I found the recipe book and the rest of it,' Mary rattled breathlessly on. 'As far as possible we'll use organic ingredients. We've yet to source those, of course.' Business-speak. How foreign it sounded coming from her lips. She was getting used to it, however. Benny rarely spoke anything else. Conversations with him were all about heads ups, curtain-raisers, blue-sky thinking, flashing the kimono. The last had left her particularly baffled until he explained it meant showing people a little of something to intrigue them. In this case the kimono had been the onion tart.

She glanced out of the window at the weeds sprouting between the flagstones outside. Benny had promised she could borrow his tractor to spray them, but if everything went well, Mary thought gleefully, she might even be able to afford her own eventually. It was not, she recognised, that she expected to become rich overnight. There was an almost unthinkable amount of hard work to do, from setting up the production to dealing with the marketing. But if all went as well as Benny seemed convinced it would, she would have help, advice and of course, now, money.

And please, please let it go well, Mary prayed several times a day. Having been so doubtful at first, she was now desperate for it all to happen. She felt excited, jumpy, full of plans and enormous, sudden, unprecedented levels of energy ready to pour into the project as soon as it got, as Benny put it, green-lighted. She must make a success of it for Benny's sake, for Lady Amelia's sake and for the sake of Weston Underwood. Would Lady Amelia's Pantry save the rest of the house? What a miracle that would be.

'It's just such a shame,' she added, 'that the ground here at Weston Underwood's unusable. It would be so wonderful for the label to utilise – I mean use – items, sorry, vegetables, actually sourced – I mean grown – on site. In the garden, I mean.' She grinned, exasperated and delighted, at Mrs Shuffle. Business-speak was so hard to get out of your head once it got in.

Chapter 51

The next Saturday night, around eleven o'clock, Beth and Benny walked up to the allotment field by the light of the silvery moon. Too goddam silvery by half, Benny thought. It was too bright and would shine like a spotlight on their activities, but Beth pointed out that everyone would be inside, in bed.

Benny wished that he was in bed, too. But Beth had consulted the calendar and decided that tonight was the night for the earth closet to be moved. Given her tolerance of his recent working hours, Benny realised he must obey if he wanted to keep the peace. Still, not all his efforts had been in vain. His client, Mr Persson, was very keen to meet Mary to talk about her food business, and a date had been set for the following week.

There was a hell of a lot of peace out here, that was for sure, Benny thought. Too much, if you asked him. It was pretty spooky and still, with the normally green grass looking black and the moon shining on the pale limestone ridges of wall. Looking back at the village, which showed like a black and white photograph now, all the usual colour drained,

Benny saw how the moonlight picked out the gravestones in the churchyard; gleaming on the spiky black railings surrounding the columns and obelisks, lying flat on the older tombs, where slipped stones revealed terrible yawning gaps.

Nor was that the only thing that worried him. As they ascended the stepped path up the hillside, the image of the brimming bucket in the closet loomed ever larger. They had not discussed between them whose job it would be to remove it, but Benny had a feeling it would not be Beth's. So far in their marriage she had never done as much as put the rubbish out.

'Here we are,' giggled Beth excitedly, stepping on to Alexandra's allotment and shining the torch she had carried from the house across the undulating, rusting surface of the earth closet.

'Here we are,' agreed Benny reluctantly.

'Look, why don't I stand here and shine the light while you pull the walls down?' Beth suggested.

Gee, thanks, thought Benny. His wife, it was clear, really had not anticipated making an effort of any sort. He rattled the iron surround of the closet. 'Hey,' he muttered, dejectedly, 'it's a bit firmer than it looks. I think we're going to have to dig it out.'

'What – both of us?' Beth asked, horrified.

Benny felt a stir of irritation. 'It won't take long,' he said firmly. 'We just need to dig out round these four posts in the corners. It'll come out easily enough after that.'

Beth reluctantly took up position and began to dig a hole around her appointed post. For a few minutes there was nothing but the sound of heavy breathing. While boring and uncomfortable, the undertaking was not so bad as Benny had feared. As well as the moon, Fortune had shone on their enterprise at least to the extent of ensuring there was no wind and therefore, despite the warmth, very little smell.

'You need to make it a bit deeper,' Benny advised his wife after about ten minutes. 'The reason it's stuck into the ground so hard is that Morag's put some sort of spike on the end of the posts, to anchor them in position, I guess. They're a lot deeper than the posts themselves. We'll have to go quite a way down to get them out. A lot deeper than Morag and those other freaks dug originally.'

Beth muttered something rude under her breath. She was starting to wish she had not had this idea. Or that she had paid someone else to do it for her, that skinny boy who was always hanging round the allotments, for example; the one who had been interested in their car. He looked as if he needed the money.

'Look, just stop complaining, will you?' Alexandra snapped at Petra as they came off the motorway. 'The whole point of being personal stylist to a celebrity is that, from time to time, you're asked to do things that are a little out of the ordinary. You've got to think out of the box, yeah?'

Petra, huddled in the front seat under several layers of khaki pashmina, snorted sulkily through her nostrils. 'It's the box that's worrying me,' she replied. 'It's got a bucket of poo in it, you said.' Petra had not been best pleased to be told that her Saturday night, earmarked for a party due to be attended by Kate Moss, was to be spent digging in some muddy field in Derbyshire. As she had told Alexandra, she hadn't dug since she was four on St Ives beach. But Alexandra's word was law, or at least it was if Petra wanted to continue receiving a regular salary.

Alexandra pressed her foot harder to the metal in irritation. The pearlised four-wheel drive roared through the thirty-mile-an-hour zone as if the hounds of hell were after it. 'Yeah, but the bucket of poo's where Imelda comes in. Right, Imelda?' Alexandra threw over her snakeskin-bomber-jacketed shoulder. While Petra's bad mood had not permitted a conference on the perfect outfit in which to remove an earth closet, she had dressed with an eye to practicality. White jeans were, for example, obviously out. She'd put a pair of new Earls on instead and teamed them with sensible black patent mid-heel ankle boots.

In the darkness of the back seat, the Filipino cleaner clutched at the safety handle and shuddered. She didn't care what Alexandra was asking her to do at the end of this journey. All she cared about was getting to wherever it was in one piece. Working for the demanding, imperious Alexandra Pigott was bad enough in the penthouse. But that was sweet bliss and ease compared with working for her on the move, with her driving. Imelda closed her eyes and prayed to the Virgin as the overhead lights shot past.

'Ooh,' Benny heard his wife grunt from round the other side of the shack.

'Anything wrong, honey?' he called.

'No, nothing, I've just dropped some cash . . . Hang on, no, it's okay, I can see it in the moonlight.'

Below the allotments, in Allsop village, a woman, unable to sleep, was staring moodily out of her window into the warm night.

It had not been a good day for Morag Archbutt-Pesk. Her mind churned with acid, indigestible, curdling frustrations. First of all Merlin had flatly refused to eat her home-made, ultra-high-bran-content version of Weetabix. Then the girl, whose birthday was approaching, had asked for a Disney princess party complete with tiaras, fluffy pink shoes and glittery plastic goblets. Morag, who had been thinking in terms of a home-made papier-mâché piñata filled with sustainable gifts, had almost choked on her soya and echinacea shake. 'Capitalist crap!' she had screeched at the five year old. 'Over my dead body.'

Merlin had shrugged. 'Okay. I don't mind having it in the garden.'

'In the garden?' gasped her mother.

Her daughter had fixed Morag with a steely grey-brown gaze. Morag bent forward slightly. Was that mascara on her daughter's lashes? Her heart rate increased. And was that heightened colour on her plump, pale cheeks, which Morag had smugly attributed to all the houmous and raw carrot Merlin ate, actually *blusher*?

'You're always saying you're going to be buried in the garden in an eco-efficient cardboard coffin,' Merlin announced, tossing hair that was not only longer than Morag would like, but looked suspiciously as if it had been tonged and possibly even had some gel in it. *Glitter* gel.

'Well that's right. I *am* going to be buried in the garden in an eco-efficient cardboard coffin,' Morag stated, trying to focus on the facts.

'That's cool. Well your dead body would be in the garden then,' Merlin said with the relentless and rather icy logic that was increasingly characteristic of her. 'So we'll have the party there. Over it.'

Morag stared, reeling at the thought that her own flesh and blood could contemplate her demise with such equanimity. 'Well you're always saying there are too many people on the planet,' Merlin breezily reminded her. 'And can I have a toy riding school with a showjumping course for my present?'

'No you bloody can't,' Morag had shouted. 'You're having an eco-tepee made out of cardboard from sustainable forests.'

Merlin's eyes had widened. 'I didn't know there were cardboard forests.'

School, Morag knew, was to blame for all this. As was Gid, whose idea it had been to send Merlin to Allsop Primary, where, Morag thought hotly, Catherine Brooke made it her business to thwart and ridicule her at every opportunity. Recently, the headmistress had poured scorn on more of her initiatives. She had completely refused to support Morag's idea that the village's carbon footprint could be reduced by replacing the fuel-emissions-choked school run with a pony-and-trap service and funded by the council. The council, it had to be said, were no more helpful.

And her idea that this Christmas the school should celebrate the festive season in a more socially inclusive manner had received even shorter shrift. 'We are a church school,' Catherine Brooke had pointed out in her snotty voice. 'So we are to some extent obliged to offer that repressive Christian bullshit, as you put it, Ms Archbutt-Pesk. And while your idea that we celebrate certain African tribal rituals instead is interesting and can possibly be incorporated into a study of alternative Christmases across the world, I regret that it cannot be the main focus.'

Bloody fascist, Morag thought now. Did she want someone like that teaching her child? And not teaching her all that well either; Merlin was only middle in the class, a considerably lower ranking than her obviously extremely high intelligence deserved. How dare that bloody headmistress imply that Merlin's progress could not really start until Merlin had been retaught all the spelling and maths her mother had taught her wrongly at home.

In the frame of the bathroom window, Morag shook her head. Sometimes it just felt as if she carried the entire burden of the world on her shoulders. Even Gid had let her down today, being less than enthusiastic about her suggestion that they spend the summer in India and see the world through the eyes of a cotton farmer. It turned out, incredibly, that he had been thinking about Center Parcs.

Morag turned her boiling gaze up to the allotments. There was another source of frustration. No one seemed to realise that without her, those plots simply wouldn't exist. They had been her idea from the start, whatever credit St John bloody Goodenough tried to claim for himself. And yet people were abusing the earth left, right and centre. Slug pellets. Rotivators. Genetically modified crops, for all she knew. Her brow creased angrily as she remembered that smartarse solicitor telling her that all crops were genetically modified to some extent, just like people were. He could speak for himself, Morag had hit back. *Her* genes were untampered with.

'Impossible, I'm afraid,' the solicitor had said wearily. 'Otherwise you'd be an amoeba in the primordial soup.' He'd then looked at her consideringly in a way she had not liked.

There was a light on the allotment, Morag noticed now. Dweeb and Vicky, most probably, having sex by rushlight on their fertility symbol. It was a full moon after all and they had still had no luck at conceiving. Hardly surprising, Morag thought patronisingly, given how irritated Dweeb was getting with the arrangement. 'Great sex is impossible if you're tense and stressed, yeah?' she'd informed him recently. In reply, he had muttered something she suspected was not complimentary.

But the light was not on Dweeb and Vicky's plot, Morag now saw. It was further down, more towards Beth and Benny Ferraro's. Towards Alexandra Pigott's. Towards the earth closet, in fact. Her eyes narrowed and her lip curled. Just what the hell was going on up there?

There was only one way to find out. She would have to go to the allotments and investigate.

Morag reached for her purple drawstring trousers, hanging over the bath side, and pulled them grimly on.

Chapter 52

Alexandra drove the pearlised four-wheel drive into Allsop. The village was silent in the moonlight as she roared up the main street. Every light was out and the silvery glow from above emphasised the feeling of emptiness and remoteness. Stripped of its summer colour by the night, the village looked a different, altogether less friendly place.

'God, it's really spooky,' Petra observed fearfully.

'Don't be stupid,' Alexandra snapped as she reached the village cross, ripped up the handbrake and opened the door. 'Come on,' she urged, her Iced Skinny Latte'd lips twisting impatiently.

'I don't want to,' whimpered Petra, huddling in her pashminas. 'I'm scared of the dark.'

Alexandra looked into the back seat. Imelda, who felt horribly sick from the journey, as well as terrified, gazed back at her in dumb misery. She had never been into the English countryside before and had not the faintest idea where she was.

'Oh for God's sake,' Alexandra growled impatiently. She tossed her platinum mane and glanced up towards the allotment fields, the reflection of the moon skidding agitatedly across the surface of her sunglasses.

'Hang on a minute,' she said. 'There's a light up there.' There was not quite moon enough to see exactly what was happening, especially given the additional complications of her sunglasses, but it seemed to Alexandra that whatever was going on was going on somewhere in the vicinity of her own patch. If not on her own patch itself.

For all her failings and self-delusions, personal courage and conviction were qualities Alexandra possessed in abundance. 'You stay there,' she instructed her reluctant co-conspirators. 'I'll be right back.'

'Don't hurry yourself,' muttered Petra rebelliously as Alexandra slammed the door.

Benny continued to dig. The spikes at the bottom of the earth closet posts were almost entirely exposed now. It was time to lift the frame and carry it over to Morag's end of the plots. All that remained then was to pick up the bucket and carry that too. He tried not to feel sick at the thought.

Ten minutes later, he and Beth were staggering across the field with various large pieces of wood and corrugated iron. Benny was surprised at his wife's strength. He had never previously seen her carry anything heavier than a shopping bag, although admittedly some of those had been pretty hefty.

After the last piece of frame had been moved, they walked slowly back to the original site of the earth closet. The bucket within was now exposed. Its metal sides glowed in the moonlight. As he approached, Benny could see that it was, as he had feared, full to the brim. They paused.

'Yuck,' said Beth.

They moved closer to the bucket. As the scent, faint but definite, wafted up, Beth stepped back. 'I'm sorry. I just can't.' She didn't, Benny thought, sound in the least bit sorry. But there was no doubt about the can't.

'Well why should it be just me?' Benny expostulated.

'Because you're the brawn behind this operation,' Beth explained. 'And I'm the brains.'

Benny decided to get it over with. He took a deep breath so he would not have to breathe for a few moments, seized the handle of the bucket and lifted it up. It was even heavier than he expected, but he did not want to think about possible reasons for this.

'Oooh,' said Beth, as he walked away. Her eye had caught a few more glinting coins in the dug-up bottom of the earth closet. 'More cash. I didn't realise I'd dropped so much.' As the moon was now half obscured by cloud, she reached for the torch. Bugger. Where was it?

Benny, sweating profusely, had by now almost attained his goal. He was practically at Morag's allotment, where he planned to deposit the bucket next to the piles of wood and corrugated iron. The whole undertaking had been much harder work than he had anticipated and he had no intention of rebuilding the whole shack tonight. His plans now extended no further than going home, having a thorough bath and returning to the bed he had been obliged to vacate.

Not far now, he told himself, the handle of the bucket cutting into his palm as he staggered the remaining few yards. The heavy container swayed and lurched as he walked. He was beginning to wish he had worn wellies.

Beth, at the other end of the field, had by now found the torch. She shone it on the handful of coins she supposed had dropped from her pocket. As the beam caught the shining metal, she frowned. Then she gasped. A feeling of volcanic excitement possessed her.

Benny, nearly at his goal with the swaying bucket, did not notice the shadowy figure rapidly mounting the stepped path up from the village. Nor did Beth, lost in astonishment at her discovery. 'Oh my God,' she breathed.

Three things then happened at once.

'What the fuck's going on?' hissed Alexandra Pigott. 'This is my allotment.'

'What the hell do you think you're doing,' roared Morag's voice. 'That's *my* earth closet.'

'Benny! Benny! Come over here!' screamed Beth. Certain his wife was being attacked, Benny dumped the bucket all over Morag's random vegetable patch and ran to the rescue.

'Well I've heard of pots of gold at the end of the rainbow,' Beth remarked softly, a few minutes later. 'But never in a . . .'

The big flashlight shone into the hole. Nestling in the bottom was a mass of gold coins, dazzling against the dark soil.

'Well you do hear of people turning up treasure in bogs, I guess,' Benny muttered, dazed. 'But not in, like, literal bogs.'

He shook his head slowly, still having difficulty believing what his wife had found. A sackful of dough, basically. And all right underneath where that crap bucket had been. You couldn't make it up, you really couldn't. There literally had been gold in them thar hills.

He slid a glance at Alexandra and Morag. They, too, were staring at the gold. Both had stood without speaking for several seconds; a record, Benny thought, especially for

Morag. Since her first, outraged, lioness roar she had been as quiet as a mouse.

It was of course entirely possible, Benny reflected, that someone with Morag's eco-sanctimonious, anti-consumerist mentality might find the presence of actual money on the allotments offensive. That strange, fixed look might be disgust.

'It's mine!' roared Morag, bursting into sudden life. 'Mine! Mine!'

The noise was enormous and made Benny jump. He was grateful not to be still holding the bucket.

'Yours?' Beth gasped. She had thought it was impossible to be surprised by Morag any more, but Morag was proving her wrong.

'Yes, mine,' Morag panted, dropping to her knees and scooping the gold into her hands. Her wolfish teeth gleamed yellow with the reflected metal.

'Of course it's not yours,' Beth objected. 'I found it.'

'On my allotment!' hissed Alexandra Pigott.

'Hey, guys, *guys*,' Benny said in a jittery voice, trying to sound reasonable above his hammering heart. 'We're not sure if it's anybody's.'

The three women's heads flew up. '*What?*' they roared in unison.

Beth glared at him, her expression accusing him of rank betrayal.

'We're not even sure what it is,' Benny added firmly.

'It's buried treasure, stupid,' Morag snarled at him.

'But is it?' Benny demurred. It had occurred to him that it could be a hoax. Money was his job, after all.

'Course it is,' Alexandra snapped. She flung out a snakeskin-covered arm. 'What does it look like?'

Benny considered this. Certainly, with the authentic-looking coins spilling everywhere, and that ancient, rotting pot right next to them, it did look rather as if Beth, Alexandra and Morag might be on to something. It looked old, it looked gold, it looked the business, frankly. Besides, who in their right mind would stick a hoard of fake coins under an eco-sustainable john? Then again, he thought worriedly, who in their right mind would stick real ones in the same place?

'Yes it is,' Morag snarled. 'And it was buried under *my* earth closet. That makes it mine.'

'But you didn't find it when you dug the earth closet foundations, did you?' argued Beth. 'Benny and I dug deeper. You would never have found it yourself.'

'It's on my allotment, anyway,' Alexandra said heatedly. 'That's the point.'

'And it's not your earth closet anyway,' Beth challenged Morag. 'You're not the only one who's been using it. You've been trying to get everyone to.'

'Yes, but it was my idea, wasn't it?' As Morag gave her a deadly glare, Benny feared for his wife's safety. It was, after all, the middle of the night and they were in a remote country location. Anything could happen. Morag might try to strangle Beth – perhaps him as well – with the drawstring waist of her purple trousers.

'Hey. Girls. *Girls.*'

Morag's eyes flashed murderously in the torchlight. 'Don't call me a girl, you sexist pig.'

Benny was at a loss. Then inspiration struck. 'Okay then, females. Members of the female sex, c'mon. Let's calm down and try and think about this.'

'What's there to think about?' Morag demanded. 'It's mine.'

'No it isn't,' Beth argued. 'If it's anyone's, it's mine. Finders keepers.'

'It's mine!' shouted Alexandra, her sunglasses flashing dangerously in the torchlight.

As Morag looked ready to spring on Beth, and Alexandra on both of them, Benny moved protectively in front of his wife. 'Listen,' he said quickly. 'There are rules about this kind of thing. Laws. We need to find someone who knows about them.'

'But who?' Beth demanded. 'And what are we going to do with all this until we find them?' She gestured at the coins. 'We can hardly leave it all here, can we? I'm not leaving it, anyway,' she added firmly.

'Me neither,' Morag stated equally categorically.

'Nor me,' growled Alexandra.

The rain, which had started soft and misty some few minutes ago, suddenly gathered force. Benny felt it smack him about the eyes and forehead and hated it. There was something so intensely, nastily personal about rain, the way it got into your every nook and cranny. He looked miserably back at his wife, Alexandra and Morag. Alexandra's straightened platinum mane was curling in the downpour and Morag's was rat's tails already. Were they really going to have to stay here all night in the pissing wet?

It was stalemate. The three women glared at each other for a few defiant minutes. Then, quite suddenly and unexpectedly, a brainwave struck Benny. 'Hey. That solicitor guy!' he exclaimed. 'He'll know what to do.'

'Yes, that's it,' Beth cried. 'Good idea.'

'We need to go and get him,' Benny mused.

'You mean go and get him now?' demanded Alexandra. 'At God knows what time in the morning?'

Benny shrugged. 'What else can we do? We need a decision. The alternative is that we all sit here all night.'

Beth's bottom lip came stubbornly out. 'I'm not leaving this.' Her eyes glinted in the torchlight as she faced Morag and Alexandra over the golden treasure.

'Nor me.'

'Nor me.'

And if you think I'm leaving you . . . Benny thought, imagining gladiatorial combat as soon as he had turned his back. For all Morag's overt nature-loving credentials he had no doubt he would come back to find his wife and Alexandra battered to death with the cane currently supporting Gid's bid for jam supremacy. 'Well we'll just all have to go then,' he said.

'What about the treasure?' Morag demanded.

Benny stared at the glimmering gold, to which the rain had lent a new intensity of brilliance. 'It'll have to come with us.'

Chapter 53

Philip Protheroe always had difficulty sleeping these days, but it had got much worse lately. He lay awake long into the night before drifting into fitful slumber full of piercingly real images of his lost wife. Recently, in the hazy slot between waking and sleeping he had felt almost close enough to touch the red shimmer of her hair as she tossed it back in that beautiful, once-familiar gesture. Her green eyes, turned laughingly to him, had been full of sunshine. As always, she had seemed happy. She seemed almost to be talking to him although he could not hear what she was saying.

Philip's heart ached. The twelve months between then and now made no difference whatsoever. He still missed her agonisingly.

Tonight, as he rolled restlessly about the bed, the noise of the cotton duvet crashed loudly in his ears. When, suddenly, he stopped moving, the crashing continued and Philip slowly realised that the noise wasn't the bedcover at all. It was the front door. Someone was banging on it hard.

Philip swung his legs on to the floor and groped for the alarm clock. Half past midnight. What the hell was going on?

His first thought was Mrs Palfrey next door, but his second was that she was away in Skegness visiting her sister. And Mr Palfrey, as always in his wife's absence, had been taken in temporarily by the local old people's centre.

It was unlikely that it was work. While clients occasionally got aerated, full-scale middle-of-the-night meltdowns were unheard of.

Philip flung on his dressing gown, shoved on his glasses, went downstairs and opened the door cautiously. He would have been surprised whoever it was – the circumstances did not allow otherwise – but he was particularly amazed to see, so directly behind the door as to almost fall inside when he opened it, the American woman from up the road. The flowery one with the obviously moneyed husband, the colossal four-wheel drive and the allotment that looked like the Roman Forum.

'Tell me it's mine!' demanded the American. Her usually immaculate hair, Philip saw, was soaked with rain. Her floral T-shirt was wet and clung to her slim frame. Philip averted his gaze.

'No, it's mine,' shouted someone else, and to Philip's amazement, Morag Archbutt-Pesk now appeared in the door frame, also dripping wet. Philip looked away from Morag's nipples, clearly visible through the rather grubby white T-shirt she wore. Not only were they mesmerisingly thick and prominent but also much lower down than one might have expected.

'It bloody isn't. It's mine!' exclaimed a strange accent Philip nonetheless recognised as belonging to that improbable blonde, Alexandra Pigott. Improbably blonde in the sense that hardly anyone's hair was naturally that colour. And improbable, full stop. That scene on the allotments with the film crew and the pink Wellingtons had to be seen to be believed, and even then it hadn't seemed entirely possible.

Alexandra was fighting hard to get a look-in. He could see her head, straining to peer round Morag. Incredibly, even in the middle of the night she still had her sunglasses on. And her lipstick, although it looked somewhat smudged.

There was someone behind, straining to peer round them all. A man, Philip saw. The American woman's husband, he recognised in the next instant, the one who had come to see him about the document. Benny Ferraro. But looking very different now from the brisk, businesslike, smart-suited Benny Ferraro he had met the week before. This one had wild, wet hair and a harassed expression. He also looked naked, or as naked as it was possible to be given the thick black chest hair that almost entirely covered Benny's stocky torso.

Philip backed away slightly. It was all a bit much for this hour of the morning. It would have been a bit much any hour of the day.

'It's mine!' yelled Alexandra, again.

A couple of lights snapped on in windows further up the road.

Exasperation mingled with Philip's tiredness. 'What's yours? Have you any idea what time . . . ?'

'The gold!' Beth chortled, cutting a mini-caper in the street and narrowly missing knocking over some milk bottles.

'Gold?'

'I've struck gold. Gold! Loads of it.'

'No, *I've* struck it,' Morag shouted furiously.

'The hell you have,' roared Alexandra. 'I have.'

More lights snapped on.

Struck gold? Visions of bearded men panning in

Californian streams nonsensically assailed Philip. He did not especially want to let these people in. They were obviously in a state of intense mental disturbance and it could be dangerous. On the other hand, it was raining pretty hard now.

From the threshold, Benny gave Philip an appealing, man-to-man glance. 'Hey, look, I'm sorry. I know it's late and all that. But do you think we could come in?'

Faintly reassured by his tone, and by the fact that he could now see Benny had trousers on, Philip stood aside to let the group in. As, in the hall, everyone but Morag removed their footwear, Philip noticed that Morag and Benny were holding something between them.

It was the handles of a large and rather muddy wheelbarrow. Which seemed, on first glance, to be heaped with gold coins, but that could not possibly be the case.

Philip tipped up his glasses and rubbed his eyes again, unsure that he was not, after all, imagining it. He replaced his spectacles, looked at the barrow more closely and realised that yes, it was full of gold. A mass of small, gleaming gold coins. A man's checked shirt peeped from under them at the edges.

'I didn't want them to get scratched in the barrow,' Benny explained. 'It was pretty jerky, getting this lot down the steps.' Particularly with Morag, Alexandra and Beth all fighting over it. Once or twice the laden barrow had threatened to go right over. Pushing it up the hill from the market cross towards Philip's cottage near the church had been even more of a challenge. Benny's every sinew had strained, his forehead had poured with sweat and his heart had pounded fast and loud in his ears.

Benny had never imagined gold could weigh so much. He

was accustomed in his daily life to moving large amounts of money; millions quite often flicked between bank accounts at the touch of a button or the click of a mouse. But this was financial transfer of a completely different, altogether more traditional and utterly back-breaking kind.

Unsteadily, Benny, hindered by Morag and the two others, now lifted the barrow handles and dragged it into Philip's hallway.

'Hey, sorry about your carpet,' Benny muttered.

'It's okay,' the solicitor said. Compared to what else was happening, a bit of dirt on the floor seemed irrelevant. 'It's not a very nice carpet anyway,' he added.

'No it's not, it's vile,' Beth agreed cheerily.

As they followed him into the sitting room, and tipped up the barrow, a pool of gold swooshed over the floor. It looked, Philip thought, like something out of a fairy tale. A golden carpet. A sea of coins. A mass of treasure. As if Midas had pressed his hand right into the middle of the cottage's fake Axminster.

There was silence as everyone stood looking at the glittering expanse in awe. The dazzle was overwhelming, especially in the powerful overhead light. Philip finally accepted that he was not dreaming and that something significant was happening. 'I'll put the kettle on,' he murmured.

'I found it,' Beth explained matter-of-factly as he returned with a teapot, four mugs, a bottle of milk and a notebook. She was sitting on the black plastic sofa with her legs curled up, regarding him with glittering eyes.

'It's not yours!' hissed Morag and Alexandra in unison.

Alexandra's legs in their tight jeans sprawled over the black plastic armchair. Her now wildly curly hair rioted over her shoulders. Was it like that naturally? Philip found himself intermittently wondering. She was tugging at it irritatedly, as if trying to straighten it out. She had taken off her snakeskin bomber jacket to reveal a tight pink vest with the sequinned legend 'No Shit' across the front.

'It's mine,' Morag insisted. She was on the floor and had spread herself over the money in what she clearly considered was a guarding fashion.

Philip was now sufficiently awake to recognise some behavioural inconsistency here. Hadn't this woman always positioned herself as a dedicated eco-friendly anti-capitalist? The two blondes' greed wasn't too attractive either, but at least neither of them had ever seemed anything other than rampantly consumerist.

'I just want to be sure it's mine, that's all,' Beth continued, ignoring Morag and Alexandra. 'Apparently there are laws about it,' she added, rolling her eyes as if she considered this the most tremendous bore. Which in point of fact she did.

'Treasure trove, yes,' Philip nodded.

'Okay, so what happens?' Beth demanded.

Philip rubbed his eyes beneath his lenses. 'Er . . .' Treasure trove law was not one of his areas of expertise. He wasn't sure any area was at this time of the morning. 'I'd have to check, obviously, but . . .'

'Yeah?' Beth, eyes eager, had edged to the front of Philip's sofa.

'Yes?' Morag rasped, edging further on to the coins.

'Yeah?' Alexandra stood up, stalked to the pile and stood protectively over it.

'Obviously the person all this belongs to is whoever buried it.' As Philip reached for a handful of coins, Morag glared warningly. 'But it looks pretty old,' he continued. 'I'm no expert, but it could be medieval, Anglo-Saxon, that sort of thing. So obviously we're not going to find the actual person who left it.'

'Anglo-Saxon,' Benny breathed. 'Awesome.' Fancy Beth turning up something like that. 'So what happens now?'

The solicitor let the coins slither through his long fingers. It was, even at this hour, genuinely amazing to think how much time had passed since they were last handled, and by whom. The historian in him longed to know the circumstances in which they had been buried. Why? Did whoever had put them there expect to come back and get them?

'Well,' he replied to Benny. 'If it's an important historical find, then museums get involved.'

'Museums!' Morag snarled. 'What right have they to come in and grab other people's treasure?'

'I think they have to buy it, or contribute something at least,' Philip said quickly. 'But if they don't want it for whatever reason, I think the treasure belongs to the person who owns the land. Where was it found?'

'Under my earth closet,' Morag said swiftly.

Philip blinked. 'Under . . . ?' She had to be joking. And if she wasn't, who the hell had been under it? And why? He looked nervously at the three people in his sitting room.

'By me!' Beth asserted.

'On *my* plot,' Alexandra interrupted heatedly.

'Under the eco-sustainable lavatory facility that was *my* idea and which *I* constructed,' Morag shouted.

'But without Benny and me deciding to move it, this money would never have been found!' Beth shrieked.

'Hey, cool it, girls, erm, I mean members of the female sex,' advised Benny, from over by the window where he was standing. Philip's sitting room was small, and there was no room for his burly frame near the coins. He shrugged in an I'll-tell-you-later sort of way as the solicitor gave him a surprised glance.

Philip's sitting room was strange too, Benny thought, with fake beams everywhere and bright overhead lights. And the carpet, of course, but that was mostly covered with gold now. Together with the late hour and the general hysteria, they were doing strange things to his eyes. Funny, the Protheroe guy had always seemed kind of tasteful. He wouldn't have thought a dump like this would have been his scene.

'You are saying,' Philip deduced, 'that it was found on the allotments?'

Beth nodded.

'The allotments *I* championed and brought to fruition,' Morag added forcefully.

'Mmm,' the solicitor mused. He doubted this, having caught some of St John's opinion on the matter. He was aware the parish council chairman's view was that without Morag the allotments would exist a good deal more happily and productively.

'No you didn't,' challenged Beth immediately. 'St John did.'

'The hell he did,' Morag snapped back.

'Did.'

'Didn't.'

'Did.'

'It was my allotment, anyway,' Alexandra maintained stolidly.

Philip held up his hand. 'That is irrelevant.'

Alexandra looked outraged. 'What?'

'You see!' hissed Beth triumphantly. 'It doesn't matter that it's your allotment! It's the fact I dug it that counts.'

Alexandra was glaring at the solicitor through the black lenses of her sunglasses. 'Why is it irrelevant?'

'Because,' Philip said thoughtfully, 'as far as I am aware, the allotments are common land. They don't belong to anyone.'

'There we are then,' Morag declared triumphantly. 'The treasure's mine.'

'How do you work that out?' Benny asked, incredulous.

'Well if there's no particular owner, then obviously it reverts to the most deserving case. Which is me, obviously. I built the earth closet and without me the allotments would not exist.'

They all looked expectantly at Philip.

'It doesn't quite work like that.' Philip rubbed his eyes again.

'Hooray,' cheered Beth.

'Why not?' Morag snarled.

'Well if the land doesn't belong to anyone, it's not immediately clear who the treasure belongs to. I'd have to check, as I say, but I think the whole case would have to go to the coroner.'

Chapter 54

News of the discovery of buried treasure swept the allotment like the chemical sprays Morag so disapproved of.

'Well I sincerely hope some of it's going to find its way to the church roof fund,' the vicar remarked, turning his customary smile on Catherine, the one that never quite seemed to reach his eyes.

Catherine's own private hopes had soared as far as wondering if the hoard – in whatever mysterious way it might eventually be distributed – might somehow help with her dream of a school computer suite. Or even some new books for the school library. But she did not plan to confide these – or anything else – to the Reverend Tribble.

'At the moment it's not going anywhere, is it?' she remarked to the vicar. 'Nothing's been decided.'

'So I believe. But I was rather thinking of being there when it was. It might be interesting.'

'To the coroner's court? Are you allowed to?'

'It's a public meeting. Interested parties and those with relevant evidence are, I gather, allowed,' the Reverend Tribble said pompously. 'Perhaps, Miss Brooke, you'd like to accompany me?'

Catherine looked up to see his head on one side in emphatic enquiry. While she had every intention of being there – to stake the claim for the books and the computer suite if opportunity allowed – the Reverend Tribble had not figured in her plans. 'Er, maybe,' she parried. 'Expect me if you see me.'

Some ten minutes later, after the vicar had finally got the hint behind her monosyllabic answers and Catherine was frowning over her sweetcorn, Sam Binns appeared.

'Hi, miss!'

'Oh, hello, Sam.'

'What about the buried treasure, then?' the boy remarked excitedly as he strode on to Catherine's plot and began immediately attending to some leeks. His custom on arrival was to get directly on with whatever job he considered needing doing, and Catherine saw no reason to stop him. If Sam, as he evidently did, wanted to think of himself as having a controlling stake in her allotment, that was fine with her. She had acquired it mainly as an educational experience and a means of widening her social circle, and it had not failed her, even if the methods and results were unexpected.

'I know. It's very exciting. Such an odd place to find it, too.' Catherine looked at Alexandra Pigott's plot. The scruffy, overgrown patch, the only one of all the allotments that had not yet been cultivated, looked an unlikely treasure-house.

Over on the other side of the field the corrugated iron and wood of the former earth closet lay in the haphazard heap Benny and Beth had left it in, right in the middle of Morag's free-range vegetable patch. It was, Catherine thought with an amused twist of the lips, the least she deserved.

Sam was still jabbering excitedly about the treasure. 'I thought it would be crowns and pearls and diamonds in a big chest,' he said, looking up for a moment, his face eager and, for once, open and glowing.

'And it isn't?' Catherine smiled at Sam's vision of what the treasure looked like; the pantomime, story-book image seemed touchingly innocent for a child whose experiences had been so brutal. She tried to work out what else was so different about the boy's expression, so unlike the usual one he wore: shut, wary, old beyond his years. Then it came to her. It was childlike. For once, for the first time ever, Sam Binns looked like the eight year old he was.

He shook his shorn head, grinning. 'No. Phil tells me it's just a load of titchy coins. He's got them in his house but he says he can't let me see them.'

Phil. She shook her head slightly at the unexpected friendship Sam seemed to have developed with, of all people, the rather distant solicitor.

'How's, er, Phil's allotment coming on?' Catherine asked. She was aware that she did not enjoy Sam's horticultural favours exclusively. The boy put many hours into Philip Protheroe's plot, although she had never dared to venture over to see what the results of his attentions there were. She longed to, but did not want to seem forward.

'Great. You should see his rhubarb,' Sam enthused. 'Oooh,' he added suddenly. 'I'm glad you reminded me, miss.'

'Reminded you of what?'

'Phil. He asked me to give you a message.'

'A message?' Catherine repeated in amazement. Her heart revved up its beats. What possible message could the solicitor have for her?

Sam, she noticed, seemed red-faced and uncomfortable. 'It's a bit embarrassing,' he muttered.

'What is?' Catherine was intrigued and amazed in equal parts. She felt tight in her stomach.

'He wondered whether you might, well, like to . . .'

'To what?' Catherine urged, smiling.

'To meet him.'

'Meet him!' Catherine exclaimed, as a rush of excitement roared through her, leaving her tingling all over in its wake. 'But I see him on the allotment all the time.'

'Yeah, but you never say anything, do you?' Sam challenged, his voice gathering strength and conviction. 'He'd like to take you out for a drink, you see, get to know you better. But he's very shy. That's why he's asked me to ask you.'

Catherine leant on her spade and blinked. This was frankly unbelievable. She glanced over to the Protheroe plot but it was empty.

'He's not here,' Sam supplied quickly. 'Just in case you said no and it was embarrassing.'

He looked up at her, his eyes wide and full of candid appeal. 'He's very lonely, you see, miss. Since his wife died and all that he's all on his own. I think he needs a friend.'

Catherine nodded. He isn't the only one, was the thought now flitting through her head. Although, admittedly, Sam's near constant companionship as she gardened had made her feel less lonely of late. Hearing what bits and pieces about his life he chose to reveal had engendered a new affection, sympathy and admiration for him. Beneath that surly and difficult exterior, she had discovered, beat a loving, sensitive and imaginative heart.

Was the same true of Philip Protheroe? she wondered. Not that he was difficult or surly, of course. But he certainly did not give much away. The tingle of excitement had now steadied to a glow of pleasure. As well as seeming the most sensitive and intelligent, Philip Protheroe was easily the most handsome and eligible man around. To be asked out by him was as flattering as it was unexpected.

'You see,' Sam added earnestly now, 'the only other women he ever sees is his hundred-year-old neighbour and some old bag at his office.'

His face fell as Catherine laughed. She knew the neighbour concerned. She wondered whether to seem reluctant, but her face, red with pleasure, and her thundering heart, probably almost visible beneath the thin material of her T-shirt, told their own story. She had never, Catherine accepted ruefully, been good at disguising her feelings. 'Okay,' she smiled. 'You look surprised,' she added, seeing Sam's face blank with shock.

'Er . . . I am, to be honest . . . I don't think he really expected you to say yes, you see. He's not got much, erm, what's it called? Self-belief. Sense of self-worth. Confidence.'

Catherine smiled. It was comical hearing such phrases from an eight year old. Then she realised where he had probably come across them – child psychologists' clinics, fostering assessment meetings – and her smile faded.

'Where does he want to meet, and when?' she asked.

'Er, the Crown at seven thirty next Friday,' Sam said immediately.

'The Crown?' Catherine was surprised. The Crown? That huge and hideous pub with the nightclub underneath it, in which a clientele of balloon-bellied men with rough red faces drank lager all day? She had not for one minute imagined it to be the sort of place Philip Protheroe, who struck her as stylish, as well as very attractive, patronised.

Sam was staring at her with an inscrutable expression on his face. He seemed to wilt visibly with relief as, suddenly, Catherine shrugged. What did it matter, after all? Even if the Crown was the Crown, an adventure was an adventure. 'Fine,' she said to Sam. 'Tell him I'll be there.'

So far as Gid was concerned, one moment his partner was storming out of the house in the middle of the night saying there were lights on the allotments and that someone was plundering her wisdom patch. The next thing he knew, she was back yelling about finding millions of pounds' worth of gold.

'Look, I know it's been a traumatic experience,' Gid had sympathised, yawning and rubbing his eyes. He had only just got off to sleep. But he tried not to mind too much; Morag was clearly in a state of great distress and needed his help and support.

'Traumatic?' she had repeated in a hollow voice.

Gid smiled. 'Yeah. Come on, Morag, articulate it. Face up to the horror that you've witnessed.'

'Horror?'

Propping himself up on the carbon-neutral pillows with one meaty arm, Gid had nodded emphatically. 'It's bound to have been a nasty shock. Seeing it all there. Millions of pounds – money, y'know? Just what you hate most.'

As Morag stared back at him, a stunned expression in her bulging brown eyes, Gid lay down and closed his eyes. She really shouldn't worry so much. It was only money, after all. It was fortunate, Gid had reflected, that his and Morag's friends were all such laid-back characters, such total non-breadheads and so committed to eco-respect, mutual interhuman respect and encouragement of peace, anti-greed and respect in general. Their certain response to hearing about the treasure would be lofty contempt. He wondered if he should even bother telling Dweeb about it; it might only upset him.

Now Gid, moodily inspecting his raspberry bush, felt bruised and let down. He was horrified to find that Morag blamed him for mentioning the treasure to Dweeb. He had not realised – or expected – that she intended to keep the information close to her chest.

The raspberry bush had let him down as well. It was drooping, looked weak and he was starting to accept that his hopes for it would not be realised. Far from being the founding father of a flourishing fruit empire, it didn't look likely to make it through the weekend.

But this was nothing compared to the larger-scale hopes that had been dashed; those concerning humanity in general. Now that, Gid thought gloomily, money had entered the Utopian allotment scene, everything had gone wrong. Those who had claimed to share such high ideals had proved to have feet of clay.

Funnily enough, Dweeb had been trying to scrape some of the allotment mud from his flip-flops when Gid had opened the conversation about the treasure.

'How's it going, man?' he had nodded at Dweeb; the customary greeting.

'Not so cool,' Dweeb had replied, waving the dirt-clumped item of footwear. 'This stuff gets everywhere, man.'

Delaying the great moment of revelation, Gid had looked about for an interim subject. 'He-ey,' he had said eventually, his eye alighting on the penis-shaped patch of chamomile. 'The fertility garden's looking like really fecund.'

Dweeb looked up, his hat lurching with the movement. 'Like really what?'

'Fecund.' It was a word he had learnt from Morag. 'You know. Kind of . . . well . . .' Gid struggled for a definition. 'I dunno. Healthy, I suppose. Fertile.'

Dweeb's habitually drooping expression drooped further. 'Yeah, well it's the only thing that is in that case.'

Gid squatted down beside his friend. Sitting cross-legged on the wet mud wasn't ideal, but one had to show solidarity in times like this. 'Anything wrong, man?'

'Vicky's getting nowhere with that chamomile,' Dweeb groaned. He took a deep breath as if about to make an announcement of considerable importance. 'No sign of a babe. We've decided to go for IVF.'

'IVF!' Gid was shocked. 'Oh but man, that's like so intrusive.' He imagined with horror what Morag would say about it. 'What about nature taking its course and all that, with the help of Morag's wise-woman herbs and being as one with the rhythm of the seasons and all that?' His voice held a hint of panic.

'Look, man, Vicky said the wise-woman herbs tasted like shit, okay?' Dweeb said testily. 'And as for the rhythm of the seasons, having to shag on the freezing ground inches from some burning clump of grass in the early hours of the morning didn't seem to do the trick either. *Oddly enough,*' he added in a voice which Gid might have construed as ironic if recognising irony was part of his make-up, which it wasn't.

'Oh, right,' Gid said, subdued. 'Shame you're going for IVF, though,' he added timidly.

'You bet it's a shame,' Dweeb remarked, scraping some long and not terribly-clean-looking hair back over similarly unpristine ears. 'It's going to cost a bloody fortune. Where the money's going to come from, God knows.'

'You mean Goddess,' Gid reminded him, in accordance with the respect Morag insisted was due to the supreme mother of the universe.

Dweeb cast him a look he could not quite interpret. Time for a change of subject, Gid decided.

'Hey!' he exclaimed, as if the thought had just occurred to him, which it had. 'You'll never guess what Morag found last night?'

'Merlin's dream-catcher?' Dweeb guessed, without detectable interest. Gid remembered that this window ornament had indeed recently disappeared and Morag had made a big fuss about it. His suspicion that Merlin had sold it to buy sweets represented the crux of divided loyalty.

'No,' he replied. 'Morag found some buried treasure under the earth closet.'

Dweeb nodded. His calm response was exactly as Gid had imagined. He felt a rush of satisfaction; his faith in the ideals he shared with his friends was unshaken.

'Yeah, I saw the earth closet had moved,' Dweeb said. 'What did she find then? A few jugs, a broken plate, that sort of thing?' He was accustomed to Morag and Gid overstating things.

'No, man.' Gid leant forward, grinning earnestly. 'Like, real gold, you know? Loads of it.'

There was a sudden, blurred rushing movement accompanied by a strong smell of stale essential oil. It was Dweeb leaping to his feet. Gid looked up to see his friend and spiritual brother looking down on him, eyes burning. 'She's found treasure? *Here?* Lead me to it, man. *Now.*'

Chapter 55

It was obviously ridiculous, Philip thought, to wish the treasure had been uncovered at a more convenient time for him. By this he did not mean the impromptu early-hours meeting with the discovery team, although he would happily have waived that privilege. But the work that the find had resulted in – for him in particular – was badly timed.

While the coins were fascinating, the administration they brought with them was rather less gratifying. He was overwhelmed with routine work to such an extent that he was staying late at the office every night anyway. Preparing, in addition, the presentation of the treasure at the coroner's court, not to mention fielding phone calls concerning the find from the few local journalists who had got wind of it, took up even more time. The worst offender was the ghastly Tamara Ogden from the *Mineford Mercury*. As their office was just over the road from Philip's, was on the first floor as he was and had similar large Victorian windows, he could actually see her making the calls to him. She would wave and smile with that huge red-lipsticked mouth of hers. And vice versa; Mrs Sheen, in this case, could not pretend that he was out, although he was tempted to ask her to do so.

Tamara, at least, did not seem to know much. He had feared Morag, in particular, would go to the papers without hesitation, but the seething atmosphere within the village of claim and counterclaim seemed to have encouraged an unexpected discretion – at least until things were decided. Which, thank goodness, would be in a mere couple of days when the case would be heard.

The interest – or possibly, the danger – of having the coins in his house had been short-lived. Given the rivals for ownership of the hoard – even that hippy in the velvet top hat had weighed in now – Philip had not felt able to sleep safely in his bed at night while the money had been hidden in the cottage.

But thankfully – although not without a great deal of unpleasantness from Morag, who clearly suspected his motives – he had now arranged for the treasure to lodge in a bank vault until after the coroner had pronounced.

Tonight, as Philip worked late in his office, the rich evening sun slanted across his documents and gilded the edge of the green and purple legal ribbons with which they were bound. He found himself thinking longingly about his allotment. Although he had taken it on as nothing much more than an experiment, he was surprised at the extent it now mattered to him, how central to his life it had become. Now he was not doing it as a matter of routine, he realised he actually enjoyed it; mildly, quietly, but nonetheless sincerely.

He had, he knew, not thought ever to enjoy anything again. And yet here he was in his office actually hankering after the evening walk to the field, relishing the bright air and the view of the village, the sound of the swooping swifts and housemartins hunting the day's last insects, soothing away a stressful day with the rhythm of digging. He enjoyed the metally, minerally smell of the earth and the magic – really, there seemed no other word for it – of seeing the things he had planted actually emerge.

Of course, what was currently emerging from his plot had been helped considerably on its way by the boy Sam and his seemingly endless knowledge and enthusiasm. And not just about vegetables; his interest in Roman culture was equally boundless and they had had many an enjoyable discussion of the Punic Wars over the pea patch. Philip, musing about this, wondered how his peas were doing, exactly.

His thoughts, like one of the pollinating bees he had discovered were so crucial to fruit and vegetable husbandry, now alighted on Sam. Although neither of them had done more than sketch the outlines of what had happened, he knew that the boy, like himself, had had some swingeing blows from life, and Philip felt drawn to him, protective almost.

He looked down at the documents on which he was working. He had virtually finished them; if he came in a little earlier tomorrow morning, he could see them off easily. And if he left now he could have a few minutes to himself on his plot as the sun went down.

As Philip was not actually planning to work on his vegetables, just look at them, he did not go home to change. He parked his car by the pub by the village cross and walked eagerly up the stepped path to the gate on the hillside that led into the flat allotment field. As he crossed the plots towards his own, he saw that he was not alone. A small figure was bent over his bean rows. 'Sam!'

The boy looked up, surprise and relief in his thin white face. 'Phil! You've not been here for ages.'

'Work, I'm afraid,' Philip admitted, realising guiltily, as his eyes swept the patch, that Sam had very much been here. There was not a weed in sight and an entire new area of something or other seemed to have been planted. His rhubarb, meanwhile, was twice as big as it had been the last time he saw it and so shiny with health it looked to have been polished. 'You've been busy,' he remarked gratefully.

'This and that,' Sam shrugged.

'But it's late,' Philip said, his guilt deepening. 'Have you been here this late every night?'

Sam shrugged again. 'I were hoping to see yer. There's something I wanted to talk to you about.'

'About Pompey's campaigns?' They had been talking about the great Roman general, scourge of Antony and Cleopatra, last time they were together. Philip squinted at his leeks. He had been mad to think he could see anything at this time of night.

'No. About Miss Brooke, actually.'

The light was fading fast. Philip stared at the glowing white disc that was the boy's face. 'Miss Brooke? The headmistress, you mean?' Philip was conscious of a slight increase in his heart rate.

'Yeah,' Sam replied flatly.

'What about her?' His throat felt suddenly dry and he swallowed. Philip was aware, lately, of his glance lingering on the form of the headmistress as she toiled on her plot rather longer than it lingered on anyone else. Her body looked soft, yet strong, she was slender, yet not thin, small, but not too tiny. He liked her neat and shining bob, the colour of conkers. Her mouth, up close, had been as round and red as a strawberry; her eyes wide and clear.

He rarely spoke to her, admittedly. But he felt her there on the plots, albeit at a distance, and once or twice lately he had found himself picturing her as he drifted off to sleep. A new longing for human contact, someone to hold, someone to hug, had passed through him.

'There was something she wanted me to ask you,' Sam told him.

'Oh yes?' No doubt something and nothing, but Philip's level tone masked the fact he was intrigued. Excited, even.

'She wondered,' Sam muttered, his voice low in the dark, 'whether you might . . . whether you might . . .'

'Whether I might what?' Philip urged.

'Whether you might, well, you know . . .'

'*What?*'

'Go for a drink with her.'

Philip, the sole of one shoe rocking on a large clod, now almost fell over. 'A drink?' He felt his brain processing this completely unexpected piece of information. It whooshed through his synapses with the speed of a welcome surprise, but in its wake he felt something slam shut. His interest in the idea went suddenly into reverse. Panic rose. A drink? What did Catherine mean by this? They were mere nodding acquaintances.

'That's what she was worried about,' Sam told him, reading his face with an accuracy and perception Philip might have found surprising in an eight year old, if he hadn't been finding too many other things surprising to notice.

'What? What was she worried about?' Philip muttered, his large eyes darting about behind his glasses.

'That you might not want to. That's why she asked me to ask you. Less embarrassing, she reckoned.'

Behind Philip's neat shirtfront was a whirl of guilt and fear. His pale hands were clammy. He couldn't go out with a woman. Alone. Especially for reasons that could not be screened by work and were overtly social. Possibly even . . . but no. He dare not even frame the word romantic. To even think of it was disloyal to Emily.

'She thought it might be fun,' Sam said encouragingly.

'Fun?' Philip rubbed his forehead as he did when perturbed. He didn't expect fun. He never thought about it. He didn't want it. What did fun have to do with anything any more? 'Er, I really don't think so.'

No. He felt firm about it now. Definitely not. Drinks with women were not something he did. Not now. Not unless one counted strong cups of PG Tips with Mrs Palfrey.

'Why not?' Sam riposted from the now almost complete darkness beside him. 'She's nice, Miss Brooke is. And she's all by herself, like you are. And she knows a lot about the Romans.'

'But I don't want to have a drink with her,' Philip objected. 'I don't know her,' he added, as Sam stared at him accusingly.

'Well you're not going to know her any better at this rate, are you?' Sam pointed out with faultless logic.

'But I don't know if I want to,' Philip said with more frankness than he had intended.

'Of course you want to,' Sam said briskly. 'She's all right, Miss Brooke is. Look,' he added with a hint of exasperation, 'she's not asking you to marry her.'

'Jesus Christ!' Philip shouted involuntarily. He clapped a hand to his mouth and eyed Sam over it. 'Sorry,' he muttered into his palm, shaking his head fitfully.

'She's just suggesting a drink,' Sam went calmly on, accepting Philip's reaction in a manner, the solicitor perceived with sudden, devastating clarity, that suggested he had dealt with adult histrionics many times before. 'You're on your own and she's on her own,' the crop-headed boy reasoned, his slitty eyes opened slightly in appeal. 'You can afford to spend a couple of hours together. You never know, you might hit it off. As *friends*,' he emphasised hurriedly.

Philip strove for self-control. He was thirty-five and a highly qualified lawyer, and a persistent eight year old was making him panic. But the thought of being alone with any woman under sixty terrified him. He had no desire to form a relationship, however slight, ever again. Especially not with the sort of woman who approached men using eight-year-old boys as go-betweens. It was desperate behaviour. Wasn't it? 'No.' He shook his head emphatically.

'So what else are you doing on Friday night?' Sam demanded.

'Friday night?'

'Yes. Half past seven at the Crown.'

'The *Crown*?'

'That's it,' Sam confirmed jauntily.

'Out of the question, I'm afraid.' That frankly disgusting pub?

'Why?'

'Because I'll be, er . . .' Philip wondered why he was justifying himself to this child. Surely it was his own business what he did with his weekend evenings? 'I'll be working,' he stated stiffly.

'Working?' Sam echoed.

The faint derision in his voice made Philip bridle. 'Well, yes, as it happens. I've got a lot of work to get through. More since this treasure business . . .'

Sam was silent for a few minutes. Then he spoke. 'But there's more to life than just work, isn't there?' he said.

'Well no, actually, there isn't,' Philip felt like saying. 'Not now, at any rate.' He decided not to reply at all.

There followed a short silence during which Philip hoped he had carried his point. But then Sam started to speak again.

'Don't you need friends, as well as work?' he asked, his tone pleasantly conversational. 'Or are you going to spend the rest of your life on your own?'

Irritation flared within Philip. 'I'd rather not talk about it,' he said stiffly. He knew he sounded peevish, but he couldn't help it.

'I'm not asking you to talk about your wife,' Sam replied softly. 'I'm just saying it might be nice not to be alone for once. Your wife wouldn't want you to be lonely, would she? She wouldn't want you to spend the rest of your life by yourself.'

This was too much. 'Don't tell me what my wife would or wouldn't have wanted!' Philip howled. '*Please*,' he added in an anguished whisper.

'Fine,' muttered Sam. 'Whatever. I'm only trying to say that it might be an idea to pick up the pieces and move on. Open up. Trust. Take a chance on people again. That's what everyone's always saying to *me* at any rate.'

He rushed off into the darkness. Philip remained for a few minutes afterwards, then went himself.

Chapter 56

The moment she stepped out of the train at St Pancras, London rushed up to Mary and hurled itself upon her like a long-lost friend. She gazed in wonder round the huge, light-filled station with its great arched roof, marble floors, rushing people, shining trains, coffee stands, digital clocks and general air of business and hurry.

Nothing escaped her notice. To one accustomed for so long to the slow pace of Underpants and the allotment, London was an explosion of speed, noise and fascinating detail, from the intricate patterning at the top of the station's cast-iron pillars to the shining covers of the magazines in WH Smith at the bottom of the escalator.

It was intensely stimulating; imitating the people plunging past her on either side, Mary changed pace and started to walk faster and faster, almost breaking into a trot, though to do so would have risked endangering the food samples she was taking to her meeting, all carefully packed into Tupperware boxes. Nonetheless, there was something about London that made her want to run out of the station and into the heart of it, as people at the edge of a beach run to the sea. She wanted to dive in, immerse herself.

Outside St Pancras, the noise hit her like a hammer: the roar of traffic, the clanking of construction, the growl of planes above. The air felt dry and gritty and much warmer than in the Midlands, and the sun, despite the early hour, already beat down hot on the shadeless pavements. Mary, used to space, gazed round in wonder at the buildings whose sheer sides flung up all about her. They were amazingly various: the new, the old, the recent, the not-yet-built. The ugly, the beautiful, the decorative, the functional, or a mixture, as in the crazed Victorian spires of St Pancras piercing the skies immediately above, or the gleaming, blunt glass cones of the distant City, glimpsed between the blocks on the Euston Road.

London had changed, Mary saw. St Pancras and its environs now bore little relation to the depressed, poor and dirty area it had been when she lived in London herself. It had changed even in the year or so since last she had been here, for some abortive heritage-related meeting with Monty. The new St Pancras station with its Eurostar terminal had been well under way then, but now it was complete. Great curving sheets of steel and glass blazed in the sunshine and hoardings down the side of the refurbished Victorian engine shed advertised 'Europe's Longest Champagne Bar'.

Who was providing the food for this champagne bar? Mary wondered as she hurried past. Could Lady Amelia's own patent potato crisp recipe play a part? Or her tiny cheese and onion pies? She had samples of both in her bag for Mr Persson to taste. Why not, once things had got off the ground with the food company? People were so much more adventurous about food now. They loved small, upmarket businesses like hers – Mary thought of Lady Amelia's Pantry as hers now. Anything could happen.

People shoved past her, shouting into their mobiles, but Mary did not mind. It was intoxicating, this impression of so many lives, so many conversations, all extending and intertwining over and under and around the city like a vast spider's web. She could not believe that, once, she had actively disliked London. But she had had no particular aim in life then. Escape had been her subconscious agenda; escape and marriage. But now she was back, and with a purpose. Time for London to be for her the city of dreams and promises it had been for so many others, even though she was approaching forty. But wasn't that when life was supposed to begin?

Mary smiled as a passing businessman cast her an appreciative look. She looked, she knew, pretty as well as businesslike in a new striped shirt which had been knocked down to nothing in the Boden sale and which had miraculously arrived just in time for the meeting. The chic but simple black courts, mid-heeled but feeling sky-high to Mary, and the efficient yet sexy navy skirt, hugging her slim hips and stopping just above her pretty knees, had come from the same mail-order catalogue, which Mary had formerly never even bothered to open. What would have been the point? She couldn't afford anything. Now, however, with Benny's advance, and the prospect of much more to come, it was a different and rather better-dressed story.

She even had make-up on, just a touch, but the mascara had widened her eyes and deepened the green of them, and the girlish smudge of rosy blusher had taken away years. Her black-coffee-coloured hair, trimmed for the occasion at Snips & Lips, bounced and shone on her shoulders as Mary strode happily along. It was a glorious day; she was nervous yet excited about the meeting, which Benny had assured her was the best way to be.

At the thought of Benny, Mary felt a tremor of misgiving. He was delayed, he had told her on her new mobile – bought at Benny's insistence – as she came down on the train, but he'd be there as soon as he could, and besides, she could more than cope on her own. 'You'll charm the pants off him,' Benny had assured her. 'What, with *your* looks, and *that* food, and the plan we've cooked up. It's infallible, Mary.' Knowing that she, despite being so new to the world of business, already had the confidence of Benny, a man so experienced in it, buoyed Mary again.

Benny's mobile had cut off before she could mention her plan to surprise-visit Monty at the Notting Hill house. She had timed it for late afternoon, when she had calculated he would be back from his training. Now, about to disappear down the tunnel to take the Tube to her meeting, Mary felt almost ill with joy at the thought of seeing him again.

Had she but known it, her beloved husband, elsewhere in the city, was feeling considerably less pleased with life.

Monty Longshott was dawdling up Piccadilly. He had been to visit a doctor for an expedition-related tetanus jab and his arm felt sore as a result. But this was not his only discomfort. Try as he might, he could not help noticing that the expedition on which he had pinned all his hopes seemed to be dragging its heels somewhat. The sponsoring company was now delaying and hedging to a degree that even Monty, who had a tendency to let optimism and enthusiasm immunise him against unpleasant realities, could not fail to notice. Of course, Monty told himself, nothing was wrong.

This unpleasant sensation of things unravelling, of them spiralling away out of his reach, was merely paranoia. Everything would be fine in the end.

He wished Mary were here with him, to hold him, kiss and hug him and tell him everything would be all right. He missed his gentle and beautiful wife dreadfully; had, in fact, from the beginning of his stay in London. Beth and Benny had been kind to a fault, and he was intensely grateful to them; his certain fate had they not stepped in with their hospitality, eking out these endless weeks in the cheapest bed and breakfast in Hendon, did not bear thinking about. He would have been infinitely more miserable kicking his heels in a place like that.

The house in Notting Hill, by contrast, was wonderfully luxurious. A bit modern inside for his tastes, perhaps, but he had been very comfortable there, apart from missing Mary, his nagging, increasing fears about the expedition, and being in the city in general. Rushing people and rushing traffic weren't really his thing; rushing rivers and no one in sight, on the other hand, very much were. Monty was a country boy, fond of remote spots like Underpants and the Arctic Ocean. He was, he freely admitted to himself, quite unsophisticated, which was possibly why he couldn't quite understand Beth's behaviour.

Perhaps she was just very, very interested in his expedition. She always had been, of course, right from the dinner party where she had asked endless questions, especially about his lavatorial arrangements, Monty remembered. Since staying with her he had grown used to coming back after training to the Notting Hill house to find Beth – and it was almost always just Beth, Benny seemed always to be working – lounging on the sofa in the upstairs sitting room, the blinds down and the lights low, surrounded by scented candles, her clothes slipping off her shoulders and sipping a glass of champagne.

Monty would politely pop his head round the door to say hello, sweaty after his training and his every muscle tired, and Beth would always spring up, rush over and kiss him, pressing her breasts against him and enveloping him in whatever musky scent she wore. She would insist he join her on the sofa. Monty, although aching in every limb after the workout Sergeant Potts put him through and longing more for a bath than a glass of champagne, felt nonetheless obliged to accept and sit there while Beth pelted him with admiring questions about his upbringing in a stately home and his experiences at public school. More than once, when he had finally escaped bathwards, she had offered to come in and rub his back for him. He had laughed as if it were a joke, although he was not quite sure that it was.

More than once, too, he had run into Beth on the landing outside his room at night. She would, for some reason, be wearing full make-up and a robe of some gossamer material, almost transparent, through which the rosy tips of her nipples and the trim dark triangle at the centre of her hips could be glimpsed, despite his efforts not to. She would giggle when she saw him, look at him expectantly for a minute and eventually explain she was using the guest bathroom as there was something wrong with that attached to the master bedroom. It struck Monty as odd that Beth, who had servants and helpers to do every imaginable household task, seemed to lack the number of a plumber.

Monty wished Benny wasn't away working so much. He could not help noticing that these encounters in the see-through robe never happened when Beth's husband was around. And it was obvious she was bored, apart from weekends, when she went up to Allsop, although she never had much news of Mary when she came back. Monty wished he could go to Allsop at weekends too, but Sergeant Potts insisted that seven days a week was the bare minimum required for getting him into shape. But in shape for what, Monty was increasingly wondering. Perhaps Mary's initial reaction had been spot-on; a prison security company who had lost so many prisoners could hardly be relied on. But Monty clung to his belief in them. What else could he do?

Now, on Piccadilly, trudging past the Royal Academy, he felt, despite the warmth and sunshine of the day, a leaden, chilly despair.

His mobile phone, supplied by his sponsors, suddenly rang. After a few tricky minutes Monty liberated it from the holes in his pocket lining. 'Hello?'

It was the chairman of the security company. 'I've got rather a challenge for you,' he began brightly. It was the approach with which he had broken bad news to several district chief constables.

'Great,' said Monty, not used to this ruse and little suspecting what lay behind it. 'I love challenges.'

This one, however, turned out to be hard to love. The chairman was calling to say that they were dropping sponsorship of his expedition.

Monty was speechless with shock. The ground seemed to loom up at him and for a few horrible seconds he thought he was about to faint. After a couple of devastated moments he assembled the vocal cords to utter the single racked syllable 'Why?'

The security chairman, used to a similar response from

senior police officers, pressed ahead in the usual fashion, which was to deliver the rest of the bad news quickly and get off the phone as fast as possible.

It was thus that Monty gathered that the firm had decided that 'the new black at the moment, exploringwise, well, it's moved on'.

'M-m-m-moved on!' stammered a disbelieving Monty. 'From me, you mean? It can't have. I come from a line of successful Arctic explorers. I am,' he desperately trotted out his credentials, 'the last survivor of the ancient Longshott line, holders of the ancient estate of Weston Underwood, one hundred and forty-four acres, two fishing lakes and mansion house comprising Georgian portico, medieval great hall, Tudor wings and chapel, ancestral home of the Longshotts for over five hundred years . . .'

'Yeah, but Monty, mate, hope you don't mind me saying so, but that's all a bit five years ago, frankly.'

'More like a thousand years ago!' cried Monty. 'We Longshotts go back to—'

'Yeah, yeah, but what pushes buttons now are women teams of explorers, you see, Monty,' the chairman cut in in his weaselly voice. 'Ellen MacArthur types that the press and public can get behind.'

'Ellen MacArthur – Dame Ellen MacArthur to you, actually – is a sailor,' Monty corrected sharply. 'Not a Polar explorer.'

'Whatever,' said the chairman in his smooth, easy tones. 'But she's the sort the press and public can get behind. Young women explorers, you see . . .'

It was too much for Monty. He could sense that the die was cast and the decision made and nothing he could say would make any difference. Nonetheless, he stopped on the pavement opposite the Ritz hotel and screamed into his mobile.

'I'm a middle-aged man, and an aristocrat,' he howled. 'This is sex, age and class discrimination. I should sue.'

'I wouldn't,' said the chairman, comfortably, also used to hearing the latter threat from police officers. 'No one's managed to do that successfully yet.'

Chapter 57

Beth walked aimlessly about the large, light, high-ceilinged sitting room of her house in Lansdowne Road. The first floor had once been two rooms but these were now knocked together. Throughout the house walls had been removed and those remaining painted matt white, skylights had been cut in the ceiling and glass put everywhere from the staircase to the transparent bricks in the master-suite shower. Beth had, on first arriving in London, been enthused by the concept of a cutting-edge townhouse, which had been highly fashionable at the time. That had been before the idea of a bolthole in the country had taken over and Bijou Cottage had been bought. Now she was bored with both of them.

The discovery of the treasure had been pretty thrilling, admittedly. But now all that was locked up somewhere and was no doubt going to be claimed by the government or something. Yet another thing she'd got overexcited about in this goddam country, Beth thought grimly to herself, and which had come to nothing. Still, at least she'd got rid of Morag Archbutt-Pesk's earth closet. She'd achieved that, if nothing else. It wasn't quite what she'd had in mind for her life in the country, but it had been obvious pretty early on that the long mahogany tables full of dukes, wits and beautiful women she'd envisioned herself at were not going to materialise. There was Monty, of course, who was beautiful and as near to a duke as she'd ever met, but despite her best efforts, he was obviously not interested in her. It was almost rude, frankly. She'd invited him to stay to be company for her, certainly, but she'd had a gentle flirtation in mind too, something to fill the time when Benny was working. Once Monty was away from that wife of his, a ridiculously beautiful woman who, even more ridiculously, seemed to have no idea about her looks at all, he would be easy meat, Beth had calculated. But she had calculated wrong. He had rebuffed her, albeit in the nicest and vaguest possible way, which, along with her general boredom, had had the predictable effect of making casual desire into something approaching a passion. Lately, she had even been driven to lurking outside his bedroom, churning with lust, her nipples burning, waiting for him to come out. But even that had not worked.

She wandered out into the hallway and looked up the three flights of cantilevered green glass staircase to where a slab of plate glass formed a large part of the roof above. This would, she thought, have been a good idea in California, where it was generally sunny, but in London all it tended to reveal were expanses of grey sky and spattering raindrops. Today, however, it actually was sunny for a change.

She walked back into the sitting room, straightening the many cushions. These were pointlessly small and covered in slippery silver material for what the interior designer had assured her was a wildly contemporary effect. The furniture was entirely black, and sparsely distributed. The lamps had brushed steel stands with paper shades; some made out of newspapers, which had seemed so witty when they had first been introduced. The steel banisters and handles everywhere, which had seemed so stylish, now reminded her of nothing so much as a provincial airport: utterly impersonal, dull and monochrome. Adding to this feel, although she could not see it at the moment, was the clock above the kitchen door which displayed the hour in London, New York, Paris, Berlin and Beijing, all places where Benny had business interests. Interests everywhere, she thought cryptically, apart from his wife.

For a change of scene more than anything, Beth went upstairs, the glass slabs of the steps cold against her naked soles. She wore nothing but a flimsy pale pink kaftan; she was technically in that state between getting up and dressing, but actually unable to see the point of either. The bedroom was not, however, a change of scene in any case; it was more of the same, black and white.

There was a heavy emphasis on storage in the bedroom, and in the house as a whole; even the skirting boards slid out as drawers. But the odd pile of books or slung-in-a-corner bag would, Beth thought now, hardly have interrupted the aesthetic. There were shelves for books, but they had not enough books to fill them; the shelves, anyway, were lined with suede for reasons Beth could not remember now, unless it were to ratchet up the designer's materials bill as much as possible.

Beth toned down the lighting a smidgeon more; like most other things in the hi-tech house this could be changed at the touch of a pad or a text message. The whole place was run by an electronic butler; a computer system that could draw baths, arrange lighting, adjust heating and choose music on receipt of a text message sent from anywhere in the world. She had been excited about it at the time, but now, like everything else, it bored her.

She went into the master bedroom – monochrome with a huge, low bed – and glanced with dislike at the wall-mounted, rather battered violin, viola and cello, placed at crazy angles. They looked ridiculous, she thought, although she had loved them at first. They had been the leitmotif of the interior designer, apparently.

Beth lay down on the bed, made up in granite-grey linen below the black silk cover, and stretched her arms above her head. God, she was bored. Looking at the sunshine outside the window, she sighed and slipped one hand beneath her kaftan. If only Monty was here to play with.

At a noise below, she raised her head slightly. Was that the front door? She lowered her head again. The cleaner, no doubt. Or the housekeeper. They had their own keys. Beth never bothered answering the door. There was always someone else to.

Footsteps were coming up the stairs. Not the submissive tread of the cleaner, though. The steps were slappy and stompy, evidently from large feet. Men's feet. Monty's feet? It sounded like his familiar, hurried stumble.

'Monty?' she called sharply, all suspense. Her eyes manically roved the ceiling as her ears strained for his answer.

The answer was the bedroom door pushed open. Monty stuck his head round and she looked at him, expecting the familiar polite-yet-reluctant expression he employed whenever she offered him an evening glass of champagne.

'Monty?' Beth sat up on the bed. The face looking round the door at her was as shattered a visage as she had ever seen. There was no light in the blue eyes at all. The long, wide mouth with its ready smile, and which she had so often imagined doing delicious things to her, hung redundantly below the nose. Monty looked as if all hope had drained out of him.

Beth's heart began to hammer. Had something happened to Mary? Oh God, the poor guy. 'Monty! Hey, what's up?' she asked, all sweet concern.

Monty, from the door, groped blindly to this source of light in his darkness. From the bottom of his despair, amid the shattering of all his dreams, everything appeared grey and vague and meaningless. Normal distinctions did not apply. All he could see now was that there was sympathy over there on that bed, and comfort too.

'The expedition,' he muttered. 'It's not happening.'

Beth blinked. Just the expedition? Jesus, you'd have thought the world had ended. She was about to tell him to cheer up, when another thought struck her. 'Aw, come here,' she invited, half rising to take his hand and pull him towards her.

Mary emerged from Notting Hill Tube. The explosion of mid-afternoon sunshine that greeted her matched that in her heart. The meeting with Benny's client, but without Benny, as it happened, had gone well. Mr Persson, a softly spoken Scandinavian with very clean glasses and a perfectly cut suit, had been impressed both with Mary's pitch and with what she had brought for him to taste. Her mobile had rung within minutes of her leaving the nondescript office in Aldwych where she had met what she hoped was her destiny.

'Hey there, Mary.'

It was Benny. Immediately, Mary felt her heart leap into

the base of her throat. Was he calling her because he had heard back from the client?

He did not keep her in suspense.

'You're on,' he told her, excitedly. 'He's going to put up the money. Your career as international businesswoman starts here. Best go and get your apron on!'

Mary, in an uncharacteristic gesture for her, had punched the air in delight. Now she would really have something to tell Monty when she saw him. Which, hopefully, if she got her directions right, would be only a mere matter of minutes from now.

So which one of these white-painted stucco terraces was Lansdowne Road, exactly? Notting Hill had never been her stamping ground. Mary slipped into a nearby café to buy a takeaway cappuccino to sip as she pored over what she was beginning to feel was an incriminatingly new *A to Z*.

'Have a nice day!' said the assistant as she left.

'I am doing already!' Mary assured him, and felt that it was true. Euphoria was filling her soul with golden light and love for all humankind. Already. And she hadn't even seen her husband yet.

Beth and Benny's house in Lansdowne Road was a large, thick slice of four-storey terrace, festooned on the outside with pillars and balustrades and painted in shining white stucco. Mary knocked repeatedly, ringing the bell, but there was no answer. Rather to her surprise, however, the heavy grey front door swung open, revealing a stark, white-painted hall where green glass stairs, apparently unsupported, wound up into the light like a charmed snake.

She glanced at her watch. She was earlier than she had expected to be. Everything had moved so fast, much faster than she had imagined it would. People in London did not hang about when they wanted something to happen. It was one of the many things she liked about the place.

Still, she could always wait. It didn't seem as if there was anyone about. She peered, rather awed, into the great bare sitting room. Should she wait here? Everything looked so primped and perfect. It would spoil it to sit down.

Then, amid the ringing silence of the great house, Mary heard a familiar sound. Monty's voice. She was sure it was Monty's voice. Coming from one of the upstairs rooms.

Dropping her bag on the floor, Mary gleefully climbed the glass staircase and burst into the first bedroom she came to.

The smile on her face, the happy gasp in her throat, all died.

There, on a flat black bed, stark naked, his white bottom rising and falling between Beth's pale spread legs, was Monty. Beth's head was thrown back, her eyes closed; she was panting, her breasts shaking with the force of his thrusts. He was, Mary saw, making love in a manner far removed from the tender way she knew; thrusting frenziedly, the veins on his forehead standing out with the effort, as if working out some long-held, frustrated desire. 'Oh,' Beth was gasping in ecstasy. 'Oh God, Monty. Oh. My. God.'

Mary's legs would not move. She wanted to run, but the fascination of the spectacle held her. As a female scream of orgasmic triumph rang through the room, Monty, finally, saw her. Raised above Beth's body, sweating, panting, his horrified eyes burned into his wife's.

Nausea overwhelmed Mary. Clutching her hand to her mouth, she reeled out of the room and ran downstairs, the glass steps slippery beneath her unfamiliar, skittering heels. Barely a minute after she had entered the house, she was outside again.

The door banged behind her. Then it banged again. Monty, a towel – for some reason – clutched over his penis, was running after her. 'Mary! Mary! Oh God, Mary, please, come back,' he howled.

Mary was running from him as if he would kill her. She could not bear to look at him, much less to hear him, and if he touched her she would certainly explode. Just now, in this first intensity of shock, in a frenzy of self-protection, she wanted to put all the distance she could between them. She ran to the end of the road, in the direction that the high, white, shrilling space that had formerly been her brain indicated the Tube lay. By the time Monty and his towel arrived at Notting Hill station, she had disappeared into the ground.

Chapter 58

There were, Catherine thought, even more unpleasant-looking men at the Crown than was usual. They were whiskery and undergrown and jerky and quivery, sort of terrier-like. Several of them rolled a lager-soused eye over her from time to time as she stood nervously in the corner of the bar. She had been standing outside but it had started to rain.

It was now half past seven exactly. In her schoolteacherish, over-punctual way she had been ten minutes early and now felt she had been here for ever, trying to ignore the glances of rudely staring men obviously wondering what she was doing. It was a question she had had time to ponder herself as she sipped her glass of fizzy water.

Had it been a good idea to meet Philip Protheroe? She had hoped to see him on the allotments before the date and mention it, get a feel for what he was expecting from it, perhaps even change the proposed venue, but he had been absent ever since the drink idea was mooted. 'He's just working a lot,' Sam had told her when, after some doubt as to whether she should, Catherine had asked after the solicitor's whereabouts.

Not sure whether to believe this, unsure in general, Catherine had determinedly built down her hopes for the occasion. The fact that the evening was to begin – and possibly end – at the worst pub in Mineford indicated that Philip Protheroe did not regard it as a particularly special one. Nonetheless, Catherine had prepared for it with a certain excitement. She had dressed casually but with care in her best pair of close-fitting black trousers, a black top, a slim-cut caramel corduroy jacket that was fashionably short and definitely not 'school' and the high-heeled pointy black ankle boots that the children called 'witch boots' when she wore them in the classroom.

She had washed and blow-dried her chestnut bob which, newly cut, looked snappy and pert. Her make-up was under-stated, but definite. All in all, Catherine thought, she could give every other woman in this pub a run for their money, although that was admittedly not saying much. Not many of them looked as if they could run at all. Of those present, some were huge with fat mottled arms and low-self-esteem haircuts, choppy and masculine. Others were drug-addict skinny and pale, their greasy hair scraped back with agonising tightness over their temples.

Catherine had tried to stop herself thinking beyond the first drink, although she was planning to suggest they had dinner. There was nothing particularly forward about that; their friendship was not advanced, but enough to permit the suggestion. Besides, two professionals in their thirties, like Philip and herself – she guessed his age to be similar – couldn't stand in pubs all night drinking lager like teenagers.

After dinner, if it happened, she had no thoughts whatso-ever. None she gave herself deliberate licence for, although

Philip had haunted her subconscious lately, ever since the date was proposed. It had been many months since Catherine had been intimate with a man, and there was obviously no question of sex, not after the first date and certainly not as one upstanding member of a small village community with another upstanding member of the same.

Catherine had determinedly tried to banish thoughts of upstanding members where Philip Protheroe was concerned. During daylight hours anyway. But at night, alone, in the dark, she surrendered herself to pleasure, imagining the solicitor's full, soft-looking lips on hers, the scent of his skin, the feel of being drawn into that slim yet strong-looking body. Thoughts that had her gasping in the night, her eyes flying open in the darkness when she had been on the point of sleep.

Her eye caught the fake-Edwardian station clock surrounded by fake-Edwardian beer signs on the opposite wall of the bar. It was now twenty to eight. Catherine's stomach gave a surge of misery. Where was he?

How foolish she felt now. How far removed from any possibility of realisation were her sad single-woman fantasies. Irritation began to follow her shame and disappointment. What was the point of asking her out if he never intended to turn up?

Across the road, in the darkness, Philip leant against the wall by the traffic lights. He could see Catherine at the bar. Her shiny nut of hair seemed a beacon of cleanliness and order compared to the rumpled, faded heads of those around her.

She looked, he could not help recognising, unhappy and

apprehensive. While apprehension was only to be expected in the Crown, the degree of her obvious discomfort seemed strange; it was her idea that they meet, after all. Not his.

Nonetheless, part of him, the polite part, wanted to cross the road, go in and reassure her. But a rather larger part of him, the part that was still shut as tight as an oyster against any danger of interaction, especially female interaction, kept him against the wall. This part of him could not believe he had even got this far, that he was actually a mere few feet away from a date with a woman. How could he? What was the point? He had nothing to offer any woman, and no woman, after Emily, had anything to offer him.

He had dreamt about her last night again. Again, she had seemed close enough to touch. She had whirled in his dreams, happy, smiling, hair shining, talking to him. He had the sense that she was urging him to do something, but could not make out what.

After a few minutes, he calmed down again. He was not, Philip knew, here for Catherine anyway. Much of what Sam had said had struck home with him, especially the last bit about how he, Sam, was always being told to trust again. It wasn't that Philip felt compelled to do anything of the sort himself, more the triteness of the phrase and the circumstances in which he imagined it being said to the boy, by some council official in some sterile office. The thought gave him a squeezing sensation in his throat.

So he was here for Sam. He owed the boy something for all the work he had put in on the allotment, and that he, Philip, meet the schoolteacher for the drink she wanted was obviously important to Sam. Besides, he could not forget that forlorn speech, the one about self-confidence. Seeing Catherine glance desperately, once again, at what he assumed was a clock opposite her and pick up her bag, obviously about to leave, Philip shot across the road and into the pub.

Catherine, hurrying out of the doorway, eyes determinedly downcast, could not completely avoid the tall man hurrying in. 'Sorry,' she muttered as their shoulders collided.

'No, it's me who should apologise,' Philip insisted.

She looked up at that. 'Oh. I was just leaving . . .'

'I got, erm, held up at work.'

They looked at each other in the pub entrance. Various characters squeezed roughly past, their anoraked shoulders shining with the wet. 'Excuse *me*,' Catherine said rebukingly after one particularly violent jostle.

'Er, perhaps we should go somewhere else,' Philip muttered doubtfully.

She leapt at the suggestion. 'Yes, let's.' She didn't want to sound too relieved; the Crown had been his idea after all. For his part Philip wondered at her eagerness to leave. She had suggested the place, hadn't she?

They went out into the wet evening. Catherine fumblingly erected her umbrella while Philip screwed his face against the weather, pulled his collar up and racked his brains for Mineford's least appalling establishment. While inspiration did not leap immediately to mind, he recalled that there was some sort of Spanish-themed bar the other side of the bridge. It would serve wine, at least. He doubted Catherine Brooke was much of a beer woman; at least he hoped she wasn't.

The bar, Los Alanos, was dark, loud and crammed with teenagers. Catherine felt about a hundred years old and dowdier than a thousand grandmothers compared to the prevailing heavily eye-lined nymphs in hipster jeans showing a great deal of midriff flesh. And staring unnervingly at her, as if she had no right to be here, which she by no means disagreed with. Thank goodness they were all too old to be at Allsop Primary.

Thanks to the earsplitting music – some sort of generic excitable Latin blaring and whooping – it was impossible to hear what Philip was saying, though as he wasn't saying anything, just staring around disapprovingly, this possibly was no bad thing. Half concealed in the gloom, Catherine heaved a sigh that went right to her witch boots.

What on earth was she doing here? Why had he asked her out when he seemed so grumpy and uninterested? Of course he might be shy, and of course he had suffered a lot. But even so . . . He was much more approachable in his red T-shirt and jeans, with a fork in his hand on the allotment. Perhaps they should have gone there.

Philip, trying to catch the barman's eye, was wondering much the same thing. He regretted obeying whatever misguided urge had propelled him across the wet road and into the Crown, which seemed pleasant and peaceful in retrospect compared to this pulsating hellhole. He had done Catherine no favours; it was clear from her face that she was hardly enjoying herself. What madness had prompted her to suggest this venture? What she was expecting from it, he could not guess. As for him, the evening so far grimly confirmed all his fears about social interaction with women. Perhaps they should just pack up and go home. He was about to bawl this over the whooping when the barman's eyes finally made contact with his and Philip found himself bawling for two glasses of red wine instead.

The alcohol restored some of Catherine's flagging courage. The evening was, she accepted, a disaster, but where lesser women would have given up, Catherine didn't. It was too loud to, for a start; any suggestion they go home would be lost in the blare and rattle of the music. And besides, once she started something, she saw it through to the end. Whatever it might be.

She would not, she reflected, have got far in her career if this had not been her philosophy. Improvements such as Sam Binns would never have happened for a start; she couldn't, of course, claim credit for that entirely herself, but she had certainly helped.

At the thought of Sam, Catherine felt her resolve stiffening further; he had pressed her hard to agree to the solicitor's request for a date. That the meeting took place was obviously important to him even if it no longer seemed so to Philip, and Catherine felt obliged to make as much of a success of it as she could. Besides all this, she was hungry.

'Shall we go and eat?' she shouted at Philip, deciding to take the bull by the horns. What was there to lose? It wasn't as if things could get much worse. And the one entertainment amenity Mineford had in spades was Indian restaurants. Perhaps a bad evening could be transformed with a good curry.

Philip's instinct was to refuse, and then he remembered his empty fridge. He liked curry, anyway. They drained their glasses, left Los Alanos and headed across the road to the Spice Merchant.

Tucking herself in with a stiff napkin, Catherine felt better and better. There was something immensely cheering about the acres of white tablecloth, the tinkling music, the polite and friendly waiters, the reassuring menu. Even Philip Protheroe seemed to be warming up, asking her view on whether he should have vindaloo or jalfrezi. 'Vindaloo, every time,' Catherine grinned. Deciding he wouldn't be outdone, Philip ordered vindaloo as well.

It was much easier to talk here than in the pub or the bar. And once the subject of the treasure had been breached, and the possibilities of the coroner's court where the public meeting was to be held, Catherine found herself wondering how things could have seemed so difficult before. Whilst still far from effusive, Philip was drily amusing on the subject.

The talk moved to books. Catherine told him that she was planning to take the school to Stratford-upon-Avon in the summer. 'They're doing *A Midsummer Night's Dream*, which is just the best play to take children to see. So funny and magical. It was the first one I saw and I've never forgotten it.'

Philip looked up from snapping poppadoms with his long, bony fingers. 'So you like Shakespeare?'

Catherine's face glowed. 'Like it?' She paused, thinking that for anyone interested in literature it was a bit like being asked whether you liked breathing. 'Yes, I like it,' she smiled. 'Do you?'

Philip nodded. 'I'm no expert, but I've enjoyed what I've read and seen. My wife was the book-lover . . .' He stopped suddenly.

Catherine dropped her gaze to her own poppadoms and wondered what to say. As he had brought up the subject, ignoring it did not seem to be an option. 'I'm sorry,' she said simply.

He nodded, his eyes still downcast. His fingers drummed on the table as he fought to get a grip on the swirling emotions within him. Sam was right. He had to be able if not to move on, at least to get through a perfectly normal meal with a perfectly normal and really very nice woman.

Oh no, Catherine thought in anguish. He's crying. Oh, the poor man. The poor, poor man.

Then he looked up. To her surprise his eyes, behind his

glasses, were now what could only be described as twinkling. 'I must say,' he grinned, 'I'm very much looking forward to hearing Morag Archbutt-Pesk at the coroner's court. I think, for comedy, it's going to give even Shakespeare a run for his money.'

Chapter 59

At that exact moment, in a cottage some few miles from where Catherine and Philip sat, Morag and her cohort were discussing that very subject.

His suggestion that they all just meet and talk the whole treasure issue peacefully over across the kitchen table was not, Gid saw, going well. He had served his wholemeal, not-too-sweet scones but no one had taken as much as a bite. He had made pot after pot of nettle tea but it didn't seem to be having the calming effect it was famed for. Rather, the opposite. Dweeb looked with distaste at the greenish liquid in the bottom of his Fairtrade mug and asked, 'Haven't you got any Twinings?'

It was, Gid thought sadly, more proof of the corrosive influence of impending money that Dweeb now went for big-corporation beverages. An illustration of the extent to which the eco-idealistic brotherhood of the allotments; a brave band against a greedy world, had conclusively collapsed. 'You're going in the wrong direction, man,' he warned Dweeb. 'By striving after the fruits of wealth we lose the ability to savour and taste.'

Dweeb looked affronted. 'Yeah, well I don't like the taste of nettle tea, yeah? And some jam wouldn't harm these scones, either.'

Gid sighed. He could read the signs. The desire for affluence was corrosive and destructive. Time was, Dweeb had loved his nettle tea. He had not lusted after jam.

Did none of them realise, Gid mourned silently, that wealth was bad for you, that money meant misery and that the simple things in life were the best? He had tried explaining this to Morag, but she had replied witheringly that if he thought that, he was one of the simple things in life himself.

Gid could not believe the change in her. From eco-goddess to disciple of greed. Did she not realise that personal growth was more important than money? Perhaps it was significant that her own personal growths had been eradicated. She had started shaving her armpits and her moustache had been bleached into oblivion.

He cringed as he heard her shouting at Gudrun now. 'That's such crap to say you have any right to the money,' she bellowed. 'You hardly came up to the allotment at all. You were always in that pink shithole of yours smoking pot.'

Gudrun's nose was blazing with fury. 'How dare you?' she blared at Morag in her distinctive honking voice. 'How the hell do you know when I came up? You weren't there every bloody hour of every day. You were off sticking your nose in someone else's business at least *some* of the time.'

'Sisters, sisters,' murmured Gid, his buttocks tight with misery.

Dweeb now waded in. 'Look, man. It's obvious who deserves the dosh.'

Everyone stared at him. For all the joss sticks and relaxing oil burners, there was, Gid felt, tension in the room.

'How?' demanded Morag with savagery, her lips drawn back over her teeth. In the candlelight, with her bulging eyes and wild hair, she looked, Gid thought, like some terrifying medieval gargoyle.

'It's whoever has used the earth closet most,' Dweeb said airily. 'Which narrows it down to us, obviously. No one else ever really went near it.'

'That's not true,' Morag started to bluster before realising that Dweeb's idea might have something in it, and if it did she was arguing in the opposite direction.

'I used it most,' Gudrun asserted immediately. 'I went five times a day.'

'I went four times a day before it was taken down,' Vicky claimed.

Tecwen, who saw himself as the brains of the group, now roused himself to contribute to the debate. 'Well if we can't work out who used it when, perhaps we can project it through a process of supposition,' he remarked in his lazy fashion from between his blubbery lips.

'Eh?' said Dweeb, suspiciously.

'We can take another contributory factor, such as diet. Frequency of earth closet use can possibly be proven by looking at what each individual eats. I can probably make up a formula for it – bran over peas divided by mung beans equals four earth closet visits a day, for instance.'

'We eat a lot of brown rice,' Vicky said, nodding emphatically.

'Gudrun and I enjoy a very high-bran diet,' Tecwen maintained.

'Gid and I have lentil soup at least six times a week, don't we?' Morag twisted her neck round to glare at her partner. 'And we eat a lot of Jerusalem artichokes.'

'I can't see how we can prove any of this,' Dweeb said crossly.

Chapter 60

The vindaloo had arrived. Catherine was now openly chuckling at Philip's attempts to eat it. 'It's hotter than I thought,' he gasped, flailing for the water and watching Catherine with something approaching admiration as she forked hers in with apparent enjoyment.

Catherine smiled back. Philip Protheroe really was handsome – and looked so much younger – when he smiled like that. He had wonderful eyes. Probably even more beautiful without the glasses on. She imagined herself lifting them off, imagined them slowly closing, his mouth opening, in a long, shuddering moment of ecstasy. And that tumbling, beautiful, altogether deliciously schoolboy hair. So thick, so dark. She longed to knot her fingers in it, and pull his mouth to hers.

Catherine hiccupped and stared accusingly at her drink. Stop. This was too soon. But he had asked her for a drink; presumably he felt some attraction. He wanted to get to know her better. And he was having fun too, she was certain. He had been reserved at first, but after a couple of bottles of imported Indian lager he had warmed up, removed his really rather nice black and white checked tie, and been amusing and even charming company. Perhaps, Catherine was starting to think, just *perhaps* they might even see each other again after this.

Philip too was enjoying himself. Catherine, with her neat, small, curvaceous figure and wide and shining eyes was an admirable sight across the table, especially now she had taken her jacket off. He noticed what long eyelashes she had, and how her strawberry mouth was more intriguing even than he remembered; here bunched with amusement, here in mock disapproval, here open, plump and inviting as she laughed. Catching sight of a small tongue, he had swallowed.

Her teeth were very white. He imagined her breath, warm, slightly minty. For a split second he wondered what her underwear was like; he had caught a glimpse of pink bra strap as she had reached over for the lime pickle. He pushed away such unworthy thoughts and concentrated on the conversation. But then the thought ebbed back that she had asked him for a drink; she must feel some attraction, or an interest that might develop that way. Fantasies of physical closeness, even if it was just a peck on the cheek at the end of the evening, were not too far-fetched, surely. Anything could happen.

Perhaps he should let it, Philip considered as he ordered another bottle of lager. Catherine was not only pretty, after all, but, as she had shown over the Morag horse incident, brave and resourceful. Now, listening to her speak, Philip found his admiration growing. Not only was she far more erudite than he was, but also wryly amusing and, on the subject of state education especially, impressively impassioned. Briefly, immediately, he imagined her impassioned in other, more physical situations, then instantly suppressed those imaginings too, admiring instead her obvious commitment to her work and the ability she exhibited generally at remaining upbeat whatever the circumstances.

And her circumstances, he now knew, had occasionally been difficult and painful. She had ruefully admitted to having little luck in love, and it was the collapse of a long relationship as much as the desire for professional advancement that had prompted her to leave her previous post and come to Allsop. 'I did wonder,' Philip smiled at Catherine in an unguarded moment. 'It seemed surprising that a woman like you . . .' he paused, wondering what he was trying to say, 'you know, an attractive woman . . .' he blundered on, reddening, 'should be by herself.'

Catherine shrugged. 'There are all sorts of reasons for being alone,' she had said, in a voice so gentle he had found himself suddenly looking away.

They had so much in common, he realised. It was clear that for her, as for him, the village was occasionally a lonely place. And yet she seemed endlessly positive.

They were now talking happily about the allotments, in particular about their mutual wonder, as former non-gardeners, at what fun it all was, and swapping tips about vegetable growing.

'Although of course,' Catherine added, at the end of a sermon about mace-planting, 'I can't claim these are my ideas. I get all my information from Sam.'

'Me too,' Philip chuckled, taking another swig of lager. It seemed years since he had felt so loose and relaxed. A year ago, to be precise, he remembered with a violent pang. He looked down so Catherine did not see the pain in his eyes.

'He's an amazing boy,' he said, when the pang had passed.

'He certainly is,' Catherine agreed. 'He's improved so much at school it's unbelievable. I gather,' she added, shooting Philip a shy smile, 'that you've been helping him with his Romans. It's made a lot of difference.'

'I wouldn't call it help, Catherine,' Philip replied, gratified that this had been noticed. 'When someone's that interested, it's a pleasure.'

Catherine nodded, noting his easy use of her name and glowing with pleasure. She would say 'Philip' at the first opportunity. 'Phil', as per Sam, was obviously impossible. She wasn't sure how much of a Phil he was anyway.

'Although,' she added with a chuckle, 'I must say I wondered what Sam was about to ask me when he came over with the message from you suggesting a drink.'

She was astonished at Philip's reaction. His relaxed, smiling face disappeared in an instant to be replaced by its old expression of suspicious hauteur. 'The message from me suggesting a *drink*?'

He recoiled with the speed of a snail seeking sanctuary in its shell. Shame flooded him at the carnal thoughts he had had. She was here not because she had any interest in him, but because that boy had asked her to. And there he had been, almost beginning to enjoy himself, almost about to open up to a woman for the first time since . . .

Christ, Philip thought, mentally passing a shaking hand across a perspiring brow. He had had a close escape.

'Er, yes,' blundered Catherine, wondering what she had done wrong. Was she not supposed to mention it out of respect for his male pride or something?

'I didn't send any such message,' Philip pronounced sternly. He was no longer slumped over the table cradling his lager but sitting stiffly upright as if interviewing one of his clients. 'On the contrary. Sam came with a message from *you* asking if I would meet *you* for a drink.'

'A message from *me*?' Catherine repeated, now utterly flummoxed. What was Philip talking about? 'But I didn't . . .'

'Apparently you did. Why else would I be here?' Philip snapped.

He was tired, slightly drunk, confused, angry and suspicious. The panic he had felt before the meeting rushed back twofold. Most of all he was disappointed, and this made him savage.

Catherine stared at him, her wide eyes unhappy. She could not bring herself to come out with the same line, even though she was entitled to. She was astonished by the violent suddenness with which the evening, going so well, had been derailed. She felt an ache of shame, of misery, of frustration. And a flash of anger at his rudeness. Had it been her fault? No, it had not.

Philip stood up. She found herself thinking, somewhat irrationally, how very tall he looked beneath the low ceiling, dark and stern against the colourful scenes of Jaipur rioting on the wall. 'It would seem,' Philip remarked with stiff sarcasm, 'that your star pupil has not quite dispensed with some of his unfortunate habits. Clearly this is his idea of a joke.' He sprang up, dashing his napkin to the carpet, dragged his wallet out of his pocket and threw some crumpled notes down on the smooth white surface of the table.

'Good night, Miss Brooke,' he snapped as he stumbled out.

Catherine drove home in a fury exactly divided between injury to her dignity and the bitter dashing of her hopes. She and Philip had been getting on so well. She had even started to wonder if there might indeed be a future; another date, at least. How wrong could she possibly have been? He was not interested in the least. He despised her. It was now painfully, crushingly clear that it would never have occurred to him in a million years to ask her out had not Sam Binns intervened.

Sam Binns. Of course, he was not entirely to blame. Philip Protheroe had been horribly rude. Being left in the Indian restaurant after he had gone, to gather her coat and pay the bill, had been humiliation of the highest order. Well, perhaps the second highest order after the humiliation Philip himself had heaped upon her.

But Sam Binns, all the same. He had been the one who had set the traps. It had been his idea, this whole hideous evening. Catherine's face sizzled with anger and shame. The misfit boy in whom she alone had believed, who she had nurtured, encouraged and imagined to have improved. And all the time he had been plotting this devastating trick. It was far worse than the 'enormous cow' moment in the Norse class. Such things occasionally happened in schools and teachers had to brace themselves and deal with them. But tonight's incident, out of school, in her own private time, was entirely unexpected and had resulted in complete humiliation.

Just wait until the next time she saw him, Catherine vowed. She would hold nothing back in conveying the full extent of her fury. She had defended him, encouraged him, even, she realised with an acid spring of tears to the eyes, started to love him. And this was how he had thanked her.

Of course, perhaps it was understandable that Sam wanted to cause misery. He had suffered a lot himself. But that did not give him the right to behave as he liked, to revenge himself on the world.

Feeling let down and betrayed was, Catherine felt, the tip of the iceberg. She felt stupid too. She had not seen this coming, had trusted Sam despite his history of rudeness and intransigence, had never guessed he might act in this fashion, and consequently, for the first time in her career, seriously doubted her own judgement. Perhaps she was in the wrong job. Perhaps the school she fancied she had almost turned round was actually worse than ever. Perhaps she was a fantastist, an incompetent. Perhaps she was losing her grip.

Catherine, who rarely drove fast, relieved her feelings by putting her foot down harder than normal on the accelerator of her sensible black Golf. She roared into Allsop safe in the knowledge that no one was ever out on the roads at this hour, least of all any of her pupils, although there was admittedly one pupil whose mowing-down she would not, at this moment, mourn.

She slammed her car door to realise, looking up, what seemed like the final irony. As her own evening had got worse, the weather had improved, and what had been a grey and rainy end to the day had bloomed into a fantastical scene from the background of a particularly effervescent classical painting. Behind the stabbing black spire of the church the sky had cleared and the sun was sinking into a bed of yellow glory, fringed with clouds of brightest duck-egg blue and edged with gold.

School House and the church opposite wore the strange grey-yellow, otherworldly sheen of buildings caught in the odd mood between sunshine and showers, day and night. It added to the turbulence in her own soul as she nudged the half-open gate and stomped up the slippery path to her house.

But then, as she fumbled for the keys, she heard a sound.

The sound of sobbing. Someone very close to where she stood was crying. Catherine, who was not far from tears herself, looked up, half fearful, half surprised. She scanned the small patch of her garden in the fading light and then, to her amazement, spotted, beneath the glowing mopheads of a white hydrangea that hunched at the point where the house met the bordering rectangular garden wall, Mary Longshott. Crouched on an upturned bucket and sobbing as if her heart would break.

Chapter 61

Catherine dropped her keys in amazement. 'What on earth's the matter?' she gasped, scrabbling for them in the gathering darkness. 'Has something awful happened?' She realised as soon as she said it what a stupid utterance that was. Clearly something awful had happened.

Mary's face was buried in her hands. She now looked up. Even in the dying beams of the sinking sun Catherine could see that the long, pale face was blotchy, the dark eyes swollen and thick with tears. She had clearly been crying for some time.

'Has someone died?' Catherine urged, her throat dry with panic.

Mary raised her head. Her eyes were so red they hardly showed up against the rest of her hot, swollen face. 'Yes,' she sniffed.

'I'm so sorry,' Catherine murmured. 'Who?'

'My marriage,' spat Mary. She outlined the scenes in Notting Hill. 'I got straight on the train and came back,' she finished. Catherine's eyes swept the dark outlines of what seemed to be various bags Mary had with her. There seemed to be some Tupperware containers on the path too, for some reason.

'But . . .' Catherine, standing brandishing her keys, was confounded. 'I, I mean, I just can't believe it. I thought Monty was supposed to be going to the North Pole.'

'I think he had a different sort of pole in mind, or Beth certainly did,' Mary said bitterly, thinking of philandering Uncle Hengist and how Monty, who had seemed so different, had turned out to be a chip off the old adulterous block after all.

'You mean he never had any intention of going?' Catherine gasped. 'That it was all a lie?'

Mary raised wide, miserable eyes in the faint light. 'Who knows?'

Catherine was good in a crisis. She had had to be many times during her career. And in her personal life too, most recently less than half an hour ago. But she would put that aside for the moment. Mary's need was obviously greater than hers. 'You'd better come with me,' she said.

Fifteen minutes later, Mary lay on Catherine's sofa cradling a glass of single malt. 'You need to drink a lot of this,' Catherine advised. 'The hurt will go away and when you sober up you won't be able to tell whether it's your hangover or Monty which is making you feel worse.'

Mary half wondered, as she sipped the whisky, through what set of unhappy circumstances Catherine had found this recipe for dealing with pain. That it would not work for her she was sure. It would take more than whisky to obliterate what she had seen.

She had cried herself out now, there were no more tears. Now she felt numb, disorientated and cut off from everything that had gone before. Being in Catherine's cottage, a place she had not previously been, reinforced this sensation. She never wanted to see Underpants ever again. Or Monty. And if Beth ever had the misfortune to cross her path, Mary thought savagely, she'd bludgeon her to death with one of her own designer trowels.

Had Beth homed in on Monty that fateful night of the dinner party and decided then and there to have him? How far back did the relationship go, exactly? Years? Weeks? Hours? Mary had no idea. She had not been in the least interested in Monty's explanations, as he ran after her down the road and had eventually given up.

Nothing mattered, Mary thought. Her excitement over Lady Amelia's Pantry was now dust and ashes. A smoking ruin. Nothing mattered beside what she had seen. Her husband making love to another woman. She started to close her eyes in despair but then forced them back open. All she saw, when they were shut, was Beth's slender body, her long stomach, white thighs, raspberry-tipped breasts, her eyes closed and mouth open in gasping ecstasy.

Rage began to build within her, along with frustration. But there was, Mary knew, no real point in blaming Beth. Monty was the one who was her husband.

'I only have one piece of advice to give you,' Catherine said gently.

Here it comes, Mary thought. All men are bastards. You should never trust them. She roused herself, expecting welcome into the bitter sisterhood of women who had had their fingers burnt. She sensed Catherine had had little success with men.

But Catherine said none of the anticipated things. Instead she said: 'You're thinking about divorce, I imagine.'

Mary nodded. When she stopped feeling angry and empty

for long enough to frame a thought, this was indeed the thought she framed.

'Well before you put a lawyer on your speed-dial,' Catherine said, 'don't.'

'Don't?' Mary echoed, staggered.

'It's an irrevocable step, once it's done. Take your time. Think.'

'Why?' Mary demanded.

Catherine shrugged. 'When you've married someone, you've married them. It's a serious thing. You have to try everything to make it work.'

'Monty hasn't,' Mary burst out bitterly.

'Yes, I know. But one of you has to be grown-up about it. Believe me.' Catherine slid off the seat in which she sat before the other woman and dropped to her knees despite her best black trousers. Taking Mary's hands, she looked earnestly into her eyes. 'I've seen the results of divorce, Mary. I've worked with them. It can be terrible.'

Mary stared. Her mouth felt dry and her heart thumped. Somewhere in her head was a high, keening scream. 'You're talking about children,' she gasped.

'Yes. But the parents too.'

Mary stared at her friend. Why was Catherine bringing up the subject of children? Reminding her of her failure, of the wish that had never been granted? Did she want to make everything worse than it already was?

'But Monty and I,' Mary howled, her face crumpling, the sobs tearing from her body, 'we don't . . . we don't . . . have any children.'

Chapter 62

The coroner's court – a room in the upper floor of the Town Hall, to be strictly accurate – was small and stuffy, and despite the warm sunny morning outside, had that cold, dusty smell of a place unused for some time. The foregathered were ranged on rows of chairs which faced a raised dais. On this was a chair behind a table where the coroner would sit.

Tamara Ogden of the *Mineford Mercury* sat, notebook in hand, one plump, black-stockinged leg heaved with difficulty over the other. She felt what was rare in her job, anticipation. Excitement, even. That buried treasure had been discovered in Allsop was nothing short of staggering. And that to whom it belonged was in dispute was a joy. If the allotment meeting was anything to go by, there would be some juicy scenes. Dramas, no less.

The cast looked good, Tamara thought, working on her metaphors and wondering whether to describe the whole proceedings in theatrical terms. Derek Savage would probably be horrible about it, but he was horrible about everything. He was horrible, full stop. Roll on the glorious day when she would be out of his nasty nicotine-stained clutches. But there seemed little hope of that at the moment, despite her applications to various London papers. The editor of *The Sunday Times* did not appear to be in need of a deputy at the moment, and the same went for the editor of the *Daily Mail*. Tamara could not understand it. Did these men not realise what they were turning down? Or not bothering to turn down, to be precise.

There were a lot of people here. Most of the village of Allsop, by the looks of it. She recognised some of them from the original allotment meeting: that crazy bloke in the blue velvet hat, for instance, plus the woman with the big nose and the bright pink vest top. That Morag Archbutt-Pesk was present Tamara had realised before she had even gone into the building. On the kerb outside was a filthy, battered decommissioned ambulance.

There was the old chap with impressive moustaches, whose idea the allotments had been in the first place. St John whatsit. He didn't look well, either. He'd lost some weight, Tamara thought. Had he been ill? His once-red face now looked quite yellow.

And here was the headmistress with her auburn bob, inching along one of the rows. She was looking about her with what struck Tamara as a mixture of caution and defiance.

Catherine was, of course, sweeping the room for Philip Protheroe. Her eyes were lowered, hooded, ready to snatch away at any minute if they encountered the cool, bespectacled gaze of her least favourite solicitor. The room, full as it was, seemed empty of him, however. Was he, knowing she would be here, avoiding having to face her? And so he should, she thought indignantly, as various details of her humiliating evening rose to assail her once more.

In normal circumstances, Catherine supposed, she might have confided the sorry tale of the night with Philip to Mary when they met on the allotments. She was bursting to confide it to someone, certainly. But that was before finding a devastated Mary sobbing in her garden after finding, in turn, her husband in bed with Beth Ferraro.

Beth was not here, Catherine saw, glancing up and down the rows. Nor Benny. Hardly surprising that Beth wasn't showing her face, of course. Benny could be absent for the same reason, but it was equally possible he was simply away again being high-powered and had no idea what had happened.

What, Catherine wondered, was the point of being high-powered if you couldn't trust your own wife? Perhaps the Ferraros needed to put some time into their marriage. Was Benny to blame as much as Beth? As Monty, even? Had Benny paid Beth more attention, which she had clearly required – Mary had sobbingly related the conversation in the kitchen at the dinner party – perhaps none of what had happened would have happened. However, it had.

Catherine had wrestled with her conscience about leaving Mary Longshott, in the state she was in, alone in her cottage while she went to the Town Hall. What if Mary decided to put her head in the gas oven? This seemed unlikely, however; Catherine had left her asleep in the little white bed in the small, white-painted spare room, where she had been for the past few days.

But Mary seemed little better, for all Catherine's sympathy. Her eyes, red in pools of tired purple, shone with tears at all times and she shook constantly, as if chilled to the bone and unable, despite all the fires Catherine banked up and despite the summer weather outside, to get warm.

She slept badly, too. After hours of sighing, tossing, turning and the occasional sob – much of which Catherine could hear through the thin walls – finally, worn out with whisky and misery, she would fall asleep.

While she was obviously grateful for Catherine's kindness, it was equally obvious to the headmistress that Mary's mental state was becoming increasingly unravelled. There had been a desperate conversation the night before on the subject of children, which seemed to be obsessing Mary. 'Did you never want them?' Mary had asked, her eyes burning feverishly in the firelight, brimming over a glass of the whisky she seemed rather to have come to rely on.

Catherine, stifled by the kiln-like heat she felt obliged to supply for her shivering friend, had shrugged. 'I suppose I did at some stage. But I've always had children at school, you see. And the right man's never come along.' She remembered Philip Protheroe – not that the shameful evening was ever far from her thoughts – and scowled.

'The right man came along for me,' Mary had said quietly. 'But children never did. And now they never will.' She put her glass swiftly down on the carpet and her raw, bony hands to her face.

'You don't know that,' Catherine had soothed. She hoped Mary was still asleep now, and not trying to do anything rash. With difficulty she prevented herself from getting up and rushing out. She had to stay here now, whatever happened. If the money was declared treasure trove and given to the village to go in aid of a good cause – a scenario Philip Protheroe had considered the most likely when they had discussed it during the civilised part of the evening – she needed to be present to put the case for the school computer suite. She owed it to the children, to the school.

She owed it to Mary as well; being an allotment-holder, her friend obviously had an interest in what was being decided. By being here she could, Catherine thought, defend or represent Mary's interest if necessary, too.

Oh no. Here he was. A shock of embarrassment shuddered through Catherine as, now, she half glimpsed someone with spectacles, floppy black hair and a grey suit stride swiftly down the hall between the banks of chairs. She looked away, training her gaze on the chair back in front of her, her fingers tightly knotted in her lap. Tamara, on the other hand, followed the solicitor's straight, moving figure with interest. Having observed him for some time now through her office window, which looked into his, she was certain that his neat, precise, rather repressed surroundings disguised a volcanically passionate nature.

Philip's nature was habitually proud, but at the moment, feelings of shame and self-recrimination were sweeping across it with the regularity of windscreen wipers. He had done his best to justify to himself his behaviour in the restaurant with Catherine Brooke. Advocacy and the persuasive representing of interests were, after all, his profession. But something within himself, like a particularly pernickety, difficult magistrate, seemed reluctant to accept his version of events. Yes, this magistrate said. You were deceived by the Binns boy who had obviously played a trick. But that did not give you licence to be as rude to a woman – and a nice woman at that – as you were to Catherine Brooke.

Philip did his best to argue his inner magistrate down. Catherine Brooke may not have been telling the truth about her side of the story. What if she had put Sam Binns up to it, urged him to ask for the date, and then for strange reasons of her own tried to pretend she hadn't? That would point to a streak of madness. Philip had done the right thing by getting away as fast as possible.

But the inner magistrate insisted that he hadn't and now, glimpsing the back of Catherine's neat, shiny bob as he came down the aisle between the chairs, Philip felt a wave of shame, followed by helplessness. Embarrassment on this scale was not something he was used to. He had not the least idea what to do about it, or even whether he should do anything.

Tamara's eyes were still snapping about the company. Here, one of the last to arrive, came the Reverend Tribble, patting his scrapeover, his pointy, yellowish face expectant, shuffling along one of the lines of chairs and sitting right next to Catherine Brooke, who gave him a rather strained smile of welcome.

There was a cough and a shuffle. The coroner had arrived. He came trotting in; a short, brisk and very clean-looking man in a grey suit. He had a shining bulbous head and the type of sloping features, Tamara thought, that seemed to be falling off his face. Nonetheless he looked friendly enough and gripped an armful of documents as he ascended to the dais. There was a rumpus as everyone stood up. Everyone, that was, apart from the woman in purple trousers.

'Stand up!' Gid hissed at Morag.

She shook her head and glared at him. 'I don't do respect for patriarchal institutions.'

Morag was exultant. To her amazement, neither the American incomer nor Alexandra Pigott had appeared to challenge her unchallengeable right to the treasure. And, as the coroner's doleful, jowly, brown-suited assistant now closed the double doors at the back of the hall, they were obviously not going to.

'You don't do respect for patriarchal institutions?' Gid

repeated, puzzled. 'But *this* patriarchal institution might give you the money.' He had now realised that, incredible though it seemed, the money was what Morag wanted, although spiritually he was still finding coming to terms with it difficult.

'Where *is* the money?' Morag hissed, looking wildly around. 'He hasn't brought it with him, has he? He's probably nicked it, the—'

'It's not necessary for the actual treasure trove to be present at the hearing,' Philip Protheroe leant over and hissed from the row behind. 'Not when there's as much of it as there is of the gold.' The grooves dug by the laden wheelbarrow when crossing his carpet could still be seen. He had cleaned out the mud, but the indentations remained.

As Philip's remark was conveyed in whispers throughout the room, Tamara heard and was disappointed at the non-appearance of the treasure. She had been imagining a large, brass-bound wooden lidded chest out of which glittering crowns, jewelled tiaras, huge rings, gleaming ropes of pearls and sparkling rubies and diamonds all spilt as in a scene from *Aladdin*. But now she gathered it was just a lot of old coins anyway and she wouldn't even be able to see them.

The coroner slipped a hand in the inside pocket of his suit, produced a spectacle case and, with both hands, placed a pair of bifocals on his short, fat nose. He stood up, cleared his throat, placed one hand on his papers and made some opening remarks.

Just as he was getting to the end of them, there was a tremendous banging at the opposite end of the hall. Someone – a woman by the sound of it – was shouting to be let in. The doleful assistant, eyes downcast and expression unmoving, proceeded in funereal fashion to the double doors and opened them with slow ceremony.

Something black and white skittered in.

'The courtroom all turned and stared, fascinated and amazed,' Tamara Ogden scribbled in a frenzy of admiration, 'as, like a fabulous bride on her wedding day, Alexandra Pigott proceeded down the aisle between the chairs. Her shining white-blond hair was twisted up in a smooth and supremely elegant chignon, into the back of which one black and one white feather had been expertly inserted. Her black backless minidress was restrained and yet sensual, exposing as it did a pair of perfectly smooth brown shoulders and of course Miss Pigott's famously long brown legs, which ended in a pair of four-inch black stiletto sandals enlivened with crystals. Diamonds flashed in her ears and in the brown valley of her cleavage nestled a magnificent pearl and diamond pendant fashioned in the shape of a cross. She accessorised the look with a black silk clutch, and of course a pair of her favourite black sunglasses were perched on her exquisitely made-up face . . .'

Chapter 63

'I'm going to appear in court,' Alexandra had told Petra. 'So you know what that means.'

Petra had stared back apprehensively. In the world in which she moved – fashion, fame, celebrities – a court appearance could mean anything. Drugs, usually. Divorce, almost as usually. Motoring and public order offences occasionally. But never before, she thought, eyes wide as Alexandra tossed out selected details, had she known a celebrity client go to court over an allotment.

'It means,' Alexandra informed her speechless stylist, 'a suitable court outfit.'

Petra had shot to the wardrobe. Ten minutes later, Alexandra picked herself up off the chaise longue on the terrace where she had been meditatively sipping a glass of champagne and came to view the selected outfit. 'Bloody idiot!' she exclaimed, seeing Petra had laid out the gold shorts and pink high-heeled Wellingtons again.

Petra twisted her curly blond hair and eyed her employer sulkily. 'I thought gardening clothes. It's about an allotment, you said.'

Alexandra grasped her hair in both hands in a gesture of frustration, but did not tug as she was tempted. Robby Trendy had only replaced the extensions the day before. '*Celebrity* court appearances,' she hissed at her stylist. 'What does that say to you?'

Petra put her tousled head on one side. 'Er, Michael Jackson?'

Alexandra glared through her sunglasses. 'I'm talking suing *Hello!*.'

Petra was completely confused now. Why would Alexandra sue *Hello!*? She was desperate to be in their pages, Petra knew. Was she planning legal action because they wouldn't put her there?

'I mean *Catherine Zeta Jones* suing *Hello!*,' Alexandra growled, seeing the more than usual degree of incomprehension on Petra's face. 'I'm talking Paris Hilton in court. I'm talking subdued style, understated glamour, sexy but discreet. Do you understand what I mean?'

Petra nodded. She had got it now. She understood fully. The only doubt was that Alexandra's wardrobe could fulfil the brief. Understated and subdued were not terms one readily associated with it.

Alexandra stared boldly at the assembly in the makeshift courtroom as, now, she strode in. She felt tired – she had been up since the first rays of sun struck the patio heaters on the penthouse terrace in order to make it in time. But, given the highly sensitive and secret nature of her mission, she wanted to drive herself up here. Tired as she was, she was determined. And she knew that she looked magnificent.

After Alexandra had settled herself in the front row, in which there was in fact no space and so several people were forced to move along to create it, Mrs Goodenough ending up hanging off the other end, the coroner resumed.

'An interesting case,' he remarked. 'And one to which there is no obvious answer.'

Morag shot to her feet. 'Yes there is. It's mine. It was found under my earth closet.'

'On my allotment!' Alexandra leapt to her feet and swayed there, balancing precariously on her heels.

The coroner looked amazed, then disapproving. 'Ladies, ladies. Please. This is an official hearing. I must ask you to respect procedure.' He motioned the two on their feet to sit down. Reluctantly, each checking to see the other had complied, they did.

'Now.' The coroner looked over his bifocals at Morag. 'What did you say you found it under?' The papers he had been given did not mention the words she had used. That the treasure had been found on an allotment that was part of common land were the details he had been supplied with.

'Earth closet,' repeated Morag.

'I beg your pardon?'

'An earth closet,' Philip Protheroe said, slowly and clearly. As the member of the allotment scheme with the most legal experience, he felt it incumbent upon him to act as spokesman when required. There may also, he was aware, have been an element of wanting to redeem himself in the eyes of Catherine Brooke by being helpful to the community.

'And what, exactly, is an earth closet?' the coroner asked.

'It's a sort of outdoor loo. That you don't flush,' Philip replied. 'It's eco-friendly,' he added, catching Morag's furious eye.

'I see,' murmured the coroner, looking disturbed. 'And the trove was found underneath it?'

Philip nodded. 'It was.'

'In my allotment,' Alexandra said warningly.

Tamara licked her lips and began to scribble again.

The coroner looked thoughtful. 'But of course no one owns the earth closet as such.'

'I built it,' shouted Morag.

'You mean I did,' interjected Dweeb, his velvet hat nodding in agitation. 'And him.' He jerked a thumb at Gid, who looked miserably downwards.

'On common land,' pointed out the coroner.

'On my allotment!' yelped Alexandra.

'Squatter's rights!' Morag yelled.

'Given the circumstances,' scribbled Tamara Ogden in her notebook, 'there was no doubt squatter's rights had a certain relevance . . .'

'So it's mine!' Morag declared.

'It's *mine*!' roared Alexandra.

'At least some of it's mine,' stated Dweeb.

The two women looked daggers at each other, then both looked daggers at Dweeb.

The coroner sighed. 'May I remind everyone that we are here to establish ownership. No one, at this stage, has a definite right of any sort.'

'There followed murmurs of dissent from the various interested parties . . .' scribbled Tamara.

The coroner continued. 'As you know, when the owner of an archaeological find cannot be traced, any find belongs to the owner of the land on which it was discovered.'

'Me!' shrieked Alexandra in triumph. She leapt up again and began jumping up and down on her perilous heels. 'Me, me, me!'

At the slightest of motions from the coroner, the brown-suited, inscrutable assistant glided to Alexandra's jiggling side.

'Please sit down, madam, or proceedings will have to be curtailed.'

Alexandra sat down with a thump. She wasn't sure what curtailed meant but she was not risking things being stopped when they were going so well. For her, that was. She shot the mutinous-looking Morag Archbutt-Pesk a gloating grin.

The coroner lifted his eyebrows. He cleared his throat. 'As I was saying,' he continued, with a stern look at Alexandra, 'any find belongs to the owner of the land on which it was discovered. In the case of treasure trove, however – basically gold and silver, where the owner cannot be found – special legislation applies. It belongs to the Crown . . .'

'The Crown!' echoed Morag in fury. 'But the monarchy's a repressive, exploitative, fascistic institution that I personally have big ideological issues with.'

Wasn't everything, in Morag's view? Philip wondered wearily. Personally he thought the description fitted no one better than Morag herself.

'The Crown!' Alexandra shouted. 'But the Queen's got billions of pounds' worth of gold and jewels already. And she looks awful in all of them.'

'That's not very patriotic,' muttered St John into his moustaches.

The Crown, Philip thought, his thoughts inadvertently jerking to the unattractive hostelry, the scene of the start of the evening with Catherine Brooke. He sensed she was avoiding his eye even more than he was hers. He still had no idea what to do about it. But about one thing he was absolutely certain. If he ever saw Sam Binns on his allotment again, or anywhere else for that matter, then the devil help him.

The coroner sighed. 'The number of jewels owned by Her

Majesty and what she looks like in them is really neither here nor there. Ownerless treasure trove belongs, as I say, to the Crown. And when it is discovered it is, as now, subject to an inquest at a coroner's court to establish the circumstances of its loss or deposition. I would now like to ask Mr Parsnik, the county archaeologist, to step forward and outline his findings. Mr Parsnik has examined the trove during its time in the bank.'

An earnest, generally beige young man with straight fair hair and owlish glasses now stood up at the back of the hall and walked to the front. He flinched nervously as he walked past Morag and studiously avoided the sunglassed glare of Alexandra as he stood before her and the rest of the gathering.

Both women, Philip saw, despite their obvious intellectual limitations, had effortlessly sensed that it was on the strength of Mr Parsnik's pronouncement that the coins could go to an institution like the British Museum and be forever out of their reach.

With no such concerns on his own mind, Philip listened with interest to what the architect had to say. The trove, Mr Parsnik thought, dated from the late Roman period. His guess – and it could only be a guess – was that the person who had buried it was a member of the late Romano-British aristocracy who had seen the writing on the wall in terms of the crumbling empire and the rise of the Anglo-Saxons. He had no doubt intended to return and retrieve it in less dangerous times.

Mr Parsnik paused. Alexandra and Morag, who had yawned conspicuously during the archaeologist's explanation, now stirred. Their eyeballs hardened and they licked their lips.

'The verdict,' Tamara breathlessly scribbled at the back of the hall, 'was coming.'

Under their laser stare, Mr Parsnik nervously dropped his eyes. 'While it is a fine collection of coins, mainly notable for its volume,' he said hurriedly, 'it is by no means unique. Many such collections were buried in a similar way and for similar reasons and several fine examples already exist in both national and regional museums. My recommendation therefore is that the state need not exercise its claim and that the finder be allowed to keep the trove.'

'There arose a loud cheer from the alternative lifestyle sector of the audience,' Tamara scribbled. ' "There is a God!" exclaimed the Reverend Alan Tribble apparently involuntarily, although he immediately looked round at the staring multitude, smiled weakly and said, rather uncomfortably, "A joke, of course." While Miss Alexandra Pigott again jumped up and down, exposing the full length of her elegant brown legs and the fact that she wore a sequinned hot pink thong. "I could kiss you!" she shouted at the county archaeologist, who blushed conspicuously . . .'

Back to square one, then, thought Philip.

'Thank you, Mr Parsnik,' said the coroner as the beige young man scurried back to his seat. To judge from his face and mien as he passed them, avoiding their arms outstretched to embrace him, bearding the pleasure of Alexandra and Morag seemed to be an even more terrifying experience than bearding their wrath had been. His pupils were still shrunk with shock following the exposure of the thong.

The coroner addressed the room in general. 'As the trove was found on common land, there is no owner as such. We therefore need to determine a fair and just method of determining ownership. One option of course is for the trove to be divided among the local community.'

There were a few murmurs of approval, Philip's among them.

'No!' roared Alexandra. 'No!' shouted Morag. 'No!' agreed Dweeb, Gudrun, Tecwen and Vicky. Gid, meanwhile, looked troubled.

The coroner sighed. 'I was about to suggest we put it to the vote, but a large contingent looks set to disagree. The other alternative is for it to be donated to one good cause in the village.'

'The church roof!' yelped Reverend Tribble, bobbing up in his black.

'The school computer suite!' cried Catherine, shooting an arm up from beside him.

'Now hang on a minute,' yelled Alexandra, rising to her feet once again.

Morag leapt up too, hands on lilac hips. 'Neither of these are good causes in my view,' she snapped. 'There is no way this treasure is going towards literally supporting the fabric of organised religion in which people like myself, having alternative beliefs, have no stake.'

The Reverend Tribble narrowed his eyes. If there was a God, Catherine thought, she didn't fancy Morag's chances of making it through the Pearly Gates. She would be doing so without the nod from the vicar of Allsop. But then, who did get the nod? The Reverend Tribble, Catherine had noticed, might find it easy to praise the Lord but he found it very hard to praise people. She had in fact never heard him say anything nice about anyone. She yanked herself back from this reflection as she heard Morag shouting about the computer suite.

'As for the school computer suite,' Morag thundered, 'I

don't see why this treasure should be used to fund local children to meet paedophiles in chatrooms.'

Catherine jumped to her feet in defence of her pet project. Philip now plucked up the courage to cast her a nervous glance. She looked, he thought with a pang of something like regret, quite magnificent as she defended the interests of her school. 'Her eyes glittering with anger, her cheeks flushed with indignation, her shining hair tousled with agitation, Miss Brooke looked both noble and arresting,' Tamara Ogden scribbled.

'That's not the idea at all,' Catherine informed Morag with all the politeness she could muster, which was not much. 'The point is the information superhighway.'

'Superhighway!' snorted Morag. 'We need fewer roads, not more of them.'

'Order, please,' rapped out the coroner. He waited for the excitement – in other words, Morag – to subside. 'Well, ladies and gentlemen, I have to say that this is an unprecedented situation in my experience. We need to make a decision about ownership and yet there seems to be no basis on which to do so. My proposal, therefore . . .'

'The court held its breath,' scribbled Tamara Ogden.

'. . . is that we adjourn the meeting pending further advice and evidence. Mr Protheroe, is it?'

Philip nodded.

'A word with you, please,' said the coroner.

Chapter 64

The meeting over, Catherine joined the disappointed flood leaving the courtroom. The sense of anticlimax was almost palpable.

Alexandra, the feathers on the back of her head nodding agitatedly, shot out first in high and furious dudgeon, Tamara Ogden in hot pursuit.

'It's *outrageous*!' Morag Archbutt-Pesk was snarling to anyone who would listen. 'Typical of the repressive, greedy, opportunistic, *fascistic* state we are compelled to live in. But if,' she added, looking back over her shoulder, eyes glittering, to the empty courtroom, 'if *he* thinks he's heard the last of *me*, he's in for a shock.'

'Steady on, Miss Brooke!' joshed a familiar voice as Catherine, pushed aside as Morag exited with violent suddenness, found herself cannoning into the vicar in the Town Hall doorway.

'Sorry, Reverend Tribble.'

'Not at all, not at all . . . lovely day, isn't it?' trilled the Reverend Tribble, who seemed to have quite got over his unfortunate moment at the meeting and was now standing

515

on the Town Hall steps with his hands outstretched as if he alone could take credit for the admittedly beautiful sunny blue morning around them.

Catherine agreed, passing on down the steps, hoping the Reverend would get the message that she was in a hurry. But the vicar was not in the business of earthly messages, especially ones that he wanted to ignore.

'I'm glad I've seen you, Miss Brooke,' the Reverend Tribble smiled, keeping up with her as she scuttled downwards. He seemed to speak with particular meaning.

'I'm in a bit of a hurry—' she started to say, but he cut in.

'I was wondering,' he cried in pleasant, upbeat tones, while his hand firmly gripped her arm, 'whether I might ask your opinion about something. Do you have the time for a coffee?'

'Er, not really.'

'I'm so sorry to hear that,' he sang, not releasing his grip in the slightest. On the contrary, Catherine felt the fingers grasp more tightly. 'I really wanted to ask you something rather important.'

As he was to all intents and purposes making a citizen's arrest, Catherine grudgingly agreed to 'a very quick one, then' and together they headed for the nearest café.

'I was wondering about chintz,' the vicar smiled, leaning over the café table which the sour-faced waitress had just wiped with an equally sour cloth.

Catherine looked at him over the rim of her chipped mug of coffee. 'Chintz?'

'For the sitting room,' the Reverend Tribble intoned with a strange gravity, as if he were explaining the meaning of one of the trickier parables. 'I understand it is enjoying something of a revival at the moment. The Church needs to move with the times,' he added roguishly.

'I'm sure that will be fine,' Catherine muttered, not caring to the extent she would have thought it impossible not to care. She wished desperately she had not agreed to a coffee. She had avoided this café until now; it had always looked, from the outside, a depressing place. From the inside, it was even worse. It was empty, although traces of earlier customers were still present in the great pile of greasy plates on the counter and the overwhelming stench of fried breakfast in the air.

It was a disgusting place to come. Even the Crown seemed like the Ritz in comparison. Catherine suddenly found herself thinking that even Philip, rude and hurtful though he had been, was nonetheless a good deal easier on the eye than the yellowish face and spongy scalp of the Reverend Tribble. He was staring at her with an unnerving directness.

'You may wonder,' the vicar intoned, 'why I keep asking you so many questions about my interiors.' He put his head on one side. 'It's because I was hoping you might be persuaded to have more than a passing interest in what the vicarage looks like, Miss Brooke.'

Catherine's alarm grew. What did this mean?

The vicar smiled, his unblinking eyes still trained relentlessly on her face. 'We get on very well, do we not, Miss Brooke?' he asked in persuasive tones. He seemed, she noticed, entirely unconcerned by the fact they were in a public place, although the volume of the radio behind the counter, half tuned to something riotous on Radio One, made it unlikely anyone there could hear.

'Certainly, I feel that in recent months, as we have both toiled in our respective vineyards, to use a Biblical allusion, ha ha . . .'

Catherine blocked any further thought and just stared, waiting for the blow she sensed was coming.

'. . . that we have perhaps many things in common. That we have become close and might, in fact, become closer.' The Reverend was certainly closer. He had leant over the table and his face was almost up against hers now. She could smell his breath, which was garlicky with a top note of garlic-masking mint.

Still the vicar's calm vibrato continued. 'You must by now realise what I am leading up to, Miss Brooke – or can I call you Catherine?'

She shot him a terrified glance which he interpreted as permission.

'Will you marry me, Catherine?' asked the Reverend Tribble.

The sun, which had been shining brilliantly outside and sending shafts even into this turgid café, chose this moment to slip behind a cloud. Catherine leant backwards slightly. After her largely sleepless night there was a hallucinatory edge to most things, and to this most of all. The vicar was asking her to *marry* him? The Reverend Tribble wanted her to become his *wife*?

'Will you marry me?' the vicar repeated, a melting expression on his face.

Catherine closed the mouth that had fallen open. She stared at the vicar in amazement. He was in love with her? She had never had the faintest idea. Her first instinct was to be repelled. This spongy, flaky man in dusty black – in bed with her? She pictured his kisses, imagined the fumbling, too-red lips. She glanced at his hands; they had an unpleasant, puffy look. She imagined the sweaty palms against her breasts, his panting rasps for breath.

It had been all very different, she remembered, when she thought of Philip Protheroe. It was not how she had pictured being proposed to, an approach in a stinking, sticky-tabled café from a man in a dusty black dress who she didn't even like very much.

Catherine had never had marriage as her goal. A loving partnership with respect on both sides had always seemed to her more important than a ring and a title. But neither was she opposed to weddings and once or twice, over the years, the idea of swearing in public lifelong fidelity to someone she loved had seemed a possibility.

Fortunately she never had, as the relationships had ended, usually acrimoniously. Yet that marriage could be a blessed state she knew; Mary's grief over her beloved Monty was one instance of it, and of course Philip Protheroe, whose still-obvious aching for his dead wife was the only excuse imaginable for the way he had behaved.

But a good excuse, nonetheless, Catherine found herself thinking now. Perhaps she had judged him harshly. He had been unpleasant, but perhaps understandably. His unpleasantness was, in any case, a different and somehow more comprehensible variety from the fathomless, rather creepy Reverend Tribble.

'Oh come on now, Miss Brooke,' sallied the vicar in teasing tones that clashed horribly on her ear. 'You dissemble, surely. This cannot be entirely unexpected.'

After the first horrific proposal had emerged, Catherine had not imagined anything still more unpleasant could be lurking. But now she found she was wrong. Was the Reverend implying she had somehow encouraged him, participated in a courtship she had been all the while unaware of? Had her monosyllabic answers to whether he should have cream or grey sofas been interpreted as billing to his cooing? There was something terrifying about this.

She had no idea what to say yet felt impelled to speak in case he interpreted her silence as assent and somehow, in some secret vicarish way, married her there and then over the café table without her even realising it. She did not trust the Reverend Tribble as far as she could throw him, but this was only one of the reasons she would never have contemplated marrying him.

'I'm awfully flattered, but actually, Vicar . . .'

'Call me Alan,' he suggested cosily.

'Er, I really don't think I'd make you a very good wife, *Alan* . . .'

'And why is that exactly?' asked the Reverend with a rather steely pleasantness. She sensed that refusing him was not going to be easy. Or, to be more precise, he was not going to make it easy.

Catherine searched wildly for reasons that were not insultingly personal. 'Well, you know I'm a bit undecided about Believing . . .'

'That can be addressed,' smiled the Reverend.

Addressed? Catherine stared at him. In what way? Hypnotism? Electro-cognitive therapy?

'Look,' she said flatly, 'I'm sorry, but I've really got no plans to marry.'

The Reverend gave rather a stagey chuckle. 'Plans, my dear Catherine? Plans are what we make and then God gets in the way.'

Catherine frowned. Hadn't John Lennon said something similar? Only not about God. She stared at the Reverend Tribble almost appealingly. She had turned him down, hadn't she? How could he still sit there, arguing the toss over the grubby bottles of brown sauce and ketchup? Had he no sense of embarrassment?

Apparently not, she realised as he remained there smiling persuasively. But wasn't there something odd about it all? She did not for one minute believe that he loved her – she might have lost her grip, but not to the extent of complete self-delusion. So what were his reasons? 'Why do you want to marry me?' she asked bluntly.

'Why?' The vicar raised his hands exultantly to the café's battered ceiling. 'Why would I not? To see you, Catherine, to work beside you as we toil together on our allotments, to talk with you. All this is to want to marry you,' he finished extravagantly.

As well as looking like something from a nineteenth-century novel, he spoke like something from one too. Catherine had never heard such blandishments outside of period drama. 'No, but why do you want to marry me *really*?' she persisted.

The vicar shrugged his black-clad shoulders. 'I'm a single man. You're a single woman. I need company.' He cudgelled his brains for the phraseology the Bishop had used. 'The work of the Lord can be a lonely life – except for the constant companionship and cheer of the Saviour, of course,' he added quickly.

Catherine did not reply.

The sun now slid out from behind its cloud and sent some shafts through the café's smeared window to illuminate the Reverend Tribble's balding head. It also lit what seemed a speculative expression in his eye as he looked at Catherine. 'There is also the small matter of advancement,' he murmured. 'I'm ultimately in the frame for a bishopric and marriage won't hurt that one bit.'

Catherine stared. He wanted to use her to climb the greasy ecclesiastical pole. Could she be hearing properly? Double no chance. She wanted to laugh almost, yet still she felt the need to be polite.

'I'm sorry . . .' she muttered.

The vicar's face now held a hint of exasperation. 'Catherine, my dear. I would ask you to think carefully before you refuse me.'

'Would you?' Catherine returned, reeling at the implication that he was the best offer she was likely to get. Yet this, it turned out, was exactly what the Reverend was saying.

'Just think,' he urged her. She felt as if his garlicky breath was crawling over her face. 'Consider what I can offer you. A large, comfortable house, a good position . . .'

There was a clanging in Catherine's ears which made it hard for her to listen. She had a horrible, claustrophobic sense of being one of those women in Jane Austen novels, satellites round the glamorous, headstrong heroine, who were plain, dull and poor and forced to marry curates as their only chance to avoid the workhouse.

'Of course, if you want to hang around waiting for a better offer . . .'

There was no mistaking the scorn in his voice.

Catherine stood up. After the evening with Philip Protheroe, this was just too much.

'So what do you say?' smiled the Reverend Tribble to the horrified headmistress.

Chapter 65

It took some days for Philip to find Sam. It finally happened on the Sunday morning, three days after the coroner's meeting and more than a week after the date with Catherine. Sam had been setting off from Mrs Newton's, obviously bound for a morning's digging, when the solicitor had spotted him in the distance.

Philip was angry anyway. But the fact that the boy was whistling, apparently happy, no doubt in triumphant, amused contemplation of the trick he had played, made him angrier still.

'I suppose you're very pleased with yourself,' Philip barked, striding vengefully up behind Sam.

He had not expected the boy to look as absolutely terrified as he did. He shrank against the wall in a way that made Philip swallow despite his fury. There was something so instinctive, so well rehearsed about the movement. Sam had obviously shrunk in terror like this many times in the past.

Philip sighed. Telling Sam off was going to be harder than he had anticipated.

'What's up?' the boy mumbled once he had recovered himself slightly.

'My night out with your headmistress,' Philip said, downgrading the tone of his voice from furious to stern. 'It turns out that she didn't ask you to ask me out at all. In fact you told her that I'd asked you to ask her . . .' He paused, wondering if he had got this quite right. Even for one with his lawyer's skill at précis it was a challenge.

The boy stared down at the asphalt road. He did not speak.

'Do you have nothing to say at all?' Philip demanded, his anger rising again as he remembered the embarrassments of the evening. 'It made for a very difficult night, I can tell you. Miss Brooke was horrified when she realised the truth of the situation, as indeed was I.' He stopped, remembering what his own horror and panic had precipitated – the unpleasant, ungallant things he had said to Catherine. Of all the things he regretted about the evening he regretted those most. He was regretting them more all the time, even though he was trying not to dwell on them.

'Your idea of a joke, eh?' he snapped now at the still silent boy. 'Think you're very funny, I suppose. Only *I* don't see what's funny. Miss Brooke and I – apart from your unfortunate foster mother – are about the only people in this village who have any time for you at all . . .'

Sam looked up at this. His face paled.

'. . . and this is how you treat us!' Philip finished. 'You're an irresponsible idiot, messing about with people and causing damage that you could never understand, even if you did care.'

Sam said something Philip could not quite catch.

'What? What was that?'

'I said it weren't meant to be a joke.' Sam was looking at him quite levelly now. He spoke quietly, his tones almost plaintive. 'I were only trying to get you two together. A blind date sort of thing. I thought – well – you'd probably work out what I'd done but you'd see the funny side. And you'd have a good time anyway, like, so it wouldn't matter.' He looked at Philip in a manner half resentful, half appealing. 'I weren't being nasty. I didn't mean to be, um, irresponsible, honest.'

'Well that's the way it turned out,' Philip said crossly, feeling nonetheless that some of the heat had been removed from his argument.

Sam shrugged. 'I didn't mean any harm. You would never have got together otherwise.'

'But is there any reason why we should?' Philip demanded, exasperated. 'What makes you think we have the slightest interest in each other?'

Sam bit his lip. He seemed to be struggling with his feelings. 'Because you're nice and she's nice,' he muttered eventually. 'And because, like you say, you've been the nicest to me of anyone in this . . .' his eyes narrowed, '. . . bloody village. I were only wanting to do something to make you happy. You both seemed so lonely, and I know what that's like . . . oh, what's the use? Nothing ever works out.' The boy gave a huge sob, threw his spade on the floor and ran off down the road.

Immediately, a great wave of guilt and misery crashed over Philip. He, with all his power and advantages, had made someone whose life had been a series of challenging circumstances cry. He, who regarded himself as such a sensitive soul, had caused a vulnerable, parentless eight year old to weep and run away.

He walked home slowly, thinking hard. Of course, the

person he was really angry with was not Sam. It was himself. His own rude treatment of Catherine was what lay at the heart of his fury. It was a guilt that would not go away and which informed all his other perceptions. He had dreamt of his wife again last night and she had seemed worried and sad, not smiling. Something had happened to upset her, he had sensed. Now he wondered whether it was him and what he had done. What a hypocrite he was, Philip told himself, writhing with self-loathing. What a selfish, blinkered, self-absorbed fool.

Well, he had to make amends. To Sam *and* Catherine Brooke. There was nothing else for it.

He watched the boy as, still running, he became a smaller and smaller speck on the road leading out of the village.

The following Monday morning, Catherine stood looking forlornly out of her cottage window. She shrank suddenly into the shadows as a group of elderly hikers passed by. Unnecessarily, she knew. Despite occasional concerted efforts on the part of some walkers, no one could actually see into the room at all. It looked very dark and shadowy from the outside. From the inside, meanwhile, the square of light provided by the window seemed a brilliant burst of colour and light.

For Catherine, however, her view of Allsop through her window currently seemed anything but positive. So far as she was concerned, the pretty grey-stone village nestling in its gentle dip of hills was not a scene of bucolic perfection, but a theatre of humiliation.

'Must you go, really?' Mary murmured regretfully from the sofa behind her.

Catherine, turning to face her, smiled wanly at the other woman, who managed a twitch of the lips in return. Mary was beginning to resume some of her old calm now. A sad stoicism, occasionally shattered by tears, had started to replace her hysterics.

Turning back to the window, the headmistress felt mildly hysterical herself. The Philip and Sam experiences had been bad enough. To be proposed to, on top of all that, by the Reverend Tribble looked like carelessness. Which was why, even though it was still the summer holidays, she was going to go in to school, perhaps today, but if not then tomorrow, clear her desk and hand in her notice to the governors.

How was she to continue at Allsop Primary (Church of England Aided) with the Reverend Tribble, as it were, just next door? She had never found him particularly attractive and now there was the possibility, by no means remote to judge from his tactics and determination, that he might press his suit again. Repeatedly.

And then there was Sam. His betrayal had, subtly but significantly, changed her attitude to the school and her job. Vainly, stupidly, she had thought Sam had improved his behaviour, become happier and more receptive, through what she had contributed to his life both in understanding and in tillable soil. Of course, she could not take all the credit. The patient Mrs Newton deserved a great deal of that too. But Catherine had fancied she had had some significant influence, and that influence good. And all the time he had been laughing at her, possibly hating her, plotting this humiliation for her.

But perhaps, Catherine thought, she had been foolish to expect anything else. Someone who had suffered as Sam had couldn't afford to trust, be friends. He had learnt early that it was not worth expecting anything of anyone and that the only way to avoid pain was to bail out of all relationships if people showed signs of getting close. Perhaps, Catherine thought, he was right.

She felt dull and hopeless. The day, which had never seemed really to get going, reflected these sensations. It looked as if some universal dimmer switch was turned permanently down.

'I don't see why the vicar can't leave instead,' Mary lamented. 'Why shouldn't he go and you stay?'

Mary was right, of course, Catherine knew. The easiest thing would be if the Reverend Tribble resigned his own post out of shame. But this was obviously not going to happen. For one thing, he was clearly incapable of shame. For another, he had explained his ambitions in the Church; he was hardly likely to do anything to hamper his own progress. For a third, as she knew in hideous, unwanted, uninvited detail, he had forked out not insignificant amounts on refurbishing the vicarage.

Catherine knew, for all her inner conviction that she loved and cherished her flock at the school far more deeply and genuinely than the Reverend Tribble did his at the church, that he would not be the one leaving.

'But I don't want you to go,' Mary said, standing up and walking to the window to stand beside Catherine. She squeezed the headmistress's hand. Catherine squeezed back. She guessed that what Mary did not say was that she wished it had been in different circumstances.

'On the other hand,' Mary said, her sunken, purple-circled gaze dragging round the room, 'it's not as if I'm definitely staying here myself. What the hell am I going to do with the rest of my life?' Catherine saw the tears start to her eyes and, feeling a mirror response in her own, looked down.

'What about the food business?' she asked. 'You were so excited about it . . .' she took a deep breath, '. . . before.'

'Yes, I was,' Mary said heavily. 'But that was then and this is now.'

'But won't Benny want to know what's going on?' Catherine pointed out softly. 'He had a client lined up and everything.'

Mary shrugged. 'I haven't heard from him. I haven't seen him since . . . before . . .' She heaved an exasperated sigh and pushed one long, bony hand back through her unbrushed hair. 'I mean . . . I've no idea if he knows about . . . Oh, anyway. What does it matter any more? What does anything matter any more?'

She looked, the headmistress thought, shrunken and vulnerable in the jeans and black poloneck, clothes Catherine had lent her and slightly on the big side despite Mary's superior height.

'But it seems a shame. You were so thrilled about the whole Lady Amelia's Pantry thing,' Catherine persisted, hoping to strike the spark that would begin the process of bringing Mary back to life.

Mary's wide green eyes flashed warningly. 'Yes, but that was before. And now . . .' she made a helpless gesture with her arms, 'I just don't have the energy. Or, frankly, the inclination either.' She rubbed her eyes and yawned. 'All that sourcing of vegetables was going to be so complicated. It would have been different if the old vegetable garden at Underpants . . . if the ground hadn't been . . . Oh, what's the point?' she suddenly demanded angrily. 'Even if everything went well and I could restore Underpants, I would still be sharing it with . . .' she fought to retain control of her face, '*him. He*'d never move out. And then, after we're dead, what would happen to it? It's not as if there's anyone to hand it on to, which I suppose is just as well.' Her face, as she stared unseeing through the windowpane, was startling in its bleakness.

Catherine's heart ached for her friend. She knew that Mary found it impossible to accept what had happened. It was, she told Catherine, too big, too painful, too awful to absorb. The very foundation of her existence had been shattered. She had struggled to describe the symptoms: how she could hardly frame a thought. How her head was filled with a white blare, a prolonged trumpet-blast of agony. How the pain inside her pulsed constantly, getting, if anything, worse. And all because the person she had married, had loved for years, had thought she knew inside out, was really someone else altogether.

Catherine had listened and sympathised, awed by the scale of Mary's grief. Her love for Monty had obviously been the real thing. But, that being the case, could it really be eradicated so utterly, by one selfish and stupid act? It was this aspect that Catherine, personally, found the most impossible to accept. The veteran of many selfish and stupid acts herself, she had learnt to pick up and carry on, but Mary had obviously no intention of this. Not with Monty, in any case.

'You're sure you're definitely not going back to him?' Catherine asked gently, knowing full well what the answer would be. In the face of all Catherine's efforts to persuade her to give the marriage another chance, Mary had adamantly refused. She refused now.

'No. Never. Nothing would make me.'

Catherine greeted this dramatic announcement with the silence she felt it deserved.

'And what about your allotment?' she asked after a few minutes. Catherine had noticed that Mary held in her hand a gardening magazine. She now let it drop to the floor, as if she had just realised there was no point reading about such things any more.

Mary rubbed her eyes and yawned. 'My allotment? I don't know.'

'But you loved it,' Catherine cried. 'It was the inspiration for everything. Come on. You can't give up now.'

Mary eyed her steadily. 'You are.'

'That's different,' Catherine maintained stoutly. 'Staying here would be . . . difficult for me.'

'Yes, well, it's difficult for me as well,' Mary said bleakly.

Chapter 66

The phone trilled in the Goodenoughs' lamplit lounge. Veronica, sitting over her embroidery, looked up from an aubergine and eyed the instrument balefully. If it was Morag Archbutt-Pesk at the other end — yet again — Veronica felt finally ready to give her a piece of her mind.

Morag Archbutt-Pesk's blithe assumption that St John would agree to her latest demand and stand as a character witness to persuade the coroner to give her the treasure was, Veronica felt, unbelievable even by that woman's incredible standards. For one thing, what reference could St John give now that Morag's former position as eco-conscience of the village had suffered a violent reverse into fully paid-up disciple of Mammon? 'The politest thing one could say,' he observed, 'is that she's a schizophrenic.'

Veronica, however, had no thoughts of being polite. Morag's brass neck exceeded anything she had ever encountered before; had ever imagined possible. What she personally would like to say about Morag's character turned the inside of Veronica's head blue. She had not realised she knew such language, even if she didn't say it out loud. And she a churchwarden, too.

She was particularly outraged that Morag's endless, bullying telephone calls about the character reference had proved the last straw for St John. He had now suffered a minor breakdown. He had been in bed for the last three days diagnosed with nervous exhaustion and incipient alcoholism and under stern medical instruction not to go near the allotments or even to think about them. Veronica, heaving herself up from her armchair, crossed to the telephone with the intention of giving Morag the same advice with regard to St John.

The caller, however, was not Morag. It was an extremely pleasant and intelligent-sounding young man who spoke for quite a few minutes. 'I see,' Veronica said consideringly when he had finished. 'That does sound very interesting, I agree. I think what you propose would be absolutely fine.'

'That's great,' said the eager young man. 'But don't I need to check with Mr Goodenough? I understand that he is President of the Allsop Allotments Association.'

'Yes he is,' Veronica confirmed. 'But he's indisposed at the moment. I have no doubt, however, that he would be happy to give you permission.' As a matter of fact, Veronica knew that St John, battered into nervous-wreckdom by Morag, would actually dither hopelessly on the question. It was time, she felt, for her to make decisions on his behalf.

The young man still sounded doubtful. Veronica was surprised and impressed at his scrupulousness. 'There isn't a deputy or any other person in charge that we should check with in Mr Goodenough's absence? A vice-president of the allotments, perhaps?'

'*Absolutely not,*' Veronica said violently. She had no

intention of referring this pleasant man to Morag, who would be sure to say no just for the sheer joy of refusing someone something. And what this young man and his friends were proposing to do, Veronica thought, would be a good thing for everyone if it came off. A line could be drawn and they could all get on with their lives.

'You're sure?' pressed the young man. 'You see, we're all so fired up about this. I'd hate us to have to stop.'

'Quite sure,' Veronica said firmly. 'Just go ahead,' she urged. 'And good luck.'

'Oh, wow,' said the young man excitedly. 'Thank you. That's great.'

'My pleasure,' said Veronica. She replaced the receiver and returned to her aubergine.

On Tuesday morning, Catherine heaved herself out of bed in the knowledge that today was the day she had to face her own problems, not take refuge, as she rather suspected she had been doing, in those of Mary.

She had to go to school, clear her desk and tell the governors what they would not particularly want to hear. Then, afterwards, Mrs Watkins and Miss Hanscombe would have to be told. At some stage Catherine would call her old boss to sound out the possibility of returning to her previous job in the London primary. When they had last spoken, as they regularly did, her former headmistress had still not found a satisfactory deputy and was making do with a series of inadequate-sounding supply teachers. It was unlikely the situation had changed.

Catherine left Mary in the cottage, slumped, dead-eyed before Lorraine Kelly on GMTV. She had not, Catherine knew, slept particularly well the night before and had mentioned feeling sick this morning. 'I dreamt about Weston Underwood,' she had said sadly, pushing away the bowl of cereal Catherine had set before her. 'I don't think I could ever bear to see it again.'

'Never mind Weston Underwood,' Catherine had answered robustly. 'You won't be seeing anything ever again if you don't eat. You have to keep your energy up. You need it.'

But Mary had shaken her head, pleading nausea. Catherine, realising her efforts were pointless, had waved a brisk goodbye.

She walked slowly to the school, trying not to notice the beauty of the early sun on the ancient stone of the houses, the ecstatic singing of the birds, the impossibly radiant green of the trees and the heart-surging blue of the open sky above. It was a morning almost Italian in its brightness and clarity. The weathercock atop the church's medieval steeple blazed brilliant gold as she approached. Catherine told herself fiercely that she would not miss Allsop. Finding this unconvincing, she told herself firmly that there was no point grieving for it as she could not possibly stay. She had made up her mind.

As she turned in through the school gate and headed for the familiar red-painted door, Catherine took a deep breath and held her head high.

Realising that, most unexpectedly, there was a figure leaning against the school's bright red arched front door, Catherine stopped short in surprise. The figure was tall and thin and looked, from a distance, very rough. It was a man in creased clothes, unshaven, with a fugitive, desperate, exhausted air about him. Catherine approached cautiously. Was it a tramp? She had never seen tramps in Allsop before.

Indications of life's more challenging aspects were few – apart from Sam Binns, of course.

She approached cautiously across the grey playground. The figure, who had been staring into thin air with fixed desperation, suddenly saw her. It was then that Catherine realised that this man was Mary's husband.

She had seen him only a couple of times before, had registered his golden good looks, his blue eyes and ready smile. But now he looked different, much as the once-beautiful Mary did too.

Stronger than her immediate suspicion of him, her dislike, even, was Catherine's amazement at his changed appearance. Never had she seen anyone looking so shattered, so quickly. From refined medieval angel Monty had turned to medieval vagrant. He looked bleary, blasted, like a man who had not slept for a long time. He wasn't dirty, exactly, but his clothes were chaotic: crumpled, buttoned up all wrong, ends hanging out, as if he had dressed in a whirlwind. His hair was straw-like, clumped and almost as wild as his bloodshot eyes. It was as if, Catherine thought, he had slept in a ditch for a week, although presumably, as he was up here, he had been at Weston Underwood since the scene in Notting Hill.

The whole of his face, as she came up to him, seemed to scrabble to compose itself; hope, grief, despair, curiosity all spasmed across the thin features. He clearly wanted to ask her something, but was having difficulty getting it out.

'I went to her allotment,' Monty croaked, in the same tones, Catherine thought immediately, as if saying he had been to her grave. 'They said to ask you, but I wasn't sure where you lived.'

Thank God, Catherine thought with a rush of relief.

What might have happened if he had did not bear contemplation.

His eyes were fixed on her as if she was his last hope on earth. Which perhaps, Catherine realised with some awe, she actually was. 'Do you know where Mary is?' Monty demanded. 'Is she okay?'

'Yes,' Catherine said immediately. 'She's fine.'

'Oh, thank God.' He collapsed against the Victorian dogtooth carving of the doorway, his face the sudden, blazing red of relief. 'I thought,' he muttered, 'that she must have gone off to a hotel or something and that she'd get in touch.' He shook his head. 'But she hasn't.'

'She's staying with me,' Catherine told him, bracing herself against a possible onslaught.

But there was no bitter speech demanding to know what right she had to get involved. Rather, Monty looked relieved. 'Thank you,' he said, to her surprise. 'Thank you for looking after her. It must have been . . .' he lifted red, exhausted eyes to Catherine's before swiftly dropping them again, 'a horrible shock for her. I'm glad she's been with a friend.'

'You'd better come in,' Catherine said, as she had not long ago to Monty's wife. 'Come in to the school and have a cup of tea.'

When Monty, settled in her office holding a mug printed with the Ofsted logo, started to talk, his words fell over themselves. He was, Catherine found, desperate to explain himself. Staring unflinchingly, pleadingly, into her eyes he confessed, in tones which swung between high emotion and steady rationality, his bottomless, boundless regret at what he had done and the hurt occasioned by his foolish actions. He was fully, horribly aware of how stupid he was. He had been flattered, seduced, an idiot. He had been desperate; the disappointment of the expedition had hit him like an avalanche, he had not known what to do. Beth, semi-naked in her bed, had offered immediate comfort, which he had immediately regretted.

He would, he told Catherine, never find another wife like Mary; he had utterly failed to appreciate her, had consistently undervalued her loyalty, her love for his house, her love for him, her unending support, her cheeriness and her resourcefulness. He did not, Catherine saw, even know about the food business, and as its future looked just as hopeless as his did, there seemed little point telling him about it.

Nonetheless she listened, awed, wishing she had a tape recorder. It would probably not change Mary's mind, but it would at least have made an impression. Again, she fought with herself over feeling sorry for him. This man was a proven deceiver; was he trying to manipulate her too? Was it all true about the sponsor pulling out of the expedition? Had there been a sponsor at all, or had Monty been trying to expedite explorations closer to home, in the marital bed of another man?

'Your affair with Beth is over, then?' Catherine asked sternly.

'It wasn't an affair,' Monty pleaded, obviously anguished. 'She was always quite keen to . . .' he dropped his eyes, '. . . but I stupidly didn't realise. I would never have stayed there if I had. But eventually I gave in, like a bloody idiot. Oh God,' he suddenly roared, making Catherine jump in her swivel chair. 'Oh God,' he roared again, like a penned bull, the cords on his neck standing out.

Monty got up from the chair reserved for visiting parents, the one Julia Cooke had sat on. He took the few steps over to Catherine and clasped her hands with both his cold and shaking ones. 'Tell Mary I love her,' he stammered, the struggle to remain composed and not cry again setting his head bobbing in a slightly dislocated fashion. The kindly schoolteacher wondered how long it was since he had eaten.

'Does she want to see me, do you think?' Monty asked, fixing Catherine's steady grey gaze in his own wild blue-red one.

The headmistress shrugged and shook her head. 'I don't really think so,' she said gently. 'Not yet.'

He nodded uncontrollably. 'Of course,' he gabbled. 'Of course of course of course.' He swallowed, his thin throat working agitatedly. He took a deep breath. 'Tell her,' he said slowly, his distended, bloodshot eyes ricocheting between both of Catherine's. 'Tell her,' he gulped, 'that I understand why she doesn't want to come back and why she doesn't want to see me any more. I've been a fool. An unforgivable fool.' He took a deep breath and shoved a shaking hand backward through once-thick locks, now dry and lank. 'But she's all I have.' He had cast a despairing look round the yellow-painted room, hanging with staff playground rotas and the subject areas for the forthcoming term. A term, Catherine half registered with a pang, that she would not be here to see.

'I can't live here without her,' Monty ended, brokenly. He stopped short of saying that he didn't want to live at all. But the words, Catherine felt, showing him out, had been in the air.

She watched him, walking slowly, beatenly, across the playground and realised that, for all her suspicion of him, she wished him well. He seemed genuinely shattered; utterly remorseful. His anguish at his own stupidity showed in every line and lineament. She hoped Mary would not divorce Monty; that they would try, despite the problems, to overcome their difficulties. It was, as Catherine knew and had seen from her work, so easy to get divorced. It was not so easy to carry on afterwards, either for the divorcees or the others involved. And, as she also knew, it wasn't easy to get married in the first place. Meeting the right person – someone you liked enough to marry – was terribly difficult. Mary, if she dumped Monty, might never find anyone again. Monty likewise. Particularly looking like he was at the moment.

Catherine lost no time. As soon as Monty had shuffled off down the high street, she shot across the road back to School House. Mary, still in the armchair, the sitting-room curtains drawn against the brightness of the day outside, looked blearily up at her in the gloom. 'I still feel sick,' she said faintly. 'And I've got a headache.'

Mary's face did look green, Catherine saw, although it could have been its proximity to the armchair, upholstered in a tasteful shade of sage. Or perhaps the whisky to which Mary seemed to have become mildly addicted. Whatever it was, Catherine had news to jerk her out of her malaise, and did not beat about the bush. 'You'll feel better after what I've got to tell you,' she exclaimed, eyes shining with excitement, voice warm with a confidence she hoped was justified. It was all in the presentation, she knew. That was the first rule of teaching.

Mary listened to her account of the interview with Monty with a flat and inexpressive face. She said nothing for a few minutes when Catherine had finished. Then she raised the wide eyes which had once been so beautiful, pursed the formerly rosy mouth and uttered the bitter sentence of wronged wives through the ages. 'He should have thought of all that before.'

'Oh, but Mary . . .' Catherine began. But the other woman had turned her face away into the pale green covering of the armchair.

There was nothing for it, Catherine saw. She had tried her best. Perhaps she would try again later. But for now, there was nothing to be done. She may as well go back to school and continue the desk-clearing.

Back across the road to the school and once again in her office, Catherine had only just opened her file drawers when a terrific banging at the door sent her heart racing.

She approached the front door cautiously. Was it Monty again?

Through the safety glass, cross-hatched with wires, could be seen not Mary's agonised husband, but Mrs Newton, Sam's foster mother. Catherine flushed red with embarrassment. Did she know about the night out? she wondered.

Reluctantly, Catherine slid back the catch and opened the door.

'The lady at your house said you'd be here,' Mrs Newton stammered.

Catherine realised the woman's kindly hamster face was anxious and tired. Her normally tidy hair was wild and dishevelled and her creased clothes added to her general air of disorientation. While not in as extreme a condition as Monty, she did not look as if she had slept much either.

'Mrs Newton! Whatever's the matter?' Catherine could guess, however. Sam had driven his foster mother to the edge; his behaviour had reverted. Mrs Newton had come to brief the school to expect the worst in the forthcoming term. So far so unsurprising, thought the newly cynical headmistress.

'Oh, Miss Brooke,' Mrs Newton cried.

'What's the problem, Mrs Newton?' Catherine asked resignedly.

'It's Sam.'

Catherine nodded. 'What about Sam?' Her stomach clenched, imagining his triumphant contempt, his sneering pleasure at the success of his plan to embarrass her.

'He's gone,' wailed Mrs Newton.

'*Gone?*' Catherine stared. 'Gone where?'

'I don't know,' Mrs Newton gasped, wringing her hands. 'He's been missing since Sunday.'

'*Sunday?*' Two days ago?

'Yes. The police know. I've been in constant touch with them. But I thought you should know too.'

Mrs Newton sobbed, pulling the bottom of her cardigan up to her nose. 'Oh, Miss Brooke. I know he started off a bit difficult like. But we've really grown to love him, Dave and me. He's a good boy underneath, he really is. We're both out of our minds with worry.'

Chapter 67

Mrs Ramsden was having a lot of difficulty understanding the various clauses of her recently deceased husband's will. This was hardly surprising, Philip thought. She was extremely short-sighted, for a start, holding the document up to her nose and peering at the small print uncomprehendingly.

He rather hoped the incomprehension would continue, although he knew that it could not. Not least because it was his professional duty to elucidate things. And unfortunately for Mrs Ramsden it was clear – to Philip at least – from the document listing Mr Ramsden's possessions and his intentions for them that at least some were intended for a long-term mistress Mrs Ramsden clearly had no idea about. Sooner or later – in about five minutes, Philip estimated – this was going to come fully out into the open where even Mrs Ramsden could not be confused about it.

Feeling vaguely anxious, Philip drummed his long fingers on the polished surface of his table. It would be a shock and require delicate handling. It needed tact and diplomacy. All of which, as recent events had proven, he was hopeless at. He was, Philip now accepted, no good with women. What small skills he had once possessed had now gone utterly.

His treatment of Catherine Brooke haunted him. Because of work he had been unable, as he now knew he must, to visit the school in the hope of seeing her and saying he was sorry. He had more than his own reasons for this. He was now certain that Emily, in his dreams, was urging him to apologise to Catherine and that Emily liked her.

And not only Emily. He had been hanging out the washing in his back garden when Mrs Palfrey had beckoned him over. 'Hear you were out with that schoolteacher the other night,' she croaked, coming straight to the point as usual. As she gave him a conspiratorial grin, her ancient face creased into an uncountable number of lines.

Caught, hands in the air holding a pair of his boxer shorts, Philip felt guilty and resentful. Did everyone know? And if so, what business was it of theirs?

'Nice woman, that Miss Brooke.' Mrs Palfrey nodded meaningfully at him. 'Lovely girl. Done amazing things at that school, I'm told.'

Remembering the passion with which Catherine had spoken of her job, Philip could believe this. The fact that even Mrs Palfrey, who approved of practically no one under the age of seventy, was one of Catherine's fans made him feel even worse about the remarks he had made.

'Bonny looking, too,' Mrs Palfrey added, a twinkle in her eye. 'She'd be nice for you.'

'Nice for *me*?' Philip repeated indignantly.

The old woman nodded, pursing her lips roguishly. 'Go on! You don't want to be on your own for ever, do you?'

'Mrs Palfrey, *really*!' Philip expostulated, deciding this familiarity was too much. She may have lent him gardening tools but that did not give her the right to dig into the most private areas of his life.

But Mrs Palfrey did not hear, having chosen that moment to sweep back indoors with a speed surprising for her age. Philip looked after her, his worst fears confirmed. He was an idiot. A rude and unforgivable idiot. Catherine Brooke was special; it was official. Mrs Palfrey had spoken.

He had to apologise. He could not rest easy until he had; and neither, it seemed, could Emily.

As strong gusts of mothballs wafted across the table towards him, Philip returned his attention to Mrs Ramsden. She had clearly decided one had to dress for the occasion when visiting a solicitor. She was resplendent in a musquash coat of funereal black with huge shiny buttons and a fur collar that seemed to be made of cat. It was a coat of the sort his own grandmother had worn for best and which Philip had not imagined existed any more. He felt it suggested something about Mrs Ramsden's approach to life that made her late husband's decision to look elsewhere for excitement if not excusable then at least understandable.

'Eeh, I'm all discombobulated,' Mrs Ramsden said, sighing heavily at her late husband's will.

Philip nodded. 'Wills are very, er, discombobulating,' he allowed generously, by way of a run-up to sensitively handling the about-to-explode situation.

Mrs Ramsden looked at him, her eyes a faded duck-egg blue through her large and thick bifocals. 'It's not just t'will, young man. I'm all upset because of my neighbour.'

Philip nodded again. 'Noisy, are they? That's terrible.'

Mrs Ramsden shook her head. Her thin, permed grey hair moved rigidly with it. 'It's not that. She's lost 'er little boy. 'E's gone missing.'

Philip felt a clutch of real horror. 'How absolutely dreadful,' he said, alarmed. He felt as if something piercingly cold had penetrated the stuffy atmosphere of the office. 'They've no idea where he is?'

Mrs Ramsden's curls continued to move stiffly from side to side. 'No idea. It's a terrible business. The lad's parents – they're foster parents, mind you – are in a dreadful state. Can you imagine?'

'No,' Philip murmured. For him, a non-parent, to suggest he could share anything of the agony of a parent who had lost a child would, he felt, unforgivably trivialise it. But he had often wondered what it would be like to be a parent; he and Emily both had. They had hoped to begin the process of finding out before the accident. Now, of course, there was no hope and it was another thing Philip tried not to think about. Nonetheless, in his dealings with Sam Binns, he had from time to time felt the buried urge stir. No longer, of course. Not since the Crown incident. Although compounding Philip's guilt about Catherine was the possibility that he had been rather harsh on the boy as well. But hopefully Sam had forgotten about it by now.

'I'm not saying Sam were any sort of saint, like,' Mrs Ramsden continued, 'but now 'e's not around I miss 'im dreadful.'

Philip's spine, which had been curved explainingly over the desk towards his client, now shot rigidly upwards. A thousand fire drill alarm bells shrilled in his chest. 'Sam, did you say?' he gasped. 'Sam?'

'That's right.' Mrs Ramsden shook her head. 'No one's seen him since Sunday morning. I'm not saying 'e weren't difficult at first, like, but—'

'*Sunday morning?*' Philip stammered through a suddenly

dry throat. Oh God, no. No. Just after he had seen him. Had Sam run away because of what had been said? But would it, he realised in the same instant, be any better if it were someone else's fault?

Philip was across the room in an instant. The coathanger on the back of the door ricocheted wildly as he snatched his mackintosh. 'I'm awfully sorry,' he barked at an astonished Mrs Ramsden from the open door of the office. 'But I suddenly have to go out. I'll leave you in the capable hands of Mrs Sheen here,' he added, stumbling past his amazed receptionist and heading for the stairs.

He took the distance to the ground floor in one huge Superman leap, the impact against solid stone reverberating painfully in his soles and ankles. But Philip, as he sped out of the door, hardly noticed. There was but one thought in his mind, and one image, that of a small, skinny, sobbing figure running down the road that led out of the village.

Catherine was up at the allotments. She had gone there immediately she had heard the news about Sam.

Sam. Vulnerable, hot-headed Sam had run away. Who knew where? Anything could have happened.

Catherine's throat was permanently choked. She wanted to cry out to the blue sky, beg the beautiful morning to help him, to bring him back safely. She wished that she had been more definite with the Reverend on the subject of the Almighty. 'If there is a God,' Catherine whispered, her eyes fixed yearningly on the blueness above her, 'then please protect Sam. He's only eight, he's only little, oh please God, don't let anything . . .' She could not bear to think any further. The possibilities were too cruel. Had not Sam suffered enough already in his short life?

Bitterly she berated herself for being angry about the evening with Philip Protheroe. What did it matter? She would have forgiven Sam much worse now. She would have forgiven him anything.

But what had happened to Sam? No one seemed to know. He had, Mrs Newton tearfully reported, seemed perfectly happy when he had left home that Sunday morning, getting out from under her feet so she could listen to *The Archers*. Her addiction to Ambridge goings-on was only one of the many things for which, in her anguish, Sam's foster mother was bitterly blaming herself. None were remotely serious, but no doubt, Catherine thought, Mrs Newton had to direct her terrified energy somewhere.

Catherine now knew that the police were working on the theory that Sam had been abducted. Although, it being a Sunday morning when he disappeared, the village had been devoid of activity and no one seemed to have seen anything. People were starting to be questioned now, however. From where she knelt, distractedly dragging out weeds, Catherine could see the brilliant lime-green livery of a police vehicle.

She was vaguely aware of activity elsewhere on the allotments. For some reason two of the plots – the vicar's and Beth and Benny's – seemed to be full of brawny young men in T-shirts. She had no idea why and cared less. Even Mary and her problems faded. She and Monty were at least alive and accounted for. Only one thing mattered to Catherine now. The safe return of Sam Binns.

Chapter 68

Tamara Ogden of the *Mineford Mercury* was beside herself about the missing boy. Here, at last, was a story worthy of her talents; a human interest tale par excellence. It was impossible not to go over the top about it; even Derek Savage had been heard to sniff when the story had reached the *Mercury* of how an adopted boy from a broken home had just vanished overnight from Allsop. Tamara seized on this as licence to write the most heart-rending account she was capable of.

And it was all happening on her patch as well. Really, Tamara thought, it was incredible to remember how dull Allsop used to be. New York's most happening precinct frankly paled, these days, beside what was going on in this small, unassuming Derbyshire village. After Tamara's account of the allotment treasure-trove story had appeared in the *Mercury* – another amazing Allsop story, incidentally – various nationals had picked it up. Tamara had had an exciting morning giving an account of events to reporters from the *Mail*, *Times* and *Telegraph*, and although not all of them had run the story in the end, the one in the *Telegraph* had actually name-checked her: 'local journalist Miss Tamara

Ogden'. She might, Tamara thought, actually ask for a job there on the strength of that mention.

Tamara had little doubt that the same papers would pick up the Sam Binns story. She was here this morning in order to report on any progress, or, preferably, lack of progress. The heartbroken foster parents were making satisfactorily juicy copy; the mother in particular banging on endlessly about *The Archers* for some reason.

As she went about the village this morning interviewing anyone she came across and asking their views on the subject, Tamara's attention was attracted by a group of extremely fit and handsome young men, stripped to the waist to reveal pronounced biceps and tanned torsos, currently digging up the Allsop allotments. As she stumbled up the steep steps to the field, Tamara, gasping with the effort, managed to drag herself away from contemplation of the approaching muscles enough to notice that part of the plot area was surrounded by fluorescent orange string which looked rather official.

Tamara's heart leapt into her mouth. The dreadful but professionally thrilling possibility that Sam Binns had been buried under one of the vegetable patches swept through her.

'You looking for a body?' she yelled at the group, hanging over the gate. 'I'm from the local paper.'

They looked up. There were five of them, all young gods and a far cry, Tamara considered, from the usual type of man available in the area. It was not an opportunity – five opportunities, to be precise – that she intended to let pass. One of them, whose hair was shaggier, curlier and blonder than the others, stepped forward. He placed a hand over his eyes to see her, exposing a tuft of hair in his armpit that sent a thrill through her.

'A body?' He shook his head soberly. His curls bounced in

the sunshine. 'No. Not one buried fewer than seventeen hundred years ago, anyway.'

Tamara slumped against the gate, feeling disappointment almost as much as relief and feeling rather ashamed as a result. She looked at the shaggy blond god again and felt her spirits rising. After all, she had a reason to linger and talk to them. She was professionally entitled to ask them questions.

She slipped through the gate and sashayed towards the blond god. 'I'm from the local paper,' she simpered.

'I'm Ptolemy Montgomery,' grinned the god.

Five minutes later she had found out that, far from being from the regional constabulary's forensics department, Ptolemy and his crew were from Cambridge University's Archaeology and Anthropology Department. 'It's just a hunch, obviously,' Ptolemy told her. He had an upmarket voice she found deeply exotic and a big, toothy, boyish smile. He reminded her vaguely of Prince William, but with much more hair. 'But we reckon that the buried money might be part of something a lot bigger,' he added.

'Something a lot bigger,' Tamara repeated, licking her lips and making a concerted effort to keep her eyes from slipping to Ptolemy's crotch area. 'What big thing could it be?' she purred, batting her eyelids and folding her arms to force her plump breasts upwards.

'A Romano-British complex!' Ptolemy told her as if it were the most exciting thing in the world.

'A what?'

'The house of the guy who buried the money,' Ptolemy explained. 'Built around the third century AD, just as the Empire began to collapse in this country. Which was probably why he buried it.'

Tamara nodded. 'I think that archaeologist bloke said

something about that at the coroner's court,' she remembered, hoping to impress the student.

Ptolemy smiled. 'Steve Parsnik, that's right. He's an old boy of our department. That's how we found out about the whole thing.'

'Oh. Not from my stories in the national papers then,' Tamara said disappointedly. She had been priding herself on this possibility and was about to mention it.

Ptolemy looked vague. 'I don't really read papers, I'm afraid.' He gave her a wide, apologetic grin.

'So you really think there's a house under here?' Tamara said doubtfully, looking at the neat rows of vegetables nearby.

'Absolutely. Just look at the lie of the land.' The student extended a muscular brown arm across the flat plateau on the side of the hill. 'This has all been levelled from the hillside, right? That's usually a sign someone intended to build here. And we've found enough bits and pieces of brick about on the plots to make us think someone did.'

Tamara tried to look interested in Ptolemy's project and not in what was potentially in his trousers. 'Wow,' she breathed in what she imagined was a convincing manner.

Ptolemy looked at her. 'Well you might not be interested now,' he said. 'But once we start hitting some serious foundations you will.'

Tamara nodded. She was very interested in foundations. She put a great deal on every morning.

'And actually,' Ptolemy added, 'so will everyone else round here. Especially those people planning on getting their hands on the dug-up loot.'

'Oh really?' Tamara was all ears now.

Ptolemy flashed his sexy grin again. He tossed back the sun-bleached surfer curls that dropped fetchingly over his somewhat long-jawed face. 'Because if there really is a Romano-British villa under here,' he stomped a large boot into the soil, 'this whole place will be reclassified as an Ancient Monument. They'll probably build a small museum, either next to the site or somewhere close by, to house the finds and the treasure will go in it. The state will claim it back as being of educational importance.'

It slowly dawned on Tamara what this meant. Her eyes widened. 'So no one will have a right to that money?'

'That's about the size of it. If it reverts to the state, all bets are off. All claims will be redundant. As will, unfortunately, everyone's allotments, but there you go.' Ptolemy shrugged. 'Though from what I can gather from talking to people round here, that might not be such a disaster. They're all so fed up with that madwoman in purple trousers bossing them about, they'd probably be quite happy just to start again somewhere else.'

Tamara grinned. 'You've met Morag then, have you?'

Ptolemy rolled his delicious hazel eyes. 'She turned up here yesterday morning shouting her mouth off. But I soon shut her up.'

'You shut Morag Archbutt-Pesk up?' Tamara looked at Ptolemy in wonderment. He seemed more of a hero as each minute passed.

'She was a pain,' he confirmed. 'Came storming up wanting to know what we were all doing here and why she hadn't been consulted.' Ptolemy wonderingly shook his handsome head in remembrance of the scene. 'I told her we had been given permission by the president of the allotments. Well, his authorised representative, anyway. She really blew a gasket at that, but fortunately her husband or her partner appeared and sort of led her away. Poor sod. He obviously has a hell of a life. I'm not sure she's well up here,' Ptolemy tapped his shaggy temple. 'My girlfriend's doing research into bipolar disorder at the moment, and old Purple Trousers looked like a classic case if you ask me.'

'Your girlfriend?' Tamara echoed, crestfallen.

Chapter 69

Philip, taking the steps up to the allotment field in double-quick time, was disappointed but unsurprised to see that Sam Binns was not there. He experienced a lurch of horror when he saw that the area around Beth's patch had been roped off and that people were digging. Surely not. Surely no one thought . . .

He spotted Catherine tearing weeds out of her plot and strode straight up to her. His embarrassment had disappeared, replaced by a fear so agonising it made his shame about their evening seem delicious luxury.

'They're not . . .' he muttered, gulping with fear. 'They're not . . .' He nodded his head violently towards the diggers. 'They're not . . . digging for . . . Sam, are they?' He locked his gaze tensely on hers. He felt the answer to this question would inform the rest of his entire life.

Seeing Catherine shake her head violently, he felt his legs buckle beneath him with relief. Now the worst of all possibilities had been lifted, the next bit of business was easy. Sinking to his knees in the soil beside her he said, 'Catherine, I'm sorry. I behaved like a complete pig when we went out. I was unforgivably rude and I didn't mean it. You didn't deserve it.'

There was a silence. Catherine did not reply. On the other hand, she hadn't immediately risen to her feet and stormed off, as he had half feared she might.

'Do you forgive me?' he pressed. For Emily's sake as well as his own he needed to hear her say yes.

'I suppose so. It really doesn't matter,' Catherine said dully. It seemed impossible now that anything so trivial could have had any importance.

'It's my fault,' Philip muttered, still on his knees in the earth. 'It's all my fault.'

'Oh come on,' Catherine said impatiently. 'It doesn't matter. It was just a night out. I don't care, I just told you.'

'Not you, not the evening,' Philip gasped, trying to control his voice. 'Sam. I was the last to see him, I'm sure. It was probably because of me that he went.'

Catherine screwed up her eyes, uncomprehending. 'What?'

Philip uncomfortably explained. She listened no less comfortably, biting her lip. He did not spare himself. Every word they had exchanged was faithfully transmitted. Noting his honesty, even as she regretted what he was describing, Catherine could all too easily imagine the proud, passionate boy, burning with resentment, rushing out of the village on those skinny legs of his. Oh Sam, she thought. Where did you go?

That their disastrous night out was bound up in Sam's disappearance made, Catherine thought, both things worse. What had seemed a farce on the one hand was now tinged with tragedy, and the same applied in reverse to the boy having gone. It also meant that to an inextricable extent, they were in this together.

With the exception of the Newtons, she and Philip were the people in the village who had cared most about Sam. She had seen with her own eyes the relationship the boy and the solicitor had had. And at this time of supreme trial, that was a bond superseding any other consideration. They could wait for what news might come together.

Philip Protheroe needed to speak to the police, obviously. But there was nothing in his testament that would get them any further. Barring a miracle, they would just have to wait until Sam – or news of him – came back.

A light drizzle had begun.

'Come on,' Catherine said gently, leaning and patting Philip on the shoulder. 'Let's go back to my cottage for a cup of tea.'

In Catherine's cottage, at that very moment, Mary Longshott was in the bathroom. The nausea she had felt over breakfast had not improved and she was looking in Catherine's bathroom cabinet for a remedy. She had opened the door quickly; its mirrored surface, showing the dull, dry hair that had been so glossy, the eyes sunken and mud-coloured which had been as wide and green as the Weston parkland itself, had made her feel worse. But Catherine seemed to have nothing for upset stomachs and so Mary, as another wave of sickness took hold, sat down suddenly on the seat of the lavatory and took some shuddering deep breaths.

As she did so, she gazed stupidly forward, straight into the still-open cabinet, whose contents she found herself examining in psychedelic detail. Catherine's bathroom cabinet was, typically of the institution, a mixture of the much-used and never-used. In the former category were small plastic drums of aspirin, roll-on deodorant, facewash and razor attachments. In the latter were tiny, wrapped, useless bars of soap, possibly from hotel bathrooms.

A rush of misery overwhelmed Mary as she recalled her own bathroom cabinet, or the one which had until recently been hers, at Weston Underwood. She shut her eyes tightly and stuffed her fingers in her ears as an attempt, once again, to block out the sight and sound of Beth and her husband locked and grinding together, a memory that assailed her at least a hundred times a day and more at night. No wonder she felt ill, Mary thought.

Once again her entire inner core resounded with the wail of how he could have done it, and why; it was not, after all, as if the physical side of their marriage had died. The opposite, if anything. The last instance she could remember of herself and Monty making love, Mary thought with a twist of agony, was one of the most passionate she could remember. And it had only been about a month ago, on the way back from Beth and Benny's dinner party, most ironically. Could so much, she thought, really have happened in so few weeks?

It seemed a lifetime had passed since then. Before Monty had left for London had been a blessed time in retrospect, when all she had to worry about was a ruined mansion set on poisoned land. Which now, of course, seemed a metaphor for her marriage – what had that been but a vast and vulnerable edifice constructed on a worthless plot? From a distance – the distance of ignorance across which she had viewed it – it had looked impressive. Up close it was wrecked and rotting and useless.

Mary was still staring into the bathroom cabinet. Her eye now alighted on something long in a blue plastic packet. With a strange, knotted feeling, she realised what it was. A pregnancy test.

On the loo seat, Mary slumped slightly. Of course, many women had pregnancy tests in their cabinets, the same way that men had condoms in their bedside drawers. There was nothing especially unusual about Catherine having one. For Catherine, no doubt, the packet symbolised a sort of hope – she may, from what Mary had gathered, be having something less than luck with men in Mineford, but she was still optimistic. Whereas the blue packet brought forth for Mary the unwilling recollection of days when, buoyed with hope after each late period, she would crouch over the lavatory with just such an instrument, the results being invariably negative.

What a difference it would have made, she found herself thinking, if they hadn't been. What a difference it would have made to how she felt now. A child would not have reduced the shock of Monty's betrayal. But an affair, a meaningless fling, or so Monty had claimed to Catherine, a terrible, regretted mistake, a moment of madness – would that alone have broken up their family? If they had had one?

Mary chased the thoughts away. They were useless speculation. What had happened had happened, and by the same token, what hadn't happened hadn't. Perhaps the latter had made the former inevitable.

And yet Mary's glance still dwelt on the kit. There was something poignant about its having evidently been part of a two-kit pack, the first of which had presumably been used some while ago. In happier times, perhaps. And Catherine, Mary guessed, had kept the other just in case. A just-in-case which had never been justified, not since she came to Allsop anyway.

As Mary stood up and shut the cabinet, there flitted across her mind the reflection that her monthly period, due round about now, was rather late in coming. But that must be due to all the stress, Mary told herself. There could not possibly be any other reason; never, for all their fervent lovemaking before he left, and even before that, had she and Monty even got near conception. Month after month had wheeled by, and period after period.

On the other hand . . . her period was late. Really very late. And she had been feeling sick. If only . . . could it be possible . . . ?

With a racing heart, her sluggishness and sickness suddenly evaporated, Mary opened the cabinet again. The pale blue plastic packet lay innocently on the middle shelf, half hidden behind some lipsalves. She stared thoughtfully at it, and raised her hand in its direction. Then she let it drop.

No. It was a ridiculous thought. And she had had enough, lately, of seeming ridiculous. Mary closed the cabinet firmly.

Arm in arm, Catherine and Philip progressed slowly down the stepped path from the allotments back to the village. They did not speak. What was there to say? Nonetheless, as they passed the police van, they both flinched. 'You'll have to go and talk to them, you know,' Catherine muttered.

Philip squeezed her arm. 'But not yet. A cup of tea first.'

As was usual in Allsop, few people were about. Both Catherine and Philip had learnt early on in village life that this was deceptive; while the streets were indeed empty, the lace-curtained windows often disguised watching eyes and nothing was missed. No doubt, Catherine thought, many a watching eye was widening in surprise at the sight of her arm in arm with the solicitor.

She did not care, however. They would be wrong in their

assumptions, and what did it matter when she was leaving the village anyway? Her decision had gathered a hideous additional momentum in the light of recent events. Allsop seemed more than ever an unlucky place, especially now a weepy late-morning rain was once again beginning to sheen the streets.

As they progressed slowly up the lane leading to School House, the headmistress noticed a small girl hanging about her gate. It was Olivia Cooke, whose mother had taken her from Allsop Primary and sent her to St Aidan's. But Catherine, eternally fair, did not hold this against Olivia. She had always been a sweet and willing girl, and what had happened was her mother's fault, not hers. Although, to some extent, the absent Sam's; at least, he had been the excuse.

'Hello, Olivia.' She smiled as best she could. The girl was obviously waiting outside her house for some reason, but Catherine was sufficiently versed in child psychology not to ask directly why. She guessed, from the look Olivia cast Philip, that she had been hoping to see her alone. But of course there was Mary in the cottage too; whatever Olivia had to say would be witnessed by quite a crowd.

'Nice to see you,' she told the girl. 'Not in school today?' But of course, Catherine reminded herself, neither was she. Again. It was just lucky Miss Hanscombe had been in a position to take over.

Olivia shrugged. She looked pale and worried and her blond pigtails, formerly so shiny and fat, looked straw-like and drooping. She was clearly unhappy.

'Want to come in?' Catherine asked. The girl nodded hard.

The three of them went inside. Catherine piloted Philip to an armchair by the radiator where he sat hunched up, his bony hands thrust between his thighs. Then she went into the kitchen. As she had intended, Olivia followed her. Mary,

Catherine was rather relieved to notice, was not in the cottage after all. But she had not left altogether, Catherine noticed; the hideous patterned jumper she had arrived in still hung on the clothes airer in the kitchen. Perhaps she had gone for a walk to get some fresh air; that she felt up to such an excursion struck Catherine as the only bright spot in what was otherwise the most miserable of days.

'Tea or orange juice, Olivia?' Catherine tried her best to sound bright and normal. 'And I think I've got some biscuits . . . oh, darling!' she exclaimed, a sound catching her ear. 'You're crying! Whatever's the matter?'

Olivia's tears, initially silent, quickly progressed to great painful ragged gulps. She raised red eyes to Catherine. 'Oh, Miss Brooke!'

Catherine crouched down and put her arms round Olivia's waist. 'What is it, darling? Tell me.'

'S-S-S-Sam!' Olivia gasped eventually.

The headmistress nodded. Her grip round the girl tightened. While it seemed slightly strange for Olivia to be upset – she had not known Sam very long, not shared a classroom with him for many weeks now, and had suffered his hair-pulling when she had – Catherine supposed it was understandable. Children were highly sensitive, imaginative and sympathetic creatures.

'Don't worry,' she soothed, with a conviction she did not feel. 'I'm sure he'll be back soon. It's just that no one's quite sure where he is at the moment . . .' As her voice threatened to break and her eyes welled, Catherine stopped.

She felt something struggling under one of her arms. It was Olivia, violently shaking her head. 'No,' she gasped. 'You don't understand, Miss Brooke. I do know where he is at the moment.'

Chapter 70

Mary Longshott had walked out of the village and had reached the moortop road. Her legs, propelling her swiftly along, were pumping with an energy that, after all that had happened, she had not realised she still possessed.

The rain had stopped and the sun was shining with increasing strength in a sky that was becoming more and more blue. The warmth began to soak through the black cotton poloneck she wore and snatches of sharp, herby scent from the fields punched at her nostrils. Her feet in the old reliable hiking boots were heating up, but her awareness of these things was marginal. The incredible possibilities now tumbling through her head were all she concentrated on. Those, and the direction in which she was going.

The beauty of it all pressed in on her. It seemed she had gone for weeks without seeing her surroundings. It was high summer still; its last gasp perhaps, the hot, green, shining, scented peak of it before it tipped over the edge and descended into autumn. As she walked, she noticed, either side of the rapidly drying road, bunches of shining moorland grass swaying like samba dancers as the wind tickled them.

She saw the flowers; the yellow scatter of buttercups. The demure, pink-tipped daisies . . . 'He loves me, he loves me not . . .'

She walked faster, the warm hilltop wind blowing about her ears, and here and there the unmistakable fizzing noise of the ascending lark. The hurrying sound of her feet, her rapid breathing. Her own beating heart.

Reaching the gateposts of Weston Underwood, she turned in and hurried up the drive. At the first bend, she paused, as she always did. Or had. Or did.

The grey classical façade, which had, even in the worst weather and her own worst moods, never struck her as less than magnificent from this point, spread across the green parkland before her much as usual. It looked, however, different. Whereas before it always had appeared proud even in decay, it now seemed to exude a vulnerability, a fear almost. Irresistibly springing across Mary's mind came the thought that it looked like someone who had lost their protector, who stood alone in a hostile world.

She hurried towards it. As she covered the distance, leaving the drive now in order to cut across the open parkland and gain the house more quickly, Mary noticed a figure at the bottom of the sweep of steps before the portico.

A shock of relief shuddered through her. Monty was here, as she had hoped he would be. After what Catherine had reported, she feared he might have left Underpants altogether already, unable to bear the prospect of living there alone for the rest of his life. Or of living, full stop. Catherine had not spared the detail. But at least now she would have the opportunity to tell him, to say what she had come to say.

Mary's heart rate doubled in speed and volume. Her palms, already moist in the heat, began to sweat.

She got closer, rehearsing her speech. The moment was almost on her now.

He had been out in the rain, or so it seemed, from his hat. How strange. He never wore hats, Mary thought. Or so she had always imagined. But then, much of what she had imagined about Monty had recently proved to be false; his headgear preferences were the least of it.

He was bending, too, as if he was examining closely some aspect of the ground, as if he had spotted something. Or perhaps dropped something.

She was close to him now. He had different clothes on, she noticed. His trousers were not the usual red corduroy or tatty blue moleskin, but a mildewy green, and his shirt was white. He seemed to have shrunk, got thinner, become old and worn. Catherine had said that he looked terrible, but, oh God, thought Mary, catching the profile before her. She'd never imagined he would look *this* terrible. He looked *ancient*. Close to death. She could not move with the shock.

Then, in a flash, she realised, and a huge, warm rush of relief surged through her. For the man before her was not, as she had assumed, her erring husband, Monty Longshott. His was not this large, purple-veined nose, these red flaps of ears, these small, yellow-brown eyes . . .

'Ernest!'

Ernest Peaseblossom, whose back was to Mary, turned slowly round. He smiled at her and raised an arm in greeting.

'HELLO, MARY!'

'What . . . are you doing here?' she gasped, aware of the unoriginality of the query and hoping she didn't sound unfriendly, but nonetheless completely derailed by the encounter. She had been building up to a meeting so unimaginably different from this.

'I THOUGHT I'D COME AND INVESTIGATE, LIKE,' Ernest now shouted, champing his toothless gums at the end of the sentence.

'Investigate?' Mary gasped, trying in vain to collect up her scattered concentration, her rehearsed words, her mettle, her sense of drama and importance as opposed to that of the absurd. Ernest Peaseblossom? Investigating . . . what? Did he take a stern line on infidelity and had come up to lecture Monty? Surely not; that was her prerogative.

'I'VE BEEN MEANING TO COME UP ALL SUMMER,' Ernest declared. 'EVER SINCE YOU TOLD ME ABART T'LEAD POISONING, LIKE.'

'Did I?' Mary could hardly remember doing so. But she supposed she must have; they had talked about all other possible matters horticultural. And yes, she had a dim memory now of mentioning it, and perhaps, too, she had even offered to show Ernest the offending parkland.

'YER ALLUS SAID YER'D SHOW ME IT BUT YOU 'AVEN'T BEEN UP ON'T PLOTS FOR A WHILE,' Ernest confirmed now. 'SO I THOWT I'D BRING MESELF UP 'ERE, IT WERE A NICE AFTERNOON, AFTER ALL.'

'It is now,' Mary chided. She noticed now that his shirt was damp from the rain, although it was drying rapidly in the sun. She doubted he would have benefited from the drenching.

'BUT WHAT WI' ME BEING TEKKEN ILL AN' ALL, IT'S TEKKEN UNTIL NOW TO GET 'ERE,' Ernest added. He coughed slightly, then harder. Mary sprang forward and took his arm, as if the act would relieve some of his discomfort.

'But how did you get here?' she asked.

He regarded her with his bright amphibian eyes. 'WALKED, O' COURSE. WHAT ELSE ARE ME LEGS FOR?'

'You walked all the way from Allsop?' She had imagined, at the least, that he had come on the bus. 'Ernest,' she said sternly. 'You've got to be careful. You've been ill. You're almost ninety.'

The old man waved her words impatiently away. 'WELL I'VE FOUND SUMMAT OUT,' he told her, after his breathing apparatus had calmed down sufficiently to allow speech. 'ABOUT THE LAND.'

'What?' She glanced at his papery yellow hands; the dry nails were black, and on the underside of both palms, dirt showed heavily in the creases. One or two bare patches of soil, their topping of grass removed, showed by his feet, black amid the green.

With difficulty, Ernest now bent and scooped some of the earth from the holes. He raised it to his large purple nose and sniffed loudly. Some dirt flew off the pile in his hand and adhered to his nostrils.

He grunted, satisfied, then proffered the handful of earth in Mary's direction.

'THIS EARTH,' Ernest declared loudly.

Mary nodded. 'I know,' she said with a sigh. 'It's poisoned. You can't grow vegetables on it.'

From under his green-brown flat cap, the old man regarded her for an instant with his bright eyes. Then he shook his head. His red ear-flaps flicked up and down with the movement. 'THERE'S NOWT WRONG WI' THIS MUCK,' he cried.

Mary blinked. 'But . . . there must be. It's been poisoned for ages. Everyone in Monty's family always said so.'

Ernest was swinging his arms about like a cricket umpire. 'NAY. IT'S ALL REET, THIS MUCK IS. I THOUGHT IT MUST BE WHEN I SAW HOW WELL THE GRASS WERE GROWING ON IT. THERE'S NOWT WRONG WI' IT, I SAY. YOU COULD HAVE AN ALLOTMENT THE SIZE O' MINEFORD 'ERE,' he added, his bright eyes scanning the parkland before the house with satisfaction.

'You're joking, Ernest!'

'LEAD POISONING!' Ernest raised one of his sodden old boots. 'LEAD POISONING, MY FOOT! FINE GROWING LAND THIS IS. THE BEST!' He sniffed again, with the relish a wine master might have allotted a Petrus.

Mary scratched her head. 'But I don't understand. I was told that the vegetable garden was a write-off. That nothing could be grown there.'

Ernest tugged on the brim of his cap. 'AYE. THAT'S RIGHT.'

'You mean the vegetable garden *is* poisoned?'

'I'VE BEEN ROUND T' BACK AND 'AD A LOOK AND IT'S BELLAND THERE, ALL REET,' Ernest confirmed. Belland, Mary knew, was the local term for lead-infested land. 'SOME ACCIDENT OR OTHER. SOMEONE PUTTING PART OF A SPOIL 'EAP IN INSTEAD O' FERTILISER OR SUMMAT. LIKE I SAID,' Ernest shook his wrinkled head regretfully, 'BLOKE THAT USED TO RUN T' GARDEN 'ERE WERE A DRINKER. HE COULD A DONE ALL MANNER O' DAFT STUFF.'

'Are you saying,' Mary frowned, one hand to her still-throbbing forehead. 'Are you really saying, Ernest, that even though the vegetable garden is unusable, the rest of the land is fine?'

'I AM THAT!' Ernest cried with satisfaction.

Mary felt as if something inside her had exploded. An enormous set of possibilities soared like a display of fireworks.

'Ernest, I don't know how to thank you,' she gasped eventually, still shaking her head in amazement.

'DON'T THANK ME, MARY!' The gnarled old hand, its yellow skin smeared with rich black soil, gestured in her direction. 'THANK THE SOIL. THE ANSWER'S . . .'

'In the soil!' Mary giggled, the tears welling at this most potent of reminders of golden days. She pulled Ernest to her in a hug. He felt smaller and frailer even than she had expected; almost nothing there beneath the white shirt and the baggy green-brown trousers held up by the familiar braces. Another lump followed the procession up her throat.

'What's going on here?'

The voice that now came from behind was cautiously friendly. After all, Monty reasoned, seeing his wife – still his wife – hugging some elderly man on the grass in front of his steps did not, overtly at least, seem like a bad omen. Shyly, reluctantly, like someone not wanting to look into the sun because it would hurt them, he glanced into Mary's eyes. Her expression was not, as he expected and knew himself to deserve, full of blame, hurt, recrimination. It contained a sort of tremendousness. She had clearly reached some enormous decision. Monty swallowed, fearing the worst.

Whether from nicety of feeling or mere elderly inattention, the old man had wandered off now, muttering and peering at some other patch of parkland.

Monty was surprised to feel, in a sure, swift movement, Mary taking both his hands in hers. Her look was deep and serious, and seeing the tears well to her eyes, he fought off the urge to cry himself. He must hang on to the scattered rags of his self-control. 'Monty,' Mary said softly. 'Everything's changed.'

He took a deep, gulping breath. 'I know. I know. And I'm so sorry.' He closed his eyes. 'You don't know how sorry I am.'

She was pumping his hands agitatedly up and down now. He opened his eyes. Her pale face seemed full of suppressed excitement. Had he not known better, known it to be impossible, he would have almost called it joy.

'No, no. You don't understand. It's all changed because . . . I'm . . . Oh God, Monty!' She flung herself into his shaking arms. Her eyes, as green as the Weston parkland once again, blazed into his. 'Can you believe it? I'm *pregnant*!'

Chapter 71

Tamara, still up on the allotments, was trying desperately to string out her interview with the leader of the Cambridge archaeology team. The news that Ptolemy had a girlfriend had been a setback at first, but one from which she had since recovered. She would have to be even more fascinating, that was all.

She pushed out her breasts again and smiled at him. 'And you say your interest in archaeology was first sparked by—'

They were interrupted by a shout behind them. 'Tolly! Hey! Tolly!'

Yet another handsome twenty-something now appeared; one Tamara had not seen before. He was leaping up the steep steps to the allotment field, the ones that made Tamara feel she was about to have a heart attack, with the grace of a young gazelle. A young, very sexy and extremely muscly gazelle, the reporter thought, eyeing the newcomer avidly. Did *he* have a girlfriend? she wondered.

'You'll never guess, Tolly.' The new arrival, whose white T-shirt strained over his wide chest in a way that made

Tamara swallow, strode up to the team leader and struck his hand in a high five.

'Sebastian, hi,' Tolly grinned. 'What's the news?'

Sebastian shook his dark fringe back from his square and handsome face. His green eyes gleamed. He looked very pleased.

'Well it's looking pretty good. I've just been on a long walkabout as you know, checking out the boundaries.'

'Yep.' Ptolemy was nodding, seriously. Tamara hopped from foot to foot with impatience. What about *her*? Here she was – by happy coincidence – in her tightest skirt. Her heels were high and her tits were practically hanging out, for Christ's sake. Did that mean nothing to them? Why weren't either of these red-blooded males taking any notice of her?

'Well I've just been up the lane opposite the church, right to the top,' Sebastian continued. 'And guess what I found there?' His voice had risen with excitement.

Tolly's eyes were shining too now, Tamara noticed. She felt jealous of whatever Sebastian had found. She would have given a great deal to provoke a reaction in Ptolemy like that. 'What?' the team leader urged.

Sebastian paused. 'Only an altar!' he burst out.

'No!' shouted Ptolemy in a hysterical bark. 'Oh my God!'

'Well I'm not entirely sure whose god,' Sebasian grinned. 'I did try to make it out, there are a few letters on the side, but it's almost completely overgrown and largely sunken. But it looked like it was to Mars. Second century BC, I reckon.'

'Which actually pre-dates the coins,' Ptolemy interrupted urgently. 'There could have been a Roman settlement here for a few centuries. Covering an extensive area. Wow. We really are on to something.'

Sebastian nodded. 'That's what I thought.' He shook his

hair again. 'I was pretty thrilled to find the monument, I tell you. It was in a rather unlikely spot. Complete wasteland, opposite the rusty old shack that some mad sod's apparently planning to rebuild as a footballer's palace.' He snorted. 'Well, if we think what's going on here *is* going on here, they can forget that. It'll get Ancient Monument status and then wham, bam, goodbye double garage and indoor gym.'

A switch flicked in Tamara then. She had been listening, unable for the most part to understand what they were talking about. Or to imagine where a monument in Allsop could be. The only monuments she had seen were in the graveyard. Now, with the mention of double garages, indoor gyms and rusting tin shacks, she realised.

'The betrothal stone,' she blurted.

Ptolemy and Sebastian stopped staring at each other and looked instead at her. 'Eh?'

'That monument you're talking about,' Tamara supplied breathlessly, delighted to be able to contribute at last to the learned conversation. 'It's the betrothal stone. It's a sort of tradition. Women in Allsop can ask men to marry them at the stone. Or so they say.' Her gaze swept longingly over the two young men. She pouted slightly and pushed a strand of thin dark hair back over her ear. 'It's all rubbish of course,' she added, breathily.

'Not at all. It's fascinating,' began Sebastian earnestly.

'Yes, isn't it?' Ptolemy interrupted. 'Because by the sound of it, something that originally honoured a Roman god was afterwards used as a site for another, essentially pagan superstition, the betrothal myth.'

'There's a definite, possibly coincidental but nonetheless significant continuity there,' Sebastian agreed.

Tamara, who was feeling confused and beginning to wish

she had never said anything, was almost glad when, now, they were distracted by another shout. One of the other gods, Tamara saw, was jumping up and down on the vicar's former plot as if he had won the World Cup and the Ashes single-handedly. 'Hypercaust! Hypercaust!'

'Is he all right?' Tamara exclaimed. Was hypercaust a medical condition?

Ptolemy gave a whoop and bounded over.

The gods were now hugging each other and pointing excitedly into a hole about four feet square. It was dug deep, and at the bottom Tamara could see small, stumpy square brick columns placed at regular intervals about a foot from each other. What could possibly be exciting about that?

'Hypercausts!' Ptolemy said wonderingly. 'A Roman central-heating system, in other words. They only bothered putting them in luxurious villas, baths and the like. This means we really have hit something big.' He shot a muscled arm into the air. 'Yessss! Result!'

In the School House, Catherine now held Olivia's shoulders in a grip of iron. Her heart thumped violently and the blood rushed loudly in her ears. She thrust her face close to the child's. 'What? You know where Sam is? Where? Is he . . . ?' she stopped and swallowed, unable to go on. 'All right?' she muttered, eventually.

'He's fine,' Olivia yelped, her eyes wide with terror. 'He's hiding in our summer house. He's been there since Sunday. He didn't want to go home and so I thought—'

'In your *summer house?*'

The next thing Olivia knew, Miss Brooke had detached herself violently, leapt up and rushed out. She could hear her shouting in a high, strained voice somewhere. This scared Olivia even more. Miss Brooke never shouted. 'Philip! Philip!' she was yelling. 'Sam's safe! He's been in Olivia's summer house all this time!'

The terrified Olivia followed her former headmistress. 'I didn't mean any harm, Miss Brooke,' she whimpered. 'But with all these police and everything I'm really scared. I felt I had to tell someone.' Tears flowed afresh down the girl's cheeks. Compounding her fear was the sudden remembrance that Miss Brooke's friend – the man with the muddy suit – was something to do with the law. 'Will they put me in prison, Miss Brooke?'

She reached the threshold of the sitting room to see Catherine and Philip whirling round in each other's arms.

Chapter 72

The Reverend Alan Tribble waited apprehensively outside the Bishop's office. The demand that he present himself had come suddenly, peremptorily. Like an act of God, in fact.

That acts of God usually had some vengeful or destructive aspect — as opposed to acts of Jesus, who tended to be gentle and more helpful, turning water to wine and the rest of it — was something the Reverend Tribble was in a better position than most people to appreciate. It was something on which he pondered anew as he sat in the portrait-lined corridor on the red velvet cushion atop the linenfold-panelling bench awaiting the Bishop's pleasure.

Or, more likely, his wrath. For the Reverend Tribble was all too aware of having failed to fulfil the brief the Bishop had charged him with when last they had met within these imposing walls. Despite eye-popping effort, he had not noticeably increased the numbers of Allsop churchgoers. The opposite, in fact. One of his regular old ladies had died, scything the congregation down by twenty-five per cent. His attempts at a youth group had resulted in just one person turning up, the plump, ill-favoured, heavily bespectacled daughter of a local farmer who had plainly – in every sense – only come for the free biscuits.

His attempt, as per instructions, to get married had met with similar lack of success. The headmistress, who he had selected as the most obvious candidate on the grounds that she was single and, being effectively his colleague, he saw a lot of her, had not responded to any of his hints. His consequent hope that she was either stupid or merely playing hard to get had been conclusively flattened amid the egg-smeared plates and ketchup squeezers of that unappetising café in Mineford.

Catherine Brooke had been brutally frank about his chances, or lack of them, and it had not been an uplifting experience. Nor much of a return on all those hours he had put in at the allotment trying to attract her attention. All he had to show for his efforts, in fact, the Reverend reflected crossly, were a few wilting lettuces and recurring backache. As well as a possible part share in some pagan treasure, but the way things were going he would probably have to mud-wrestle Morag Archbutt-Pesk to get anywhere near that.

The marriage situation, which no doubt the Bishop would be focusing on, was so desperate that the Reverend was even considering asking the ill-favoured farmer's daughter to oblige. In a fairy tale, of course, he would get his reward by his lumpen bride turning into a beauty when he kissed her. But this was Christianity; while miracles occasionally occurred, they were rarely of a sexual nature. He sighed and stared gloomily at the Victorian Gothic carved oak door of the Bishop's office. No doubt he was about to be told he was being sent to the Outer Hebrides. Excommunicated, even.

The Reverend jumped as the carved oak office door opened. The Bishop appeared, and the Reverend Tribble scanned the ancient face anxiously for advance clues to his fate, but the thin, waxy countenance with its bony forehead and shrunken, veiny temples was as serene as ever. The Bishop even gave a distant smile as, stumbling slightly on his elderly limbs, he waved the Reverend in.

Five minutes later, the Reverend was looking over the vast, carved desk at his boss in astonishment. He had expected demotion, not its opposite. 'You're offering me a bishopric?' he repeated, flabbergasted. 'With immediate effect?'

The Bishop inclined his head gravely. 'The present incumbent,' he emitted in his quavering voice, 'has not proved himself suitable, I regret to say.'

That was putting it mildly, the Reverend thought. The present incumbent – bishop of a West Country diocese – had got into a most unsuitable muddle involving the church-warden's wife, her furious husband and several other ladies in the parish whose favours the priapic prelate had been enjoying. The Reverend had read all about it in the *Daily Mail*.

The Bishop, the Reverend now noticed, was saying something. He leant forward with extravagant attention. 'What's that you say, Your Grace?'

'Women,' the old man quavered, lifting a finger. 'Keep well away from them. They're more harm than help, take it from me.'

An incredulous beam stretched the Reverend Tribble's face. He nodded violently. 'Absolutely, Your Grace. I couldn't agree more.'

Chapter 73

Alexandra was checking her mobile phone messages in the VIP area at Robby Trendy's. She had last checked them five minutes ago in the taxi from the penthouse to London's first and only all-blond salon, and there had been nothing then. Nothing from Max, most annoyingly. He hadn't called for days. The last time they had spoken he had warned her that interest in her was at an all-time low and she should have thought twice before turning down the chance to be the face of British Sausage Week. 'It would have been a platform at least,' he had suggested.

'A platform into sausages,' Alexandra had snapped. 'Big deal.'

'Hey, come on. You could have worked your way up to bacon. Steak. Chicken. The possibilities are endless.'

'Thanks but no thanks,' Alexandra fumed. 'Is this really the best you can do?'

'Hey, babe,' Max had replied easily. 'You know me. I tell it like it is. You don't pay me to flatter you.'

It was the first Alexandra had heard of it. She thought she paid everyone to flatter her.

Now, in the salon, awaiting the attentions of a Robby fawning over the fat daughter of a rock star who he was assuring was the most beautiful creature that had ever lived, Alexandra found that someone had indeed called her as she skittered in her high white heels from taxi to stylist. Unfortunately it was nobody interesting. No one, not even his own mother, could call Barrie Hemsworth, Deputy Chief Planning Officer for Mineford Town Council, interesting.

Nonetheless Alexandra, short of calls, felt obliged, in the VIP area, to look and act like a VIP. To be on the mobile sounding important. And in the absence of a call to return from Steven Spielberg, Leonardo DiCaprio or even her own bloody agent, the one from Barrie Hemsworth would have to do.

In his office at Mineford Town Council, Barrie picked up the ringing telephone and was alarmed to hear someone husky and urgent-sounding on the end of it. 'Barrie!' it breathed.

'No thank you,' said Barrie firmly. 'I don't take these sort of calls, thank you.'

'What sort of calls?' squawked Alexandra indignantly.

'Whatever *you* are,' Barrie replied baldly, still not recognising the voice. 'One of those chatlines from the *Daily Star*, that's what you sound like.'

Alexandra was aghast. Her career was indeed in the doldrums, but she had not yet sunk to the level of providing the voice for porn chatlines. It occurred to her to wonder what Barrie Hemsworth knew about such chatlines anyway.

'What did you call about?' she asked the deputy chief planner, frowning behind her sunglasses and chewing hard on her pearlised gum. If Barrie was ringing to tell her that, for all Hassock and Hemp's confidence in their new plans, they had nonetheless been rejected, she would scream.

The whole Allsop thing was a complete disaster. At this rate she and John would not be moving in until they drew their pensions. Even the treasure, which was hers by right, had been denied her, or that was what it looked like after that ridiculous bloody meeting.

'It's about Betrothal Cottage,' Barrie began. Alexandra's tanned hand gripped the stem of her glass of complimentary champagne.

'Go on,' she instructed grimly.

'Planning permission has been withdrawn,' Barrie sighed. It was a shame, he thought. He would miss his regular conversations with Alexandra Pigott. Being on the inside track of the A-list had been a heady experience.

In Robby Trendy's VIP area, Alexandra gulped. Her fears were realised. Her head spun for a second. Then she let rip. 'What?' she shrieked, making Robby drop his scissors and the fat rock star daughter spill her crisps in her cleavage. 'Again! If it's that bitch Morag Archbutt-Pesk, I'll . . .'

A ripple of excitement ran through the salon. Lips moved in mirrors, repeating the name. Morag Archbutt-Pesk? Who was she? A bitch! How interesting!

Alexandra's other brown hand clung disbelievingly to her mobile as Barrie now explained that Morag, incredibly and unprecedentedly, was not to blame. Great swathes of Allsop village, including the allotments, were being requisitioned for archaeological research in the informed belief that they were a Roman site. The most thrilling find of all to date had been an altar to Mars directly opposite Betrothal Cottage.

'Crap,' was Alexandra's robust response. 'There's no bloody Mars altar up there.' Funny, though. She had never realised Mars bars were that old, although it didn't surprise her at all that the Romans worshipped them. If she ever allowed herself to eat chocolate, she would probably worship them too.

'There's only one monument up there,' she assured Barrie confidently. 'I should know, it's my effing land. There's the betrothal stone and that's it . . . What?'

Over the course of the next couple of minutes, Alexandra's frosted mouth opened and shut. She could hardly believe what Barrie Hemsworth was saying. When he had finished saying it, she rushed in with her objections. 'Oh *puh-leese*. The betrothal stone isn't a betrothal stone at all, it's a bloody Roman altar? You're joking. You really have to be joking.'

Robby Trendy's salon was at a standstill. Or rather, as most people were seated, a sitstill. Everyone was riveted. No conversation remotely like it had been seen or heard there before. Alexandra Pigott, WAG supreme, wannabe celebrity and unflinching blonde, was sitting in a black leather miniskirt and white high heels, sunglasses on as usual, covered in make-up, champagne glass in hand, under a heater hardening the adhesive of her extensions, having an impassioned and informed-sounding exchange about, of all things, historical monuments.

Ensconced in a taxi, Alexandra headed home soberly despite the copious amounts of champagne she had drunk. For all her buoyant blond hair, she felt flat and empty. Most uncharacteristically for her, she felt defeated.

Everything she had touched in Allsop had turned to shit, not gold. The gold certainly had. Barrie had just told her that the treasure was going to a museum that would, if excavations continued the way they were going, be built near the village.

It looked, he had said, sounding excited, as if Allsop was an important Roman site.

Which might be great news for Allsop, Alexandra reflected bitterly, but it wasn't so great for her. Planning permission for her house had been withdrawn as a result. She had also, Barrie had informed her, lost her allotment to the archaeologists – although, to be frank, that was no great loss now that it was obvious no one was interested in making a *Simple Life*-style programme about her.

And now, thanks to those bloody archaeologists as well, the betrothal stone had turned out to be not a betrothal stone but something else altogether. No longer could she ask John to marry her – crucially – in a place where he could not say no. And the likelihood of him asking her seemed more remote than ever.

Especially now he had no house to move to. The summer was marching on, John would start permanently at his new club soon and even sooner he would be expecting her to hand to him, with a happy, excited smile, the keys to their new house. Their dream home. Oh God, groaned Alexandra, gripping the handle above the taxi window and staring out through her sunglasses with anguished eyes. What the hell am I going to do?

John, in the penthouse sitting room, heard Alexandra return. He heard her kick off her shoes and throw her coat on the floor. As she pushed open the door to the sitting room, he retreated even further into the gold and white cushions and eyed her with something akin to terror.

She was going to hate it. But he had to tell her. He swallowed and felt sick at the thought of how she would react. Coming out of the players' tunnel to face a seventy-thousand-strong Wembley crowd was nothing on this.

Alexandra's first thought, on entering the room, was to go straight to the champagne bucket for Dutch courage. Then, to her amazement, she spotted John, almost hidden among the cushions. Her heart performed a tremendous loop, first zooming to the soles of her feet, then roaring upwards into her throat. She gripped the back of the nearest sofa. Oh God. She had to tell him. Come right out with it. Now. There was nothing else she could do.

'I've got something to tell you,' they announced as one, staring fearfully at each other.

'Oh,' they both said then, surprised.

'You go first,' John suggested quickly. Anything to delay things.

'No, you,' Alexandra insisted. She was in no hurry to confess her miserable failure at absolutely everything.

'You.'

'No, you.'

'Okay then,' John said resolutely. He twisted his hands, spread his knees and stared at the floor. Forcing back down the gulps of nervous nausea he felt, he began to speak. 'There's been a change of plan, I'm afraid,' he said quickly. 'I'm not moving clubs after all.'

Alexandra froze to the spot. Her nails dug into the back of the individually hand-made white-damask-covered sofa. 'What?'

He flinched at her grating whisper. Of course, she would be furious. She had put everything into their move. She'd been up there every five minutes it seemed, taking on stroppy locals, fighting over planning permission – he didn't know the details but he had vaguely gathered it was happening. She'd even got an allotment in order to immerse herself in village life, and knowing Alexandra, that was one hell of a concession. And now he was turning round and telling her all she had done had been pointless. That all the difficulties she had overcome, all the challenges she had faced – alone, mostly; he was guiltily aware of being no help whatsoever – had been one huge waste of time.

'I'm so sorry,' he whispered, trying to assess her expression behind her sunglasses. 'But we're getting a new manager at the club. Top secret at the moment of course, but it turns out he wants to keep me. Wants to give me more of a chance, he says, make me part of his fighting force. So I'm not washed up after all . . .' With difficulty, John reined himself in. What was triumph for him was, after all, the opposite for Alexandra. 'So I'll be staying here,' he finished, staring uncomfortably at the white deep-pile carpet once again. 'I won't be moving up north after all.'

Ears on stalks, he heard Alexandra take a deep, shuddering breath. Then she said something.

It didn't sound good. He swallowed. 'What was that?'

Alexandra, still by the sofa, shrugged. She was twitching, he saw. 'That's fine,' she repeated softly.

John's head flew up. 'Fine?' he cried, relieved.

'Fine, yes.' Alexandra spoke softly because she felt if she allowed any volume in her voice she would lose control altogether. She would scream with relief. She had been saved.

John was looking at her, she noticed, in an unusually attentive way. His brown eyes glowed with warmth and love. Unfolding his long, athletic body from the sofa, he walked over and pulled her tenderly into his arms. 'Oh babe. I was so worried about telling you. After everything you've done up there. You've worked so hard. You must be gutted.'

Alexandra smiled at him. 'Oh well,' she said, trying her best to sound breezy. 'These things happen. I'm just glad for you, babe, that's all. That's such wonderful news about the club.'

'Oh babe.' He felt awash with love for her suddenly. That she would react with such calmness, unflappability and generosity was the last thing he had expected. Rather, tears, shouting, bitter accusation. He had misjudged her, John realised. He owed her an apology. And perhaps more.

He peeled her sunglasses off tenderly.

'I love you, babe,' he told her softly. 'Will you marry me?'

Chapter 74

A few weeks after these events, Catherine Brooke sat across a restaurant table from Philip Protheroe. It was not, however, the Indian restaurant.

Philip, declaring he wanted to treat her, had booked a table for two in the most expensive restaurant in the area, a place of potpourri and leaded panes where tapestries hung against stone walls, a fire leapt in the ancestral grate, white linen glowed and silver cutlery shone in the candlelight. Eighties, but nice, Catherine thought on entry; but keeping this thought to herself. She didn't want to hurt Philip's feelings. She had altogether different ambitions for Philip's feelings.

'Eighties, but nice,' Philip grinned as they entered. 'But I like this sort of place. Sense of occasion.'

Catherine looked beautiful, he thought, admiring her creamy skin against the caramel lace top she wore, which was threaded with tiny pearls and diamonds and glittered as she moved. Her neat red-brown hair and steady grey eyes shone, all trace of unhappiness gone.

Beneath this approving scrutiny, Catherine glowed. Philip

looked so handsome. His slightly tired pinstripes and bent collar gave him an appealing air of helplessness, and that schoolboyish way he had of looking shyly up at her through his floppy dark fringe made her heart twist. She was aware, however, of not feeling towards him as a headmistress towards a schoolboy ideally should.

They had walked outside before dinner, round the green lawns and lavender beds of the hotel garden, arm in arm except when one or other of them bent to examine a plant. The feeling of him close to her, next to her, had been delicious. She had almost lost the struggle with an almost overwhelming desire to snuggle into his shoulder.

She contented herself with, at any excuse the conversation offered, stretching her hand over the table to him in apparent spontaneous excitement. With similar apparent spontaneity, he would seize it and grab it hard. Fortunately for them both, reviewing recent events was full of hand-grabbing excitement.

'It's all just so amazing,' Catherine said happily, admiring the candlelight reflected in her crystal champagne glass. 'I had no idea Olivia was a friend of Sam's. To think they kept in touch after she left the school – became better friends afterwards, by the sound of it. After all that hair-pulling as well.'

She shook her head at the memory of the two children standing scared, guilty, but hand in hand in the doorway of the Cooke family summer house. As Mrs Newton swept her foster son passionately into her arms, various police officers wrote things down and murmured into walkie-talkies and Julia Cooke, plastered in make-up as usual, flounced self-importantly around.

Philip smiled ruefully. 'Hey. There's nothing unusual

about becoming better friends with someone after you've been nasty to them.'

Catherine flashed him a shy look and felt herself redden.

'Anyway,' Philip said, filling Catherine's champagne glass, 'all's well that ends well. Sam's fine. You're not leaving Allsop Primary.'

'How could I?' Catherine's blush deepened. 'After the entire school – parents and children – signed a petition begging me not to?'

'Apart from Morag Archbutt-Pesk, of course,' Philip pointed out.

Catherine's hand went out and cuffed his playfully. 'Don't be horrid. She can't sign petitions from the wilds of Scotland.'

Philip nodded. Morag, who had suffered a spectacular breakdown after the archaeologists' arrival, had been subsequently diagnosed by a specialist as having severe bipolar disorder. Her manic depression, the specialist concluded, would be best treated by temporary complete removal from the site that aggravated negative feelings. Morag had therefore left Allsop and was now, Gid had told Catherine, receiving treatment in the form of six months' enforced recuperation at what he described as 'a holistic therapy centre run by some gentle people on Skye'.

'Poor old thing,' Catherine remarked ruefully. 'Her insane behaviour all seems a bit different once you realise she really was insane.'

'I know,' Philip agreed. 'But she's getting better, apparently.' The reports from Gid, who had visited, were positive.

'I only hope she doesn't have a relapse when she sees Merlin,' Catherine grinned. With her mother gone, Morag's rebellious daughter, irrespective of her tender age, had taken to wearing full make-up, glittering hair accessories, designer labels and T-shirts bearing slogans of which 'Buy Me Stuff' and 'Gold Digger' were typical. All provided, Catherine had learnt, from the proceeds of Merlin's successful trades on eBay. 'She buys things and resells them immediately at a profit,' Gid had confided in Catherine. 'She's an arch-capitalist I'm afraid,' he had sighed. 'I can't imagine where she gets it from.'

'It was nice that Olivia Cooke asked you if she could come back.' Philip broke into her thoughts.

Catherine felt a rush of pure pleasure at this. 'Oh, that was because of Sam. She probably wanted to come back to be with him now they're such friends.'

'You're being modest,' Philip teased. 'He told her the school had got better than ever after she'd gone, and she hadn't wanted to leave anyway. Her mother had made her. That's what she said to me.'

'He probably only felt that because the vicar's left,' Catherine grinned. 'Sam and the Reverend Tribble never did get on terribly well.' She took a slug of champagne. That the vicar's new job could be so well timed was unbelievable. But what *wasn't* unbelievable about recent events?

The first course, some sort of white fish rolled up, skewered with an olive and swimming in buttery sauce, was placed ceremoniously before them.

'Sam's thrilled about being able to help on the dig,' Philip remarked, poking the mixture with a silver fork. 'Ptolemy says they've never seen such an enthusiastic eight year old.'

'Did he really?' Catherine felt a sense of awe. It was unimaginable anyone would have said such a thing when Sam first came to Allsop.

'He's all fired up about becoming an archaeologist himself

now,' Philip chuckled. 'Keeps telling me it's one of the most important Roman finds for years.'

Catherine smiled fondly, her eyes suddenly welling. 'He's going the right way,' she said proudly. 'His marks are excellent. And it'll make all the difference to his stability now it's been decided his family really can't look after him and the Newtons are to adopt him permanently.'

She sounded brighter about this than she felt. While of course she was thrilled for Sam, this news had revealed to Catherine a wish so private she had not realised it existed at all. Somewhere within her, she now understood she had nursed the possibility of adopting Sam herself. Still, Mary and Monty had already asked her to be chief godmother to the new baby, which was apparently a boy and was going to be called Ernest. She felt a rush of pure joy at the thought, and of gratitude that Mary and her husband were not after all parting ways. The baby had changed everything, and Mary was working fast with Benny – by telephone from New York – over setting up as much as possible of Lady Amelia's Pantry before, as she put it, she disappeared under a pile of nappies. 'Although actually, Monty's going to be doing most of that,' the newly businesslike and motivated Mary had added firmly. 'So I can get on with some work. But I have to say,' she confided, 'I'm amazed at how much he seems to be looking forward to it. He's even stopped talking about exploring. Maybe he realises that looking after a baby's going to be the biggest adventure of his life.'

Catherine was not amazed, however, and she could guess what else Monty Longshott had realised. Having seen him in his most desperate hour, she knew he knew how close-run a thing it had been. Fault and recrimination had all been gloriously subsumed in the much greater stroke of luck that had only emerged when Mary had been driven back to the bathroom cabinet by curiosity and perhaps some greater and more mysterious imperative.

'I'll rather miss Benny and Beth,' Catherine mused now. 'But it was obvious he had to put some time into that marriage. Trying to seduce Monty was Beth's cry for attention, in a way, although admittedly not the nicest way.'

Philip took a sip of wine. 'Do you think it'll survive? Their marriage?'

Catherine shrugged. 'It's damaged, sure, but taking her back to New York and starting afresh seems a good way to fix it. If anyone can fix it, Benny can. Beth's lucky, really.'

'I'm lucky too,' Catherine heard Philip say now.

He was looking steadily into her eyes. She took a hasty mouthful of champagne, which failed to calm her. She felt weak at the knees, even though she was sitting down.

Philip's pale face was, she noticed, tinged with a growing pink. 'I never thought I would say that,' he said softly. 'I never thought I would feel lucky again. Once, not long ago, in fact, I used to feel like the unluckiest person in the world.' He stopped and looked down, then, with an effort, met her eyes again and pushed himself on. 'Until I met you. And our relationship . . . well, that is, if we have one . . .' His face was bright red now. 'If you think we could have one . . .'

Catherine felt oddly breathless. 'Oh – well – yes. Yes. Why not?' She nodded encouragingly and smiled widely. Immediately she wished she had not said the last two words. They sounded ridiculous, given the context. As if he had just asked her to do a shift on a charity cake stall or something. But she couldn't help it. Having an inkling of what it had cost Philip to say what he just had, she knew it was vital not to respond with too much tremendousness.

He did not seem to mind, however. On the contrary, he looked relieved. 'I thought I should take some time off,' he told her briskly now. 'And some new people on. I've been driving myself like a slave since . . . since . . .'

He stopped. Catherine reached a hand across the table and pressed his. 'It's all right. You can say it,' she whispered. 'You *should* say it. *Since Emily.*'

Philip's head remained bowed for a minute or two. His fingers clutched hers hard. Then he looked up and smiled.

There was silence for a while, although it wasn't, Catherine felt, an awkward one. She felt no jealousy or competitiveness with the dead woman. Just pity for Emily and Philip both. Wherever the relationship with Philip went from here, Catherine vowed, there would be room for Emily in it. If he wanted to talk about her, she would listen.

'So the treasure's going to be displayed in the site museum after all,' she remarked after a while. 'No one in Allsop's getting any of it.'

'Not in that sense,' Philip agreed. 'But obviously they can still look at it.'

It seemed, Catherine thought, almost too poetic that the treasure question had been solved by the trove being reclaimed by the state as part of an entire important site. But it seemed to her now that the coins were far from being the only – or even the most important – thing of value that the allotments had yielded. There had been treasure in abundance in the end.

'I suppose it's a bit sad that the allotments will be destroyed,' she remarked.

'It's not that sad. The parish council have pledged to find some more. There's a lot of interest. There's a meeting in the village hall about it this week, in fact.' Philip shot her a teasing look. 'I take it you'll be there.'

'Don't!' giggled Catherine. 'I've had enough of allotments for now.' She smiled and raised her glass. 'Here's to the future. Here's to us,' she added shyly.

Philip reached over. His hands, slightly shaking, touched her face. A sudden feeling of happiness rushed through him, as if Emily, somewhere, was applauding.

WENDY HOLDEN

The School For Husbands

Sophie's not happy with her husband.

Mark works late, never phones and leaves all the housework and childcare to her. She's also sure he's up to something with his sexy publishing colleague. Things come to a head and she moves back to her parents. Her mother never liked Mark anyway.

Desperate to save his marriage, Mark enrols at the 'School for Husbands', a residential college which transforms pathetic partners into husbands from heaven. Classes include love skills, sparkling conversation and the finer points of chocolate. But will this be enough to reunite him with Sophie? Especially now a rich old flame is after her . . .

Praise for *The School For Husbands*

'Riotous' *Daily Mail*

'A great summer romp' *Grazia*

'Guaranteed to make you smile' *Woman & Home*

'Giggles galore in this lively romp. A perfect bathtime read' *OK* magazine

978 0 7553 3409 4

headline
review

WENDY HOLDEN

The Wives of Bath

A tale of yummy mummies with flat brown tummies . . .

Four parents-to-be seem ante-natally sorted. Flash Hugo and Amanda have booked a chic private clinic and royal maternity nurse. Right-on Jake and Alice want an all-natural home birth with whale music and tree hugging nappies.

But nothing goes quite to plan. Amanda finds motherhood less glam than the stars make it look and disappears back to her career. Which leaves Hugo with the child and without a clue what to do.

Alice has problems too. Bringing up baby to Jake's eco-fascist standards means home-made organic everything and a recycled cardboard cot.

Will nappiness bring happiness to anybody? Not before bedhopping spouses, beastly bosses and bitchy nursery mothers have all done their dreadful worst . . .

Praise for *The Wives of Bath*

'Irresistible rom-com meets devilish satire . . . hilarious portrait of modern parenthood' *In Style*

'Fab' *Heat*

'Babies, bedhopping, booze and bad behaviour in this latest romantic comedy from *Cosmo* favourite Wendy Holden' *Cosmopolitan*

'Sly puns, sassy one-liners . . . infectious delight' *Literary Review*

'A frothy, funny read' *Company*

'If you want a deliciously funny book, then this is the perfect pick!' *Real*

978 0 7553 2629 7

headline
review